MARK

IN THE COMPANY OF SNIPERS
Book 2

IRISH WINTERS

"The first chapter of this romance suspense
will touch your heartstrings and leave you
hungry for more. Grab a box of tissues and
hang on for the ride of your life."

"Just when you thought you could not
possibly fall more in love with Mark
Houston—you do!"

"Irish Winters has done it again. She
continues to craft tales of tender warriors
who charm your socks off—and maybe
Libby Clifton's, too. Mark Houston is
irresistible, Libby is as much a warrior as he
is, and Alex Stewart continues to surprise."

"This sweet romance is a lesson in karma.
We really do reap what we sow, and every
once in awhile if we're lucky—what we reap
could last forever."

COPYRIGHT

MARK; In the Company of Snipers, 2

Edited by Katie Johnson, Editing Services.

Cover design and author photo by Kelli Ann Morgan,
http://www.inspirecreativeservices.com

Interior book design by Bob Houston eBook Formatting

ISBN Paperback: 978-1-942895-05-3
ISBN eBook: 978-1-942895-06-0
Library of Congress Control Number: 2013958282

Irish Winters can be contacted at
http://www.irishwinters.com or irishwinters.blogspot.com

In the Company of Snipers

You can find Irish Winters on Facebook: https://www.facebook.com/author.irishwinters

On Twitter: https://twitter.com/irishwinters1

For news on upcoming releases, sign up for Irish Winters' Newsletter at IrishWinters.com.

For more information about all my books, visit IrishWinters.com.

IN THE COMPANY OF SNIPERS

This series revolves around ex-Marine scout sniper, Alex Stewart, and his covert surveillance company, The TEAM, home-based out of Alexandria, Virginia. An obsessive patriot and workaholic, he created the company to give ex-military snipers like him a chance at returning to civilian life with a decent job.

This is not a serial with each book ending at a cliffhanger. I wouldn't do that to you. *In the Company of Snipers* is a collection of passionate love stories involving women and men who are tough enough to take on the world alone. Each is a stand-alone read, where in the course of an active TEAM operation, one agent comes face to face with his or her demons. The men and women I write about are all patriots and warriors, dealing with what they've lived through or the mistakes they've made

Spoiler alert: Every novel contains adult scenes including sexual situations (some explicit), language, and violence. I don't write sweet romance, so be forewarned.

At the end of each story, it's my hope that you, along with my heroes, will come to realize...

Love changes everything.

One

Slow down. You have plenty of time. Just do it right.

USMC Sergeant Mark Houston stood too long at the heavy oak door on Libby Clifton's front porch. Shaking his nervousness off, he inhaled yet another measured breath. If he didn't knock soon he would be in trouble. The sun was high and the humidity higher. A red-faced Marine in full dress uniform would not be a respectable sight so early in the morning.

Chaplain Kenny, his wingman, stood to his left, ready to pick up the pieces. Still, Mark faltered. Today was one of those hard days, the kind a person never forgot.

Where were you when JFK was killed? Where were you when the towers fell? Where were you when Mark Houston told you …?

A thousand ways he didn't like the answer to that final question.

Gentler memories flooded his mind. He had stood here before during a kinder visit to Spencer, Wisconsin when he'd followed his buddy, Jon Wells, home on a ten-day pass. They'd spent most of that ten days swimming and fishing at nearby Lake Wissota with Jon's fiancée, Libby, or visiting her family.

The Clifton's welcome had been warm with unexpected hugs from her mother, and a gripping handshake from her father that evolved into a bear of a hug. Her two sisters, Faith and Marie, had flirted and teased. They'd all barely met him, but in an instant, Mark belonged. They'd loved him like a son. Then ....

The circle that began with Jon ended with him today. Good old Jon. Best buddy. Brother. Mark and he could have passed for brothers with their same dark looks, only Jon was the taller, handsomer one, while Mark was the stocky, muscular brother. They'd met the day they joined the Corps, two young men with stars and stripes in their eyes, intent on serving their country after 9-11. Some of the guys they survived boot camp with called them twins. Some called them Mutt and Jeff. It was all the same. They were on their way to glory.

The world was different then. America was in a hurry to hold someone accountable. For Mark, it was a matter of pride. He had enlisted to right a wrong, to take justice across the ocean for all those lost. Together he and Jon hit the road less travelled. They studied hard and drilled harder. Before long, both were known for their relentless dedication and fierce patriotism.

In the hardscrabble, accelerated military life after the towers fell, Mark found himself in Afghanistan within the year. The last time he saw Jon was the day a Taliban rocket-propelled grenade blasted his Black Hawk out of the sky. The memory of charred remains haunted Mark still.

Chaplin Kenny coughed politely beside him.

Mark jerked himself out of the past. *Yeah. I know I've got to do this. Give me a minute.*

Fast forward to the Clifton porch. That was the one thing Jon had done right before he deployed. He'd listed Libby right after his parents to be notified in the event of his death. Even now, another team of two stood at Jon's parent's home announcing the same sad news.

No longer a welcomed guest or conquering hero, this morning Mark came as the destroyer. Thief in the night. Bringer of death and sorrow. USMC Notification Officer.

He stalled, his eyes glued to the brass door handle while sweat stung his eyes. Yesterday the handle opened doors. Today it kept Libby Clifton in her happy, carefree world. Until the moment it turned, she could believe. She could dream.

"Are you okay, son?" the chaplain asked kindly.

"Yes, sir," Mark answered. *Hell, no. I'll never be okay again. What kind of question is that?*

With one last breath, he rapped his gloved knuckles against the oak. Muted sounds of the household came to life.

"I'll get it," a feminine voice declared. Sounded like Faith. Not Libby.

"Beat you to it, little girl."

Damn. Mark recognized that teasing baritone voice. The brass handle turned. He stood face to face with Libby's father. Warm recognition and surprise crinkled the corners of Jerry Clifton's sharp eyes. He looked Mark up and down, processing the sight of two full dress Marines on his front porch. Jerry nodded once, but said nothing. He already knew.

Mark stepped forward. He was bad cop. Chaplain Kenny remained steadfast behind him. Good cop. Come to offer support after Mark's awful deed was done.

"Mr. Clifton." He licked his dry lips and kept his voice steady and low. "May I please speak with Libby, sir?"

The aroma of coffee and breakfast wafted through the open door. Breakfast was another one of those commonplace things about to change. Jerry turned away without inviting the Marines into his home.

Mark felt Kenny's hand on his shoulder. If it was intended to offer strength, it missed.

This porch was where Jon had first kissed Libby, where he had asked for her hand in marriage. He'd been scared that day, a cocky young man humbled by a taciturn father. The same day he proposed marriage to the sweetest girl in the world. First the brass door handle, then breakfast, now the porch. What next?

Libby came timidly to the doorway. It had been a year, but the sight of her took Mark's breath. He flinched when the scent of baby powder filled his nose. Her scent. It had haunted his dreams for months. The draft of the open door teased the white blond tendrils around her face, adding to the child-like innocence he had come to crush. Cobalt blue eyes begged him not to speak. His heart pumped too fast and too hard as his fight or flight response kicked in.

Stop. Don't do this. Run. Never tell her. Never break her heart. Run!

But duty ruled. Honor prevailed. He steeled his heart and reached for her slender hand, letting the official pronouncement roll from his lips. "Libby Clifton. The Commandant of the Marine Corps of the United States of America has entrusted me to express his deepest regret. Your fiancé, Jonathan William Wells, was killed in action in Afghanistan on June second of this year when his Black Hawk helicopter was struck down by a Taliban rocket. The

Commandant extends his deepest sympathy to you and your family in your loss."

Libby stood blinking as she struggled to process the one hundred and eighty degree change in her life. Jerry held her elbow. Rosemary, her mother, stood behind her, wiping her own tears with a corner of her apron. Daisies and bunnies. Her apron was printed with brightly colored yellow daisies and brown fuzzy bunnies.

The things a man remembers ....

"Libby, I am so sorry," Mark choked. He'd been trained to bury his emotions, to stand and stare and never show weakness. Never blink. Two centuries of military tradition, the stare was the battle-hardened Marine's mask. Not today. Standing this close to a delicate flower of a girl, and watching his words break her heart—he blinked.

She pulled her hand out of his and took a step back.

"No. You're wrong. This was not the plan. I'm in nursing school. Jonathan's in Afghanistan. That's the plan. He's on a special assignment. He told me. When he comes home this time, we're going to be married." She looked to her father and then to her mother as if searching for a way out. "He promised. Mom? Dad? Didn't he promise? This time he would really come home? You heard him. That's what he said, didn't he?"

Rosemary clutched her daughter's shoulder.

The tone in Libby's voice ratcheted higher. She stomped her foot, glaring at Mark. "No. No. No. This. Is. Not. The. Plan!"

By now her sisters, Faith and Marie, stood sobbing behind her.

She stood defiant; her hands clenched at her side, breathing hard and ready to fight. Mark saw the tear. The moment it slid out of her eye, he took a step forward, longing with all his heart to take her in his arms and speak other words.

"I hate you. I hate you!" She flung herself through the door and pounded his chest. "You're wrong. You're supposed to be his friend."

He took it unflinching. This was everything he had expected, his loss come back a thousand-fold. And more.

At last, Jerry and Rosemary got hold of her. They pulled her back into the house, but she slipped out of their hands to the floor.

"You have to be wrong. He promised," she whimpered.

Mark stepped back, gulping down the gorge rising in his throat, and pivoted on his heel. The deed was done. Her family would have to love her through it. His heart broke. Gone was the one sweet memory in his life. They would never dance on the beach again. She would never look at him with starlight in her eyes. All she would see forever more would be the monster who had destroyed her world.

It was Chaplain Kenny's turn.

He made it down the first step when a firm hand clutched his jacket sleeve. He stowed his emotions, bit his lip, and willed his tears away.

"I need to leave now," he muttered thickly without turning around.

"Mark." Rosemary's voice cracked. She held him fast and made him turn, still on that precarious first step – where he could walk away. Gentle hands cupped his clean-shaven chin, tilting his head up to face hers.

"Ma'am," he ground out, defenseless to this older woman's kind blue eyes – just like Libby's. He blinked. Moisture clouded his vision. The strong. The brave. Yeah, right.

"I'm sorry," she whispered kindly. Like his mother might have done a long time ago, she gathered him into her arms, her hand to the back of his head and held him tight against her heart. His white cap tumbled to the porch. "You poor boy. Jonathan was your friend, too."

He squeezed his eyes shut. Anger he could handle. Not this.

Two

He let Libby have her space. She needed it. So did he.

Jon's body was scheduled to arrive from the Port Mortuary at Dover Air Force Base to the Chippewa Regional Airport in Eau Claire. Mark had intended to drive alone to the airport, but Jerry wouldn't hear of it. Only now, there wasn't enough room in the back seat of Jerry's Jeep Patriot for the wall of grief between Mark and Libby. She stared out the window, wordless and crying. Clenching his jaw, he stared at the back of the front seat, willing the ride to be over and the day to be done.

While the most difficult task of notification was behind him, the following days would be just as hard. Funeral arrangements needed to be made. Chaplain Kenny had done an amazing job, but today he'd gone on ahead. He was already at the airport while Mark accompanied the Cliftons.

He stared out his window, too. Thinking. Jon's parents would receive their son's death gratuity, the one hundred thousand dollars for service members killed in a war zone, as well as any unpaid salary Jon had not received yet. Mark found it interesting Jon had not designated Libby as beneficiary to his life insurance policy. They were engaged. It would have been easy enough to take care of that before he had gone overseas. Mark would have, but then, he would have married Libby long ago, too. What was up with that?

Was Jon afraid he might get a Dear John letter? Was that why he hadn't taken those important steps?

Give me a break. She wouldn't do that, would she?

He stole a sideways glance. No. Not Libby. She loved Jon. And yet ….

The words she had hurled at him on the porch returned for closer scrutiny. *Didn't he promise? This time he would really come home?* What had she meant by that?

He didn't have the heart to tell Libby about Jon's will. No. Let John's lawyer be the bringer of that bad news; that his assets were left to his aged parents, even his brand new Mustang convertible. Jon had forever declared his love for Libby, but his actions?

Mark pushed that disquiet out of his head. What he thought didn't matter. He'd be gone in a few days, maybe a week at the most. Besides, he had broken Libby's heart. She would never want to see him again once this was done. He understood.

"I'm sorry I hit you." Her voice came thin and sad from the other side of the car. Mark turned to her, but she still faced the window, not seeing the newly planted cornfields rolling by, and not looking at him either.

"Don't worry about it." Empathy washed through him. She had wrapped her hair in a clip that barely contained the sunny mass of curly gold. He wished she would look at him. Maybe that would make the difference, and they could at least part as friends. He placed his hand palm down on the seat between them—just in case. She didn't move.

"You were his best friend, you know," she whispered to the glass. "I think he would've wanted you to be the one to tell me. He used to say you were brothers from different mothers."

"Sounds like something he would say." *Please Libby. Look at me.*

"He always made me laugh," she said wistfully. "He told me about the time he put boot polish on your rangefinder."

"I looked like a raccoon for days." *Turn around. Just once.*

"He loved the Corps, you know." Her voice was light as air with less than a puff of strength behind it, barely enough to cloud the window with the vapor of her breath. "He said it was his real family. I always thought that was kind of odd, but maybe because he was an only child ...."

Mark heard the remorse in her voice. Did she think Jon loved the Corps more than her? "He loved you, Libby. You were all he talked about. You have to know that."

"I do." With those two words her voice cracked. She covered her mouth as if to call them back, but they tolled again and again, the lovely vow now robbed of its wonder. "I do. I do."

It was all he could do to not reach across the seat and pull her into his arms while she unraveled. Every muscle in his body yearned to hold her, his tongue to tell her that she was going to make it through this, his hands to soothe her furrowed brow. Mark steeled himself and did nothing. Physical comfort was not his to offer. She belonged to Jon, not him.

Rosemary stifled a sob. Jerry's sharp eyes saw everything from the rear view mirror. "Are you okay, baby girl?" he asked Libby gently. "Do you want me to pull over to get you a drink or something?"

"I'm fine, Dad." She wiped her eyes and smoothed her hair. The moment had passed. "Really. I'm fine."

Miles went by in silence. Mark sat remembering and regretting. Her parents commented on the weather and the possibility of another road construction project through central Wisconsin. Small talk had a way of distracting tender feelings. Rolling fields with freshly plowed furrows passed by, unseen normalcy to an obscenely abnormal day. At last, the green and white water tower that brightly proclaimed the City of Eau Claire, Wisconsin, rose into view ahead of them. The Chippewa Valley Regional Airport was minutes away. He breathed a sigh of relief.

Unexpectedly, her hand reached across the seat and upset his careful control. She clutched his fingers tightly.

Mark loosened his seatbelt and shifted to her side. "I'm right here, Libby. What do you need? What can I do for you?"

"I'm scared." Grief etched the delicate features of her face. Her sad eyes melted his heart and all his resolve with it.

"I know you are," he soothed. "I'll be with you every step of the way."

"But I don't want to do this." Her ragged voice pleaded. Blue eyes gripped his as tight as her trembling fingers on his hand. She bit her bottom lip, and he wanted to caress her cheek, kiss that soft full lip, and carry her far, far away.

"We never want to do these kinds of things, do we?" He bowed his forehead to hers.

"No." Tears glistened on long lashes as her voice squeaked. "We were supposed to get married, you know."

He nodded. He knew.

"Not this." She turned to the solemn spectacle outside her car window as her father pulled through the chain link gates of the airport runway and drove slowly to his designated parking spot. It seemed the entire state of Wisconsin had shown up to welcome their fallen hero home. People were everywhere. Red, white, and blue banners waved in the soft morning breeze. Some held American flags while others held signs that simply stated love for Sergeant Jon Wells. His high school band filled the air with patriotic background music while an honor guard waited in solemn formation at the open ramp of a nearby jetliner.

Jerry parked the car as directed by a young police officer. Chaplain Kenny promptly escorted Jerry and Rosemary to their reserved seating on the tarmac. Sharon and Clark Wells had already been seated. Both gray-haired and tall, Jon's parents were an elderly couple that clung to each other for support. It was obvious he was their son. He had their height and elegant bearing, his father's handsome movie-star face and his mother's quick smile.

Mark hurried to Libby's side of the car and opened her door. He reached inside for her hand. When she didn't take his hand, he ducked his head into the car, his cover barely clearing the door as he faced his sad friend.

She sat frozen, her eyes staring straight ahead and breathing hard. She wouldn't look at him.

"Are you ready?" he asked softly.

She didn't turn his way. The waterfall of tears had breached the dam she'd tried to maintain and now ran freely down her face. She trembled, and he stifled a groan. He wanted to climb in beside her, hold her, and make time stand still. No. Who was he kidding? He wanted to turn back the hands of time and love her first, kiss her first, and marry her before Jon knew she had ever existed.

Instead, he knelt at her side, his knee to the hot asphalt and his hand resting lightly on her arm. The words of friendship they'd hurled at each other while jumping off her parent's raft into cold Lake Wissota came to him now. "You take all the time you need, Libby. No hurry. No worry. When you're ready, I'll jump with you, okay? You say when."

She looked at him, and he choked. He was falling again, but not off the edge of some raft on a lake. No. This felt more like a plunge into eternity, a fall he would never recover from. How could she not feel this intense energy between them, this magnetic pull that sucked the breath out of him?

Mark bit his lip. Reality slapped him down and woke him up. *She belongs to Jon. That's why.*

Her teary eyes were suddenly lit with that memory of a happier day. His words of comfort must have helped. How funny that a foolish childhood dare brought her strength now. But it did. The sunshine of her love came out for the first time in days. A timid smile tugged at her lips. There she was again, Libby Clifton, the woman of his dreams—and another man's girl.

She wiped her face and clasped his hand. Mark pulled her gently up from the backseat, their eyes locked on each other's.

"Thanks, Mark," she said quietly. "I think I can do this now."

He acknowledged the sudden strength in her voice. "Yes, ma'am. I know you can."

All eyes were on the striking blond fiancée of the fallen hero, escorted to her seat by his proud Marine friend and brother. Together Mark and Libby joined the rest of the family. The Clifton's chaplain went to the head of the casket, and the band played The National Anthem. After that the chaplain thanked Jonathan's parents for raising such a fine young man. He commended Jon's friends for their loyalty and friendship. Lastly, he honored Libby's devotion to the man she loved. The brief service concluded with a prayer.

When the band began the soft sad strains of *'Til We Meet Again,* Libby reached for Mark's hand. She whispered in his ear. He nodded, took her arm, and together they walked to the casket. Reverence silenced the watching crowd as the heart-rending music continued softly.

Libby stood at Jon's side again, quaking. She placed her palms face down on the flag draped casket over the sea of blue and stars of white – over the place where his heart should be, gulping back tears. It seemed she had fainted when her knees buckled, but she'd simply thrown herself onto the casket, the way she would have thrown herself into his arms if he had come home alive. One last time she embraced the man she loved.

Mark stood blinking hard and fast, listening to her whispered words to the flag. "Why Jonathan? Why wasn't I good enough? I would have loved you forever."

Through the hushed crowd, Rosemary's quiet sobs joined her daughter's. Another woman sobbed, but all Mark cared about was Libby. Every sinew and nerve in his body urged him to pull her back from the casket and protect her, to take her away, to hide her some place where she would never be hurt again. But that was not a notification officer's duty. Mark stood like the soldier he was and stared, his jaw clenched tight and his heart tighter while she sobbed, seemingly unable to let Jon go.

Mark reached for her shoulder, and she nodded, but the poor thing had no tissue, and neither did he. Mark peeled one glove from his hand and pressed it into hers. She looked up, for a moment not understanding. Tentatively, she lifted it to wipe her nose. He offered one small wink.

Take my glove. Take the shirt off my back. Take all of me. You already have my heart.

With that accomplished, and her sad face blotted semi-dry, he secured her hand over his arm once more. Slowly, they resumed their place with the family. The lovely strains of the hymn ceased. Another call to attention sounded, and the honor guard carried the fallen hero to the waiting hearse. Jon's high school band played *God Bless America*.

People cried and offered condolences. Libby accepted hugs and handshakes with tearful grace. Mark stayed at her side. The hearse pulled away.

Jonathan William Wells was home.

Three

"You're coming over for dinner tonight."

Jerry reached into the room to shake Mark's hand, extending the invitation like it was already accepted and a done deal. Libby's father looked like most farmers, tanned from years of work in the weather, strong as an ox, and bright eyed. His handshake was the same—firm, solid, and no-nonsense. "Can't have you sitting here all by yourself now, can we?"

"The girls would love to see you again." Rosemary referred to Libby and her two sisters, Faith and Marie. The four women in Jerry's home looked more like quadruplets than a mother and her three daughters. They might be separated by a few years, but all were blond-haired, blue-eyed, and pretty. "Besides, I made that dumplings and tomato sauce you liked so much last time you were here. You'll come, won't you?"

He hesitated. He'd taken a room at a motel in the nearby city of Eau Claire. A good hour's drive from Spencer, he kept a respectable distance from the families he had just dealt a devastating blow to. So he was surprised to see Libby's parents standing there, Jerry in his farmer's overalls, and Rosemary in her Sunday go-to-meeting dress. But tomato sauce and dumplings? The thought alone was enough to make a man drool. Darn, that had been a good meal. He had almost forgotten.

"You folks are very kind, but—"

"Good. Mother serves dinner at 5 PM sharp. Be there. We'll be waiting. Don't be late." Jerry clapped his back with a hearty smack, and left Mark standing at his motel room door wondering how he'd lost control so quickly.

He wasn't late.

As required in the Clifton household, Mark's hands were washed, and he was seated in his appointed chair at the dining room table by the time the blessing was offered. Faith and Marie sat across the table. Libby sat next to him, close, but withdrawn, and a definite wall between them.

Apparently Chaplain Kenny was either not invited or had other pressing responsibilities. That didn't help. Mark planned to eat fast, make up an excuse to leave, and hightail it back to the motel before dark. There was no sense staying. Libby didn't want him there.

Jerry passed plate after plate of delicious food as they served themselves. The platter of hot bread dumplings was followed by a steaming bowl of rich homemade tomato sauce full of tender chunks of beef and herbs. That aroma was filling enough, but then came cauliflower drenched in melted Colby cheese, slices of fresh-from-the-hothouse early tomatoes, a relish tray of last fall's spiced crab apples, sweet gherkin pickles, and pickled herring. It might have been June, but Mark could not have imagined a better feast at Thanksgiving.

"You want another Leinie?" Jerry asked. "I've got plenty. Amber Ale? Berry Weiss? Maybe some Summer Shandy?"

Mark had already downed one of the tasty beers from the famed Leinenkugal microbrewery in Chippewa Falls. He lifted his second brown bottle. "Still nursing this one. Thanks."

"I'll bet you haven't had home cooked food in a while, have you, son?" Jerry eyed the young man at his side. "There's plenty more. You eat up."

"Not since the last time I was here." Mark passed the homemade bread to Libby at his left. She took the wooden tray without looking at him. Their fingers never even touched.

"Rosemary will send some back with you to your motel. You do have a refrigerator in that little room they got you crammed into, don't you?"

"Dad," Faith interrupted as she smiled fetchingly across the table. "They don't have refrigerators in motels. Besides, he'll be coming back for dinner tomorrow night, too."

"He is?" Jerry asked at the same time that Mark asked, "I am?"

Both men looked at each other in surprise, but Faith continued as if the impromptu invitation were already cold, hard fact. "I don't know why you're surprised. There's no sense in him eating all by himself in Eau Claire when we've got plenty to share, now is there?"

"I guess you're right as rain, little girl." Jerry looked to Mark in amusement. "Looks like you're coming for dinner tomorrow night, too."

"I really shouldn't." Mark started to politely refuse, but Rosemary's hand was already on his arm as she stood behind him to fill his water glass.

"No sense arguing with these two." She winked kindly. "You won't win. Besides, we'd love to have you join us. We have plenty."

"That's the spirit," Jerry exclaimed. "We might be going through a tough time right now, but we've always got room at our table for a good friend. Besides, you're more like family, Mark. You oughta know that by now."

Mark lowered his head and gulped. Jerry meant well, but that day was done. Family didn't do to each other what he had just done to the Cliftons. He caught Libby's glance, her blue eyes sad and tired. For one nanosecond, she had actually looked at him. His heart pounded. *Who does she see when she looks at me, the beast who broke her heart – or me? Should I leave? Should I stay? Why did I come here?*

"Please come," she said softly. Cobalt blue forgiveness spilled between them. Her fingers strummed the table beside her plate of uneaten food like she might reach for him again.

Before he could answer, Jerry shoved the platter of dumplings into his hands. "Help yourself. So how long are you in for? And how's the Corps treating you?"

Mark turned back to Libby, but she was gone.

He speared one more dumpling to make Jerry happy more than anything else. The appetite he had come with had vanished. Early departure became an urgent need. Just like her insistent father, Faith offered the bowl of tomato sauce, her blue eyes lit with gentle flirtation. Her eyes were lighter than Libby's, more pale than full of the deep color of Jon's girl. Mark accepted the serving and set the bowl on the table.

"Actually, I'm leaving the Corps at the end of summer, sir. It's been good to me, but I'd like to try my hand at something besides the military for a change."

"And what will that be?" Jerry passed the relish tray, his brow arched.

Mark scooped a couple spiced crab apples and passed the tray along. "I'll be working for an outfit that specializes in security for federal agencies. I start with them the same week that I out-process from the Corps."

"Sounds interesting. What's the job about?"

"They'll keep me busy with surveillance, bodyguard duties, and things like that."

"It's a good thing you've already got a job lined up. There are too many guys coming home from the service who can't find one these days."

"Yes, sir, that's what I thought. It's good money. Worth a try."

"Where will you be working? Anywhere nearby? Chicago? Minneapolis?" Jerry's brows peaked at the options he had just presented.

Mark caught the hopeful tone in his voice. "I'll be working for a company called The TEAM. They're located back east in Alexandria, Virginia."

"Darn. That's too bad." Jerry pursed his lips. "I was hoping you'd settle down around here. Last time you were here, it struck me you were a farm kid."

"Dad." Faith scowled at her father and then shot another smile to Mark. "Leave him alone. He's trying to eat."

Jerry shrugged. "I'm just making conversation."

"Actually, I did grow up on a farm," Mark offered with his mouth half-full. "My family is in Ohio, so yes. Guess I'm a farm boy at heart."

"See?" Jerry smirked at Faith. "I was right, and you was wrong."

Faith blushed, and Mark looked away. He didn't want to encourage her.

For the rest of the meal, the table conversation remained on light and easy topics. Before long, Mark was well fed and planning a polite exit strategy. He'd eaten too much, but as good as everything tasted, he was not about to overstay his welcome. Libby hadn't said another word to him, not like she had spoken much to anyone else either. Despite her need for his comfort at the airport, she didn't seem to need him now.

Rosemary foiled his plan when she brought a frosted can of homemade ice cream to the table. Libby followed with steaming apple pie while Faith and Marie cleared the dishes. Mark stood to help, but Libby pushed him back into his chair with a gentle shove to his shoulder blade.

"You're our guest," she declared quietly. "You don't get to help. You only get to eat. Besides, there are enough of us girls to clean up."

"But your family's been too kind. Let me at least help with dishes." He tried to stand again, but her hand hadn't moved.

"We have a dishwasher. Eat your pie." She sounded stern as she slipped a plate of steaming apple pie in front of him. The delicious fragrance of nutmeg and cinnamon assaulted his nose in a very good way. He breathed it in, closing his eyes as the mental comfort of it took him instantly back to another table when his mother was alive. For a nanosecond, he was just a carefree kid again instead of a battle-weary Marine. He was loved and cared about. When he glanced up at Libby, she stood watching him with a funny glimmer in her eye, the ice cream scoop in her hand suspended above his slice of pie.

"Say when?" she asked, her eyes alight with tenderness.

When. His heart responded quickly, but that's not what she had meant. He recovered the use of his brain. "One scoop will be fine. Then I need to get going."

"Why?" She cocked her head, waiting on his answer.

"Because your family's been too kind and—"

Rosemary handed him a new fork and a fresh cup of coffee. She winked at him like she knew exactly what he was trying and failing miserably to do.

"I don't want to overstay my welcome," he said.

"You men. Always leaving. Never staying." Libby shook her head. Covering his pie with three scoops of fresh homemade vanilla ice cream didn't help his exit plan, but neither did the stern expression on her face. "Shut up, Mark. Eat your pie."

So he did. The evening had taken a sudden turn for the better. She was talking to him.

After dessert, the family moved to the cool of the porch, and Mark with them. Boston ferns hung from the ceiling, their long straggly fronds draping over and around the white wicker furniture. The Clifton porch wrapped the entire house in white-rails and screens, all open to invite the evening breeze.

Mark took his place with Jerry on the stoop. The weatherman said it was going to rain. That meant Jerry would have to hurry and get the latest crop of grass hay baled and in the barn. Mark deliberated extending his visit to help with the chore. Tossing hay bales would be a nice change from soldiering. He could work with Jerry in the field and maybe catch sight of Libby while he did. That might be nice.

Rosemary, Faith, and Marie discussed the food they needed to prepare for the meal after the funeral, where they would have to store it, and the logistics of moving all that food from their place to the hall at the church. Libby sat by herself in a white peacock chair in the corner. Surrounded by family, she still seemed alone, listening to the conversations whirl around her, but not partaking in any of them. Mark noticed how quiet she was, and that she watched him.

When the sun began to lower in the western sky, he stood to leave. Fireflies sparkled at the edge of the ditch bank by the road. He thanked Rosemary for her kindness, especially for preparing a meal that must have taken all day to cook. Faith and Marie both gave him an extra long hug. He had seen their furtive glances in his direction at the dinner table, especially Faith's. Each of them was as beautiful as the other, and would make some man a great girlfriend or wife. That man just wasn't him.

With a blush, Faith handed him a box of stationary with a book of stamps taped to the lid and her address written carefully below it. She shrugged when she put it in his hands. "Just in case you need a pen pal."

"You never know. Sometimes a guy gets pretty lonely." That was probably the wrong thing, but what was a guy supposed to say when a pretty girl hands him a gift?

When he shook Jerry's hand, Libby was suddenly at his side.

"We're going for a drive, Dad." She kissed her father's cheek even as he looked at the two of them in surprise.

"You are?" Again he asked his question the same time as Mark asked, "We are?"

Jerry thumped him on the back with a chuckle. "I guess us guys don't know a whole lot, do we? Seems the women in our lives got our schedules all planned out for us. Well, you kids run along now. Don't be out too late, and remember. Dinner tomorrow. 5 PM. Sharp." He waved as he turned to go inside.

Libby looked at Mark. "Do you mind if we take your car?"

"Where to?" Mark walked down the steps to his rental and unlocked the doors. His heart pounded with this sudden shift in the evening.

"The lake." She rolled her window down the minute he pulled out of the driveway. "I need to get out of the house for awhile. I hope you don't mind."

"No, ma'am." He set the radio on a local station that played soft music. Night settled dark and quiet through the countryside as he drove through the small town of Spencer and headed west to Lake Wissota. It was a good hour's drive. He waited for her to talk, but she didn't say anything.

Mark glanced at her out of the corner of his eye. The summer air filled the car, tossing her hair in a blond stream of curls behind her. She held one arm out the window, letting it undulate in the passing wind the way little kids liked to do. Libby riding shotgun in his car – what a sweet sight.

They passed through the little towns of Colby, Thorp, Stanley, and Cadott. Before long, they were bumping along the gravel road that led to the Clifton cottage.

"You missed it." She pointed to a spot behind them. "Back up. It's over there."

"I can't see it." Her open window invited all the dust of the country road inside. He put the car in reverse and his arm over the back of the seat as he followed her directions. A patch of overgrown sumac had hidden the unmarked driveway. All he saw was dust. "Where did you say it was?"

"A little further. There, see it?" Libby pointed to a gravel driveway barely visible in the dark. Only a short post with a red reflector offered any indication there was a road there. "Turn here."

Gradually, the car parted the brush, its headlights illuminating the narrow way as they left the sumac and dust behind. A two-story, cedar-shingled cottage stood at the edge of the lakeshore, its ghostly windows staring at them in the night. By the time the vehicle rolled to a stop, Libby was out the door and headed to the private dock. With one quick tug on the knotted rope, she untied the wooden raft and jumped onboard.

Mark followed. He stood on the dock, wondering exactly what she was doing, escaping the grief – or him. The notion prevailed. He wasn't going to follow if she needed space.

"Come on. Jump," she urged, so he did, easily clearing the distance.

The raft bobbed under his added weight, but it was large enough there was no concern of tipping it over. He looked around the flat deck. "Where are the oars?"

"Where they belong." She pointed to the sides of the raft where two long hunter green oars rested snug in their holders.

"Just checking. I remember someone lost them the last time I was here," he muttered.

"I did that, huh?" Libby sat in the middle of the bobbing raft, her arms around her knees as she smiled up at the night sky. "I almost forgot. We had fun last year, didn't we?"

"We did." Mark stretched his legs out in front of him, leaning back on his hands as he looked at the sky, too. A wave of stars glittered overhead. It seemed like forever ago. "I still don't like fish for breakfast, though."

She chuckled, and it was a very welcome sound in his ears. "That was so bad, wasn't it? Almost as bad as those fish tacos you made."

"No, uh huh. The fish tacos weren't so bad for lunch, but fish and eggs together for breakfast? That really grossed me out." He glanced at her. It was good to see her smile, even if it was sad.

"You're right, but the blueberry pancakes were delicious," she said pensively, her chin tucked into her knees and her hair undone over her shoulders. "I love blueberries and cream."

"They were blue." It was his turn to chuckle.

"You guys tricked me." She punched his arm, and a real, no-kidding smile brightened her eyes this time. "I didn't know they were on my chair until I sat on them."

Mark shrugged, grinning. "It was Jon's fault. He made me do it."

"You would say that." She punched him again, but harder. "If you're so innocent then, tell what did you call me the rest of the time you were here, huh? If you would never do such a thing, then you wouldn't remember that name either, would you?"

"Smurf cheeks." He tried to say it without laughing, but the memory of her blue backside was too funny—and too delightful. He couldn't have stopped looking last year if he had wanted to. There wasn't enough material in her whole swimsuit to cover the blue stain those berries had left behind—on her behind. Besides, he was a man, not likely to miss an opportunity like that one. "Thanks for reminding me. I'd forgotten."

"Yeah, right." She reached over the edge of the raft. "I had a blue butt for a week, and my swimsuit is stained for life. You men are all the same."

With a dash of her hand, she splashed water into his face. The fight was on. Before long, they were both on their hands and knees, pulling up handfuls of water and splashing each other. It wasn't enough. Her hands were smaller. She couldn't beat him. No way. He saw it coming. She sputtered and laughed, blinking lake water out of her eyes. *There she is. There's my girl.* Another extra big handful, and she barreled into him. He almost caught her before they fell overboard.

"I'm drowning," she squealed as he ducked her head under water. "I'm drowning!"

"You, Libby Clifton, cannot drown." He ducked her again. "You're not fooling me. You're the best swimmer in your class. I remember."

This time when she came up for air, she brought a rock from the lake bottom with her. Thwack. She launched it dead center off his forehead. It bounced.

"Ouch." He winced and let her go. "You got me. Dang it. I can't believe I fell for that."

She giggled and took off in a flurry of kicking legs and splashing water to the other side of the raft. There was no way he could catch her. Libby swam on a competitive swim team in high school. Mark treaded water while he removed his shoes and set them quietly on the raft. Then he resorted to very quiet puppy paddling, trying to make as little noise as possible as he circled for his mermaid. He had to keep a sharp lookout. She was good at sneak attacks, like pulling her adversaries underwater, or grabbing their hair from the safety of the raft, not that he had any to grab.

The night was dark and quiet. No sounds of splashing water met his ears. He was nearly all the way around the raft when—

Ouch! Another small rock bounced off the back of his head. She giggled behind him.

"That's twice." He turned to see her arm already cocked and her hand loaded.

"Did they teach you to count in the Corps?" she taunted.

The projectile nailed him on the side of his head, but this time she had come too close. He gave an extra hard shove through the water and instantly had her by her wrists, then the rest of her, too. She took a deep breath, and tried to submerge, but he was having none of it. He'd caught her, fair and square. No way was he losing this fish. Within minutes, he carried her thrashing and giggling out of the water and dumped her butt on the beach.

"You got me." She blew out a big breath as she slipped out of his grasp. Libby flopped onto her back, still laughing and sputtering in the dark. "I can't believe you caught me."

He stood over her for a moment, gauging her reaction to having been in his arms for that brief encounter. If she noticed it, she gave no indication, but he had. The feel of her had enticed more than he should have allowed. He was only here as a friend. That's all. Yeah, right. Try telling his heart that.

The warm tingle remained, only it had sunk lower and burned hotter. He needed to give his body time to calm down, so he walked back into the water and pulled the raft to shore and secured it to the dock. After he retrieved his waterlogged shoes, he stripped his sand covered socks off and placed the soggy combination on the edge of the dock. The happy foolish moment was over.

Or was it?

Four

"My clothes are wet." Libby pulled at her soaking wet capris, her eyes sparkling up at him.

The words he should never say sprang to his lips. He bit them back and pulled his shirt over his head instead. With deliberate intentions, he wrung it out over her. "Hey, guess what? Mine are wet, too."

"Stop." She laughed, shielding her face from the drips raining down on her. "You're getting me wetter."

"N-o-o-o." He dragged the word out. "I've got news for you. You're already wetter."

And hotter. And prettier. And everything I've ever wanted.

He squeezed the last drips of water from his shirt while she lay there in the dark chuckling, her eyes squeezed tight. An overwhelming urge to lie beside her swarmed his thin hold on common sense. Everything about her invited him tonight. Her laugh, her eyes, even her wet body and long legs were irresistible. Instead, he sank to the sand beside her, shook the wrinkles out of his shirt, and stifled his heart.

"That's the good thing about clothes. They'll dry." He pressed his palms to his dress slacks, wishing he had anticipated the dunking. He had a long drive back to Spencer, and then the return trip to Eau Claire, not exactly what he wanted to do in wet clothes. Still – she had smiled.

"Gosh. I needed that." She folded her arms behind her head and stared at the sky. "I almost feel like myself again."

He found a flat stone in the sand and skipped it across the water. It slapped the surface of the lake once, twice, and three times before it sank. "It did feel good, didn't it? Course we could've changed into swimsuits first, and maybe brought a couple of towels with us, too. Maybe we could've taken our shoes off, you know, unimportant stuff like that."

"You always like to be prepared, huh?" she asked. "You don't like surprises, do you?"

He gave her his most devilish look, his brow raised and what he hoped was a gleam in his eye. "Let's just say I didn't plan on squishing around in wet shoes the rest of the night."

"You're so serious."

"No," he replied. "Just careful. I like to know where I'm going, that's all."

"Remember when we were out here last year?" The wistfulness was back in her voice. "Remember what Jon said?"

"Which day? You'll have to be a little more specific." He meant it playfully, but she was serious again.

"I was thinking of the night we were lying out here on the raft. Remember? We were looking at the stars and talking about our families. I was telling you guys about mine, and you didn't say hardly anything at all. Do you remember what he said?"

"Yeah." Mark sailed another skipper across the surface of the lake. He remembered that night. Being third-wheel to an engaged couple was as full of opportunities as pitfalls. Most of the time, he had felt excluded, but the important thing was that he had met her. That part was all good. "He said the Corps was his family, or something like that."

"Yes. That's exactly what he said." The smile was gone from her voice. "What do you think he meant by that?"

Mark heard the ache inside the question. "I don't know. You know how he was. Jon was always saying things like that. I think he meant he was a good fit with the Corps. It gave him structure, somewhere he belonged."

"Is the Corps really a band of brothers?"

"I guess." He skipped a couple more stones. "It does turn a boy into a man pretty quick, that's for sure. And there is a bond between those of us who've been in combat. It's hard to explain. It's just the way it is. Why? What do you think he meant?"

It didn't take any training to know she had tears in her eyes. "It's just that, well, the minute he said that, I knew we were never going to be married. He wasn't ever coming home to me."

"You're wrong." Mark shook his head vehemently. That was the one sure thing about Jon. The man had Libby Clifton on the brain. He never stopped bragging about how beautiful she was, how all his children were going to be girls, and how they would all look like their mother. "He might have loved the Corps, but he loved you more. I know he did. When I first met him, he was the biggest sap on the planet. All he did was brag about you. It was always Libby this and Libby that. No. You're wrong. Jon loved you more than anything else."

He pitched a perfect skipper that smacked the water with five strong kisses before he lost the sound of it.

"I used to believe that." She sniffed. "When he first went to basic, we had a plan. I was already in nursing school. He was going to boot camp, and then onto whatever training he had to get through to finish. We weren't going to get married until he had all that behind him."

"Right. I met him at Lejeune." Mark skipped another perfect five. "That's the same plan I heard, and I can't tell you how many times I heard it. It was always the same. Marry Libby. Have a dozen kids. Live happily ever after. He drove the rest of us crazy."

"That would have been a year ago last September," she said quietly.

He sailed another rock. It sank. Yeah, Jon loved her all right, just not enough to take care of her in the event of his death, not enough to do a little pre-planning. Most soldiers carried a what-if I die letter in their pocket or helmet for their loved ones. Jon didn't. Mark had asked about it after the remains were recovered from the crash. The medic searched. He found nothing. It could have blown away or been lost in the explosion, but Mark wondered now.

"He said for sure he would come home in December, but some kind of special training came up. He couldn't make it." The sadness in her voice stabbed him. "Not even for Christmas."

He sailed another stone. It didn't skip once.

"Each time he called to reschedule, he said he felt bad. There was always something more important going on in the world. He was promoted so fast, and then there was Afghanistan. It was his first chance to see real action. You know how it is. That's what you guys trained for. It was important. He couldn't miss it." She stuck her fingers into the sand beside her, combing four straight lines before she brushed them away. "We rescheduled again."

There was nothing to say, so Mark sat and listened.

"It's not like I was rescheduling a dentist appointment. This was our wedding. I had invitations to send out, flowers to buy, and ...." Libby blew out a big sigh. "Jon was in country by January for a six-month deployment. He couldn't come home even if he wanted to. I stopped getting letters when he left this time. The few times I heard from him, he was excited about everything he had accomplished over there. The people loved him. It was like he hated to leave them more than he wanted to come home to me. We talked about a June wedding, but I could never get him to commit to a date. It was like he had better things to do."

Mark blew out a slow breath when she paused. He was in Afghanistan by then, too, part of a special operations task force. They were searching out the Taliban in hunter killer teams, one man to spot, the other to shoot. Sometimes they were so far up in the mountains, they could see all the way to Pakistan, but they were never there for so long that they couldn't get to the rear area and send word to their families. The Corps wasn't heartless. For the most part, they took care of their men and women. Yeah, life might get real rugged for awhile, but communications weren't as primitive as they used to be in past wars.

Calling home was never an option for Mark. When he came back to the rear area, bone-weary, disgusted with war and death, there hadn't been anyone to call. No one cared that he was cold, that his government-issued body armor was a piece of crap, and he could really use something that would actually hold up under extreme conditions. No one cared whether he had been successful for the day, or that he didn't get shot, that he didn't die. It galled Mark to know that Jon had called home so seldom. *Man, Jon, what were you thinking?*

"He left me in June; he came back to me in June. I don't think he would have come home any other way but in that box." Libby wiped her face before she rolled onto her side. She came to rest on her elbow, her head in her hand so she was looking at Mark. "He'd already found what was important. It just wasn't me."

"I'm sorry you feel that way, but you're wrong. I know he loved you. He did." Mark tried to sound sure, despite the doubts piling up in his mind. He had trusted Jon with his life. How could that same dashing hero have treated Libby so badly?

"I think he loved me as much as he could." She drew a heart-shape in the sand with her index finger. "But I couldn't compete with everything the Corps offered—the adventure, travel, and that band of brothers thing. I really lost him the minute he enlisted, the minute he found his Marine Corps family." She brought her fist down in the middle of the heart, stretched out her fingers, and brushed it away.

There were no more rocks nearby flat enough to skip. Mark listened to the gentle lap of the lake against the raft, the perpetual slapping sounds of water on wood. It was peaceful, but doubt assailed him now. He blamed himself. He should've known something was wrong.

Libby pulled herself into a sitting position, burying her feet in the soft sand as she wrapped her arms around her knees. "I kept hoping he would be as excited to come home as he was to leave. I guess I have to let go now, don't I?"

He didn't answer the rhetorical question. The silence lingered. Jon was a good soldier and a damn good man. Mark just couldn't defend him. Not anymore.

"Hey." She tossed a handful of sand at his bare feet. "I have a question for you."

"Okay. Shoot." He sighed. Good time to change the subject.

"I've always wondered why you were so quiet that night. I mean, there I was bragging like crazy about my family, telling you guys all my favorites stories and all the wacko things I've done over the years. Jon was complaining about being an only child, and how much he wanted to be a soldier, but you didn't say anything. What's up with that?"

Mark stared at the water. The three of them had been sprawled on the raft after a day of sunburns, fishing, and dancing on the beach. Libby and Jon lay together on one side of the raft; Mark kept his distance on the other. The night was full of stars in the heavens, and the reflection of star shine on the lake. It seemed he was sprawled between heaven and earth, bobbing along on some celestial stream —until Libby started talking about her family. She had so many good memories of early Christmas mornings, grade school programs, dance recitals, and singing in the choir. Heck, even simple Sunday chicken dinners with her family were a treat compared to the way he had grown up.

"Guess I was wondering what it was like to have a family to complain about," he said softly.

"But you have a family, don't you?" It was the same question she had asked a year ago, only he had never really answered.

"I guess." He blew out a big breath, not wanting to answer it now. "There's my old man, but he'd as soon I don't go home anymore. He never got over my mom passing."

"When was that?" She reached for his hand in the sand, intertwining her slender fingers in his. That gentle touch jumpstarted his heart. He looked to see if it had the same effect on her, but he couldn't make out the details of her face in the dark. Only her eyes sparkled.

"I was eleven. He said it was my fault. Heck, I was just a pain in the neck kid. I didn't know what cancer was. I couldn't do anything right after that."

"And you were an only child?" Her fingers wrapped tighter as she sat cross-legged and faced him.

"Yeah. He was a lot older than my Mom." Mark turned his body to face her. "He never wanted kids. Mom had something wrong with her; she wasn't supposed to be able to have kids, but she did. I don't think he ever forgave me for being born. Guess I ruined everything."

"I'm sorry, Mark."

"Yeah, well, don't be. It's along time ago. No use in crying over spilled milk." The quicker they got off this topic, the better. His mother's death crushed him, even after all these years. Libby seemed to be listening, waiting for the rest of the story.

"I look like her," he admitted. "At least, I've got her dark hair and eyes. She was pretty. Her name was Judith Jones before she married my Dad. She had four sisters. They always called her JayJay, like the two initials of her name, only spelled like the bird. JayJay."

Somehow, Libby's fingers had become a conduit of comfort to that sad little boy from so long ago, pulling the story out of the man he was now.

"Never could figure out why she married my old man. Always seemed like she got a raw deal, like she traded her big, loving family in Tennessee to live with a guy in Ohio who couldn't carry on a civil conversation, much less …." He left the words unsaid, 'love his son.'

"How did she die?"

"Kidney cancer." He blew out a deep breath. "She was doing dishes at the kitchen sink one night after supper. I was drying; she was washing. She was telling me about the first time she had ever stuffed a Thanksgiving turkey. All of a sudden, she dropped a plate. It shattered all over the floor, only …."

Only I can't talk about this anymore.

Mark looked down at her hand gently caressing his. No touch had ever felt as kind as Libby's at that moment. Did she have any idea how much it affected him? How much it helped?

"I always kind of thought he killed her. The cancer gave her a way out of a bad situation. That's all."

"What's your father like?"

Damn. How do you explain a man like John Houston? Mark didn't want to try. He pressed his other hand to the sudden pain in his temple and willed the image of his father away. "He was a hard man."

Other pictures came. His mother's tears when she found her lovely red songbirds filled with buckshot at the foot of the birdfeeder. Her tight lip when she wiped mud and muck off her freshly polished wooden floors. The way she forever tried to please a man who refused to be happy. The way he left her alone for days on end.

Yeah. It sucks to be me. End of story.

Needing to change the subject, Mark tossed a tiny pebble at Libby. It skimmed off the top of her head. "Gotcha."

"Ouch." Her eyes lit up at that not so gentle reminder of their friendship. For all her womanly ways, there was still a little girl inside who wanted to play. "Thanks for putting up with me tonight. Guess I needed to remember some good times again."

"Well, aside from the fishy breakfast, it was the best vacation I'd ever had. But I've got a question for you now." He lifted their hands out of the sand, still intertwined as if they belonged together. "You reached for my hand that night, just like this. I was right on the edge of the raft and you took hold of it like—"

"Like you were important?" She finished his sentence for him. Her knees brushed his. There was a light in those cobalt blues again. She scooted closer. Instantly, he felt the spark. His idling heart kicked into overdrive, thumping like a runaway engine.

"Well, I was going to say like you were afraid I might fall off the raft, but, yeah. I like what you said a lot better. So why did you do that? Why did you reach for me?"

He held his breath. For a moment they were just two happy-go-lucky kids again, the smell of sand and lake surrounding them in the memories of a better day.

She turned thoughtful. "You were so quiet. Jon sounded like he was telling me goodbye, like he couldn't wait to get back, and his ten-day pass was a waste of time." She clenched

Mark's hand. "But you seemed happy here, like you didn't want to leave, and I didn't want you to go."

"Good answer." Mark sighed.

She had said what he needed to hear. The heat from her touch radiated up his arm and straight to his heart. If ever there was a right moment, this was it. Wasn't it? Desire beat a steady rhythm he instantly controlled. Was it too soon to hold her? Too late?

Closing his hands over hers, he muttered. "I think I'd better get you home. Your dad needs his rest."

He said the correct words, the polite ones that maintained propriety at all cost. He had given her a way out. Did she want more? Was there any reason to hope?

Libby chuckled softly when he pulled her to her feet. Instantly, she fell into his arms. She radiated nothing but innocence and trust, her hands pressed against his bare chest to steady herself. His breath caught. Warmth for this tender woman flooded his core. He pulled her close. At last holding her in a real embrace, all of his male instincts commanded him. *Kiss her. Taste her. Finally know the answers to your questions.*

He gazed down into her lovely face, hoping for one glimmer of invitation. The night was dark. She had lowered her eyes. He couldn't see how blue they were much less read come hither in them.

She leaned her head onto his chest. He held her carefully, tucked under his chin like she belonged there and let his fingers fill with the soft sweet tendrils of silky gold. The lake and stars fell away as the very real knowledge that he loved this woman filled his heart. Here was precisely where she belonged.

She sighed.

He held his breath. Just one word, that's all he needed, and she was his.

"You're the only friend I have right now, Mark."

Not that! His heart dropped like a ton of bricks. That was the last thing he wanted to be.

A friend.

Five

Mark had to look twice.

Libby'd finally arrived, nearly late for Jon's funeral, but what had happened since their impromptu swim? She looked visibly diminished. Smaller. More frail. Black shadows rimmed her eyes, hollowing her face. The black dress she wore enhanced her skeletal pallor. Gone was the flush on her cheeks, the smile in her eyes. Only grief showed through today.

"That her?" Lance Corporal Travis Jennings, another one of Jon's closest friends, asked when Libby walked by.

"Yes," Mark said quietly. She didn't look up, didn't see the men in uniform come to honor their buddy one last time. He didn't blame her. Everything about this day was hard; meeting strangers with grace under fire even more so. She didn't have strength enough for herself much less others.

"Jon had it made," Travis muttered, his eyes on Libby.

"He did." Mark had to agree.

"Everyone ready?" Chaplain Kenny asked, his hand on Travis's shoulder. "Will you men be okay?"

"Yes, sir," Travis nodded. "We're a ready as we're going to get."

Mark turned to his men. Sergeant Rick Buckley, Corporal Greg Padgett, Lance Corporal Chris Dixon, and Gunnery Sergeant Gil Swanson, all from the Twenty-fourth Marine

Expeditionary Unit headquartered out of Camp Lejeune, North Carolina. Each had travelled on his own dime to pay final homage to their friend. He was proud to stand with them, to honor Jon. And Libby.

They stood as the priest entered the side door and proceeded to the altar. "You may be seated," he said to the congregation.

Mark took his place, but words were just words. He couldn't focus, and he didn't feel Jon with him, not here in this austere place of worship. Something felt wrong. His eyes drifted to Libby.

Oh yeah. I'm a traitor to my friend. I want his girl. No wonder Jon's spirit isn't here.

He scrubbed a hand over his eyes and focused on the funeral mass with its readings and gospel excerpts.

She's unreachable. Give it up.

Faith cried through her reciting of the obituary, and Marie sang a touching rendition of *Amazing Grace*. His eyes sought after Libby. Even with her mother and father's arms around her, she seemed alone in her grief.

It wasn't until the end of the service that she turned and locked eyes with him. It seemed she knew right where to look. A sad smile tugged at her lips. He nodded to acknowledge her, but his heart leapt. I see you, he mouthed across the pews full of people.

She nodded once and looked away.

When the service concluded, the honor guard rose, and marched to the front of the chapel to remove the casket to the waiting hearse for transport to the West Spencer Cemetery. Mark kept careful track of Libby as she sank onto her appointed chair at the gravesite. It should have been a position of strength and support to be seated between her parents and Jon's, but she seemed more alone than ever between the strong couples. Lost. Betrayed.

She looked like a woman who had been lied to, proclaimed to be the lover of a man who had chosen something else over her. Her words from the lake struck true. *He'd already found what was important to him. It wasn't me.*

Mark drew his attention back to the somber proceedings as the Honor Guard reverently transferred the coffin from the hearse to the gravesite. It was times like this that made him damn proud to be a Marine. These rough and ready men, these forward-deployed and rapid-response warriors proved themselves all over again in times of the greatest need.

Once Jon's comrades-in-arms and poker buddies, now they moved with precision slowness and tender care, each man acutely aware of their fallen friend. The weight of the coffin was more than just a wooden box to them. It was Jon's quick smile, his practical jokes and funny faces, his loyalty and patriotism. These Marine Corps brethren knew Jon literally rested in the palms of their hands on this final journey.

At last, the coffin rested in place. The honor guard took their position opposite the family, and the seven members of the Reserve rifle guard readied their weapons.

"Ready. Aim. Fire."

Libby jumped at the first seven shot volley that rang across the grassy lawn.

"Ready. Aim. Fire."

Mark braced himself for the final salute.

"Ready. Aim. Fire."

As the echo of those loud reports faded, the Marine Corps bugler stepped forward. *Taps*. Mark blocked the hymn; it always hurt. Libby wept openly, her soft cries mingling with the plaintiff twenty-four notes of sorrow pouring from the trumpet's golden throat.

> *Day is done; gone the sun;*
> *from the hills; from the lake;*
> *from the sky.*
> *All is well. Safely rest. God*
> *is nigh.*
> *God is nigh ....*

A light summer breeze played with her hair as if someone from the spirit world had reached into the real world to comfort her.

Unexpected anger welled up inside of Mark. He wanted to slap that spirit away. *Too late, Jon. You're too damn late. Let her be.*

The notes faded. Chris Dixon and Travis Jennings removed the flag that draped Jon's coffin. After they folded it lengthwise two times, they stretched thirteen folds, one after another in crisp formation. Mark slipped the twenty-one shells from the rifle salute into the folds of red, white, and blue. At last the proud flag was wrapped into a snug triangle, its position of honor after the battle was won.

Travis nodded with somber eyes when he passed it into Mark's gloved hands. He offered his friend a brief nod, cradled the flag reverently with one palm under, the other over and turned to face the families. It was time. With the careful steps of a military drill, he carried the flag of glory to Libby, exactly as Jon's mother and father had requested.

She raised her fingers to her mouth. Their eyes locked. Tears blurred his path for this sweet woman left behind in life as much as in death. With his jaw set in fierce determination, he performed his final duty. Mark placed the flag in her trembling fingers.

"Libby Clifton." His strong voice faltered. He blew out a deep breath. There was so much more he wanted to say. Not this. His heart screamed to take hold of her, to shelter her and never let her go. His soul ached to love her like she should have been loved all along, to make up for Jon's failure every day for the rest of her life. But Mark couldn't. Now was not the time or the place. Besides, he was brother and friend, not lover.

He bowed his head, drew in another calming breath, and squeezed his eyes shut.

"Libby Clifton." He whispered the words he'd memorized instead. "This flag is presented to you on behalf of a grateful nation and the United States Marine Corps. There are no words to express my love and appreciation for Jon's honorable and faithful service. He was my best friend. My faithful comrade. My brother."

He opened his eyes as he finished, and Libby stood. With a silent nod, she accepted the flag, and cradled it against her heart. Very quietly, she whispered, "He's gone."

"Yes," Mark choked at the pain in those two words. "He's gone."

"I can't do this anymore," she whined, one glance to the side as if someone might over hear.

He heard the crescendo of grief in her words. His own heart wrung out with sorrow, and he wanted her in his arms. Maybe then he would find comfort, too.

"I'm with you every step of the way," he rasped.

"I'm supposed to be getting … married. Remember?" She pressed her forehead into his uniformed chest.

"I remember." The hurt of all that was happening sucked the life out of Mark. He had already lost Jon. Now he was losing Libby, too. As he cradled her blond head against him, Mark struggled with his thoughts. Did Jon ever truly love her? Was his death a blessing in disguise? Would their marriage have ended in divorce with Jon forever away on some mission for the Corps, doing what he really wanted to do instead of loving her?

Mark let her cry while his tears fell into her hair. He didn't care who watched or what they thought. The tenderness of the moment overwhelmed him. She fit perfectly inside his arms, the same way she already fit in his heart. He stifled his feelings to keep from doing anything more foolish—like kissing her tears away.

The other mourners walked away from the grave and back to their cars. Jerry nodded as he passed by, his arm around Rosemary on one side, Marie on the other. Faith tagged behind. Mark caught her furtive glance in his direction. He closed his eyes and shut her out. She meant well. He just did not have room in his heart for anyone else.

Mark held Libby lightly until the storm subsided. By then they stood alone in an empty graveyard.

With a sniff, she took a step back. "What should I do?" she asked timidly. "I mean everyone's watching me. What am I supposed to do now?"

"Whatever you want." He searched for the right thing to say. "I'll take you to the church, your house or out to the lake again. I'll take you anywhere you want to go. People will understand."

"Anywhere?" She looked up at him, her blue eyes awash with sadness.

He pulled the tender woman into his side, content to be nothing more than her friend for now. "Listen, girlfriend. Anywhere. Anytime. You jump; I'll jump. You say when."

She smiled through her tears.

For a moment, Mark glimpsed something else shining back at him. At least he hoped.

"Come on, *Junior Agent.*"

Mark looked up. Ember had just emphasized his new-kid-on-the-block job title as she and Mother walked past his workspace on their way to the morning meeting. Ember and Mother were the two administrative assistants in the office. Known for their genius with anything IT related, they kept the office software and hardware updated, monitored nearly every other federal agency's chatter, and a wealth of other techie-type things Mark didn't exactly understand or care to know about.

"Briefing's in five. I've got a feeling the boss is watching you."

"Yeah." Mark turned his cell phone off as he followed. "Wish I knew what his problem was."

"Aw, don't let Alex get to you. He's tough on new recruits. That's all." Ember turned her dazzling, green-eyed smile on him. "You'll grow to love him. Just wait."

"Right," Mark answered sarcastically. "That's got as much chance of happening as you showing up in your natural hair color."

"Wow. Ember." Harley rounded the corner with his usual big smile, surprise showing on his raised brows at his first glimpse of her hair color of the week. "You're, umm, kinda orange today. Didn't know it was Halloween."

"Knock it off, you guys. It's called golden umber." She fluffed her hair like a movie star, her nose in the air as she modeled her new do. "I got tired of the blue. It made me look pasty white, kind of like a corpse or something."

He reached his fingers for her head. Tall, slim, and tanned from running in the latest marathon, he delighted in teasing Ember as much as he teased everyone else.

"You touch it and you'll die, Mortimer." She shot him one of her best evil looks even as his fingers reached their target. As tall as they both were, it was an easy reach.

"And now I need a mirror," she complained. "Wow. Thanks a bunch."

"Really? You need a mirror for orange spikes? You've got to be kidding." He linked his arm through hers as she pretended to push him away. "You're gorgeous, darling. You don't need a mirror. Trust me."

"One of these days." She pushed him off in mock anger. "Wait until you need satellite footage or a new computer. Then you'll be sorry."

"Umber Ember. Umber Ember," Harley chanted, his head nodding back and forth as he kept the tease alive. "Sounds like a name for a new rock star."

"Well, I like it," Mother said as they entered the Sit Room. "How about you, Mark?"

Mark shrugged her question off. "You can all show up with orange hair for all I care."

"Golden umber," Ember corrected him sternly. "Not orange."

"What did you do to set the boss off, Mark?" Harley asked "I noticed he was at your desk the other day. He didn't look none too happy."

"He was late for the briefing on the Homeland Defense operation," Mother chimed in before Mark could answer.

"Gee, thanks," he said. "Anything else you would like to share?"

"Well, now that you mention it …." Mother's bright blue eyes sparkled like sapphires against the background of her creamy skin and white hair. "There was that phone call with—"

"Never mind." Mark cut her off sharply. As usual, she was too willing to share her vast wealth of computer knowledge, office gossip, and anything else the world might be interested in, the juicier the better. "Some guy named McCormack called to welcome me to The Team. That's why I was late. That's all."

"McCormack?" Harley's eyes lit up. "Really? Jed called you? Wow. He's never called me."

"Ha!" Ember smacked his arm. "You were in rehab back then. Remember?"

"Oh. Almost forgot about that." Harley pulled chairs out for Ember and Mother, but then he turned to Mark. "Did you tell the boss it was McCormack on the line? That might make a difference."

"I didn't get the chance." Mark grimaced. "He was on me before I could get a word in edgewise. Who is Jed McCormack anyway?"

"Just the man who funded Alex when he started The TEAM," Ember responded.

"His business is up the hill from us in Rosslyn," Mother added. "He's one of the country's billionaires and a big shot in Congress, too. Alex saved his son over in Iraq. They're pretty tight."

Mark cocked his head. Why would a man like McCormack have called to welcome a nobody like him?

"Yeah, well." A knowing look passed over Harley's face. "The boss is hell on tardiness, especially when he's giving the briefing."

"I'd like to know what he isn't hell on. Stewart's got a chip on his shoulder the minute he shows up in the morning." Mark slouched into his chair. "What was he in the Marines anyway, a drill sergeant? The man's a flaming type-A."

The room stilled. Mother, Ember, and Harley were all looking over his shoulder.

"And what type would you be, Junior Agent Houston?"

Mark jumped to his feet and did a quick about face. Mr. Stewart was not smiling. Neither was Mark. "The kind who's on time for briefings, sir," he said meekly.

Mother, Ember, and Harley flinched.

The man stood at Mark's height, and right now they were nose to nose. Mr. Stewart's expensive business suit stood out in sharp contrast to Mark's casual wear. Mr. Stewart had a way about him, maybe because of the way he dressed, always sharp, professional—and powerful.

"What did you call me?" He stepped into Mark's personal space.

"Ah, sir. Sir." Mark stared straight ahead as he answered. By now Junior Agent Zack Lennox had joined the group at the table, as well as Senior Agents Murphy Finnegan and Roy Hudson. Senior Agent David Tao stood at the door, an amused smirk on his face.

"Are you stuttering? And do not call me sir one more time unless you want to be looking for another job." Mr. Stewart's growling tone demanded respect. "Is that clear?"

"Yes, ah, I mean no." Mark struggled to answer without the offending title that sprang automatically to his USMC trained lips. "I mean, yes. It's clear."

As if it were at all possible, his boss stepped closer. "I work for a living."

"Yes." Mark's response was rapid and strong, but the man didn't back off. His eyes were piercing blue, almost pointy, like two lasers boring straight through Mark's skull and out the other side.

"Mother needs a Santa Claus for her Christmas party. Would that be you, Junior Agent?"

"Yes." Mark could've sworn a bemused glint passed through those frosty blues. "That would be me. Glad to be of service, umm, Boss."

"Then sit." Mr. Stewart hissed. He took a step back and slapped his leather organizer to the table with a loud smack. "You're holding up the briefing. Again."

Mark sat, relieved to be out of the line of fire.

Harley gave him the thumbs-up sign along with a huge, lopsided grin as he whispered across the conference table, "He likes you. I can tell. He really likes you."

Six

I'm back in the damn Corps.

Mark recognized the beat down he had just received, the tough molding of a new team member by the alpha dog. Even if Stewart had never held the title of drill sergeant, he played the part perfectly.

Well, fine. You lead; I'll follow. You'd just better be worth following.

A desecrated gravesite displayed on the overhead screen. The casket had been pulled out of the muddy ground and pried open. The uniformed body of a Marine lay face down in the mud, disrespectfully jerked out of its final resting place, and the casket's inner lining torn away. Crime scene tags littered the area.

"We're dealing with a drug smuggling ring." Mr. Stewart said. "According to Air Force and FBI intel, these guys have been smuggling bricks of opium inside the transfer cases coming stateside from Afghanistan. In order to get it out of the Port Mortuary at Dover Air Force Base, they stashed the dope inside outgoing casket linings. That's why the grave desecration."

The next slide depicted another casket, only this one was not desecrated like the other. It had been exhumed by order of the FBI. Army Sergeant Harold W. Benning lay there properly dressed in his Class-A uniform, his body untouched, and the lining undisturbed. The only thing out of the ordinary was the decapitated head wrapped in plastic and resting between Sergeant Benning's boots.

Mr. Stewart pointed to the screen without looking up from his notes. "Meet Sergeant Benning and what's left of Lance Corporal Jose Gutierrez."

Mark sat back and let the rest of The TEAM run with it. He would engage when and if he was needed. It was important to get his bearings first. He didn't need to butt any more heads.

"Looks like he could use a hand," Senior Agent Roy Hudson, a muscular African American who, unlike his boss, didn't take life too seriously, remarked drily. He had spent most of his Marine career as an explosive ordnance expert and still had all of his fingers – always the sign of a good EOD man.

"FBI believes Gutierrez was the in-country operative for an upstart cartel operating near Bagram." Mr. Stewart continued as if he hadn't heard the flippant comment.

"Man. What'd he do to get on their bad side?" Zack stared at the screen. Another junior agent like Mark, he was on the hefty side, too. And built. Mark had seen this guy's biceps—almost as big as his. Almost. Zack seemed to have an easy way with the boss. Everyone around this table did— well, except him. "Last time I saw something like this was my last tour in Iraq."

"It could be they're sending a message to their man stateside," Roy offered.

"That's quite a message." Harley was out of his seat as he grabbed the laser pointer and directed it to the cut mark along the neck of the severed head. "Look here. That's a clean slice. I'll bet this poor guy was beheaded with a sword."

Murphy and Roy were out of their seats to look closer at the screen, but Mr. Stewart dismissed the chatter. "This poor guy," he said sarcastically, "smuggled opium inside the transfer cases of our KIAs, and his buddy at Dover hasn't shown up for work the last week."

"We got a name?" Murphy asked.

"Michael Louis Castor. Ex-Marine. One tour in Afghanistan. FBI thinks that's where he and Gutierrez linked up," Alex replied. "Once Castor left the Corps, he went to work in the EOD room at the Port Mortuary at Dover Air Force Base."

"They got an explosive ordnance disposal room at a mortuary?" Mother asked in surprise.

"Wow," Ember whispered. "I didn't know that."

"Yes," Roy explained. "It's the first place every transfer case goes once they arrive at the mortuary. Booby traps and unexploded ordnance don't happen very often, but every body gets scanned just in case."

"So Gutierrez shipped the dope stateside with the remains, and once they got here, Castor was the first man on the scene. He had exclusive time with each transfer case while he scanned them for bombs." Harley muttered. "What a creep."

"But Alex." Murphy was clearly agitated. An Army man himself, he'd spent his career taking care of his men instead of Army politics. "Wouldn't the Benning family have noticed the head once they got him home?"

"You'd think." Alex sounded weary. "Benning's folks are in the middle of a divorce. They didn't show at the airport when his body was shipped home. Didn't attend the funeral either. I don't guess they cared what was between his boots when they couldn't be bothered to look at his face."

Mark listened to the chatter around him, still focused on the young man in the casket. This soldier had fought for his country only to be disrespected by his family. It wasn't right.

"Families," Roy muttered.

"Our customer wants eyes on this new cartel. Harley, you take the lead. Mark, if you're up to it, you'll support Harley."

Mark caught the snide comment. Yeah. He still had the new-guy target painted on his chest.

"How long were these guys moving dope?" Harley asked. "Do we know?"

"Castor worked in the mortuary for two years," Alex answered.

"Man. They had to be blowing some serious cash. There ought to be a paper trail," Harley said.

"Mother and Ember are looking into it."

"Wait a minute. You kids are going too fast," Murphy said. "I'm no genius, but I think what I'm hearing is this Castor fellow finds his buddy's head in one of those transfer cases instead of the usual dope. He panics, hides the head inside a casket that's leaving Dover, then he hightails it to who knows where. Is that what I'm hearing?"

Alex nodded. "Apparently he had more dope to get rid of, too. He hid it inside the lining of another outgoing casket. That's why the grave desecration."

"How does the FBI know he stashed the dope at Dover?" Roy asked.

"His locker tested positive for opiates." Alex nodded toward the screen. "Plus both of these caskets had his fingerprints all over it."

"Just when you think you've heard everything." Murphy sighed.

Mark straightened in his seat, planning to head out the minute this briefing was done.

"We're in the early stages of this investigation. Let's keep that in mind. We're not here to solve the case, just to be the State Department's eyes and ears in country. Bottom line, Harley and Mark, you're not looking for the man who replaced Gutierrez. Do you understand?"

Mark nodded. *Got it. Yes, sir. Sir.*

"You are not to engage the cartel at any time. The Air Force is handling that part of the investigation. Your job is to observe only, but by the time you're through, I want to know everything about these guys, their names, known associates, what they eat for breakfast, and their girlfriends. Everything. Do I make myself clear?"

"Yes, Boss," Mark and Harley answered simultaneously.

Alex gathered his paperwork. "These are the lowest dirt bags out there. That's what makes them dangerous. Arzad will be your in-country point of contact again. Harley, you know the rules. Get in. Be smart. Stay safe. Mark. Follow Harley's lead. Can you handle that?"

Sheeesh. This guy would not let it go.

Arzad was a humble man.

The first things Mark noticed were the elderly Afghani's bright, brown eyes sparkling from the deep-set wrinkles on his weathered face. Harley and Mark had hopped a ride on a military transport to Bagram Air Base. Alex never signed off on a defense contract unless transportation was provided. The flights might not get them exactly where they needed to be, and sometimes the trip might take a few days, but they always got close.

"You've got a new ride," Harley exclaimed as they tossed their duffle bags into the back of the dilapidated van that Arzad stood proudly beside.

Arzad smiled wider. "Yes, Mr. Harley. I do." He gestured proudly to the vehicle as if it weren't forty-years old, riddled with rust, and held together with baling wire. "My brother, he is camel trader. Needed bigger truck. He trade to me for two goats. You like?"

"I do. It's much bigger than your last car." Harley motioned to Mark. "Meet Mark Houston. He'll be working with me this go round. Mark, this is Arzad."

"Good afternoon, Mr. Mark Houston. I happy to meet you."

"Very good to meet you, Arzad," Mark said sincerely. "We are privileged to be back in your country."

"You come here before, I think. Yes? Maybe soldier?" Arzad's eyes swept over Mark's six-foot frame with a knowing look. "Mr. Alex only hires best men to be his boys."

Mark cocked an eyebrow at that respectful estimation of his boss, not yet sure if it was a good thing to be one of Alex's *boys*.

"You make my wife very happy. Gulnar cook two days since we hear you are coming." Arzad pulled away from the airfield in a cloud of dust. "You stay at my humble home, yes?"

"Thank you, Arzad. It will be our honor." Harley flipped the collar of his shirt over his mouth to filter the billowing road dust. "Ah, it's good to be back, isn't it?"

"Yeah." Mark grimaced from the heat and smell blowing through the open rear windows. "Nothing like Afghanistan, that's for sure."

"We hear there's a new cartel in town." Harley turned to their driver.

"Ah, yes, that is true." Arzad's demeanor changed from boyishly happy to somber. "They came to town one night and drove other men away. Very sad."

"Why's that?"

"The other men were neighbors. Our friends. Some were family. We not know where they are. New boss maybe killed them."

"Where did he come from?" Harley asked.

Arzad shrugged. "Maybe Russia? He very mean man."

"A Russian? Are you sure?" Harley shot Mark a look.

"Oh, yes. Russian. He big man with black beard. You will see. He has many pictures on his chest and arms, like peacock. Tomorrow I show you where he lives. You will see."

"Great." Mark stared across the arid landscape. The last thing these people needed was another Russian.

The ride was hot and bumpy, but at last Arzad stopped at a small collection of mud brick structures. Mountains rose up to the north while the city of Bagram lay in the valley to the south. His home was a humble dwelling surrounded by a low rock wall. Three scrawny goats, several brown sheep, and a tired looking donkey stood behind the rickety rail fence. A couple mongrel dogs wagged happily around the men as they pulled their gear from the rear of the van. Within seconds, a thin young girl peeked out of the door to Arzad's home. With a smile, she charged Harley.

"Najela. How's my favorite girl?" He scooped her up and swung her off her feet, spinning around twice before he set her down. "My heck. You're all grown up. What have you been eating?"

She nodded shyly. "I grow very tall."

"I hope you're not too old for a present," he teased. "I brought something. If you guess what it is, you can have it."

Mark watched the game begin. Leave it to Harley to charm the ladies.

Najela's bright brown eyes sparkled with curiosity. "I think maybe it is candy bar?"

"Do you think I would only bring you a candy bar?" He spiked his brows. "I brought that last time. You get one more guess. Remember what we talked about? Time for this, and time for that, and—"

"Did you bring me a present that is a watch?" She clasped her hands together and watched while he pulled the small, pink wristwatch from one of his many pants pockets. "Oh. It is beautiful. Is a princess?"

Harley peered into the face of the watch, his face scrunched up. "Could be. I think it's Cinderella. Hmmm. Maybe it's Snow White. Here, let me set it for you." He took the tiny wristwatch and matched the time to his watch. "There you go. Now you'll always know what time it is."

She hugged it to her cheek, her eyes obviously full of adoration for this tall man. "I will take very good care of my watch. You are my most favorite American in the whole world."

"Well, I'm not the only one who brought you something." He pointed to Mark. "This is my friend, Mark Houston."

Najela turned shy and speechless as she tucked her new present into the folds of her ground-length skirt.

"Well, it just so happens …." Mark pulled a small rectangular Styrofoam container out of his pack. "I did bring something especially for you."

She stepped closer, craning to see what was in that mysterious white box. He had always loved the children of this war-torn country, and Najela was no different. Thin and small for her age, she dressed in the soft colors of most of her countrymen and women. Brown indicated poverty to Mark. These people had so little.

He lifted the lid and pulled another smaller box from between two blue icepacks. "Do you happen to like chocolate, Najela?"

She nodded even as she turned to hide her face behind her grandfather. Arzad grinned at her sudden shyness. "She is never so quiet. Najela. Come out from there. Remember how we treat guests."

She peeked from behind her grandfather's jacket, and Mark held perfectly still. Every move she made was graceful. Feminine. This little girl was fast becoming a woman. Before long she would be married off to some young man, no doubt on his way to war like all the others. Mark hoped that young man would not be Taliban, and that he would be kind. Arzad's sweet granddaughter deserved more.

She inched closer to the gift in Mark's outstretched hand. Tentatively, she touched it with her index fingertip, but did not take it. "It is for me?"

Mark nodded. "It is only a few pieces of chocolate, but each one is supposed to taste different from the rest. Will you tell me how they taste?" As he placed the box in her hand, she nodded with serious brown eyes.

"Yes. I will tell you the taste of these chocolates," she promised seriously. "Thank you, Mr. Mark." Her skirt twirled when she turned back to Harley with another big hug. "But you are still my most favorite American in the whole world."

"What can I say?" Harley's face wrinkled with a cheesy grin. "Either you got it, or you don't."

Seven

Gulnar, Arzad's wife, welcomed Harley and Mark into her humble home with a shy smile. She was as weathered looking as Arzad, but the same light sparkled in her eyes. As soon as they ducked into the door of her humble home, she spread a huge tablecloth over the rug on the floor. Najela scampered to retrieve a copper basin and pitcher of water, speaking softly to her grandmother.

"My guests. Please." Arzad motioned Harley and Mark to sit with him on the floor. "We eat now."

"This is called aftabah wa lagan," Harley whispered as Najela brought the copper basin to each man. "We will wash our hands before we eat."

Mark nodded. He appreciated that Harley assumed the role of tour guide. It never hurt to be reminded of the simple ways of Afghani hospitality. Najela knelt quietly at his side, offering a small piece of well-used soap.

"Thank you, Najela." He washed his hands while she poured water into the basin to rinse.

Ducking with shyness, she handed him a small towel, and turned to repeat the process with Harley and lastly Arzad. When the men had all completed the washing, dinner commenced. Gulnar brought dish after dish of wonderful foods to the middle of the tablecloth—an extraordinarily large bowl of mutton stew, steaming bowls of rice and boiled potatoes. She and Najela brought trays of sliced tomatoes and cucumbers, different kinds of cheeses, salads, grapes and a variety of dried fruits, and plenty of naan with sprinkles of poppy and sesame seeds, their traditional flat bread.

"This is the dastarkhan," Harley explained quietly. "It's their table setting." He turned to Arzad's very happy wife. "This is most excellent, Gulnar. I can tell you've been baking and cooking for days. I'm not good enough for so much wonderful food."

She blushed and smiled as much as Najela, clucking as if her hard work was nothing. Before long, the men were well fed and relaxed. Mark rubbed a hand over his full stomach. The last time he had eaten a traditional Afghani home cooked meal had been during a medical visit to a nearby village when he was still in the Corps. The elders there had invited his squad to share their afternoon meal in thanks for the medical supplies and care. It was a mission of gently given assistance to simple people leery of the armor-clad men with guns. By the end of the visit, they had parted friends. He hoped.

The food was always interesting. Gulnar's version of stew was filled with mutton and onions, and what looked like turnips instead of potatoes. The sweet and sour taste surprised him, but it was good. He had learned early in life not to be a picky eater. The Corps reinforced that lesson well. The abundance of fresh fruit and vegetables at the table told him Gulnar and Najela had been to the market. He liked the spicy eggplant salad, but mostly, he appreciated the constant attention of Arzad's wife and granddaughter. His cup of shomleh, a favorite Afghani drink of water, yogurt, and mint, was never allowed to empty. The minute he drank, either Gulnar or Najela refilled it, always with a shy smile as if they were thanking him for drinking. Their humility and constant care touched him.

"Thank you again for picking us up at the airbase, Arzad," Harley said between mouthfuls of rice and stew. "They give you any trouble?"

"I show them this." Arzad pulled a base identification card out from his trouser pocket. "No problem."

Mark smiled. Alex had thought of everything. Because of his military connections, it looked like Arzad was one of the few Afghani nationals allowed on base.

"So tell me," Mark said. "How is the poppy business?"

Arzad shrugged. "Is same. Some men plant. Some don't."

"But it is still an illegal crop."

"There is much illegal in my country." Arzad looked up from sopping his naan in the stew. "A man must feed his family."

"But you do not grow the poppies," Mark said evenly. "How is it you are so lucky?"

The old Afghani's eyes sparkled. "I serve Mr. Alex."

Reaching for another serving of the tomato, cucumber, and onion salad, Harley supplied the story. "Yeah. A couple Taliban sharpshooters were taking potshots at the boss. Arzad, ahem, inadvertently started a rock slide."

"Oops." Arzad shrugged, his eyes glittering with mischief.

"You saved Alex?" That surprised Mark.

"Mr. Alex good man," Arzad said firmly, and Mark had to look twice. There it was again, that loyalty thing his cantankerous boss seemed to inspire wherever he went.

When the meal was done, he started to rise to his feet to help clear dishes. Gulnar pushed him gently back to the floor, clucking her tongue and scolding. Her English was not as good as Arzad's or Najela's, but her meaning was clear. He would have persisted, but the stern smile on her face told him plenty. This was her house, her rules. The conversation was over.

She reminded him of another woman who wouldn't let him help with dishes either. Libby had done the same thing that night at her parent's home. For the millionth time since he'd left Wisconsin, he wondered if he should call, just to ask how she was doing. Caution hindered every inclination. She hadn't answered a single e-mail message. Maybe it was too soon and too late at the same time.

After the excellent meal, Harley and Mark hauled their equipment and duffel bags to the rooftop. The house itself was a mud brick structure with a flat roof that served as a gathering place in the cool of the evening. Two rickety chairs and a table with a kerosene lamp stood in the corner. Harley reported in to advise Alex they had arrived while Mark set their gear and bedrolls against the far wall.

Arzad brought another round of chai along with a tray of rote, the sweet bread Gulnar had made especially for her guests. He also brought a bowl of pomegranates along with a small carving knife. By the time Harley and Mark were unpacked, the night was dark and dessert was served.

Still smiling, Arzad waved his arm at the sky full of stars as if he had ordered this celestial display in honor of his friends. "You see?"

"It is awesome, Arzad. We are blessed to be in your home tonight." Harley bowed slightly to his diminutive host. "Thank you for always accommodating us in such a fine manner."

Arzad gestured toward the night sky again. "We are like these children. Allah watches over all of us." His eyes twinkled as if he were teaching a great mystery. The small Afghani turned to Mark. "You are married, yes?"

"No sir. Not yet," Mark replied evenly, knowing American ways mystified the common Afghani man.

Arzad shook a scolding finger. "Too late to wait. Must marry soon."

"Maybe someday." Mark shrugged.

"Family is all there is. Like the stars of Allah, it is everything." Arzad would not let it go. Again he motioned toward the star-studded sky. "Why not married yet? You have girlfriend? Yes?"

"Sure don't."

"But you do have friend who is girl, yes?" Arzad's brow furrowed with that question.

"Well, yes. Now that you put it like that, I guess I do."

Arzad looked pleased, as if he had just solved the problem. His old eyes sparkled. "Good. That is how marriage begins. Is she pretty girl?"

Mark smiled again, thoughts of Libby a welcome distraction in the stark countryside. "Very pretty."

"Ah, good," Arzad murmured appreciatively, "but beautiful woman not always a good thing. Wise man must not forget to look with his heart. Yes?"

Mark nodded at that astute observation, trying to divert the subject. "Then you must be a very fortunate man, Arzad. You live with two beautiful women. Yes?"

"I am happy man." Arzad's eyes lit up, but he could not be distracted. He turned his efforts to Harley. "I think Mr. Harley is not married, no?"

Harley rolled his eyes. "Not yet, old friend. I'm too busy to settle down. Maybe someday."

Arzad shook his head as he looked back and forth at the two young men. "Ah. You Americans. You think you have all the time. Is not good to wait. There are many young girls in America, yes?"

"Yes, Arzad. There are many young ladies in America," Harley explained patiently, "but we've both been travelling too much to think about marriage yet. It wouldn't be fair to a woman to marry her and then leave her behind all the time, now would it?"

"Ah." Arzad scowled, obviously not buying that argument. He leaned toward Harley with his hand half-covering his mouth. "Allah has made women much stronger than us men think. Do not tell Gulnar, but it is true. I am sure. You will see when you have woman. She will surprise you. She will look soft." He made the shape of a woman's vertical profile with both hands and a big smile. "But she will be tough like you. Maybe more tough."

"No doubt." Harley chuckled. "But when I marry, I'll want to spend my time with my wife, not a bunch of ugly guys in Afghanistan."

"Ha." Arzad chuckled, pointing to Mark and then himself. "He is calling us the ugly guys."

Mark watched the exchange. Harley still suffered with post-traumatic stress disorder from an injury he had received in Iraq. Once he left the service, he'd resorted to a variety of self-medications, none of which helped with the real problem of too many memories. It was only after he came to work for The TEAM that he finally did time in rehab to get his head out of drugs and his life in order.

More boy than man, he never should have gone to war in the first place, not that any man should. His decision to take on the tough alpha EOD dogs and become a canine handler for the Army actually spoke to his gentler side. The man had a soft streak a mile wide when it came to dogs, children, and older folks. Judging by the tender look on his face now, he cared deeply for this particular friend.

Harley's answer seemed to appease the elderly Afghani, but the light in his eyes faded. "Many beautiful women and girls in my country need husbands. Men go to fight. Women and babies are left behind. War is not good thing."

"That's why we're here," Harley said softly. "This new Russian in town is a danger to your country."

"You are right. In morning you will see he is not good man. He has brought much suffering to my village."

They sat in silence as the universe revolved overhead. At last Arzad stood to leave. "You will marry soon?" he asked like he needed that problem solved before he retired.

Harley gave him a quick nod. "You don't have to worry about us. We'll know when the time is right."

"It is good thing to marry. And it is good to have many children," Arzad said quietly. "Is not good to be alone. Man alone is a sad man."

With those final words, he joined his wife and granddaughter downstairs. Mark listened to his quiet conversation with Gulnar, no doubt lamenting the marital status of his strong male guests who should have been married and blessed with a dozen children by now.

"What is he? The local matchmaker or something?" Mark flopped onto one of the bedrolls.

"Nah," Harley replied. "Family is important to these people. That's all. He wants us to be happy like he is."

"I'm surprised he's not working the poppy fields like some of the other farmers."

"He's seen what happens to the men who've gotten caught up in the drug trade." Harley sank to his bedroll, balancing yet another helping of the chai and rote as he sat down. "And he's from another generation, kinda like our boss. He's only doing what he knows how to do."

"I'm surprised there's a Russian involved. That's not good," Mark said. What a profound understatement. The evidence of Russian interference in this country still littered the hills with unexploded ordnance and charred wreckage. Of course, so did American interference. He hoped the American version had served a higher purpose and maybe did a little more good.

"Russian mobs are everywhere, especially when drugs are involved. You know that."

"Yes, but Arzad takes too many risks. I know he's not doing drugs, but he needs to get out of this business. He's still too close to it."

"I know. Alex and I have tried to get him to bring his family to America for years." The sweet bread lay across Harley's chest as he leaned against the wall and slurped a cup of hot chai. "The man won't budge."

"I would if it meant my family's safety."

"Me, too, but his whole life is here, and Gulnar won't leave her mother. He says his family is all he's got. Poor guy has already lost most of them anyway."

"Yeah. What's the story behind Najela? Where are her parents?"

Harley sighed. "Arzad lost three sons fighting the Russians during their occupation, and then the Taliban showed up with their circus. They went from town to town drafting young men at the end of a gun. Arzad's son resisted."

"They killed him?"

"And his wife. Dragged them into the town square and put a bullet in their heads to make an example of 'em. Najela was just a baby. Gulnar found her still asleep at their house."

"Damn," Mark said softly. Arzad and his fellow countrymen were the only reason Afghanistan had any hope for the future. Mark had met a few others like Arzad when he had been deployed. They didn't come much better.

"These folks have had their share of crap. Whole country has."

"She sure likes you."

"Yeah," Harley said. "She's a cute kid. Alex and I have been here a couple times. Arzad's a good friend."

"How does Mr. Stewart reimburse him for all of this? Arzad just fed us a meal fit for a king, plus he's giving us free room and board for a couple months. What's Stewart got, a bank account over here or something?" Mark asked.

"I asked him once. He told me it was none of my business."

Mark dropped the subject. There was no sense discussing their boss, so he lay on his bedroll with his arms crossed behind his head staring at the stars. He'd been especially touched by Arzad's gentle admonition, *'Family is everything.'* His thoughts turned to Libby. What was she doing? Was she okay? Had she moved on and found another man in her life? A stab of irritation poked him. He hoped not.

"Goodnight," he said, but the only answer from Harley was a soft snore. He might be a highly trained covert operator, but tonight he sounded more like a kid away at camp.

The revelation that Jon had postponed his wedding still bothered Mark. Jon had never intended to marry Libby. Come to think of it, he'd never once mentioned a specific wedding date either. He was the kind of American Arzad had just warned Mark and Harley about. Mark punched his backpack into a more comfortable lumpy pillow. Jon was wrong. The Corps was not a man's family. It was a job and a temp job at that, but Libby was forever.

His mind wandered. The first thing he had noticed when he'd met her was her hair. It framed her face like a golden halo of curly sunshine. Oh yeah, and her smile. That pretty woman held so much light inside of her that she couldn't help but glow. And her upturned nose. The sprinkle of tiny brown freckles across her cheeks and nose made her look cute in a little girl sort of way. But her eyes. Yeah. The exact moment he'd looked into Libby Clifton's eyes he had fallen.

Jon had described his girlfriend a million times, but meeting her and actually looking into those cobalt blues, well, Mark made a fool of himself that day. Like an idiot he had stared, tongue-tied, embarrassed, and totally smitten with love at first sight. If he had any blood in his brain, it drained clean, clear away. Those eyes stole his heart and his common sense along with it. He was stupidly in love with a woman who considered him—a friend.

What guy wants that? Not him. No way. Not with Libby. She did things to his insides, got him tangled up and left him wanting. He turned restless just thinking about her, restless like something in his life was missing. Mark grunted and adjusted his backpack one last time. Somewhere off in the dark, a jackal yipped, followed by the gentle bleat of the sheep in Arzad's corral. The lonely sound echoed the ache in his soul.

A falling star blazed across the midnight sky, fading back into oblivion as quickly as it came. *So, we are like those children in the sky, huh?* Arzad's a funny guy. What did he mean by that? Was he talking about mankind being as numerous as the stars?

Mark stared at his celestial family, a silent observer in the dark wondering how he fit into the grand scheme of things. *We are like these children.* Constellations spread across the universe like diamonds thrown across the sky. Some glittered brightly while some were barely visible. Even the crescent moon hung like an ornament of thinnest sliver set in blackest velvet. The sky was full of treasures. He grunted. If Arzad had meant that mankind was a treasure, then Mark was the dimmest star out there. He knew his place. Libby was the brightest. No doubt about it.

Besides, he wasn't kidding himself. She had loved Jon; she would need a long time to grieve. Maybe years. Maybe a lifetime. Mark knew he had better man up and face the truth. No way could he measure up to Jon in her estimation. He was just – that guy. The one no one really saw, least of all Libby. She had said as much at the lake. He was a friend. Nothing more.

Another small meteor flashed at the corner of his eyes. He sighed, his arms still behind his head. Anything was possible. His mother had taught him that. Maybe, just maybe, a young lady might be staring up at those same stars tonight.

The notion comforted him even though he knew there was a huge time-zone difference between them. This tiny hovel in a third world country might somehow be linked to a pristine clapboard farmhouse a world away in the dairy state through this family of stars beaming down on him now.

A man could always dream.

Eight

"He wants what?" Libby couldn't keep the spike of annoyance from her voice.

"Washington D.C.," Marcy replied brightly. "You leave in two weeks."

Libby blew an errant strand of hair off her forehead, totally exasperated with this sudden change in her schedule. As a student nurse, she excelled. If the truth were known, she was obsessive about her chosen profession. She couldn't get enough of the work, clinicals, or the studying. If she wasn't up to her neck in exams and reading, she wasn't happy, not that she cared about happiness anyway. It wasn't on her agenda. She didn't intend to go looking for it.

Marcy's news brought Libby back to the problem at hand, another conference with Dr. Wonderful, also known as Dirk Clements. He was fast becoming a problem. This was the second trip he had wormed her into without prior notice, and all because, according to him, she was the sharpest in her class. It was getting old.

"He's got the hots for you, girlfriend." Marcy chuckled.

"You think?" Libby tried to keep the sarcasm out of her voice.

"I'll go in your place if you want. All you have to do is say the word."

"I wish I could. Oh, Marcy, how can I get out of this mess?" Libby faced her friend. "Can't you tell him I've got an exam or something?"

"He's already booked the flight." Marcy scrunched her shoulders and grimaced. "Sorry."

"Darn. I guess that means I'm going. What's this one about?"

"I hate to tell you, but there are actually two, one on *Endocrinology and Metabolism*, and the other's on *Infectious Diseases*. Real snoozers if you ask me." Marcy rolled her eyes. "The good thing is they're both in Georgetown. That ought to make them interesting, huh?"

Libby watched Marcy read the conference details off the sticky note in her hand. Marcy Buffington was her confidant, study partner, and best friend all rolled into one. They had joined the College of Nursing in Chicago on the same day. Libby could have continued at the local clinic in Marshfield, Wisconsin, but after Jonathan's funeral, she had felt suffocated. Everyone knew her circumstances. The pitying stares got old fast. The day she left, she dropped her wedding dress in a Salvation Army donation box and never looked back.

"You do know all the other nurses wish they were going instead of you, don't you?" Marcy reminded. "Besides, you get to travel to Washington D.C. You ought to be happy."

"I would be thrilled if only he wasn't so, umm, friendly."

Marcy didn't understand her dilemma. Libby hadn't told anyone about Jonathan or his untimely death, not even her closest friend. While most of the student nurses were looking for Mr. Right, Libby was not. She had already been down that road. Besides, there was something creepy about Dr.

Clements. He took liberties. During a previous conference in Des Moines, he had splurged on a bottle of champagne on their first and only dinner together. At that point, she'd explained her personal rule about not mixing business with pleasure. Obviously, he hadn't taken the hint.

"Did you say in two weeks?" Libby whined again, but Marcy smiled that dreamy, sappy smile of hers, already lost in fanciful imaginations of the darling Dr. Clements.

"I'm still looking for Natasha."

Harley's reference to Boris and Natasha from the Bullwinkle cartoon of bygone days made Mark smile. He'd seen the reruns. Unfortunately, the only one in sight was Boris Seinkevitz, and Arzad was right. The man was huge. With arms as thick as small tree trunks, he was a giant compared to the impoverished men in the village. A black beard and aviator sunglasses covered his ugly face.

To help blend in, Mark and Harley had changed into the traditional shalwar kameez, the brown dress-like shirt of the common man pulled over their pajama-style trousers. Both men wore a thin overcoat as well, more to disguise their very American stature than anything else. Since neither sported much hair on their heads or chins, they already stood out like two tall sore thumbs. Caps, scarves, and upright collars finished the camouflage.

"Looks like he stepped out of a Saturday morning wrestling match." Mark peered over his dark glasses to the spectacle across the street. "Old Boris likes bling."

Ropes of gold glittered off the cartel boss's muscular neck while each finger sported more nuggets of shine. He walked like a heavy man though, not one in athletic condition like most television wrestlers. Dressing in military olive drab did nothing to hide the prodigious belly that hung over his belt. A flash of gold glittered off the hilt of the sword in the scabbard at his side. Other than that, the Russian did not appear armed.

"And ink." Harley shielded his eyes from the sun. "The man's got enough tattoos, doesn't he?"

Mark switched to his rangefinder for a closer view. "Looks like a bunch of snakes and naked women from here."

"We must be careful," Arzad whispered anxiously as they watched from behind a delivery truck on the street opposite the Russian's building.

Mark stowed the rangefinder, but maintained careful observation as they continued their stroll around farmers and other vendors selling their wares. All manner of fruits, nuts, and vegetables were laid along the street in big baskets and carts. Heavily laden trays of baked pastries, baskets overflowing with spices and herbs, and brightly colored scarves and rugs were everywhere. A donkey stood patiently with a wooden cart stacked high with bright orange and purple carrots while his young owner sat beneath the cart in the shade. He smiled, offering a shy wave Mark couldn't help but return. A kid was a kid no matter which part of the world he was in.

The variety of Afghanistan always surprised, not only with all the goods and merchandise, but the people as well. Young boys ran past him dressed in school clothes similar to many American children while their mothers wore the traditional burka, their faces hidden behind layers of gray and blue fabric. Rainbow colored skeins of dyed wool hung from the doorway of one shop while woven onion, garlic, and peppers of all colors hung from the very next one. It would have been picturesque except for the mountain of trash piled at the end of the street, its unlovely odor wafting over everything. Mark pulled his scarf up to cover his nose. The smell could be much worse. It could be from the open sewers that ran behind the buildings.

The Russian's garish hangout stood out from all the rest. Flaunting freshly painted white walls with gold trim, tinted windows lined the lower level while wrought-iron railings on the second story offered an overview for two armed guards. A dusty black Hummer parked in front of the building where Seinkevitz stood with two more soldiers and a single village elder. No vendors trespassed near the building.

Mark watched the elder man with the Russian. Dressed in simple brown attire, he stood with his head down. Seinkevitz poked a finger into the older man's chest, causing him to take a step backwards. Mark detected the Russian's threatening tone. The distinct need to lock and load irked the back of his mind.

"How many men does he have in town?" Mark asked.

"Many." Arzad wanted to leave. "Come. We go to his villa next. You see then."

"His villa?" Harley stopped walking. "This guy's got a villa?"

Arzad took a few steps back to take Harley by the arm and hurry him along. "Come. We must go."

A bellow jerked Mark's eyes across the street where the older gentleman was on his hands and knees in the street. Only

Arzad's hand gripping his arm held Mark in place. "No, no, Mr. Mark. Come. We go now. Is not safe here."

"What's he saying? Tell me."

"I do not know his words. He speaks Russian." Arzad was clearly unnerved. "Maybe he angry because harvest was small. Please. We must go."

"Who's the old man?"

"Nasim."

"Who's Nasim?" Mark hadn't moved a step.

"Nasim is father of Mohammed Khan. He was village leader. Now he is missing." Arzad hyperventilated. "Please, Mr. Harley. Mr. Mark. This is not safe place. Come with me."

"It's okay, Arzad. We're just watching. Don't worry." Mark rested his hand an Arzad's shoulder to placate him. All the town's people had moved further away from Seinkevitz, though many continued to watch the confrontation from a safe distance.

"Hey, Mark," Harley said. "Look around. We're all by ourselves right now. Arzad's right. We need to move."

"Yes," Mark agreed, taking one step into the street. "You're absolutely right."

"No, damn it," Harley growled, but by then Mark had secured his scarf over the bottom half of his face. With his back straight and eyes forward, he walked to where Seinkevitz stood berating the elderly man. Nasim cowered, his hands raised over his head. Mark crouched near him and used the few Pashto words he knew.

Nasim stared at him, then nodded, his eyes flitting back to Seinkevitz. Cautiously, he placed a gnarled hand in Mark's open palm. The Russian didn't say a word when Mark pulled the elderly Afghani to his feet. It wasn't until they had completely turned that Seinkevitz charged, kicking Nasim in the back and shouting something derogatory in what sounded like Russian. His guards laughed while Mark and Nasim sprawled face down onto the street.

Nasim shook his head and groaned, waving Mark to leave him.

"No," he whispered, shaking his head, too. "I will not leave you."

Seinkevitz bellowed another string of harsh rhetoric. Mark froze. One more kick like the last, and it was all over; he would clean this guy's plow and be glad to do it. Seinkevitz might be a big guy, but Mark was no pushover. He could give the Russian a taste of his own medicine.

Apparently, bullies were the same the world over. Seinkevitz backed off, laughing with his gang of thugs at the sport of kicking an old man in the back.

Mark glanced up and caught the unspoken order in Harley's eyes to not retaliate. *Walk away, Mark; live to fight another day*. He gritted his teeth and focused on the better part of valor.

Halfway across the street Harley and Arzad ran to assist, but by then, Mark was pretty much carrying the older man. They quickly hauled Nasim around the corner and deposited him into the back seat of the van. Mark climbed in and pulled the van door shut behind them.

Poor Arzad looked like he was having a heart attack, his face white and his hands shaking. He climbed into the driver seat, repeating for the umpteenth time, "Please. We must go now."

"That was dumb, Houston." Harley got into the front seat, slamming his door behind him.

"You're just pissed you didn't think of it first."

"Come on, buddy. Time to roll." Harley drew his pistol out of its holster under his arm while he urged Arzad to, "Step on it."

Mark watched out the rear window in case any of Seinkevitz's men followed. Arzad drove through the alley, turned sharply at the corner, and sped away. Once they made their getaway, Mark tended to Nasim. The older man's lip was bloodied, but otherwise he was okay. He spoke hoarsely to Arzad while he straightened his robe and adjusted his turban, resisting Mark's attempt to help.

"He says you are fool, Mr. Mark," Arzad translated for Nasim. "No need for you to die to help an old man."

"A man shouldn't have to die in the street like that." Fool or not, Mark would do it again. "You tell him I said that."

Arzad relayed his words. They drove through the back roads until they were out of town and on their way to Nasim's home. No one followed.

"I fear Russian will remember you." Arzad's eyes focused on Mark's in the rear view mirror.

"Good. He should."

"Nasim says you call him Baabaa." His voice softened.

"Yes." Mark calmed. "I told him it was time to come home, Grandfather."

Nasim clenched Mark's hand tighter, his dark brown eyes glistening through deep wrinkles.

"He is proud to be your Grandfather," Arzad said gently. "But you and he are both fools."

"Tashakur," Nasim said hoarsely. He bowed his forehead to the clenched hands.

Mark nodded, a hard knot of compassion in his chest. "No, Nasim. Thank you."

"What's behind the walls?" Mark peered at the concertina wire across the high concrete block walls of the Russian's residential compound. After Arzad had taken Nasim home, they had continued the tour of Seinkevitz's holdings on the other side of the city.

"I do not know." Arzad drove slowly past the compound. "Maybe that is where he keeps his men."

"We'll find out," Harley replied. "Don't worry about it."

"Could we talk with some of the farmers who work for this guy?" Mark asked.

"They are waiting for us." Arzad turned south and drove a ways out of town. He stopped the van at another collection of mud-brick buildings very much like the ones Arzad lived in. "Please. We go in here."

Mark grabbed his gear bag as they piled out of the van. Besides his trusty .9mm, he also carried a couple bottles of water, a bag of hard candy in case they ran into any children, an industrial strength version of Imodium, and his first aid kit. It never hurt to be prepared.

He followed Arzad and Harley into the center courtyard of the homes where several men of all ages were waiting. They seemed happy to meet Arzad's friends. Their wives had baked and cooked the same as Gulnar had the day before. Once again, Afghanistan hospitality surrounded Harley and Mark as they sat with the men of the village and discussed the situation of the Russian cartel. Despite the friendly welcome, Mark detected an undercurrent. Distrust and suspicion had replaced the friendly welcome.

Arzad translated their stories.

"This is Rahmin." He introduced a tall man with a dirty, red and white-checkered turban. Rahmin directed his words to Arzad, then watched intently while he translated. "The government promised wheat and fertilizer if he and other farmers would stop growing poppies. That was five years ago. He knows it is illegal, but what is he to do? There is no wheat. There is no fertilizer. The government tells him to wait; it will come. But he is a man. A man must care for his family."

Rahmin spoke rapidly. Arzad translated again. "His father taught him how to grow the poppies and make opium paste when he was little boy. It is easy thing to do. Takes four months." Arzad held up four fingers to Mark and Harley. "When Seinkevitz came, he gave all farmers big cash for promise to give him all opium. That was good day. Rahmin was rich. He bought much for his family. They grew the poppies in the winter, harvested the bulbs, and made many bricks. Rahmin gave all bricks to Russian men. More cash. But this year crop no good. Rahmin does not know why. Some say it is the drought. Others say it was a bug that eats bulbs in the ground. It is not his fault, but Russian demands same number of bricks."

Mark nodded patiently. Arzad interpreted for another farmer. "This is my good friend, Mukhtar. When the Russian sent his men to collect, they cut off one of his fingers. See him? How can a man work if they take a finger when crop is bad?"

Mukhtar held up his right hand, the red stump of his missing digit clearly inflamed and swollen. But it was the way he held up his other fingers and the blatant look of hostility on his face that spiked the tension in the group. Mark caught the intended insult. Mukhtar might as well have flipped him the American version of a derogatory hand signal. The American visitors were suddenly in a group of angry men who wanted to hold someone accountable for the Russian's abuse.

Mark stared Mukhtar down through the chaos. Mark raised his hand palm forward to speak. Arzad shrugged apologetically, so Mark ceased trying and pulled his first-aid kit out of his gear bag, his eyes intent on Mukhtar. If he accomplished nothing else today, he needed to help this particular man. Mark opened the container and gestured toward the tray of sterile medical supplies.

The angry Afghani cocked his head, his lip curled in a sneer. Mark held his breath. An offer of help meant nothing unless it was accepted it. Mukhtar looked away.

By the sounds of Arzad's attempts to translate through the bedlam, all the men had been threatened and some beaten by the self-proclaimed dictator. In the beginning, they were swayed to grow poppies by the simple economics of poverty and the lure of an easy cash crop. They did not realize there would be harsh consequences.

One farmer leaned into Harley's face, bellowing while he held up his bandaged left hand. Harley reached to shake the farmer's right hand. Instantly, a shy smile flashed across the man's face. Mark was impressed. It took less than a split second, and Harley had made a friend.

Mukhtar had seen the handshake too. He eyed Mark again, his gaze drifting to the much needed care in that first-aid kit. Pushing up from his sitting position, he came to sit cross-legged in front of Mark with a show of much bravado.

"I no like you American," he hissed the moment he sat down, offering his hand to Mark despite his angry words.

"I no like Seinkevitz." Mark met his angry glare, but he saw something else there, too. This man was damn sick.

Mukhtar grunted. Mark let it go, and proceeded to examine the injury. The index finger had been severed an inch above the knuckle and just below the first joint. One hard bump was all it would take to perforate the tender skin and invite another round of bacteria. The stump was infected, barely healed at all. The single strip of tape wrapped over and around it did nothing to prevent infection or further injury. The entire hand was hot. Mukhtar had to be suffering.

The remaining bone was not crushed, indicating to Mark that an extremely sharp implement had been used to perform the brutal amputation. He growled softly to himself. Jose Gutierrez's head had also been severed surgically, much like this. No wonder Mukhtar was suspicious. What kind of man restrains another man and forces brutality on him?

The scabbard hanging on the belt beneath the Russian's belly flashed to Mark's mind. Had Boris personally inflicted these retaliations? Mark intended to find out. Somehow.

Mark clenched his jaw as he diagnosed. He had learned a few things while in the Corps. The first rule of medical triage in the field was always to seize the opportunity. Bleeding limbs and injured men could not wait. By the looks of Mukhtar's finger and the angry redness of his entire hand, he was well on his way to blood poisoning. Treatment could not wait any longer.

"You soldier?" Mark asked.

Mukhtar nodded begrudgingly, but his eyes widened when Mark pulled a tray of sealed sterilized scalpels and pre-loaded hypos of lidocaine from the kit. Mark set the tray aside and covered the now closed kit with a clean cloth he kept bagged in plastic for just such emergencies. It made for a primitive operating table, but with the feeling of distrust from these men who were no doubt also armed to the teeth, it made sense to keep everything out in the open.

"We start now," Mark said, focusing on the medical treatment he needed to complete instead of the pounding in his chest. Helping locals always involved great risk. If this man was really a Taliban sympathizer, or a Taliban soldier, Mark might be dead within seconds. Harley too. Or worse.

He opened the bottle of antiseptic wash and poured it over the injury, scrubbing lightly with a pad of sterile gauze. Grasping his patient's hand firmly between his thumb and index finger, he injected the painkiller, not giving Mukhtar any time to realize what was happening, much less object. Mark dispensed with the sterile wrap on the scalpel and cut a quick, thin slice over the tender top of the stump again without asking permission.

Mukhtar didn't flinch. *Good man.* Either his pride wouldn't let him, or he was damn tough. Putrid fluids oozed from the opening. Mark focused on cleaning it, aware that all eyes were on him and his American-hating friend.

After expressing as much of the infection as possible, he doused it with more wash and packed the incision with antiseptic infused cotton. Finally, he wrapped the entire hand with extra layers of sterile gauze and secured it with strips of white medical tape. Not until the procedure was finished did he let out a small sigh of relief.

He handed Mukhtar a small plastic bottle of a powerful antibiotic, holding up five fingers and hoping this brave Afghani soldier would understand. "You must take one each day. Five pills. Five days."

Mukhtar rattled the bottle with his good hand and nodded. A bemused light flickered over his face. The arrogance was gone, probably because of the wonder of lidocaine. "I will take."

"Keep that hand clean. Understand?"

Mukhtar pulled his hand against his chest, cradling it with his other hand. "I do what you say. I think maybe you good American GI."

Grasping his shoulder, Mark offered the hard man a quick nod. "Today I make you my friend."

"Yes. Friend." Mukhtar still eyed him. The distrust was gone, but something else was going on now that the operation was over. "I not hurt you."

Mark smiled. Mukhtar must have picked up on his nervousness and interpreted it as fear. Well, okay, so maybe some of it was fear, but mostly, Mark didn't want Mukhtar going to sleep with that throbbing wound for one more night.

"You no hurt me." He chuckled as he pointed toward the Kalashnikov that had slipped partially into view from beneath Mukhtar's robe. "That might hurt me."

Mukhtar shook his head solemnly. "No. You friend. Mukhtar no hurt you."

All eyes were still on Mark and his new friend. Harley shot him a quick wink.

Mark shrugged.

This was why he loved Afghanistan.

Nine

"What do you think? Over or through?"

Mark sized up the very impressive wall around the Russian's compound. It stood around twelve feet tall, not the kind of barrier a man could easily breach. It was late in the afternoon by the time they left the farmers, but not too late to do a little impromptu surveillance. Arzad had dropped them off near the home of Seinkevitz. They stood crouched behind the camouflage of several scraggly pines. Mark had his gear bag slung over his shoulder. Now was not the time to be tired.

"Through," Harley said as he walked up to the wall. "Let's get going."

The problem with 'through' was that it was still daylight. Mark glanced around. He would feel a hundred times less obvious if they waited until dark. The only good thing about this spur of the moment plan was that this place stood apart from the village. There were no prying eyes watching and reporting; neither were there innocent people who could get hurt if things went south. Aside from the pine trees, a fairly large orchard stood between the compound and the nearest home, which was a mile or two away.

"How through?" The wall appeared impenetrable.

"The thing about these mud brick walls." Harley flattened his body against the wall and—he disappeared.

Cool trick. Mark approached the same part of the wall. What appeared to be solid was actually two sections of the same wall, one overlapping the other to provide a hidden passageway. Mark entered sideways, blowing out his breath to make himself as thin as possible in order to follow. Once he eased his bulky frame between the two walls, he inched along. Harley made it look easy, but he had the bulk of a willow. Mark was an oak. When the narrow passageway cornered, he ran smack into his buddy's back.

"Shhhhh." Harley held a hand up signaling Mark to stay put, like he had a choice. He peered over Harley's shoulder.

They had entered the interior of the compound behind a vine-covered fence that ran the length of the back wall except where a large gate opened outward. A gravel driveway extended from that gate to a large metal building in front of them. Another building, this one with windows, stood across the way and paralleled the adjacent wall to their right. Rakes, shovels, and other gardening implements leaned against the wall of the building.

"What do you think? Barracks and garage?" Mark asked.

Harley nodded in agreement. "Looks like it. You've got the stuff?" he whispered.

"In my gear bag."

"Give me a few of them gizmos." Harley held his open palm over his shoulder. "Man, it looks awful quiet."

"Shut up, Mortimer." Mark squirmed to reach into his gear bag, which was difficult for a big guy like him in such a cramped position. At last, he reached a handful of bugs and passed them forward. "Don't jinx us."

If the law of averages worked like it usually did, the moment anyone said that an operation was too easy or too quiet, it suddenly wasn't. Going into a hot spot was never simple, and maintaining any level of secrecy in broad daylight was another problem all by itself. Still, plain sight did make for the best hiding place. Mark understood Harley's thinking. He just hated the acid pouring into his stomach.

Harley stepped out from the false wall and strode to the gardening tools, dragging them behind him as he proceeded to the front corner of the windowed building, what they thought might be the barracks. He planted the first miniscule listening device under a window frame when he paused to rake alongside of the building.

The thing about these particular bugs was that Mother had invented them. Patented under the name on Tattle Tales, they were small enough eavesdroppers to escape notice under most conditions, but powerful enough to transmit farther than others on the market.

Mark gulped at Harley's audacity. The man had nerves of steel, strolling around in broad daylight like he had a right to be there. *Damn. He's good.*

Two Russians exited the end door of the barracks, their heads bent together in earnest conversation. They barely glanced at their new gardener scratching his rake over the hard ground, collecting a small pile of rubble while planting yet another bug, this one on the upright post to the stair rail. Then another. Looking up, he waved for Mark to exit the wall, pointing to the other building.

Mark blew out a deep breath. Again, Harley made this look easy, but he could. He was skinny. He could blend in. That could be a problem. Still, if Harley could do it—

Mark gathered his nerves, and walked calmly to the space between what looked like a garage and the wall behind it. A large, corrugated steel Quonset-style building, the garage was large. Sidling between the rear of the building and the compound wall, he planted one bug at each corner for two opposing views. They might relay nothing from this location. No problem. Better to be safe than sorry.

He paused to catch his breath. His initial foray into enemy territory brought him toward the front of the compound, opposite where he and Harley had entered. The view was impressive. Seinkevitz lived in a lavish whitewashed home, again with the obscene gold trim. The place took up the entire northeast corner of the compound. A turret at one corner of the building over-looked the front gate, which could have easily accommodated a large truck's passage, maybe even a tank's. It was wide enough. Two wooden doors on massive iron hinges barred the way at the moment. Mark studied the doors.

A pulley and chain system provided a way to manually open and close them. There was no guard at the gate, in fact there were no guards anywhere. Where had the two Russians gone? He looked around, wishing he'd paid closer attention to them instead of Harley.

A patio comprised the yard west of the house. Within a circle of flowering trees gurgled a three-tiered fountain set in a concrete basin. The sounds of water would have been soothing except for the very real thing Mark had to do next. It was time to play gardener like Harley had done, only Mark didn't have a rake to hide behind. No matter.

He slouched, pulled his scarf up to hide his one day's growth and his cap down to hide his eyes. One step to the first tree and his adrenaline kicked into overdrive. Make this quick. He stuck the first bug high in the nearest tree trunk, thankful it was camouflaged. A man would have to look very hard to spot these babies.

Mark rounded the circle of trees, placing another bug on the opposite side. Video and audio was now very much alive and well inside the Seinkevitz lair. His hands shook, but he was done. Pretty good work for a dumb farm boy. Only the mansion was left. He looked up and straight into the snarling face of a uniformed guard.

The man barked something at him in Russian.

Great. What do I do now? Mark stood silent, shifting his feet and keeping his head down, hoping plain old ignorance would fool the man.

Harley ran to him, calling something from across the compound, but Mark's heart was pounding so hard, he couldn't understand a word. Harley pushed a rake into his hand, which was plenty sweaty by now. Grunting, he took the rake and kept his head down.

"Is your dumb brother?" the Russian spoke in English while he poked a stern finger into Harley's shoulder, pushing him back a step.

"Is yes." Harley shrugged apologetically, mumbling through his scarf as he accepted the push.

"You should teach him to mind his business. These trees from motherland. Too good for you."

Harley shrugged again, pushing Mark along with him back toward the barracks. Fortunately, the Russian did not follow. He had turned on his heel and walked into the mansion through the side door.

"I didn't know you spoke Afghani that well," Mark muttered.

"I don't."

"What'd you say then?"

"You don't want to know. Keep moving. We need to get inside that mansion."

Harley's calm façade had evaporated. Mark saw his hands shaking, too. Their window of opportunity was about to close.

Mark glanced sideways at the whitewashed building with its obscene gold trim. Entry through the front and side doors was definitely not feasible. He headed to the rear of the mansion, still dragging his rake in case anyone might look out the window at the two goofball gardeners. Rounding the corner, he stopped cold.

"Sonofabitch."

"Focus, Houston." Harley had seen it too. His grip on Mark's elbow was the only thing that propelled him forward.

That backdoor looked like the servant's entrance all right, but it was the heavy wooden chopping block planted on the ground between the door and the barracks that held Mark's attention. His father kept a much smaller version outside the barn back in Ohio. It was a butcher's block, a place of slaughter. Long, deep grooves marked the blackened top. Death had struck here. Often.

Mark got that. A kid raised on a farm grew up knowing that animals eventually made their way into the family freezer, but chickens, pigs and lambs didn't need leather straps or leg irons. Neither did they leave bloody human handprints smeared down the side of the wood. That was where Mukhtar had lost his finger. Those might be Mukhtar's bloody prints. Other's had been killed there, too. Mark could tell. He could feel it.

"Don't look," Harley growled. "We've got to get inside. Now."

"How?" Mark tore his eyes away from the brutal crime scene. There was no doubt what would happen if they were caught inside this compound now, but he couldn't get the image of Mukhtar's angry brown eyes out of his head. He'd suffered. Recently. Right damn here. In this very spot.

"How do you think?" Harley stepped to the backdoor of the mansion. "We do it damn fast."

Mark followed, dragging his dread with him. They were running on borrowed time. His gut churned out enough acid to eat a hole through his stomach. There was no time to strategize. He sucked in another breath, wrapped his scarf nearly up and over his nose, and into the mansion he went.

Three Afghan women looked up from their work at the kitchen counters, their eyes bright with concern. He shrugged, trying his best to look halfway daft. It was a short trip with the all the strong emotions running through his head.

Bowing, he stepped backwards as if he was just confused and needed to leave. He pressed a miniscule listening device beneath the edge of the marble cabinet. One down. Time to go. Mission accomplished.

His hand was nearly on the doorknob when one of the women grumbled. They were older, and judging by their quick conversation, they had all agreed on something. The one who had spoken waved him over and opened the very nice, stainless steel refrigerator.

Mark took one step closer and nodded, careful not to look her in the eye. She clucked softly, shaking her head, her mouth twisted in that womanly way when confronted with a foolish man.

He only leaned against the refrigerator for a brief second, but it was enough. By the time she had wrapped a hefty slice of goat's cheese in a napkin and waved him out the door, the deed was done. Not only was another bug attached to the refrigerator door, but a third was stuck to the underside of the serving cart next to the refrigerator also.

And who knew where that would go?

By then, his heart was an out of control brass band. He and Harley had to move. They made it to the hidden passage in record time. Once outside, Mark blew out a heaving sigh, his mouth open as he sucked in enough air to finally fill his lungs. Neither spoke, their only task to put time and distance between them and what they had just seen.

"Holy hell, Houston," Harley growled as they hurried into the cover of the pines. "You got a death wish or something?"

Mark shook his head instead of answering. He shouldn't have entered the mansion without at least mentioning his plan. He would have – if he'd had one. It just kind of happened. Harley had a right to be angry.

"That's twice today, three if I count the chance you took with that Mukhtar fellow." Harley kicked at a dirt clod on their path, still plenty pissed off. "You could've gotten us both killed."

"You're right," Mark conceded. For a man who didn't like to take risks, he'd certainly filled his quota today. He'd been on the receiving end of too many bullies over the years. All that past humiliation had evolved into a hair trigger of sorts. Zero tolerance. Blam. Instant reaction. He'd have to watch that. "When I saw that butcher chop block, I—"

"Forget it," Harley cut him off. "I know. You thought you had to do something. I get it. Just don't do it again."

They walked in silence for a mile or two on the dusty road back to Arzad's. The afternoon was late. Mark kept a close watch over his shoulder. No one followed. The Russian's mansion was no longer in view. He wanted to keep it that way.

"Looks like Seinkevitz is ready to start a war," Harley muttered finally. "I estimate those barracks could hold thirty men or more. Wish I'd gotten a bug inside."

"We'll know what's going on when we fire up the laptop and study the feeds." Mark tucked his cap into his belt and brushed a hand over his dusty head. Infiltration always brought bone-deep exhaustion. Finding that butcher block didn't help. "The garage looks like it could be an airplane hangar."

"But there's no runway," Harley said. "You sure surprised the heck out of me walking straight in the backdoor like you did."

"I'll tell you what surprised me."

"That chopping block," Harley said. "I know. It surprised the crap out of me, too."

"He needs to be stopped," Mark answered.

"That's why we're here."

"No. We're only here to watch. I'm talking about—"

"I know what you're talking about. You want to go charging in there and save the day again. You think I don't?"

"I don't want to go charging back in there," Mark argued. Okay, so, yeah, maybe he did. He was actually more prepared than Harley knew, but now was not the time to reveal the ace up his sleeve. This time he'd pave the way before he took another risk.

"What then? Waltz? Tiptoe?"

Mark caught Harley's sarcasm. They were both still shaken from the macabre discovery. Harley was just blowing off steam. Mark deliberately changed the subject.

"What'd you say to me back there?"

Harley cast him a sideways smirk. "You really want to know?"

"Yeah. Spit it out."

"It's just something I picked up on an operation in Turkey."

"And?"

"I just said, 'Hey sweetheart.'"

Mark chuckled. He should've known.

"It's the first thing that came to my mind," Harley said. "Knock it off. It's not like I like you or anything."

The more he tried to explain, the funnier it got. Mark laughed.

"I needed to know stuff like that back then." Harley was still at it.

Mark shoved him away, trying to regain his composure, and darn glad that particular Russian guard hadn't known the difference between Pashto and Turkish.

"Say it again," he told Harley. "I might need those words someday."

"Hey tatlim." Harley pronounced the two words slowly. "I think that's right anyway. It's been awhile."

Mark committed them to memory. "You needed those words a lot, did you?"

"I also know some bad language. Keep it up, and you're gonna hear that, too."

The banter alleviated the stress of their daring escapade. Before long they were back on the subject of Seinkevitz.

"Man, he's an arrogant pig to come in here and treat these people like that," Harley muttered.

"He's a sick bastard is what he is."

"What were you thinking walking up to him like that this morning?" Harley asked. "That could've gone so bad. I could be sending you home in a body bag."

"I was thinking of that little old man on his knees, and don't give me that bullshit," Mark came back at him. "You would have done the same thing."

"Yeah, you're probably right," Harley agreed. "I've been known to be stupid like that once or twice myself."

"It's not stupid." Mark kicked a stone on the crooked goat path they had turned onto. "It's right. If more people stood up to bastards like Seinkevitz, he'd be out of business. The world would be a better place."

"Alex says people are like wolves or sheep."

Mark glanced at his walking buddy. Harley sounded unusually pensive. Their escapade must've gotten to him, too. "Which are we?"

"Neither. We're the guys who stand between the wolves and the sheep."

"We're what? Shepherds?" That comparison actually felt right. Maybe Alex had gotten something right after all.

"Yeah, maybe."

"You served in Iraq, didn't you?"

Harley nodded. "Right. First time I came to Afghanistan was on a mission with Alex. He introduced me to Arzad. It's crazy, but it kinda felt like I'd been here before. I've always liked these folks. Most of 'em are good people."

"I agree," Mark said. "Could I interest you in a little insurance policy for these good people?"

Harley's raised eyebrow was enough answer, so Mark continued.

"I know this whole poppy business is wrong and everything, but a man like Seinkevitz shouldn't be allowed to run rough shod over poor folks who are just trying to survive. It's not like they have a lot of choices."

"What are you thinking, Houston?"

Mark grimaced at what he was going to say. "I just think that maybe it's time the little guy had an equalizer."

"And what would that be?"

"Fireworks, Mortimer. Just a little fireworks."

"You brought something extra with you on that military transport, didn't you?"

Mark grinned. Harley wasn't a tough sell in the slightest. "You in?"

"Hell, yeah. The only thing is—"

Mark was a step ahead of him. "I know. The staff. We've got to get those women out of the mansion first, huh?"

"Well, yeah," Harley muttered. "I don't mind taking Seinkevitz out, but I'm not going to smoke innocent women just to get him."

"Already thought of that." Mark smiled his most devious smile. "Did you know some of these folks believe that giants live in the mountains?"

"What are you talking about?"

"It's true. It's an old legend that's been around forever. I was thinking of planting a giant footprint or two beside that backdoor, maybe a few more around that chopping block, too. Some of these folks are real superstitious. It's worth a try. Finding giant footprints right inside the compound might scare the hell out of those women. Seinkevitz could lose all his hired help."

"Hmm. Fireworks and Sasquatch feet, huh?"

Mark shrugged. "It could work."

It took the rest of the day and most of the night to retrieve the contraband fireworks, return to the Russian's compound, and plant their fictitious evidence. By the time sunrise edged the eastern horizon, Mark and Harley had left an improvised giant handprint in the middle of the backdoor where the women could not miss it. They also made it look as if the giant had leapt over the wall right near the chopping block and then tried to get into the kitchen.

That wasn't all they left.

One thing Mark had learned in a country where improvised explosive devices caused most military deaths was to make friends with the nearest EOD man. Roy Hudson, the explosive ordnance expert on the TEAM, was a real good friend. Fortunately, he was as good at building tiny, but powerful explosive devices as he was at disarming them.

The nondescript mini-bombs now hidden inside the compound were remote-controlled and packing enough SEMTEX to end most discussions. Before they called it quits, Harley insisted on adding two more video bugs up high in a tree a half-mile away.

"If we ever use this little insurance policy of yours, I want to know for sure this bastard's got no death benefit," he muttered as he jumped down from the tree.

Mark clapped his hand to Harley's back. His friend hadn't been this happy all day.

"For sure he's got no hazard insurance that will cover this," Mark joked.

"And his deductible is going to go sky high," Harley quipped. "Through the roof."

"You mean the turret," Mark teased.

Harley gazed back at the walls of the Russian's complex. Only the turret glowed over the top of the wall. "Guess this is what you call term life insurance?"

Mark shrugged. "Sounds more like whole life to me."

Tired or not, he grinned as he walked back to Arzad's. They might never use their equalizer, but it felt damned good knowing that Seinkevitz could be dealt with if push came to shove.

And old Boris deserved a shove.

Ten

I can't believe I'm here!

Libby had to admit it. Washington D.C. was an exciting town. Even her trepidation over her travelling companion couldn't squash the thrill she felt when she stepped off the jetway at Reagan National. Just standing at the airport windows took her country girl's breath away.

"Impressive, isn't it?" Dr. Clements stood at her elbow, his briefcase in hand and a rolled newspaper under his arm. Tall, blond, and handsome, he flashed a row of straight white teeth, his face beaming. Yet he took liberties, and always seemed to be inside her comfort zone.

She shifted a step sideways from him. *Back off.*

"It looks awesome," she admitted, wishing she could hide her country bumpkin enthusiasm. She hadn't known how much she loved to travel until she had moved to Chicago. The bustling energy of the Windy City made her very aware how quiet and boring her little hometown had been. And now she was in Washington D.C. She, little nobody, Libby Clifton, was actually in the place where George Washington had walked, where Thomas Jefferson orated, and where the founding fathers once lived. Excitement shivered over her shoulders and down her arms again. *This is so cool!*

"It is quite the city." He offered his elbow for her to take, like she had ever done that.

Instead, she raised her hands full of her purse, the light jacket she had brought just in case, and the extended handle to her carry-on. An annoyed look crossed his features before he smiled again, but there was no way she was falling into that trap. The line between them was thick, black, and permanent.

He might be the perfect age and the quintessential catch of the year, but this was a business trip. That's all. They weren't a couple. No way. No how.

"Baggage carousels are on the lower level," he said curtly. "Let's get out of here."

Even the walk through the airport seemed interesting. Libby found herself in a sea of international languages and people. Diversity chatted everywhere. She found herself craning to see beyond everyone and everything to the city outside. The nation's capitol energized her. It even smelled different.

"Excuse me." She paused at one of the souvenir kiosks as they hurried past.

"Yes ma'am?" The young man behind the counter stepped into the concourse to assist. His dark skin and eyes betrayed his mid-eastern culture. "How can I help you?"

She pointed with her one unencumbered index finger to the view outside the broad plate glass window, aware that Dr. Clements stood next to her huffing his irritation over the delay. "Is that the Washington Monument over there?"

The young man turned to the view outside and then back to her, his face full of a wide open smile. "Why yes, it is. Is this your first time visiting Washington D.C.?"

"It is." Libby was making a spectacle of herself; she just couldn't stop. She was that kid on her way to the county fair with too few coins in her pocket and so many rides.

"We have a shuttle to catch." Dr. Clements latched onto her elbow, tugging her back into the flow of passengers. "We don't want to miss it."

"Thank you," she called back to the friendly clerk as she was pulled away.

"You are most welcome," he called after her and waved. "Enjoy your visit. It is a wonderful city."

Gently, Libby extracted her elbow from Dr. Clements's stern grasp.

"If we miss this shuttle, we'll have to wait for the next," he muttered.

"I've never been here before," she explained. "I wanted to—"

"There'll be time for sight-seeing later," he snapped, but then he must have thought twice. He offered another one of those dazzling smiles that she saw right through. "Don't worry, Miss Clifton. I'll take good care of you."

His presumptuous words made her skin crawl. *Yeah. I just bet you will.*

After picking their bags off the serpentine baggage carousel, Libby and Dr. Clements walked outside the ground level doors to wait for their hotel shuttle. The October afternoon weather was perfect. Glancing over at the line of waiting taxi and hotel buses, she noticed the metro train pulling to a stop on the upper level track. This one headed west. She made a mental note. *I need a metro schedule. Maybe I'll stay a couple days longer. Maybe I'll—wait. What am I thinking?*

Dr. Clements had taken a seat on a concrete bench. He sat with his nose in his newspaper again, unaffected by the sights and sounds like she was. Libby bit her lip. That wouldn't work. Any mention of an extended stay would complicate things. He would stay, too, and Libby knew where that would lead. He might think she was interested in him. They would have breakfast together, travel the metro together, and he would assume that I'm-in-control-and-I-know-what's-good-for-you boyfriend persona. He might even touch the small of her back like he had any right to, and he'd toss those lingering looks in her direction. Dr. Clements had already tried most of those moves at O'Hare on their outbound flight. It was only Monday. She was already tired of dodging him.

Never mind. I'll come back some day when I'm on my own. Later. A lot later.

Their hotel shuttle arrived, and soon she was onboard a speeding bus destined for Crystal City, Virginia. Even that name sounded magical. Pulling up to the hotel, the driver announced his schedule. The shuttle bus ran every half-hour with stops at the airport and the King Street metro station. Her ears perked up. Maybe there was a way to see something besides the inside of her hotel room and Dr. Clements's disgruntled face.

The power struggled ensued the minute the shuttle driver unloaded their luggage. Darn. Clements was a smooth operator. Latching onto her roller bag, he belted it to his suitcase and proceeded to take her small carry-on as well.

"I can carry my own bags," she said, trying hard not to sound annoyed as she followed like some good little girlfriend behind him.

"Already got it." He smiled that cheesy smile again. "Let's get checked in, shall we?"

There it was again. That word. *We.*

Libby gritted her teeth. There had to be a polite way to get through to this guy.

Check-in went smoothly, like she had a choice. He'd stepped up to the counter and tossed his VISA card to the clerk. When it was her turn to register, the clerk smiled and said, "Your companion has already checked you in."

"Excuse me?" Libby turned to Dr. Clements.

"Don't worry. It's all university expense. We'll sort the details later."

The woman at the counter handed both room key cards to him, still smiling.

"No." Libby stood her ground, handing her credit card to the clerk. "My room goes on my card, and I want my own key. One will be enough, thank you."

Dr. Clements exhaled a long-suffering sigh when he turned to the confused clerk. "Excuse me, but it appears my companion will cover her own room. Please reverse those charges."

Once check-in was corrected, Libby faced the man she had just aggravated. "I like to keep close track of my own expenses. That's just the way I am."

He nodded one curt nod toward the elevator. "Point well made. Lead on."

"And I'll take my suitcase if you don't mind."

With a moment of drawn out hesitation, he studied her before loosening the belt on his bag and handing over her luggage. "You've got quite a stubborn streak, Miss Clifton."

"Not really." She softened her attitude. He was, after all, her department head. It wouldn't do to alienate him right off the bat. "I do prefer making my own way though."

They boarded the elevator in silence. A prickle of unease commenced at the second floor when he didn't get off. It increased at the third floor, but by the time the elevator doors opened at the fourth and final floor, she was concerned.

He wouldn't have reserved the room next to mine, would he?

She glanced at the sign that directed her to her room, number four-eighteen. He turned with her, following close behind. At room number four-eighteen, she was in trouble. He had stopped too. At four-nineteen. Directly across the hall.

What a snake. He did this on purpose.

Libby focused on her key card, opening her door as quickly as possible. She rolled her suitcase inside and glanced toward the man who was quickly becoming a bigger problem than she'd anticipated.

Dr. Clements stood with his door barely opened. He looked smug, and that aggravated her all the more. She'd run the risk of facing him every time she stepped one foot into the hall.

"Would you care to join me for a drink?" He nudged his door open further with his foot, his invitation clear. The man was suave, she had to give him that. He looked good in his business suit, his blond hair trimmed and neat, and his body always spritzed with whatever that nice aftershave was. *The snake.*

She shook her head. "Sorry. I don't date co-workers, and I don't drink."

And then because this unexpected development frazzled her last nerve, she shut the door in his face.

What was I thinking? Why'd I say that? He hadn't asked for a date.

Now her rudeness compounded the problem. For all of one second, she deliberated opening her door and apologizing for her abrupt behavior.

I can say it slipped. It did, kind of. Not.

Instead, she slid the chain lock into place and flipped the deadbolt as quietly as possible. Her fingers trembled. She didn't offend him. He offended her.

He seemed to interpret even the simplest courtesy as a come-on. She didn't want to hold his arm, he shouldn't have paid for her room, and he certainly should not have booked a room across from hers. Good grief. The man should be in a room on ground level, the back dock if this place had one, or at least way down in the parking garage. Way down. He was too suave, too presumptuous, and too close.

Her confidence rattled, she turned to view her room. It was exactly like all the other hotel rooms across the country, clean, generic, and quiet. She turned the television on. Not until the room filled with the background noise of a brainless sitcom did she relax. Libby blew out a big breath, and gathered her wits. The conference was only Tuesday through Thursday. Friday was another travel day, and then she would be home. Yeah. She could make it.

But—he was right across the hall.

With a shiver, she unpacked the three dress suits she had brought with her, and hung them in the closet. Everything else could wait. She needed distance between herself and the doctor, and she needed it right away. Taking a deep breath, she opened her door, and peeked out.

It was cowardly, but she was okay being a coward. If she waited too long, good old Dirk would be knocking at her door wanting dinner—or something else. Travelling companions usually ate together, but this man made everything seem like a date.

Thankful that the thick hallway carpet cushioned her footsteps, Libby made her way back to the elevator and down to the front desk. The concierge suggested a couple activities for the rest of the day. If she was up for a lot of walking, there was time to visit the Smithsonian, which would entail a quick shuttle ride and then catching the metro into D.C. He recommended an excellent restaurant in China town, but there was also nearby King Street in historic Alexandria, with all its tourist shops, museums, and restaurants.

It took all of two seconds to decide. Opting for King Street, she left a note at the desk for her travelling partner, so he wouldn't think she was completely thoughtless, and off she went.

The concierge was right on. King Street was an interesting place to walk, shop, and see some of the sights. Libby found an Irish pub where she enjoyed a tall glass of sweet tea while a band of Irish rogues played the night away. The little pub was lined with pictures of various celebrities, including a couple past presidents. It reminded her of Malone's Diner back home in her favorite little hick town.

Sitting alone with the familiarity of the nostalgic pub around her brought back happier memories. When the band took a break from their rowdy songs, she called home and spent the next few minutes chatting with her mother and sisters. Her dad was in town at the feed store buying chicken scratch, so she had missed talking with him, but hearing her mother's voice was exactly what she needed. For a moment, Alexandria felt like home – until her mother strayed into tender territory.

"Have you heard a word from that handsome Mark Houston?"

"Mom." Libby was surprised at that nosy question. What was her mother thinking? "No. I mean, yes. He's sent me a few e-mails, but I, umm, I haven't answered them yet." She cringed. *Here it comes, Mom with that sixth sense of hers. How does she always seem to know what's really wrong?*

"Why on earth not?"

"I've been busy with classes, and ...." She let her voice trail off. Thinking of Mark brought so many conflicting emotions to the surface. She was supposed to be the grieving fiancée, not the happy girlfriend. "It's too soon."

"Too soon to be a friend?" Rosemary scolded all the way through the phone. Libby could tell. "That boy's just come home from the war, and he's moved to a big city. He's all by himself. Think about someone else for a change. If he's anything like you, he could use a friend. He's probably wondering why you won't answer him."

"I know." Libby sighed.

Her mother's voice softened. "You're not the only one who lost Jon, you know. Mark lost him, too. He's grieving the same as you are. Call him. At least answer his e-mail. Tell him what you're doing. Be a friend."

Sheeesh, Mom. Not now. Libby turned from the merriment of the pub. The band was back from break. They were laughing, tuning their instruments, and ready for another go. She wasn't.

"For goodness' sake, give the boy a break." Her mother sounded so sure of herself. "You might be surprised how good it makes you feel, too."

That's the problem, Mother. I shouldn't feel good yet, should I?

"Okay. I'll do it," Libby promised, wiping her face. Mark's gentle hug at Jonathan's graveside came back to her. He did care for her, but the timing was bad. Way bad. "I brought my laptop with me. I'll send him a note when I get back to my room."

"Good." Her mother had that satisfied tone of accomplishment in her voice. "Didn't he say he was taking a job someplace around Washington D.C.?"

Libby nodded, glancing around like she might actually see him sitting in a nearby booth, watching and waiting. She wouldn't put it past him; that was his way – to be watching and waiting. "Alexandria, I think he said."

"Well, isn't that where you are right now?"

"Yes, Mom, but I'll be in a conference all week. I won't have much time to visit." Libby cringed. Her mother was right. How would she feel if Mark had come all the way to Wisconsin and hadn't stopped to visit with her? Yikes. She had been a bad friend, only was Mark just a friend?

"Libby Clifton, you stop making excuses right now, do you hear me?"

"Okay. Okay. I'll e-mail him. At least then I'll know if he's even in town."

"Good." There was that problem-solved word again. It made Libby smile. Her mother acted like she knew exactly what was going on in her daughter's heart. Now she just had to figure it out.

The band blasted out a few discordant notes as they began again.

"I've got to go, Mom," she shouted into her phone. "Tell Dad I love him."

"You take care. Love you, Libby."

"Love you too." She ended the cell phone call, grabbed a couple napkins, and dabbed her eyes. She would have been okay if the Irish rowdies hadn't started their second round with a tear jerking version of Danny Boy, like the evening wasn't already tragic enough.

Libby gathered her purse, left enough cash on the table to cover her tab plus a tip, and ran for the exit. Enough! Between her mother's scolding and the storm she had been carrying for months in her heart, she was exhausted and red-eyed. Leaving the pub behind, she hurried downhill to the busy Potomac waterfront. Standing against the dock railing, she closed her eyes and took a deep cleansing breath. Instantly she was back at Lake Wissota, the fishy smell of the waterfront in her nose, the screech of gulls in her ears. The memory of her last visit enfolded her.

Mark. He'd been so serious, and quiet as usual, letting her dictate the course of the evening. Content to be the guy in the background, he had always let Jonathan take center stage. Of course, she and Jonathan were engaged. What else could Mark have done? Still, the moment Jonathan had introduced her, it seemed as if an invisible someone had physically tapped her on the shoulder and said, "This is the one, Libby. Listen up. Pay attention."

She shivered. As her engagement to Jonathan had unraveled, she'd shared that memory with her mother. Rosemary had wrapped her arms around Libby like she was a little girl again, and told her to always trust her heart. She hadn't understood then what her mother meant. She had trusted her heart with Jonathan. Did that tapping sensation mean she'd promised her heart to the wrong man?

Peace welled inside. After too many months worrying, grieving, and trying to catch her balance, she was herself again. Libby glanced around, wondering why that sense of balance had decided to return in a strange town on the east coast.

The autumn sunshine cast long shadows. Time to head back. She turned west and began the walk up the hill. Under the soft glow of historic Old Town Alexandria's street lamps, the shuttle returned her safely to the hotel. She walked through the lobby a new woman. Men would come, and men would go. Strong-minded parents had raised her to be self-reliant. It was happening. Her heart was healing. She was going to live.

The elevator pinged on the fourth floor and without even peeking to see if her nemesis was stalking the hall, she walked to her room. Once inside, she ordered an early wake-up call from the front desk, showered, and brushed her teeth. The television provided its usual drone. Dressed in her pajamas, she climbed under the clean sheets of the comfortable queen-sized bed with her laptop. Now for that promise she had made.

Opening the latest e-mail from Mark, she noted the date. As faithful as clockwork, he had written every single week, always Sunday night around 6 PM. His persistence tugged at her heart. Every message always ended the same way. 'Thinking of you. Wish you were here. Your friend too, Mark.'

Sounds just like him. My friend too, not only Jonathan's.

'Hi,' she typed. 'It's about time I answer my e-mail, huh? Guess what? I'm in Crystal City this week for a medical conference. Are you busy? It would be nice to see you again. How about dinner one night? I fly home Friday morning. Hope to hear from you soon. Libby.'

Her fingers lingered over the keyboard. Her note sounded so blah, like she didn't care if he answered or not. She read it one last time. It was good enough, but the ending felt kind of abrupt. Hmmm. She inserted a word right before her name. *Regards.* That was a good word. With her fingertip on the send button, she gave the note another look. It still fell short. Something was definitely missing.

What's the matter with me? Send the darn thing. It's just a note.

Still....

Tapping her fingers, she searched for the words that felt better. Sincerely? No, too over-used. Respectfully? Too impersonal. With love? *Hmmm.* Her lips turned up at the corners. She tried it on for size, slowly typing L – o – v – e. Libby leaned back into her pillow, smiling at her screen. Warmth from that one tingly word flooded through her body. She cocked her head and looked at it sideways, like that made any difference.

Her heart pounded. *Should I send it? What will he think?*

She squeezed her eyes tight and hit 'send,' snapped her laptop shut, and then opened it again, powering back up in case he had responded in the last nanosecond. It could happen. Anticipation shivered across her neck. Ducking under the covers, she watched the screen. No e-mail notification pinged her in-basket.

Well, that was anti-climactic. This is just plain silly.

She set her laptop on the bed next to her and settled down. He would answer eventually, and if they missed connecting this trip, well, there was always the next trip she planned on making to actually do some sightseeing. Still, her mother was right. Answering his e-mail had lifted her spirits.

Libby nodded off to sleep while the television provided the perfect level of white noise. A memory floated into her drowsy mind. The riveting smile of a handsome dark-haired Marine in dress blues gazed down at her. His gentle hand gripped hers, holding her steady. Strength to endure flowed into her. She recognized those eyes. They weren't the far off, 'I've got somewhere else to be,' eyes of Jonathan. No. They were brown—so dark brown they were nearly black, and their message clearly said, 'There's nowhere else I'd rather be.'

She stretched and sighed.

They were Mark's.

Eleven

The satellite phone jangled before dawn.

It took Harley a minute to fumble the phone out of its holder, then another minute to pick it up when he dropped it. Mark chuckled. Harley blinked, scrunched his face, and blinked again as he tried to figure out which end of the phone was which. The man looked like a scarecrow waking up, his hair on end and his eyes mostly shut. After two weeks of walking the streets of the village, monitoring the Seinkevitz cartel, and talking with more farmers, neither man had much sleep.

"Yeah, Boss," he muttered thickly into the wrong end of the phone.

"Turn it around," Mark whispered, motioning what he meant with his finger.

"Huh?" Harley peered across the rooftop like he couldn't see Mark either. "Turn it … What?"

"The phone. Turn it around. You're talking into the wrong end."

Harley pulled the phone away from his ear and looked at it, one eye open and one closed. "Oh. Yeah." He flipped the handset to the appropriate position, mouthpiece down and earpiece up, and turned the speakerphone on so Mark could participate.

"Who's this?" Harley mumbled.

"Took you long enough." It was Alex, loud, clear and annoyed. "You need a cup of coffee or something?"

"Ah, nope. Sure don't ... I mean ... ah, yeah, maybe on second thought." Harley brushed his hand over his head, down his neck, and back over his head again, still trying to wake up.

"Put Mark on," Alex ordered.

"Here, Boss." Mark already sat cross-legged near Harley. "What's up?"

"We've had a couple developments you two need to be aware of."

"We're listening." He leaned into the handset as Harley flopped back to his bedroll and groaned.

"First of all, good job with the video feeds. We're getting steady intel from the compound. FBI is impressed you guys got in there. So is the State Department."

"Sure. No problem." Mark flipped open his laptop to view the latest feed while he talked. "We took care of that the first chance we had. So far we know he's got thirty-four men working for him, a chopper, a tank, and a good-sized arsenal."

"Any idea why he needs the fire power?" Alex asked.

"No one's willing to talk to us yet."

"Find out."

"Will do. One thing is clear. Seinkevitz doesn't need it to intimidate folks around here. Everyone's already scared of him."

"Hey, Boss?" Harley chimed in. "Why are you at the office? It's four in the morning. That makes it what? 8 PM over there?"

"I'm working." Alex was his usual brusque self. "Do you two remember the casket with the decapitated head?"

"Kinda hard to forget," Harley muttered.

"The FBI just informed me a total of nine transfer cases arrived at Dover the last day Castor showed for work. He had access to all of them. They all tested positive for opium, too."

"In that case, the FBI is looking for a lot of dope. If it was stashed in outgoing caskets, they should be easy to locate. How many are they looking for?" Mark asked.

"Four. You saw the first two grave desecrations. There's been three more—Florida, Kentucky, and West Virginia. All had the same MO. Castor's on the move."

"They tested positive for opium, too?" Mark asked.

"Yes."

"This guy is unbelievable," Harley growled.

"Sounds like he's also got help," Mark commented. "That's a lot of ground for one man to cover. Still, if the FBI knows where the caskets are, what's the big deal? All they have to do is wait for him to show."

"Ah, Boss?" Harley pulled himself back into a sitting position, holding his head in his hands as he waited for an answer. "Where did the last four caskets end up?"

"New York, Wisconsin, Idaho, and Oregon."

"Wisconsin?" Mark hoped he had heard wrong, but Alex was a step ahead of him.

"Mark. Didn't you have a friend from Wisconsin, a Sergeant Wells who died in Afghanistan recently?"

"Yes. Funeral was June." His whole body shifted into high alert.

"Didn't he have a fiancée?"

"Libby Clifton." Swallowing was impossible with a dry throat. "Why? Does the FBI think there's dope buried in his casket, too?"

"Listen." Alex's tone deepened. Mark tensed. The worst was yet to come. "About the soldier from West Virginia. FBI found his family murdered in their home yesterday. Throats cut. His widow and their two small children."

"Say what?" Harley bolted upright.

"There were several sets of prints at the scene, but Castor's was definitely one of them. The Bureau's still processing the evidence."

"Why kill his wife and kids? What's up with that? Didn't Castor find his dope? Wasn't it in the casket?" Harley was wide-awake now.

Now it was Mark's turn to sit back. His mind had already pinged to Libby. What if she were at Jon's grave when Castor arrived in Spencer? What if he was after more than the dope? If he had searched out this family and killed them, was he insane? Mark tried to listen over the tirade in his mind.

"The FBI doesn't have all the answers yet. Mark." Alex cut to the chase. "Change of plans. Need you stateside. Today."

"I can be in Wisconsin by—" Mark jumped to his feet. He didn't need any urging.

"Negative." Alex cut him short. "Your Miss Clifton is at some medical conference in D.C. Find her."

All Mark heard was, 'your Miss Clifton.' *Damn straight.*

"Now I know why you're working late," Harley said, subdued.

"The FBI's already got the Wells and Clifton families in protective custody."

"On my way." Mark stuffed his few travel items into his bag, his mind mentally estimating the circuitous travel route out of Afghanistan, and how he would go about locating Libby once he got to D.C.

"Call when you get in." Alex paused. "And Harley."

"Yes, Boss?"

"You were right. These guys are something else. Both of you be careful."

Before midnight twenty-four hours later, Mark was thirty-five thousand feet above sea level with a long flight ahead of him. It had taken awhile to hook up with an Air Force chopper out of Bagram to the international airport in Kabul. From there he wrangled a seat on the first available flight to Dubai and from there to JFK. The waiting and stand-bys pushed the limits of his patience. Sheer determination drove him.

Finally over the Atlantic, only the flashing lights along the huge jetliner's wings were visible outside. When the flight attendants came through the cabin offering drinks and snacks, he allowed a sigh of relief. He was headed home.

The reality of all Libby meant hit him. Mark couldn't suppress his feelings. He didn't even try. Fear had crystallized his priorities. Yes, Jon was gone. Maybe she'll need more time to grieve. *Too bad. She'll have to learn how to do that with me in her life. No more of this best friend business either. I don't want a friend. I want a wife. My woman. My life.*

Relief washed over him.

I love you, Libby.

Dr. Clements was an expert at the cold shoulder, like Libby cared what he thought.

"I'd think you would be grateful." He didn't look up from his morning newspaper and coffee as he grumbled. "I could've selected anyone to attend this conference. Anyone. And they'd be glad to be here, too."

Apparently she didn't merit eye contact either. *I am grateful, just not the way you want.*

"From now on, we do everything together. Got it? That means dining, sightseeing, and anything else we might decide to do." He emphasized the word *we* again. This time he glared across the table, his cup suspended in his hand. "For all I knew, you could've been kidnapped or mugged last night. Did you ever think about that? Did you ever think I might be worried sick while you're out gallivanting all over town?"

"I left word with the hotel desk," she reminded him for the third time. The only thing he was worried sick about was a missed opportunity.

He looked away, the cup to his lips as he dismissed her reply.

Libby bit her tongue instead of giving him a piece of her mind. *Whatever.* She was sick of listening to an adult male's whining and posturing. Dropping her napkin to her plate, she pushed away from the table.

"Ready to catch the shuttle?" she asked brightly. It was going to be a long week.

As they stepped outside, she took one last look at her reflection in the plate glass hotel window. Yesterday she had dressed in slacks to travel, but today she wore her navy blue suit dress with white piping along the collar and the short sleeves. She had chosen well, achieving a crisply professional but still a classy look. Her mother's pearl earrings finished the ensemble.

She pinched her cheeks one last time, hoping to add a bit of color to her too pale cheeks. It didn't help. Swimming had once been her life, but this summer she hadn't spent any time in the sun, much less the water, and it showed. She frowned at her pallor, promising herself a long weekend at her parents, and some sun at the lake the first chance she got.

The shuttle whisked them across the Potomac, toward the National Cathedral in western Washington D.C., and on to the hotel where the medical conference was being held. She couldn't help but wonder why they hadn't stayed at this hotel instead of the one so far away in Crystal City. It would have made better sense, but maybe there wasn't room. Oh well.

She brushed the thought away as all the sights she wouldn't have time to appreciate flew past her window. *I am missing so much!*

Tucked away in what looked like an older part of the city, this hotel boasted a nearby garden bordered by a dark green hedge and full of ornamental trees, a fountain and bushes. She made a mental note to at least visit that garden – hopefully without what's-his-name grouching at her.

The beginning conference was way over her inexperienced head. Infectious Diseases was a topic she was interested in, but with all the unfamiliar terminology and acronyms, it seemed the instructor spoke a different language. Clearly, he had no business being at this course. Libby was a novice among experts, but she was determined, so she made a list in her notebook of every term she didn't recognize. Amidst all the handouts and preliminary notes, she highlighted questions and procedures she didn't understand. If nothing else, this class in the deep end of the medical pool had created a flood of questions she was excited to learn the answers to.

Libby smiled to herself. Marcy was right. She should be thankful. This was a once in a lifetime opportunity to network and hobnob with some of the brightest in her field. It also made her reconsider her goal of nursing. *Maybe I should become a doctor? I'm smart enough. I could do it.*

Of course, she could have easily asked Dr. Clements for help, but that would have been like giving the devil a toehold and saying, "Come on in." Even a simple question would stroke his humongous ego. She took more notes.

At noon, he zeroed in on her again. Instead of joining new friends and meeting more people, she found her presence expected at his table with a tray of food already selected for their lunch.

Her blood pressure spiked at his presumption. His arrogance! The man was unreal. She couldn't bring herself to sit despite the charming smile to his handsome, treacherous face. The time for being nice was long gone. Libby gritted her teeth.

"I'm not eating with you," she said, her voice low and steady. There was no need to make a scene. She could make herself perfectly clear without throwing the tray of food at him like she wanted to. "I came here for the conference. Not you."

"Sit." He nodded toward the chair, his lips pursed and tight. The charm was gone. She'd made him mad. Too bad.

"No." Libby straightened. "I'll meet you at the airport for the flight home. Until then, you need to stay away from me, is that understood?"

She didn't wait for an answer. Pivoting on her heel, she walked away. She'd probably be flunked out of nursing school now, but good old Dirk needed to know once and for all where he stood. Hints certainly hadn't worked.

Once outside of the hotel, she evaluated her new predicament. Dirk might never speak to her again, but he wouldn't flunk her, would he? Blowing out a deep breath to steady her nerves, she shook her head at that notion. She knew plenty of other teachers and department heads at the College of Nursing. Her academic reputation was stellar. No. She didn't have anything to worry about. If anything, she felt relieved for finally standing up to him.

I should have done that weeks ago.

Fortunately, she had exited through the backdoors of the hotel, just across the parking lot from a vine covered arbor that seemed to invite her into the garden. With a sigh of relief, she accepted the invitation and was soon inside the comfort of ornamental bushes, trees colored with autumn splendor, and the peace of nature. She checked her watch to mark how much time before the next session started.

Regret for not being able to tour the monuments and historical sights panged her. So many tantalizing views had beckoned from every window. She wished she were twins, one to attend the conference, the other to play. For now, this secluded garden would have to do.

"Work now. Play later," she reminded herself as she investigated the delightful retreat.

Those words made her smile. The last time she had done anything resembling play was the night she'd pushed Mark off the raft. That was fun. He had such a cute I-can't-believe-you're-doing-this light in his eye when he went overboard. Although he had never said it, she could tell he'd been annoyed that she had gotten his shoes wet. Silly man. What did he think would happen at a lake?

Even now she didn't know why she did that. It seemed the only way to break the walking-on-eggshells feeling that had sprung up between them since Jonathan's death. She shouldn't have reacted so badly to that news. All of her dreams came to a screeching halt that morning. It might not have happened the way Jonathan intended, but it happened just the same. He had no intention of coming back. Mark brought more than bad news that day. He'd brought the truth.

Libby cringed. Her real dilemma began that night at the lake with Mark. While she poured her heart out, he had made real good excuses for Jonathan's shortcomings. He'd also listened, another trait unique to Mark.

Poor guy. Did he have to walk around in soggy dress shoes the rest of the week just because of her confused state of mind? And what about his clothes? There was something sexy about a man in wet clothes, especially after he took his shirt off. A half-naked man who actually listened? Yikes. She was in trouble. A man didn't get any hotter than that.

But none of it mattered. He hadn't answered her e-mail and was probably too busy with his exciting new job. She had another year and a half of schooling. After that, she would return to Spencer, maybe get a nursing job at the nearby Marshfield Clinic and settle down like all of her girlfriends.

She would find someone to marry, probably have a half-dozen kids, and—

Ugh! How depressing!

Worse, she and Mark lived in two different worlds. They would never meet again. He didn't even know that he had broken her heart simply because he left. How unfair was that?

She relived the memory as she strolled through the garden, taking in sights of the late summer roses against a background of tall, russet-colored ferns. He'd come out to the farm to say goodbye and to thank her parents for the kind way they had treated him. Faith and Marie were moping around, still hopeful he would look at them like they weren't just friends. He promised to write Faith. After all, she'd given him a box of stationary. He had to say something.

Silly Faith might have thought she'd set a clever feminine trap with that gift, but Mark had kindly deflected the hint when he told her he wasn't much of a letter writer. She shouldn't hold her breath.

Like a coward, Libby had stood behind the kitchen door, listening to the small talk. Hiding. Afraid what she might see in his eyes.

Before long, he said he really needed to get on the road. She listened to another round of goodbyes and knew exactly the moment when her mother and sisters hugged him one last time. Her father told him he was always welcome. Don't be a stranger.

Mark promised to keep in touch.

Libby gathered her wits, sucked up a shred of courage, and stepped out of the kitchen just as her father closed the front door. Mark was gone.

She panicked. In a rush, she nearly pulled the door off its hinges.

What have I done? I need to at least say goodbye.

He stood at the bottom of the steps, his head turned toward the barn like he was looking for something. Or someone. The moment he turned and saw her, his eyes lit up. The thunder in her heart at his gentle smile took her by surprise. He looked so genuinely happy.

"Wait. I … I," she'd stammered, not sure what to say to the man who had told her Jonathan was dead.

"I was hoping you'd show up." His tender words cajoled.

"I was just …." Flustered, she couldn't come up with anything that sounded even remotely authentic. *What? I was hiding? Scared? Just suddenly aware that I care about you a lot more than I should?* It took all her willpower not to run to him, bowl him over, kiss the daylights out of him and make him promise he would return.

"I have a flight out of O'Hare this afternoon." He offered his hand when she came down the steps.

Libby nodded. Of course she knew. The kitchen door wasn't that thick.

"I just …." With a lump in her throat, she couldn't speak. Shaking like a leaf, she took his hand and joined him at his car door. "Have a safe flight."

I don't want you to leave.

"Yes, ma'am." He squeezed her hand, his eyes so full of the unsaid. "I intend to."

"Do you have to go back ... over there?" She stalled, her fingers itching to hold onto him.

Do you really have to go so soon? Can't you stay?

"Do you mean Afghanistan?" he'd asked. "No. I'm too short for an overseas assignment. I'll out-process from the Corps in a couple weeks and start my new job. I'll be stateside from now on."

"Where?" He had to catch a flight, but her mouth kept asking questions.

Please don't go. We need to talk. There's so much I have to tell you. Still so much I don't know about you.

"East Coast. I'll be working for a company called The TEAM. Guess it's one of the best jobs around for a guy like me."

A guy like him? A caring, wonderful, handsome guy like him? What kind of a job is this?

"Will you …." She paused. She didn't want to sound needy like Faith. "Will you email me or something and let me know you made it home?"

"I will." He still held her hand, his fingers clenching hers like he might ask her to dance at any moment. She would have. On the lawn. In the barn. Anywhere, as long as it was with him. "Will you be okay now, Libby?"

Ahh, she loved the way her name sounded on his lips, so much like a prayer. She'd nodded then because she couldn't speak, but her heart cried, *'No. Not if you leave me, too. I'll never be okay.'*

"You'll make a very good nurse. I have faith in you."

The knot in her throat tightened. Her feelings had been tender that June morning. If he would've tugged her even one millimeter closer, she would have jumped into his arms and buried herself there. She'd have made a fool of herself yet one more time. It was probably a good thing that he'd only squeezed her fingers and let her go.

She had to bite her lip to keep from crying. He had seen enough of her tears. She tried to be strong, but even now, remembering hurt.

Her lip hurt, too.

Twelve

Healing takes time.

Libby knew better. That's all this emotional bond with Mark was about. He represented a happier time, nothing more. She took another deep breath and enjoyed where she was today. This garden was a beautiful place to heal.

She pushed up on tiptoes to reach a flowering branch of dark magenta flowers. Despite the late season, the tree was full of blossoms. She had barely inhaled when, seemingly out of nowhere, Dr. Clements was behind her. She hadn't heard a footstep. It happened so fast.

"May I help?" He pulled the branch down, which would have been nice, but his hand rested too quickly on the small of her back.

She spun around startled that she wasn't alone. That put her directly in his arms. He reciprocated as if she had done that intentionally, pulling her close. Indignation clutched her throat.

"No!" She stepped back, away from him.

"Come on, Libby," he coaxed, one hand on her wrist, the other bending the branch closer. "I think we've gotten off on the wrong foot. I'm just here to help."

There was something creepy about his choice of words.

"I don't want to fight with you, but I meant what I said." She took another step to distance herself from him. He let the branch go.

"Your hair smells better than those flowers any day." He took a step toward her, not acknowledging he'd heard her. "They're crepe myrtle by the way. Lovely, aren't they?"

Apprehension slithered through her mind. "I'm going back inside. I want to be in my seat before the next session starts."

"I know what I'd like to do." Despite his insinuating words, he removed his hand from her wrist. "But, have it your way."

Instantly, she brushed the sensation of his touch away. Goosebumps wiggled across her shoulders. What was it about this guy? Weren't doctors supposed to be smart? Didn't he understand English?

"Come on then. I'll walk you to class." He was saying all the right words, but he had her backed into a corner of bushes and trees. "After you." He made a polite flourish for her to walk ahead.

She quelled the rising panic that clutched her throat. This man was her department head. He was safe. Responsible. Trustworthy. He wouldn't hurt her, would he? All of her internal alarms were blaring at her to run. When she turned her body to step around him, he grabbed her wrist and spun her back into his arms.

"Not so fast."

With his breath in her face, she turned away. "Listen—"

"No. You listen." The man moved fast. With one hand fisted in her hair and another at her back, he jerked her head until she had no choice but to look up at him. "You got away from me once, but don't think you can avoid me every night. And what's this bullshit about not being good enough to eat with me? What? You don't think every one saw that?" he hissed.

"Let me go," she breathed, her heart pounding in her ears. All that nice men's cologne didn't smell so nice with terror clutching her throat.

He towered over her. "Listen, and listen well. I can make you, or I can break you. Remember that the next time you decide to take off on your own for a little late night rendezvous with God knows who. I didn't come all this way to spend my nights alone."

She gasped, his threat clear. "You – you can't do this."

"Oh, little girl, you have no idea what I can do." His eyes narrowed as he inhaled deeply. "You smell better than these flowers, and I intend on collecting. If I can't have you at night …."

His threat hung between them.

Writhing to pull away, all she managed was to give him a better handhold. With her hair twisted in his fingers, and her hands sandwiched between them, she was trapped. He pulled her closer.

"Stop it." She squirmed, but he responded by pushing his body into hers. Desperately, she scanned her surroundings. There was no one else around. In the process of retreating from him, she had stepped beyond the view of the windows, deep within the cover of the very bushes and trees she'd come outside to admire. The fear of her predicament rocked her. No one could see. No one would know. No one would help.

With a growl, he bent her backwards, his free hand inching her dress up with his fingers.

"Let me go!" she cried.

"Come on, Libby." He moved in for a kiss. "Call me Dirk again."

"I'll scream."

His hand clamped over her mouth. With a sharp jerk, he pulled her head back. Salacious eyes glittered over her face and down her neck to the v-neck collar to her dress suit. "Of all my nurses, you're the biggest tease. I've dreamed of you for weeks now. Come on. Fight me. Scream for me. That's what I—"

"I think the lady said no." A deep male voice boomed directly behind them.

Instantly, Dirk pressed her face into his chest. She couldn't speak with her mouth mashed against his suit jacket, but she squirmed with everything she had. At last, she glimpsed the bearded man who had spoken. Dressed in a black top and fatigues, he stood within arm's reach, almost close enough to help. Dark glasses masked his eyes.

Dirk clamped his hand tighter over her mouth.

She tried to bite him, but managed nothing more than a muffled growl.

"Shut up," he snarled.

That second of breathing room was all she needed. With a shove, she was loose. Libby darted behind the stranger, smoothing her dress down over her thighs as she trembled.

He reached a steadying hand to her arm. "Is this man bothering you, ma'am?"

"No. We were in the middle of a silly lover's spat until you butted in." Dirk waved the stranger off.

"N - n - no, we're not!" She pushed her hair out of her eyes, her teeth chattering. "He was going to—"

"It's none of your business what I was going to do," Dirk shouted. He shoved the stranger's shoulder, but the bearded man didn't budge an inch. It looked more like Dirk had tried to push a wall.

"I'm making it my business." The man hadn't raised his voice, but Libby heard the menacing power in his tone. By then, he'd planted himself squarely between the good doctor and her. "Ma'am? Is this man your husband?"

"No!" she cried. *What an odd question.* "God, no. He's a—"

"If you must know, I'm her psychiatrist," Dirk roared out another lie. "Restraint is a known method of treatment. She was hysterical. I was simply restraining her to—"

"You lie! You were hurting me!" she screamed, "and I'm not hysterical either!"

Libby glanced at the man in fatigues, afraid he might never believe her now. If anything, she had just made Dirk's case for him, but then she really looked at the stranger. His dark beard did not hide the square line of his jaw. Muscular shoulders roped his broad chest before it tapered off to a trim waist. The way he stood so sure of himself, his hard body shielding her from danger, gave her a déjà vue kind of feeling, like she had seen him standing exactly like that before. He looked confident. Proud. Honorable.

When he took a step forward, Dirk took a matching step backwards.

"Where I come from, we treat women like ladies," the stranger said evenly.

"Where I come from, we mind our own business!" Dirk shot back. He ducked his shoulder to pass the stranger. He didn't get far.

The man moved so fast that Libby yelped. In a flash, he had hold of Dirk's lapels, his fist curled inward as he angled Dirk's face into his. The doctor's feet were nearly off the ground, and his back was to the same bushes where he had just cornered her. Now he was the one in danger.

"If you ever, and I mean ever, touch this young lady again …." the man hissed.

Libby tugged at his elbow. He'd changed so drastically from calm to ferocious.

"B-b-but …." Dirk found his squeaky voice.

"If you so much as dream of laying a finger on her," the stranger rasped. "I'll rip that finger off and make you eat it."

Dirk's jaw dropped. He sputtered, his lips moving in a good impression of a silent movie.

"Do I make myself clear?"

By then, the men were nose to nose. Dirk's toes were pedaling the sidewalk. His head bobbed in response. "Y-y-yes," he answered meekly.

"Then get the hell out of here." The stranger pushed Dirk backwards into the bushes. Without stopping to tuck his shirt back into his pants or to tell another lie, Dr. Clements beat a hasty retreat. He had almost gotten away when the man called after him.

"Hey! You forgot something!"

Dirk spun around, his eyes wide with fright. "I, I what?"

"You forgot that these things take amazing videos." The stranger waved his cell phone high in the air. "I am a witness to what you did here today, and I can find you any time I want."

Dirk nodded once before he turned and all but ran back to the building.

Libby stood alone with the stranger. He had just rescued her, but he had a scary side, too. Smoothing her hair out of her face, she was a little afraid to look at him.

"Th-thanks," she muttered, still trying to stop her shaking. "Thank you—"

"Libby," he said softly, lifting his dark glasses to the top of his head. "Don't you recognize me?"

The change in his voice brought her face up.

"Mark?" She clutched his sleeve. "Is that you?"

He stood rock solid as she barreled into him, his open arms wrapping her tight and safe. Relief flooded her. These arms she knew. Her heart pounded, making her voice squeaky and weak. "Oh, thank you, thank you, thank you."

"Believe me," he muttered into her neck. "The pleasure is all mine."

A shiver of panic shuddered through her body. She had come close to being assaulted. "He was going to hurt me."

"He's gone now." Mark tucked her under his chin. "I've got you now. Don't cry."

Like she could have stopped if she'd wanted to. He handed her a cloth handkerchief, which she promptly saturated. She eased away from him to blow her nose. "Gosh, I'm a mess."

"Looks like I got here just in time." He tucked a loose curl behind her ear. Tenderness shone in his dark eyes. "Who was that jerk?"

Libby glanced back to where she had been trapped a moment earlier. Her throat dried just thinking about it. "Dr. Dirk Clements. My department head at the university. We're attending the same conference, only he's got a different kind of conference in mind."

She blew her nose one last time, her hands trembling so hard she was afraid she would drop the handkerchief and end up blowing her nose on her bare fingers. "I've never been so happy to see anyone in my whole life. It's been too long."

"You didn't answer any of my e-mails." The way he blurted those words out sounded sad. Disappointed.

"I did. Last night ... I'm sorry. You're right. I've been busy. I didn't know if I should. If we—" She stopped spouting her lame excuses.

"I missed you," he said softly, closing the distance between them again.

He didn't get another word out of his mouth. Too many months of wondering where he was and how he was doing fell away. One moment she was wondering what it would be like to kiss him, and the next, her lips were on his. Her fingers gained easy access to the sides of his head, combing through dark locks of more hair than he had last time she'd seen him. His sunglasses slipped back farther on his head. She kissed him hard, and he kissed her with the same hunger. The surprise on his whiskered mouth quickly changed to *welcome home, Libby*. He tasted wonderful, minty, salty, and—him. His beard tickled, but his lips—soft, warm and incredibly satisfying.

He lifted both of her feet off the ground. Her knees bent and even her toes arched in feminine surrender. Mark was all she felt from lips to toes, and he felt very, very good.

The kiss deepened. When he groaned softly, she wholeheartedly agreed. For one breathless moment, the warmth and taste of another man on her mouth consumed her. An unexpected appetite for this man roared to life. She wanted more. She wanted—

What am I thinking? What have I done?

Libby pushed away. She'd just overstepped the limit of friendship in too many ways.

Mark placed her feet back to the ground reluctantly, his hand still circling her wrist.

"I'm sorry. It's just that ... it's just that—" Embarrassment strangled a sob out of her. She lowered her eyes. "Gosh, I've missed you, and you look so good. I shouldn't have done that though. I'm sorry."

"Well, I'm not." Mark pulled her back under his chin, his hand flat between her shoulder blades. "Don't apologize."

He stroked the back of her head like he needed to calm her. It worked. His gentle side released all of her confused emotions, and once again, her tears got the best of her. She wasn't crying for herself anymore, but for all the wasted months waiting for a man who didn't really want her, all the lies she had tried so hard to believe, and all her broken dreams. The gate to her grief had opened, and Mark was the only one there to witness. She snuggled into his arms, the smell of him filling her nose with memories from the lake, the airport, and the cemetery. He'd been there during every painful time in her life, quietly and steadfastly waiting for her to notice.

"I used to think he loved me," she admitted. "He lied, Mark. Jonathan lied."

"Shhhhh," he soothed. "I know. It's over. It's done. You're safe now."

And there it was. She heard what Mark had not said. Yes, she was safe from Dirk, but now she was also safe from Jon. Libby blew out a big sigh. The weight she'd carried for a long time lifted out of her. She could breathe.

Mark tipped her chin up, kind eyes taking in every feature of her blotchy, tear-stained face. She saw the question in those dark browns, and the hesitation. Very slowly, he leaned in, as if asking permission. With that sweet question silently posed, she raised her lips, and he closed the distance. The tenderest feelings flooded her when his mouth touched hers. Realization struck home. She was done with regret and anger. She was done with friendship, too. She wanted more.

He ended the kiss, whispering hotly against her cheek. "I am so glad I showed up."

She stroked the beard on his chin. It was no wonder she hadn't recognized him. This man had some gorgeous hair on his head instead of that uptight military cut. Pushing her fingers into his scalp, he sighed, and she paused. This rescue could turn into some serious petting if she didn't knock it off. With one last stroke of her index fingertip along the edge of his ear, she pulled her hand away.

He shivered, closing his eyes for a second.

Oh, yeah. She needed to stop tempting him. And her.

"Did you really catch all that on video?" she asked shyly as she changed the subject.

"Nope, but he doesn't know one way or the other, does he?" Mark chuckled as he swayed back and forth with her in his arms.

Libby turned in his arms to face him, stoking the whiskers on his chin again. This touching seemed a little less intimate, but it still ignited a steady glow all the way to her core. "So why are you here? You didn't come all the way to Washington D.C. just to rescue me."

"Let's sit down while I explain." He latched onto her hand and led her to a nearby park bench. "I've been looking for you since I got into D.C. I called your friend, Marcy. She told me you would be here. Then it was just a matter of finding you."

"But why did you need to find me?" Libby turned to face him. He'd restored his sunglasses to the top of his head again. Everything about him looked so good, all that tanned skin and the laugh lines crinkling at the corners of his eyes. She reached out to touch him, and he clasped her other hand, too.

"Remember I told you about my new job?"

She nodded, her eyes drinking him in.

"My boss sent me to Afghanistan to investigate a new drug cartel," Mark explained. "They've been smuggling opium stateside when soldiers' remains are shipped home. Some of that dope was hidden inside a few of the caskets that left Dover. We're fairly sure that includes Jon's."

"But how could they do that? Wouldn't those nice people at the mortuary—"

"No, not unless they had a drug sniffing dog."

"But I—" Libby couldn't finish. Of course, they hadn't looked inside Jonathan's casket. His body wasn't there. There was nothing inside but a heavy-duty plastic bag of remains beneath a USMC dress uniform. Tears came with the rush of sad memories.

"I'm sorry." Mark traced a gentle finger over her cheek. "I didn't want you to hurt again."

She leaned into him and closed her eyes. "No, I'm sorry. I think I'm getting over it, and then it all comes back like it happened yesterday."

"It takes time. I know." He brushed his hand through her hair. "But there's more. I'm also taking you to a safe house until this business with the cartel is settled."

"A safe house? Why on earth?" She pulled away to look at him. "Are you serious?"

"Yes. My boss doesn't want to take any chances. For once, I agree with him. These guys are dangerous."

"But what about my family? Are they in danger too? Who's going to save them?"

"Don't worry. The FBI already has them in protective custody. Jon's parents too."

"But I need to get my things from the hotel. I need to cancel this class. I need to——."

"No, Libby. No, you don't." He braced a gentle hand under her chin. "Right now, we're going to the safe house, and that's all there is to it. Another agent will get your things from the hotel. You're not leaving my sight for a minute, honey."

Libby blinked. *He just called me honey.*

Thirteen

"This can't be the right place." Mark peered up at the giant oaks lining the residential street. "Let me check my GPS."

Libby waited patiently while he entered the address again. Yep. This was it, but there was no way his boss would live in a little cracker box home like the one Mark had momentarily parked in front of. He'd fully expected a grand mansion given the money Mr. Stewart had to be bringing down. Judging by the ultra modern office building that housed The TEAM, with its utilitarian design, black granite surfaces and polished aluminum trim, he figured the Stewart's home would be just as lavish and twice as pretentious. It wasn't.

Mark glanced at Libby riding shotgun and looking like she belonged there. After showing up just in time to be her hero for the day, he didn't want to look like a bumbling country bumpkin who couldn't navigate big cities. It was time to act like he knew what he was doing, even though he didn't.

"Let's see who's home."

"Okay," she answered.

He ran around the rental car to get her door. The moment she swung her long legs out of the vehicle, his heart flip-flopped. The navy blue dress and heels enhanced her already slender figure, but the way she smoothed her hands over her hips to push the wrinkles away didn't help. He was already mesmerized, and very aware of her curves. She looped her arm through his, smiling up at him on their way to Alex Stewart's front door, if this really was his home. Mark stifled his lustful thoughts of Libby, and prepared to find out the hard way who lived here—by knocking.

"This is a nice quiet neighborhood." Libby glanced down the sidewalk where a bushy-tailed squirrel hopped on its way to a nearby bush. "I like it. It feels like home."

Mental note to self, *Libby likes this place. Cool. Gosh, I hope we're not lost.*

"Mark." A smiling Mrs. Stewart met them at the front door. "I've been expecting you. Please come in."

He breathed a sigh of relief. Mission accomplished. This dinky little slice of suburbia really did belong to his millionaire boss. How weird?

The dinky little place didn't even sport a garage, only a carport and a fenced backyard. The inside seemed larger than the outside, but that had to be the artful way the furniture was arranged, that and the fact there was so little of it. The old man didn't even have a television, at least not in the front room. A bookshelf, sofa, and easy chair with end tables graced the room before it led to a nineteen-fifties style kitchen, chrome legs, red vinyl covered chairs, and all. A black cat clock hung above the table, its long tail swinging back and forth to the ticking minutes.

"Libby Clifton." He stopped surveilling his boss's home to handle proper introductions. "This is Kelsey Stewart. Very nice to meet you, ma'am."

Kelsey waved off his handshake in lieu of a hug. She was very pleasant and attractive. With her long brown hair clipped at the back of her head, she could not have looked happier.

He looked twice. Tiny scars marked the side of her face. For all her cheerful welcome, there was a haunted look to her eyes, as if she was happy but in a subdued way.

"How was your flight?" she asked. "You must have been flying all night, Mark."

"Yes, ma'am." He looked around again, his need to understand his surroundings overcoming his need to socialize. "If you ladies don't mind, I'd like to check the perimeter."

"I'll be fine," Libby said. "You go do what you have to do."

"We'll fix lemonade while you're gone," Kelsey said. "Come on, Libby. I understand you're from Wisconsin?"

The women's chatter faded as Mark let himself out the front door. He had noticed the magnetic security tape on the windows as well as the keypad for an alarm inside the front door. The outside of the home appeared in good order. No windows were left opened, nor did they appear easily accessible.

He mentally strategized. The home had the usual two points of egress, a fenced back yard, and an alarm system. In case they were under attack, he could have Libby out of there in no time at all. He ran into trouble the moment he lifted the latch to the backyard gate. Two huge German Shepherd-type dogs set up a noisy ruckus.

"Whisper. Smoke. Shush." Mrs. Stewart stepped out the back porch. Both dogs ceased barking and sat on their haunches as if waiting another command.

"Wow. You've got some huge guard dogs."

"They were EOD dogs over in Iraq," she explained. "Whisper's the black one. Smoke's the silver. You do know what EOD means, don't you?"

"Yes, ma'am. Explosive Ordnance Disposal." Mark joined her at the backdoor. "I never would've guessed Mr. Stewart was a dog lover though."

"Please Mark, call me Kelsey." She was so much the opposite of her domineering husband. The evidence that his boss had a definite alter ego was beginning to pile up. How could a woman as sweet as Kelsey stand a man as obnoxious as Alex?

"Yes, ma'am."

"Mark." Kelsey stopped him with a hand to his arm, a scolding smirk on her face. "You need to stop calling your boss Mr. Stewart, too. Just Alex and Kelsey. That's all. I mean it."

"Sorry." He ran a hand over his head, grimacing that she really wanted him to call his boss by his first name. That was going to be hard. The man didn't even like being called sir, but Alex? "Guess it's the way I was raised. Being in the military only made it worse. It just kinda pops out of my mouth."

"I know." She chuckled as they entered the kitchen through the backdoor. "It's very respectful, but we're your friends. You can be yourself with us. Now, can I pour some lemonade for you?"

He nodded, instantly distracted. Libby had just bent over the arm of the couch in the front room, reaching for something he couldn't see. It was what he could see that detonated a heated explosion in his body. Every ounce of blood fled from his brain. The sight of her very trim backside and curvaceous hips took every last intelligent thought right out of his head. He couldn't look away, his eyes memorizing the smooth curve of her profile, the gentle swell of her breasts as she leaned over, and the way the buttons of her dress parted just enough to catch a glimpse of her bra. White. Lacey. Thirty-six Bs. Hmmm.

"Earth to Mark," Kelsey teased. "Are you still with me?"

He turned back to her standing beside him with his glass of lemonade in her hand, not sure what she was talking about. His entire body was still tuned to Libby. He had to be ten shades of flaming red.

Libby joined them at the kitchen door. "What's up?"

"Ah." He squirmed. "I don't know."

"It's probably jet lag." Kelsey nudged him with her elbow, a definite twinkle in her eye. "I think Mark needs a nap. He looks kind of tired."

He grinned. Kelsey was comfortable to be around, even when he had acted like a high school kid with raging hormones. "Yeah, something like that," he muttered.

Libby came to his side, her hand claiming his arm as she peered into his eyes. "Are you tired?"

"No." He beamed, wrapping his arm around her waist. "I'm fine." He took the lemonade from Kelsey, but he caught the look in her eye. She knew very well what he had been looking at.

"So tell me all about yourselves." Kelsey motioned them back into her living room. Before Mark could respond, they were interrupted by a gentle knock at the front door. Roy let himself in with Murphy following right behind.

"Hey, Kelsey." Roy gave her a quick peck on the cheek, and set Libby's suitcase by the door. His eyes were full of mischief. "Here's all your stuff from the hotel, young lady. So Mark, you gonna introduce us, or what?"

Mark sat on the sofa with his arm around Libby. "This is my girlfriend, Libby Clifton."

The second he said those words she noticed. She hadn't pulled away or jumped, but that one word rippled between them. Libby glanced shyly in his direction, and yeah, he'd done good. He winked at her while she shook Roy's hand, loving the way her eyes lit up even when she wasn't looking at him.

"Libby, this is Roy Hudson with all the pearly whites, and that old duffer beside him is Murphy Finnegan. They're a couple of the senior agents I work with, and I do mean *senior*."

"It's very nice to meet you," she said.

"Well, it's sure nice to finally meet you, Miss Clifton. May I call you Libby?" Roy poured on the charm. The man had his nerve. He was outright flirting and doing it right under Mark's nose, too.

"We were concerned for a minute or two yesterday when all the bad news started breaking. You should've seen the boss when we found out you had moved to Chicago. Alex about came unglued. I'm sure glad you're safe and sound. My goodness but you're a pretty little thing."

"Okay, that's enough." Mark smacked Roy's arm. "Let her be. Stop pawing my girl."

"I'm not pawing." A huge smile split Roy's face. "I'm welcoming. And don't you worry about a thing, Libby. I understand this fellow here will be keeping you company for awhile."

"Oh? Mark didn't tell me that." Libby leaned into him. "I'm good with that."

"Seems only fair." He gave her a squeeze. "I mean, I am the one who found you and everything."

"And everything." She smiled knowingly as their eyes met. He stifled an urge to kiss her, not sure he would be able to maintain control once he started. The fear in her eyes when he had first seen her with Dirk whats-his-name was replaced with contentment. All she needed was a red swimsuit, and she would be back to herself again.

"You know," Murphy said, "about that senior agent crack. I might be an old duffer, but I'm still ready to whoop you young pups any day of the week." He winked at Libby. "This fellow taking good care of you, young lady?"

"He is," Libby said. "He already saved me this afternoon."

"Oh?" Murphy's blue eyes twinkled. "What's that about?"

"I intercepted a forward pass," Mark answered as nonchalantly as if that's all that had happened. "Just at the right place at the right time. It's a gift."

"And what's this scruffy stuff growing on your ugly face?" Murphy tugged the beard on Mark's chin. "Alex isn't going to like that."

"Then he shouldn't send me to countries where men are expected to wear beards, should he?" Mark said to Murphy what he would never have the nerve to say to Alex.

Murphy shot him a sympathetic look, shaking his head like he agreed.

Libby's gentle hand on Mark's cheek diffused the conversation. "I kind of like it."

"Is Alex on his way?" Kelsey interrupted.

"You know better than that. The boss never leaves his office this early." There was a mischievous smirk on Roy's face again. "Hey Mark? Can I get your help with a couple of things in the car?"

Before he knew it, they were hauling groceries, bags of ice, and a couple coolers of beverages into the back yard. Murphy fired up the grill, while Roy set up chairs and two tables. When Mark went to check on the women, Kelsey and Libby were at the kitchen sink cleaning vegetables and fruit.

"You ladies doing okay?" he asked. "Do you need any help?"

"No, we're fine," Kelsey answered brightly. "I set the front door alarm, just to be safe. If anyone tries to enter, you'll hear it. We all will."

"You're sure you don't need anything?"

"Not unless you want to listen to girl talk." With that Libby waved him out the backdoor.

He pulled her close before she got too far away. "Come here, you," he said quietly, planting a quick kiss on her lips. "Are you sure you're okay, I mean, after everything that happened today?"

"I think I'm the best I've been in a very long time." Her fingers laced around his neck. "How about you?"

"Oh, yeah," he growled playfully, his hands roaming over her shoulder blades and down her back, wishing they could run off to some place nice and quiet.

"Do you still need a nap?"

He caught the tease in her voice. Her hands were roaming plenty, too, playing with the collar of his shirt, smoothing the skin on his neck, and along his whiskered jaw. Her touch tingled, and he swore he could feel the fingerprints on each of her delicate fingers. His entire body seemed to be on high alert for this woman.

"Only if you're taking one with me."

Her cheeks turned red. Yeah, he affected her, too. A blush looked very good on Libby.

"I'd better help Kelsey," she whispered, but then she nipped his lower lip with a quick kiss, and left him standing there with his heart in his throat.

"Hey," Murphy called.

Mark turned in a daze sure he'd just been kissed by an angel. The amazing shift in her feelings toward him left him off balance and pleasantly warm all over. With her feminine fragrance in his nose and the feel of her hand lingering on his neck, he had to shake it off to make sense of Murphy's words.

He felt it before he knew it. The carefree atmosphere had changed. His boss was home. Alex had come straight to the backyard, and was already engrossed in a terse conversation with Roy and Murphy.

Alex waved his junior agent to join them. "According to the FBI, two dozen men flew into the states from Afghanistan six days ago. They've already dodged surveillance. Presumably, they've connected with Castor. FBI confirms they were involved in the murder of that West Virginia family."

"The FBI have a motive yet?" Murphy asked.

"Not yet."

"Maybe Seinkevitz is sending another message," Roy offered.

"To who? Castor?" Murphy asked. "Wasn't he with them?"

"Could be it's a message to anyone who gets in his way," Roy said.

"But this family wasn't in his way," Alex argued. "These bastards intentionally sought out an innocent family and murdered them in broad daylight. What do you think, Mark? You've been watching Seinkevitz for the last couple of weeks. What's your take?"

"The man's got no problem with torture or murder, but what's his motive? What did he get out of killing a woman and two children?" Mark asked.

Alex ran a hand through his hair. "What does that bastard want?"

"Do we know where his men are now?" Roy asked.

"Mother's been looking for them since the FBI lost track," Alex said. "She'll find them."

"You use my babies yet?" Roy arched a questioning eyebrow at Mark.

Mark glanced at Alex, not sure he should admit to such a huge indiscretion as infiltrating Bagram with a couple contraband bombs.

"What are we talking about?" Alex smirked. "You two got something else going on that I don't know about?"

Roy grinned, and Mark wanted to smack him for opening his big mouth.

"It's kind of like an equalizer," he admitted. "Seinkevitz thinks he owns the whole village and everyone in it. Me and Harley thought different."

"So I take it that you planned ahead, just in case?"

Mark shrugged. "Sure. I always go in country prepared. Don't you?"

Alex only nodded, but there was that glint of amusement in his eye again, like he knew something Mark didn't.

Roy mouthed, *'Good job,'* and gave Mark the thumbs up sign.

"How's he moving the rest of his product?" Alex asked.

"Through the silk route like every other cartel over there." Mark focused on his boss instead of the grinning black man beside him. He and Roy would definitely be having a talk later about the true meaning of covert operations. "He moves it straight north into Russia."

"He doesn't have another stateside operation?"

"Not that we could tell," Mark answered, "but you've got to remember people over there are afraid to talk with us. He runs a brutal program against anyone who gets in his way."

"Air Force investigators have Gutierrez's replacement in custody. They moved in too fast. We still don't know who Castor handed the product off to here in the states. How's Arzad?"

Mark smiled at the abrupt shift in conversation. "He's good. Real good."

"Is he still matchmaking?"

"You know about that?"

"Yeah. Of course." Alex shook his head. "He was always pestering me to get married, too. Did he do the star routine with you guys, the stars are like our family thing?"

"He did." Mark chuckled. This was his first friendly conversation with his boss, and it was all because of a gnarly little Afghani on the other side of the world. "He's quite the character, isn't he?"

"He is that." Alex clapped a hand to Mark's shoulder like they were friends. "You and Harley did damn good work over there. Sorry I had to call you home early."

The backdoor opened as Kelsey and Libby carried the fruit and vegetable trays out, ending the business conversation.

"It's about time you girls joined us." Alex went straight away to help carry the trays.

"I thought I heard you back here." Kelsey beamed to see him.

Mark watched the transformation. The second the trays were on the table, Alex whispered something in her ear. She blushed, smiling up at him with something like hero worship shining on her face. The haunted look was gone. He kissed his wife, his hands on her waist as if they were going dancing. This was no 'Honey, I'm home,' kiss. The tender scene was almost intimate, like they had forgotten they weren't the only two people in the backyard.

Alex transformed again when he turned and extended a welcoming hand to Libby, still keeping Kelsey tucked under his arm. "And you must be our missing Miss Clifton. Welcome. I'm Alex Stewart, Kelsey's husband. Good to see that Mark tracked you down. He's one of my best agents, you know. I knew he'd find you."

Mark about dropped his teeth. *One of my best agents? That was news.*

"Yes, Mark caught up with me this afternoon." Libby shook his hand, glancing around the yard. "I never dreamed that a safe house would look like this, though. I was expecting bars or something, you know, like in the movies. Maybe some guys in black suits and dark sunglasses."

"I guess if you need to be in a safe house, this is as good as any." Alex chuckled as he surveyed his back yard, too. "So tell me, how long have you known Mark?"

Mark heard the question from across the yard where he stood with Roy and Murphy. Libby's gaze zeroed in on his.

"It feels like forever."

Fourteen

Before long, the steaks were grilled to order, and everyone's plate was full. Alex and Kelsey settled at the picnic table chatting with Libby. Mark made another security sweep of the front and back yards before he sat to eat with Roy and Murphy. Alex seemed quite the gentleman with the ladies. He laughed and joked, and for the most part, was pleasant. Libby looked comfortable, so Mark took a seat where he could keep track of the entire yard. It worked to everyone's advantage. He wouldn't be able to keep his hands off of her if he sat any closer.

Kelsey was simply stunning. It seemed she had instantly become Libby's friend, and went out of her way to make her comfortable. For that matter, Alex did, too. Libby laughed at something he had just said. It looked more like she was chatting with old friends instead of people she had just met.

"Looks like you're deep in thought." Roy pulled his chair alongside Mark's.

Mark raised an eyebrow. "Yeah, guess so."

"Those two have quite the story, you know." Roy nodded toward Alex and Kelsey.

"It's nice to see there's another side to him."

"What you really mean is it's nice to see he's not always a complete ass, right?"

"Something like that."

"He was a lot worse before Kelsey came into his life. That man's been through some tough times, but he's got something special in that little lady of his. See what I mean? Look at those two kids. See how they're always touching each other? My heck, they act like a couple teenagers."

Mark looked across the lawn. Roy was right. Alex had an arm draped comfortably across Kelsey's shoulder, while her hand rested lightly on his knee. They did look like kids. He wasn't going to admit to anything. So Alex had a decent streak? Big deal.

"Guess we all have our stories."

"No. Not like those two you don't." Roy leaned in like a conspirator about to share top-secret intel. "There's a helluva lot you don't know about that guy over there."

"Whatever." Mark lowered his voice. Last thing he needed was his boss to overhear.

"Did you know his first wife and little girl were killed in a car accident?"

Mark shook his head, still watching guardedly.

"His daughter died instantly, and his wife died on the street while the paramedics were trying to save her. It happened when he was overseas, still in the Corps. By the time he got back home, there wasn't anything left to do but their funerals. Damn near destroyed him. He still blames himself. Then he went through two nasty divorces. The man couldn't win to save his life."

"Two divorces?" Despite himself, Mark was listening. "Was he nuts?"

"No." Roy shook his head sadly. "He was just hurting, trying to plug the sucking hole in his heart. You know how it is.

You just lost your best friend. It's a helluva lot worse when those best friends were your wife and your little girl."

Mark saw Alex through different eyes. That explained a lot.

"And poor little Kelsey was married to a sonofabitch who tried to kill her." Roy's voice turned to a whisper. "He murdered her two little boys."

"He did what?" Mark hissed. This was an incredibly tragic story that did not translate into the happily ever after couple who sat chatting with Libby. He shot another glance to Alex. How could the man look so—normal?

"Yeah. Those little guys were only two and four years old. Damn shame that." Roy shook his head sadly.

"So that's how she got those scars on her face?"

Roy nodded somberly. "She might not look like it, but she's one tough little cookie. Thought you ought to know since you're part of The TEAM now. Her ex had another go at them about a year after they got together. Almost killed 'em both."

By now Mark was hanging on every word, but Murphy interrupted with a pitcher of beer and three clinking glasses.

"That's another story for another time." Roy scooted his chair over to make room. "You thirsty or something that you need three glasses, old man?"

"What's this old man crap I've been hearing all night? First Mark. Now you? I was just hoping you two would help this *old man* drain a pitcher, but I can always leave."

"Sit on down." Roy chuckled. "What? You getting sensitive in your old age?"

"There you go again." Murphy poured a foamy round as he settled between Mark and Roy. "Just remember, you might not look it, but you're a year older than me. Now grab a glass you guys. You're looking awful serious over here. What's up?"

Roy took a dripping full glass and nodded across the yard. "Just giving Mark a history lesson."

"Oh, that." Murphy shook his head and poured a glass for Mark. "If I'd known that's what you guys were so quiet about, I would've stayed with the food. Get on with it."

Roy lowered his voice. "I was telling Mark what happened when the boss took her out to his cabin near Seattle."

"I thought his cabin was closer to Tacoma."

"Tacoma? Nah, Spanaway's up by Seattle."

"No, it ain't. That's why they ended up at Tacoma General Hospital."

"You sure, Murph?" Roy scratched his head like that would help him remember.

"I'll get a map if you want, but I spent a lot of time in a—"

"Guys." Mark interrupted the squabbling older gentlemen. "Get on with it. What happened next?"

"Okay, Tacoma then," Roy conceded the argument. "Anyway the week off didn't turn out like Alex planned."

"No, sir, not one bit." Murphy muttered.

"Like I said, her ex was a sonofabitch. He'd already tried to kill her and Alex once before. This time he brought some of his buddies with him. They burned the cabin down. Alex figured he could get most of them before they got him. Didn't work that way. He only got four." Roy smoothed a hand over his head.

"How many were there?" Mark asked.

"Final body count was seven. One got away."

Murphy took over the storytelling. "Yeah. Nick's mother. That's who got away. Nick was Kelsey's ex. That old broad who raised him is the one who thumped Alex with a log. Almost took his head off, she hit him so damned hard."

"Wait a minute. Nick's mother?" Mark asked. This horror story just kept getting weirder.

"That's another story all by itself," Roy interjected. "But let me tell you. That old saying the apple doesn't fall far from the tree is the gospel truth. She was a mean drunk."

Mark catalogued that story for another day, along with what Roy had already said about Nick trying to kill Alex and Kelsey once before. He glanced at the happy couple across the way. No wonder they kept their hands on each other.

"You guys mind if I go on with the storytelling?" Murphy looked sternly over his half full mug. "Like I was saying, once they got Alex, Kelsey wouldn't leave."

"Wait. Where was Kelsey all this time?"

"Boss told her to run and hide," Roy said. "She didn't."

"Those bastards would've beaten him to death if she hadn't shown herself. Poor thing." Murphy wiped his eyes. "Had to be scared to death watching all that happening to him. Look at her. She's just a little gal."

Mark couldn't help but look. Kelsey was fine-boned, a tiny thing compared to the rugged man beside her.

"You need a tissue?" Roy bumped Murphy's chair with his boot. "Come on. We ain't got all night for you to start bawling your eyes out."

Murphy wiped his face again. "Still gets to me though."

"Me, too. Anyway—" Roy was promptly interrupted by Murphy.

"So anyway, she tried to help, only Nick and his goons got to her."

"Not 'til she killed one of 'em," Roy interjected.

"Kelsey?" Mark was shocked. Kelsey a killer? No way.

"What I wouldn't give to have seen her take that shot." There was a mixture of pride and sadness in Roy's voice.

"Yeah, but then it got real ugly." Murphy lowered his voice even further. "Guess the guy she shot was Buck's brother. Nick and he were the only ones left. They hurt Kelsey real bad after that, hauled her off with them to their camp. Left Alex to die."

Roy ground a clenched fist into his open palm. "Wish I'd been there. I'd a made those bastards suffer instead of taking 'em out with a single tap."

"Wait. Single tap? How did Alex and Kelsey get away?" Mark asked. "Who found them? Who saved them?"

"Harley." Murphy took a big swallow of his beer, like that was a dumb question.

"Harley?" Mark sucked in his surprise.

"Harley." Murphy continued. "That kid dropped out of sight with all that drug crap he was into. None of us had a clue where he was. Then all of a sudden, he drops out of the clear, blue sky, and wants his job back."

"Wait a minute." Mark held up his hand. "I've been in country with him for two weeks now. Not once has he mentioned a word about any of this, and we've talked plenty."

"Yeah, well." Murphy scrubbed a hand over his thinning hair. "He'd just gotten out of rehab. Took it pretty hard when he found Kelsey. That whole night brought up a lot of the crap he was trying to forget. He don't talk about it to anyone."

Mark sat back in his chair. Harley saved Kelsey? He shot her ex? Man. That was definitely another story Mark needed to hear.

Roy jumped in. "So anyway, Harley hightails it across country in the first military ride he could talk his way onto. He's got lots of friends who'll let him fly. When he gets to the cabin, it's burned to the ground. He finds Alex damn nearly dead, only Alex won't let him stay and help. You know how he is. He makes Harley go find Kelsey instead."

Mark nodded. Sounded exactly like Alex.

"Yeah. So he leaves Alex with a gun and one of his dogs."

"You're kidding me, right?" Mark stopped Roy's story telling again. This story was unbelievable. "Are you guys pulling my leg? Harley took Alex's dogs with him on a military hop?"

"Well, of course." Murphy's forehead crinkled. "Harley's a canine handler. Them dogs are working dogs. He takes 'em everywhere."

Mark shook his head, not sure what to think.

Roy continued. "So anyway, Harley and Whisper take off to find Kelsey. To make a long story short, Harley snipes them last two bastards when he found her. Man, she was in bad shape." He turned away with a whisper. "I'm sorry, but you had to be there. I mean look at her, Mark. She's a dang little girl for hell's sake. She ain't made to take a punch."

"See. I'm not the only one who needs a tissue." Murphy thumped Roy's shoulder. "Roy's right. We spent a heck of a lot of time in Tacoma that summer."

"It was Whisper who found her, ya know." Roy nodded toward the kennel. "Harley let him run. That big old mutt tracked straight to her; would've taken those men out all by himself if Harley would've let him. I never seen a dog love someone like that Whisper loves her."

"I think you're right," Murphy said quietly.

Mark saw it too. Both dogs sat watching Alex and Kelsey, but only the black dog seemed anxious at the kennel gate.

"Anyway, Alex and Kelsey were both laid up for a long time." Roy glanced sideways at them again. "Thought we were going to lose the boss for awhile there. He kept having them mini heart attacks. Almost went blind. It's a miracle he's alive."

"Okay, enough of all this gossiping and storytelling." Murphy blew out a big sigh. "Can't take anymore. All this reminiscing's enough to make an old man cry. 'Sides, I think we're looking at the miracle in his life."

"Damned if you ain't right," Roy drawled. "Them two youngsters are straight out of a fairytale."

Mark stole another glance. Alex looked like the life of the party. Both women were laughing at whatever story he had just finished. Kelsey's eyes were bright with love. She smiled up at Alex, her hand still on his knee.

The thought hit Mark. He wanted Libby to look at him that way, like her world revolved around him, like he was the only thing she saw.

He wanted what they had.

Fifteen

"Nursing, huh?" Alex asked. "That's a noble profession. You'll get to help a lot of folks being a nurse."

"Yes. Jonathan joined the Marines, and I went to nursing school. It was a good a plan until ...." Libby looked away. "Until he was killed in Afghanistan."

"I'm sorry to hear that." Alex placed a gentle hand on her arm. "When did it happen?"

"June." She didn't want to talk about it anymore, but Alex was kind, so she gave a brief explanation. "A rocket hit his helicopter. Everyone on board was hurt or killed." Libby gulped, her throat dry and that trapped feeling suffocating her all over again. She looked for Mark, but he and Roy were busy taking dishes into the house with Kelsey.

"I know it doesn't mean much." Alex hadn't moved his hand. "But it sounds like he died a hero."

Libby nodded. She was done chatting about the thing that still hurt. Her feelings for Jonathan were muddled somewhere between love and loss, with a dash of anger and disappointment thrown in for good measure. Her feelings for Mark only clouded the issue.

Unexpectedly, Alex pulled her into his side, and whispered into her ear. "We never forget them. We honor them every day, and then we keep on living, don't we?"

She pulled back. Man, he had intense blue eyes. There was compassion there, but something else, too. The way he had said those last words made her realize. Kelsey's husband knew what she was going through.

"You've lost someone too?" she asked.

"We all have." He nodded. "Ironic as it is, death is part of life. The hard part." Alex gave her another small squeeze when Kelsey, Roy, and Mark returned. "Come on. Let's see what Kelsey can do with those dogs of hers. Have a seat."

Libby meant to take the empty chair beside Mark, but he snagged her wrist and pulled her onto his lap instead, wrapping her tight. She shivered the minute his chin nestled into her neck.

"I missed you," he muttered.

She turned so she was sitting sideways over his thighs, and snaked an arm around his neck. Her heart stalled. Dark brown eyes pulled her in. Maybe sitting on his lap was not a good idea. Hmmm. Maybe it was. It certainly felt – warm.

"I've been right here," she said quietly.

He didn't answer. He didn't need to. Emotion shone in those deep, dark browns. His hand between her shoulder blades offered support and temptation. If only they had been alone ….

Kelsey whistled to the dogs, jerking Libby's gaze off Mark and just in time. Anymore deep lingering looks like that last one, and she'd be a goner. Grieving fiancée propriety was impossible to maintain enveloped by this particular masculine body. It would only take one little wiggle and she'd combust, so Libby focused on the dogs. At least, she tried to. Every nerve in her body was suddenly alive and tingling. Make that burning.

Alex loosed the kennel latch.

Libby could barely breathe. Dogs, shmogs. She leaned back into Mark, more interested in the feel of his abs against her hips, the sensation of his pecs in contact with the side of her body. The dogs were gorgeous, but she had her own handsome beast, and she was sitting on him. Wasn't that a sign of dominance in the dog world? Her breast rubbed accidentally against his chest. He had to have felt it. His breath hitched almost as sharply as hers.

Oh, Kelsey. Get on with the dog show. I've got a man to kiss.

Whisper bounded to Kelsey. He let loose a yowling kind of bark that made everyone laugh. He was talking with her, maybe telling her it was about time he got invited to the party. Libby steadied her carnal thoughts. It was hard to watch the show with her body tuned into the signals that Mark's body was sending. He hadn't stopped looking at her, his nose still in her hair, breathing fire over the tender skin at her neck with every breath. *How does he do that?*

"You'd never know I was standing here, huh?" Alex groused loudly as if offended that the dogs ignored him.

"You big babies. Do you want a treat?" Kelsey knelt on the ground and hugged them.

"Look how cute they are," Libby said, needing to distract Mark before she melted all over him.

He blew a gentle breath into her ear. "I see them."

Goosebumps zoomed up her neck. Yeah, he was seeing something all right – her. Crank up the fire. She was going to burn.

"Okay now, boys. Settle down. Let's visit." Kelsey signaled with a circular wave of her hand. Obediently,

Whisper and Smoke trotted to each guest for a pat on the head.

Libby reached to pet Smoke when he walked by. Big mistake. Mark adjusted his sitting position. He had to. The dogs weren't the only ones who needed to settle down.

"Did you miss anyone?" Kelsey asked Whisper, her head cocked. He had returned too quickly to her feet. Smoke was still making the rounds. Whisper cocked his head the same as his mistress and barked once.

"Don't take that tone with me. Who did you forget?" She waved him off.

With his belly to the ground, he crawled his way back to Alex like he was one embarrassed dog.

"He always forgets me," Alex said, planting a firm pat to Whisper's forehead. "Damn dog."

Libby would've laughed if Mark's fingers hadn't started a slow, deliberate massage. Up they went to the nape of her neck and slowly back down again, just to the band of her pantyhose. He lingered for a second, tracing the edge just enough to let her know that he was very aware of that thin piece of elastic. Muscles clenched that hadn't clenched in a long time. Mark groaned softly and readjusted his, umm, lap – again.

This dog routine was sure taking a long time.

Whisper returned to Kelsey. Again, he and Smoke sat at her feet with undivided canine attention. Libby tried to pay attention; she really did. She clapped with everyone else. It was obvious that the Stewarts were one big happy family, dogs included, but she needed them to get on with it.

"Okay now, let's sing." Kelsey pointed her index finger to the sky.

Oh, my gosh. More tricks?

Both dogs raised their muzzles and howled in unison. For a moment, it sounded like wolves lived in the neighborhood. As long as she pointed upward, Whisper and Smoke kept the haunting chorus going. Everyone chuckled and clapped. It would have been cool if Libby hadn't been sizzling in her panties.

"Thanks everyone. They really are big babies." Kelsey leaned into their expectant furry faces. "What do we do when we're done, boys?"

Both Whisper and Smoke hit the ground, rolled onto their backs, and played dead with all four feet in the air. They didn't move a muscle until Kelsey told them, "Up."

Finally. Libby let out a big sigh. Mark's hand had wandered to the back of her neck, gently working his thumb and index finger in the most soothing neck rub she had ever felt. Blood rushed to her brain even as warmth surged to parts below. Any move he made right now stimulated. Heck. All he had to do was breathe.

Again, Whisper and Smoke thumped their tails at Kelsey's knee like two little boys waiting for attention. She sent them around the yard to visit one last time, and of course, they returned right back to her side.

"What's next?" Libby leaned into Mark's ear; sure he had to be thinking the same thing she was. "Do you think we could go for a ride or—"

"Whoa. Whoa. Not so fast." Alex snapped his fingers and pointed to the ground at his feet. "We're not done yet."

Libby groaned. Was he talking to her? She shifted her attention back to the show.

Both dogs sat at his feet now while he scanned his audience. Murphy and Roy chuckled like they knew what was coming next. Kelsey's eyes twinkled. Libby caught the expectant feeling in the air. *Now what?*

"Hmm." Alex rubbed his chin as he scanned everyone's faces. "Harley's usually around when I do this. Mark? Are you up for an exercise in canine control?"

Mark looked down at Libby. She caught the glimmer of regret flash through his eyes, but he eased her onto her feet, his hands firmly at her hips.

"Sorry. Duty calls." He pulled himself out of his chair, and handed her his dark glasses, his eyes smoldering. "Hold these. I'll be right back." Then he turned to Alex. "Sure, Boss. Anything you say."

"Good." Alex looked pleased. Libby wasn't. "I need you to stand by the back gate. That's good. Stop right there. Okay now, all you have to do is hold still and get ready to be wrestled to the ground. You good with that?"

Mark grimaced. "By both of them?"

"Come on," Roy taunted. "They're just two little puppies. Look. They're smiling at you."

"They're smiling because it's dinner time." Murphy chuckled. "Sure glad it's you, Mark, and not me."

Sure enough, both Whisper and Smoke were focused on Alex. They looked like they were smiling. Libby held her breath. They also had two sets of sharp, pointy canine teeth behind those black, licorice lips. And fangs. It didn't help when Murphy knelt near Mark with his camera and offered not so helpful advice. "This is just to document how you're going to die, son. Don't pay any attention to me."

"Real funny." Mark turned sideways, and hunkered down, his hands on his knees to offset the onslaught of the two, smiling *puppy dogs*. He cast a sideways wink to Libby.

"Relax. Go with the flow, Mark. They won't hurt you. Trust me." Alex gave a barely audible command to the dogs, "Hold."

Instantly, two furry torpedoes exploded. Libby gasped, her heart in her throat. Within seconds, they had Mark flat on his back. Whisper had hold of his neck while Smoke's mouth was clamped to his shoulder. Mark hadn't said a word. He lay there rigid on the ground, panting.

"He's okay," Roy reassured her. "These dogs are only lethal with the right command."

Libby couldn't answer. Mark hadn't moved. This part of the dog show was not funny. How could Alex do something like this to one of his friends? He must've given another command. All at once, Whisper and Smoke released their prey and returned to their kennel, their tails wagging like they really were just pets after all. It was like someone had flipped a switch. They sat with their eyes glued to Alex, waiting for another command or a treat. He ruffled their manes, latched the kennel gate, and walked over to give Mark a hand up. "Good job."

"Now I know what Harley's always talking about." Mark grabbed onto Alex's forearm and got to his feet, rubbing his neck and shoulder as he wiped the dog slobber off.

"Harley would know." Alex seemed pleased. "That wasn't so bad now, was it?"

"No." Mark shook his head. "Not now that I survived."

"You're kinda like a big old doggie toy, aren't you?" Roy and Murphy chuckled from their chairs. "Go on. Do it again."

Libby hurried to check Mark's neck and shoulder for puncture wounds. Those dogs had hold of him. He had to be hurt. "Are you okay?"

"I am now." He captured her wandering hands and pulled her into his arms instead.

"That scared me," she whispered.

"Me, too," he admitted. "They're quite the dogs, huh?"

"Those are quite the teeth." Libby traced the whiskered line of his jaw with her fingernails, not willing to release him. Not yet. "You're a very good sport."

"Nah." He shrugged with a smile. "I'm an idiot."

Libby leaned into Mark as they joined the others inside. The men had already picked up the yard, folded the table and chairs, and put everything away while Kelsey watered the dogs. It was a fun evening. Libby felt at home. Once inside, she and Mark stepped into the momentary privacy of Kelsey's living room.

"Look." She nodded toward the pictures of two brown-haired boys and one blond young girl on the mantel. The little boys were tiny versions of Kelsey, maybe two or three years old at the most. The blond girl was an easy match to Alex. Her blue eyes were his all over again. Next to those pictures stood a larger portrait of Alex and Kelsey's wedding.

He wore a black tux, silver vest, and matching black tie. Kelsey wore a sleeveless, cream-colored gown with a ruffle that dropped diagonally from one shoulder to her bare feet.

Sunset glowed behind the happy couple. It looked like they were on a beach somewhere.

She stood with her palms on his chest. They were both probably supposed to be facing the camera. Instead, the moment was caught with them looking into each other's eyes. It was easy to read the love between them. Very tanned, masculine, and debonair, Alex looked down at her with both hands on her waist, his face tender and his eyes aglow. With her hair cascading like a curly waterfall over her shoulders, Kelsey smiled up to him, the tip of her tongue barely visible on her lips, her eyes full of light.

"They make a beautiful couple," Libby whispered. "I wonder why they don't have a family picture though."

"I'll tell you about it sometime," Mark whispered back. "I didn't think coming here was a good idea at first, but now I do. You'll be okay."

She slipped her arm around his waist. "As long as you're with me, I'll be fine anywhere." Her heart thudded with what she had just acknowledged.

"I feel the same way," he breathed, his eyes gleaming. "I know it's soon, Libby, but—"

"Shhhhh." She sealed his lips with her index finger. "Your boss told me something very important."

"Alex?" Mark's brow wrinkled. "What?"

"He said we never forget the people we've lost, but we have to keep on living. Jon's gone, but I want to keep living, Mark." She rose up on her toes. He met her halfway and kissed her gently, stealing her breath with that soft contact. The house was full of people, but all she felt was his lips on hers, and his hands anchored at her waist. She circled her arms around his neck, happy with whatever he had in mind.

Someone's cell phone rang.

"Darn," he growled when she broke the kiss. "I was enjoying that."

"Me, too," she admitted happily.

They joined the others in the kitchen. Libby snuggled with her back to Mark, his arm draped casually around her neck. For all she had been through, the day couldn't have a better ending. Mark was going to stay with her. Somehow, they would find a way to be together. Nothing could upset the calm in her heart. Nothing.

Alex turned all business when he hung up his phone. "Listen up. Mother tracked Castor. He's headed north with a dozen accomplices. Looks like our Russian friends have been busy. They're driving some heavy rigs."

Kelsey had come to his side after the phone call, her arm around his waist. He looked down into her face. "Sorry, sweetheart. We fly out to tonight."

Libby caught the tender look in his eye. These two older people were very much in love. It showed. They shared a bond that seemed to answer questions still unasked. It happened in the intimate twinkle in his eye. Alex had just poured love all over his wife, and she had silently returned it in the light of her smile and a pat of her hand on his chest.

"At least I'll have Mark and Libby for company," Kelsey answered. "We'll be okay."

Libby blushed. She wanted the same with – wait. *Mark? But he already looks at me like that.* She leaned against him to test her conclusion. Instantly he pulled her close, his hand at her waist and his hips bumping her backside.

"Change of plans." Alex nodded at Mark. "Get your gear. Roy and Murphy will stay with the ladies. You're coming with me."

No! Libby cringed. What?

Alex frowned. "Have you had any sleep lately?"

"A couple days ago." Mark shrugged, tightening his hold on Libby.

"Well, you can sleep on the flight. It's a couple hours, but it's better than nothing. We leave in an hour. And Mark."

"Yes, Boss?"

"I've got an extra shaving kit in the bathroom. First drawer by the sink." Alex glanced down the hallway. "Get that dirt off your face."

Libby heard Mark's quiet grunt. Without another word, he pulled her down the hall with him. Just as well. She needed some time with this guy if he was leaving.

Darn that Alex.

Sixteen

"You're boss has a lot of nerve," Libby grumbled.

"He does." Mark pulled the extra shave kit out of the drawer and turned on the hot water tap.

The bathroom was much larger than Libby expected. A sunken tub stood out like a masterpiece beneath the frosted window, and surrounded by black tiled floor and walls like it was. An elegant vanity and matching chair, a glassed-in shower stall, and a commode completed the setting. Kelsey had decorated with seashells and peach-colored candles around the tub. Black towels were folded and ready for use at the edge of the tub. It was a very romantic setting, not that Libby would need it now that Mark was leaving.

Darn that Alex.

She made herself comfortable at the vanity, still mentally cussing. First Alex used Mark like some kind of a chew toy for his dogs, and then he ruined her plans for time alone with her friend, who she hadn't seen in a very long time. How messed up was that? Who does this guy think he is, anyway? Just because Mark works for him does not mean—

Mark stripped his shirt over his head.

Oh, my heck.

Her animosity toward Alex fled.

Libby's heart stopped. She'd never been alone with Mark like this before, not with him half-naked, incredibly sexy and—

Oh, my heck. He's ripped.

He focused on his reflection in the mirror. She focused on him.

Standing with his legs spread, he leaned over the sink and applied shaving cream. Camouflaged pants hung loosely off narrow hips, leaving the black waistband of his briefs exposed and a very nicely sculpted portion of his abdomen, too. She knew the proper term for those very handsome muscle groups, the rectus abdominus—the paired muscles running vertically on each side of his abdomen. Every student nurse knew the biology of how the tendinous intersections separated the rectus abdominus into what was popularly called a six-pack, or an eight-pack, or an – *oh, my gosh.*

She licked her lips. A thin line of hair trailed between those perfectly aligned muscles, past his navel to where those same muscles narrowed to a V. And beyond.

Libby wiggled, all at once aware of another ache in her body.

When he lifted his razor to take that first swipe, the muscles on his back rippled alongside his spine. A set of two dog tags hung off a simple beaded chain around his neck. Strong shoulders led to equally sculpted biceps and forearms. This man worked out. It showed.

Gradually, he scrapped his chin clean. The chiseled corner of his jaw appeared. When he tilted his head back, Libby watched the razor skim up and over his Adam's apple. She caught herself wanting to taste that handsome neck, to run her tongue over that freshly shaved chin. Her fingers itched to bury themselves in his dark hair, and to lace around his ears as she pulled him into her body, and—

"You're cute." He winked at her in the mirror.

She blushed. He'd caught her mimicking his actions. Every time he'd moved his lips to the left to shave, so did she. To the right, she had followed suit. She scrunched her shoulders and smiled, afraid her very carnal intentions showed.

With one last swipe up his neck, he rinsed the razor and set it on the edge of the sink. She was off the chair and in his arms before he could reach for the towel.

"I like this." She stroked his clean-shaven face with both hands, her body stretched sensually against his. "I like this a lot."

His smoky gaze spiked another surge of heat through her. Placing her hands on his wet face, she kissed him while he held her tight. This was no little kiss of impulse though. She meant it with every ounce of strength and desire she had. He smelled of shaving cream. His lips, warm and gentle against hers, melted her sorrow away, and a few inhibitions, too.

He took half a step back to steady his balance. "Hey," he breathed hotly into her face. "I think there's some people waiting for us."

"I have something to tell you," she said before she changed her mind. The hole in her soul demanded filling.

He leaned back to look into her eyes. "I'm listening."

She took a deep breath and bared her soul in a hurried rush. "It broke my heart when you left Spencer last time. I didn't want you to go."

His tender smile was all the encouragement she needed.

"And I ...." She drew in another breath. *Do I tell him? Do I say the words? Dare I? Is it too soon?*

Before she could finish, he picked her up, turned around, and deposited her on the counter by the sink. Now she was sitting, her dress hiked up in a very un-lady like fashion, and her pantyhose exposed to her hips. He looked down at her, his eyes hooded and darker than she had ever seen before. Her heart thudded when he placed a hand on each of her knees and stepped between them, effectively pushing her dress up higher and her legs further apart.

She gulped. *Yes. It's time.*

"Still listening," he growled.

"I love you, Mark," she whispered breathlessly. "I know it's too early. I know I should wait for a year ... for awhile. I can't. I don't want you to leave me. I love you so much."

Well, if that didn't sound needy, nothing did. She cringed. All she needed was a box of stationary to make it complete. *Ugh.*

His eyes lit up at her words. "Now it's my turn."

Gently, his hands moved up her thighs, over the wrinkled hem of her dress, claiming every inch of her along the way. By the time his fingers cupped her backside, she had turned into a quivering mass of desire. He had to have been able to hear the blood pounding in her veins. His eyes arrowed straight to her heart before his words did.

"I've always loved you, Libby." His deep voice rumbled over her.

Zing. The gentle tapping she had felt on her shoulder a year ago was nothing compared to the noisy *YES* she heard now. *This is the one. Pay attention.*

He did not hesitate or ask permission this time when his lips covered hers, crushing her mouth in passion. Libby poured her heart into that kiss, and Mark matched her breath by ragged breath. She had never tasted anything sweeter. The door to her heart was kicked open. *He wants me. He's always loved me.*

Her heart soared through the ceiling and clear up to the stars. There was no way to get enough. She wanted every part of him, and she didn't care if they were in someone else's bathroom.

Fire surged up from her legs, clenching her belly with need. Feverishly, she worked the snap and zipper to his pants, afraid she might spontaneously combust if she waited another second. Her dress hiked up higher, and one thing she knew for sure. All her spandex had to go!

"Libby." He clutched her against his bare chest, wrapping her so tightly she couldn't continue undressing him, but that was okay, too. She was happy to be plastered against this man. It gave her a moment to relish the sensations storming her starving heart. Judging by the hammering going on inside his chest, he wanted the same thing. She wiggled against him, planting nibbles and kisses on the skin she could reach.

Ah! He tastes good.

Mark straightened with an audible groan, exactly what she expected to hear. The sheer mass of his body added more fuel to the fire. Her feminine libido turned into a determined beast. She wanted him. Now. On the floor. Over the counter. In the tub. It was all good. Better. Best!

When her fingers dove under the waistband of his briefs, he caught her wrist and held her tight. With one hand splayed between her shoulder blades, he pulled her tightly against him again and imprisoned her. She arched against him, her hips nearly off the counter.

"I'm not going to take you in here." He shuddered, still working to catch his breath.

Not now? Not me? She groaned, her physical need painfully urgent.

"I love you too much." His hot breath scorched her neck as her brain kicked back into logic mode. "You deserve more."

She stilled. *No I don't. Don't make me wait.* As ready as she was, it was hard to slow the freight train of her desire. She took several slow breaths, listening to his heart pound exactly like hers. *Maybe I can change your mind.*

He tipped her face up until they were looking into each other's eyes. The man gazing down at her was the same honorable Mark. Even now, he had taken a step back and blew out a measured breath. She licked her lips again, hoping he wasn't in any more control than she was. He tugged her dress over her legs again and smoothed the wrinkles.

She caught his hands, knowing exactly what he was doing. He was putting her back together, keeping her presentable, and breathing hard, but definitely not stealing her virtue.

Darn it anyway.

"No," she whined.

"We will have our first time together." He leaned in and placed a chaste kiss on her forehead. "I promise you that. I am coming back soon and—"

Her heart stopped. She'd heard those words before.

"No. Really, Libby." He peered worriedly into her face as if he had read her mind. "This op shouldn't take more than a day or two. Murphy and Roy will keep you safe. We'll get these cartel guys, and I'm coming back for you. I promise."

She stared at him, her heart barely calmed from throwing herself at him. Here she was doing it all over again, putting her faith on the line for a man who was going off to battle. This time felt different. The man was Mark. He wasn't telling her what he thought she wanted to hear. He meant it. Didn't he?

"You promise?" There was that needy tone again. *What is wrong with me?*

"I promise, Libby," he whispered earnestly, fumbling in his pants pocket. "Here. Keep these for me while I'm gone."

She took the keys he offered. One looked like a door key, the other a car key.

"Your keys?" she smirked.

His eyes widened in shock as he pinched the car key between his thumb and index finger. "They're not just keys. This is the key to my '69 Camaro."

He looked so endearing. The way he had emphasized Camaro made it sound like he'd entrusted her with his child.

"So, where is it?" She stilled her wanton side and let him think he had won. For now.

His eyes widened again, this time in a smile. He pinched the other key. "It's locked up nice and safe behind garage door number 18C at my apartment. Maybe Roy and Murphy can take you over there while I'm gone. Go ahead. Drive it. You'd like it."

"What color is it?"

"Black. Of course."

How could she resist? His eyes were filled with a boyish charm that only added more fuel to her desire. There was no deceit on his handsome face, only the wide-open smile of a man in love.

"And here." He pulled his dog tags over his head. In two seconds flat, he'd slid the keys onto the same chain and secured it around her neck. "Now you have everything I own," he said quietly.

"I do?"

He nodded, his forehead pressed to hers. "My home. My car. And my heart."

Seventeen

"They what? When? Stupid fools!"

Mark caught the drift of tension when Alex stepped away to take a call. They'd barely flown into Chicago's O'Hare Airport. He hadn't realized they were headed to Wisconsin until they'd left the Stewart residence. Apparently, Alex hadn't wanted to alarm Libby.

Crowds of passengers stormed the baggage carousel. He watched for their weapons cases and ammo cases. Flying with firearms always meant extra restrictions and preparation, but he took no chances. The sooner this gear was out of the public's reach the better off he'd feel. If only he knew what his boss was ranting about.

"We need to get to Spencer. Now." Alex stuffed his cell phone into his pocket, grim and focused as he jerked his overnight case off the carousel, grabbed his rifle case and turned toward the exit. "Castor and his friends blew through the safe house."

"What are you saying?" Mark stepped to his boss's side.

"I mean they blew it up. Damned FBI only had two agents there. Both are dead. Zack thinks one of Libby's sisters might've been killed, too."

God, no. Fear clutched Mark's throat. "Are Jon's parents okay?"

"You know as much as I do," Alex snapped.

"But how could this happen?"

"Because the damned Bureau is so buried in political bullshit, they can't do anything right. Nothing like this would've happened if you guys had been there." Alex cursed all the way to the tarmac and their next ride, a private jet that would get them into the airport at Eau Claire. From there, it was less than an hour to Spencer.

Mark couldn't think. This turn of events was going to kill Libby. Zack had to be wrong.

"You see why I needed you here?" Alex fumed as they flew northward. "I need my best snipers."

The Gulfstream ate up the miles. Before long they'd secured a rental vehicle, a roomy Yukon that would hold all their gear. Mark expected a war zone when they screeched up the long gravel driveway to the Clifton farm. It was strangely quiet. Alex's cell phone rang. Mark listened to Zack's loud voice in Alex's ear.

"Boss, you gonna get your dumb ass in here or you gonna hang around for midnight target practice?"

Mark stopped in his tracks. Zack just called the boss what? But Alex did not react like Mark expected. Instead, they ran for the open front door. Zack slammed it shut behind them There were no lights inside the farmhouse, just the dim shape of Libby's father, Jerry, crouched at the open window, his rifle in hand.

"Sit rep," Alex demanded when he cleared the doorway.

"Nothing in sight. The Russians took out both FBI helicopters just outside of town. We saw the explosions from the upstairs windows. We know they're coming and they've got rocket launchers. Get ready." Zack took position at the other open window. "It sure feels like I'm back in Iraq all of a sudden. You heard from Mother yet?"

"Not yet," Alex snapped. "She can't get a decent answer from the FBI anyway."

"Weren't they the ones who told us a couple dozen Russians entered the states?" Zack asked.

"They're also the ones who lost 'em." Alex muttered while he strapped his thigh holster on. "Let's do this right. You guys know what to do."

"You find your girlfriend already?" Zack asked Mark.

"Yeah," Mark nodded, thankful Libby was far away from this warzone. He pulled his custom made, bolt action, .308-caliber rifle from its travel case and loaded the pockets of his cargo pants with ammo. Zack and Alex sported the same weapon, standard issue for every member of The TEAM. Individual handguns might be allowed, but not tactical rifles. "She's safe in Alexandria."

"That my baby girl?" Jerry asked. The fear in his eye confirmed it. He'd lost a daughter tonight.

"Yes, sir," Mark answered gently.

"Well, good." Jerry turned back to the window. "Least she's safe."

The cell phone on Alex's belt rang. He turned the speakerphone on so everyone could hear Mother.

"Boss, we've got you on satellite feed. You've got two bogeys headed your way, more behind the barn. Also watching two smoking vehicles down the road from your position. FBI said they would send agents to assist. If that's who was in that car, you can assume you will no longer receive that support."

"Got it." He clipped the phone back onto his belt. "You heard the lady. FBI support is gone. Zack, eyes on the front. Jerry, take the road. Mark and I are going to intercept."

Anger flashed in his eye. "Where the hell is Libby's mother?"

"In the fruit cellar. Where do you think?" Jerry barked. "I'm not losing my wife, too."

"Can she shoot?"

"Course she can shoot."

"Then get her a gun. We need everyone we've got."

"This is my house, and that's my wife, you—"

"Jerry!" Rosemary appeared at the doorway with a double-barrel shotgun across her arms, her blond hair braided at the back of her head. She had heard the exchange. Red-eyed and angry, she might have been shaken up by the news of her daughters, but she was not incapacitated.

"It's good to see you again," she said when she faced Mark. Clifton determination glittered in her eye. Man, she looked like Libby.

"I'm sorry," he said softly, hating the useless words.

Jerry scowled and turned away, but she nodded, fighting tears. "There'll be time for crying later," she said in a stronger voice than Mark expected. "Now let's give these Russians something to remember Spencer by."

"Libby's safe." He offered the only comfort he had.

Rosemary gulped. "I know. I stopped worrying about her the second Alex called and said he'd sent you to find her."

The evidence was stacking up. There might be hope for Alex after all.

Zack interrupted, waving Rosemary over to where he knelt by the window. "Get on over here, Mrs. Clifton. You can help me cover the front. You got enough shells?"

He'd barely finished speaking when the swoosh-bang of a rocket-propelled grenade hit the concrete front porch steps, blasting against the stone foundation, but not entering the home. Zack pulled her into his side, shielding her with his body as the windows shattered over their heads. Glass sprayed everywhere. Mark and Alex crouched behind the furniture to avoid getting hit. Flames licked the wooden porch, casting an eerie orange glow through the windows.

When Mark looked up again, Jerry and Rosemary both had their rifles pointed out the broken windows.

"Damn terrorists," Zack muttered, peering through his scope across the lawn.

"How many?" Alex asked.

Jerry's gun roared.

"Was two." Zack raised his eyebrows at his new shooting partners. He took a steadying breath, aimed, and—

BLAM. Rosemary got off a shot.

Zack glanced over his shoulder at Alex. "Now there's none. I think we got it covered in here. You two be careful."

Jerry looked up from his firing position to Mark. "You give 'em hell for me, will you son?"

"Yes, sir, I intend to." Mark turned away to do exactly that.

Quietly, he shouldered his rifle and followed Alex out the backdoor, across the back lawn, and past the rear of Jerry's two-car garage. They crept alongside the greenhouse until they could duck in between the barbed wire fencing that surrounded the cornfield that ran north of the house and the barn.

Concealment was easy in the densely tasseled stalks in the dark. In another week, Jerry would be harvesting the crop as silage for his dairy herd. Tonight it was pure camouflage with enough room between the rows that a man could easily maneuver through it. The fire at the house masked what little noise they were making in the field.

"We stop them right here." Alex dropped to the ground once the front of the house came into view.

Mark grimaced. What a sad sight to see the tidy front porch with its comfy wicker furniture now turned to smoking shambles. It hadn't been too long ago when he had sat there enjoying an evening with the Cliftons. Now this.

He dropped alongside his boss to take a solid position. Two men in fatigues were dragging the bodies of the men Jerry and Rosemary had shot back toward the barn. Nine more men in military style uniforms crept closer to the house with two RPG launchers and a couple small wooden crates.

"They're going to shell the house," Alex muttered.

"Not tonight," Mark breathed.

"You got any tracer rounds?"

"Always."

Mark rolled to his side, traded the standard rounds in the detachable box magazine for tracers and resumed a firing position. If he hit true, one hot round would light these jokers up. Back on his belly, he took careful aim. A soldier normally used tracers to assist with course corrections while firing on his enemy. The pyrotechnic charge in the base of a tracer burned white-hot, making the bullets visible to the naked eye, day or night. The problem with that scenario was it also revealed the location of the shooter, so a sniper deep undercover did not normally use tracers. Tonight was an exception to that rule.

"You need a spotter?" Alex asked quietly.

"No, sir, ah, I mean, Boss. Not at this distance." Mark steadied his weapon and quieted his nerves. This was his God-given talent. He didn't need a spotter for what came natural. The night sky sparkled with stars. He drew on that celestial solitude and the knowledge of a certain young woman waiting for him in Virginia as he centered his mind.

"I'll take the four at the rear," Alex whispered.

Mark drew in a final calming breath. Held it. Sighted one of the wooden crates. Fired. The ordnance in the crates reacted perfectly to the tracer round, exploding upwards and out, taking a few bad guys with it. He fired again. Within seconds, six Russians lay dead. Another thrashed, injured and cursing. Two fled to safety behind the barn.

"Leave him." Alex nodded toward the injured man. "Let's move."

Good call. Mark was all for that. Helping the enemy could wait 'til the battle was over.

They pushed out of the dirt and paralleled the fleeing men. Russian central seemed to be behind Jerry's red dairy barn. Bingo. Three heavy trucks were parked against the stone foundation, tailgates down, and boxes and weapons haphazardly placed on the ground. Propane lanterns cast an eerie bluish glow over another dozen men milling around the trucks. The sound of angry argument made its way to where Alex and Mark crouched watching.

"You seeing this?" Mark made himself comfortable in the soft dirt, his feet spread out behind him, his belly to the ground, and his rifle set to engage. He squinted into his scope, surprised he was facing an army in the middle of dairy country. "I count fourteen on their feet, two on the ground, another one in the truck."

"Right. Seventeen." Alex focused through his rangefinder. "More crates, too. Looks like RPG's are these guys' weapon of choice."

"Yep. Got 'em. Same as last time." Mark glanced at Alex. "RPG-7s again. What the hell is going on? These are Russian made grenades. These guys didn't come for a couple bricks of opium, Boss. This is a well-equipped army."

"Won't matter. Hit the warheads," Alex muttered. "One shot and they're history."

"Then let's make history." Mark sighted in the crates at the rear of the truck. It was an easy shot until one of the Russians stood up with a launcher on his shoulder.

Mark held his breath. The man stood the full-length of the barn away from him, but someone else had caught Mark's attention. RPG guy stood listening to the man inside the truck.

Truck Guy appeared to be furiously working something on his lap, barely looking up as he talked with RPG Guy and shook his head.

RPG Guy yelled something in Russian.

Truck Guy shook an adamant, 'No.'

"Do you see that guy in the truck, Boss? Can you see what he's doing?"

Alex peered through his rangefinder. He lay to the side of Mark, and hopefully, he could see through the open truck door to see what Truck Guy was really doing. "My hell. He's on a laptop. He's their Mother."

"Or he's listening to someone just like her."

Mark and Alex looked at each other at the same time.

"They've got eyes and ears on us," Alex hissed.

"Won't be the first time." Mark zeroed in on the box of ordnance. Live by the RPG; die by the RPG. It was time for a personal payback for Faith.

Alex fed him a second-by-second play. "The guy is angry with RPG man. He's shaking his head. We're made. Grenades and gunfire headed our way."

"Ah huh," Mark replied softly. Made or not, he was taking this shot. He had one chance only. Of all those crates on the ground, he had to hit the one full of warheads.

RPG Guy jerked the launcher onto his shoulder while the rest of the troops turned to the cornfield and hunkered down or crouched to fire. All hell broke loose. Mark heard the whir of bullets hitting too close and personal in the furrow around him. Alex fired again and again without a single word, laying down cover and giving Mark time. Men fell.

Mark whispered as he squeezed the trigger. "This is for Faith."

With a single crack of thunder, his shot interrupted the Russian assault. Blistering fire and smoke enveloped RPG Guy, along with Truck Guy and several others standing too close to the kill zone. The men not hurt in the explosion flattened into the ground to protect themselves from flying debris.

An ammo dump style fireworks show with live rounds of killer bees zinged into and over the Russian troops. The warheads exploded in a deafening roar throwing more burning wreckage into the air. Men scrambled for safety, but as soon as they recovered their wits, they turned and began firing on Mark and Alex once more.

"Reminds me of my last job," Mark muttered as he loaded another magazine. Live rounds still flashed. Nonetheless, between him, Alex, and the fire, the Russians were no longer a force to be reckoned with. All were on the ground.

Alex rolled to his back and rang Mother, the cell phone pressed between both hands to conceal the glow of the screen. "Tell me what you're seeing," he whispered. A second of silence ensued. "Good. Keep track of them."

He snapped the phone shut and pointed east to the field of oats behind the barn. "Two fleeing on foot that way. Let's go back to the house. We can finish this later."

Mark was not prepared for the sight back at the farmhouse. Smoke still billowed from the blast where the first RPG had made contact, but now the heavy oak door, the same one he had so reluctantly knocked on months before, hung splintered and scorched on one hinge.

They ran to the rear of the home only to find everyone gathered around Libby's father on the ground. Zack was on his knees and covered in sweat, performing chest compressions on an unconscious Jerry Clifton. Rosemary crouched beside the men, wringing her hands, her face red and worried.

"What the hell?" Alex exclaimed.

"Heart attack. Ambulance and local police are late as usual." Zack panted. "Glad you two showed up. Spell me. I'm beat."

Mark knelt and took over, easing Zack's hands out of the way as he continued the same steady rhythm. "Come on,

Jerry. I've got you now." He turned to Zack. "How long have you been working on him?"

"About forty minutes. He went down right after you guys left." Zack blew out a big breath and sat back on the patio, wiping the sweat off his face with a swipe of his arm. "We took another RPG. One minute he was shooting. The next he was down. Thought he got shot. Man, that's a lot like work."

"So if one of you was working on Jerry this whole time ...." Alex looked from Zack to Rosemary. Rosemary pointed at Zack just as he pointed at her.

"Zack's a very good shot," said Rosemary calmly. "I'm proud of him."

Mark glanced up at Rosemary's no-nonsense demeanor. She wasn't wringing her hands. She was simply working the cramps out of her fingers after taking her turn at performing chest compressions on her husband. The woman was amazing.

"You two get 'em all?" Zack asked.

"Two got away. Possibly a couple more in a pickup vehicle. Mother is tracking them. We'll need to move soon if we're going to stop them," Alex answered. "I think you're right, Mark. Something else is definitely going on here."

Sirens screamed in the distance. Mark kept working on Jerry. Zack and Alex located a fire extinguisher and put out the fire in the front room.

It was a helluva night.

Eighteen

"Whew." Murphy blew out a deep sigh. "How many of these danged rocking horses did you say you make each year?"

Libby sat contented and happy to be helping Kelsey at the basement worktable. Murphy and Roy had kept them up late the night before with stories of their crazy exploits over the years. They explained how they'd used C4 to heat cans of beans in the jungles of Vietnam, how they win at outrageous cockroach races, and how to keep dry in the monsoon season.

This morning was different. They were on Kelsey's turf, seated on opposite sides of a worktable while an army of wooden horse parts waited in the middle to be painted, assembled, and glued.

Murphy's job was to paint the square horse bodies a light tan, while Roy was in charge of painting the leg pieces dark brown. Kelsey covered the rockers with fire engine red, while Libby painted the head and neckpieces white. Multi-colored yarn lay off to the side for the rocking horse tails: blue for boys, pink for girls, and red for fun.

Jingle Bells. Rudolph the Red-nosed Reindeer. Deck the Halls.

Christmas songs kept running through Libby's head. Painting relaxed her. So did the friendly banter of Mark's friends. Murphy and Roy did not seem like typical bodyguards. Yes, they wore gun holsters under their jackets, and she'd seen their pistols, but their relationship with Kelsey was more on the fatherly side. They both treated her as if she were their favorite daughter instead of their boss's wife. They doted on her, which explained why everyone was in the basement painting. When Kelsey mentioned the mountain of work she had to do, these two men had quickly jumped to help her.

"He used to do twenty-five each year. Since I joined the workforce, it's gone up to fifty. We work on something all year around." Kelsey pointed to more wooden pieces stacked in the corner. "Cradles are next."

"And he gives these toys away?" Murphy asked.

"It's how we celebrate Christmas. You know how he is."

"He's a damn workaholic, that's how he is."

Libby finished another piece. She couldn't wait to put the eye decals on them. These little creatures were the cutest things ever, perfect for little children who had to be stuck in the hospital over the holidays.

"I think it's sweet." She leaned back to observe the scene. It did look like Santa's workshop, only with a couple of grumpy elves.

"Humph. Never ever heard Alex called sweet before," Murphy grumbled. "Besides, you just met him. He's a slave driver."

"Yeah. He is." Kelsey laughed.

"You think he'll ever be able to make enough cradles and rocking horses?" Murphy asked.

Libby sensed an underlying question to Murphy's words. *Make enough cradles and rocking horses for what? The kids? For Kelsey?*

"Maybe someday," Kelsey answered softly. "Even if he did, he'll still have to help me, won't he?"

There was some hidden conversation going on between Murphy and Kelsey that Libby could not put her finger on, some untold story she'd have to ask Mark about later.

"Yeah." Murphy reached across the table and patted her arm. He seemed so genuinely tender. "I guess so."

"You painted me!" Kelsey exclaimed.

"Well, so I did. So I did." He chuckled. "How you doing, Roy?"

"Fine."

Libby glanced at Roy's curt answer. He had been way too quiet, not joining in on the camaraderie. All ten of his fingers were covered in brown paint. His tongue stuck out of the corner of his mouth like he was really concentrating.

"Ah, Roy, you're doing it again," she said.

"Will you stop watching me, woman?" He licked his lips, his eyebrow spiked in comedic frustration. "You think painting these stubby little legs is easy? It ain't. They keep rolling all over the place. If I stand them on end, they fall down. I'm tired of chasing 'em."

"I'll help," she offered. "If we dipped one end of the dowels in black paint, then it would make them look like they had hooves."

"Good idea," Kelsey said.

"Oh, no, you don't." Roy pointed a threatening paintbrush across the table at Libby. "Don't you go pulling that trick on me. I know what you're doing. You're trying to make me feel guilty, only it ain't gonna work. 'Sides, those heads and neckpieces are bigger. Painting them will take me all day."

"They're already done." She stuck her tongue out at him, so he followed suit.

He also rolled a few wooden dowels in her direction, his brow spiked in evil intent. "Well, if you insist."

Murphy pushed away from the table, stood, and stretched. "I'm done. There's only so much painting an old man like me can handle in a day. I'm going upstairs to start breakfast. Anyone else hungry?"

"Since you're asking, I'd take a cup of coffee," Roy said. "Bring some cream back with you."

"I'll put a pot on, but I don't deliver. If you want it, you'll have to finish what you're doing and get your own."

"'Scuse me?" Roy's eyebrows shot up in mock exasperation. "Now listen here. You only had twenty-five square little pieces of wood to paint. I'm doing the darn legs. That's—"

"One hundred legs," Libby teased.

Roy leveled his paintbrush her way again. "I know. I can count. You keep this up, and you and me are going to be painting legs all day long."

"I'd love that." She pointed her paintbrush right back at him, cancelling his imaginary shot. "Then we could sing carols and get into the spirit of Christmas together. Won't that be fun?"

He rolled his eyes.

"I know." Libby loved to taunt. "Maybe it will snow, too. We might need to put up a Christmas tree down here while we paint."

His eyebrow spiked. "Knock it off, young lady."

Libby looked up to Murphy's hand on her shoulder. "I thought you went upstairs?"

"Where's my coffee?" Roy asked, still deep into the grumpy elf routine.

"Libby." Murphy pulled a chair over and sat down next to her, his cell phone in his other hand.

She looked up into sad blue eyes. The festive spirit fled.

"What's wrong?" The same premonition she had experienced in June strangled her once more. Long before Mark had knocked on her parent's door, she had sensed something happened with Jonathan. Her heart froze in her chest, holding back breath and time. *Not Mark. Please, not Mark.*

"Honey." Murphy sighed. "Just got a call from Alex."

She hadn't even heard his phone ring. Roy and she were too busy teasing each other. She was having fun. Her stomach lurched. *Please, not Mark.*

"I guess things went real bad in Spencer last night."

Libby blinked at him, not understanding what and not wanting to hear any more.

"The cartel hit the safe house. They killed two FBI agents and one civilian. Injured the other civilian. She's in the hospital."

Kelsey gasped. Libby couldn't process exactly what Murphy had just said. Civilians? What civilians. Who were the civilians? Weren't Faith and Marie at the safe house?

"What?" Realization struck. Her heart thumped. "No."

He took hold of her arm. "I'm sorry to have to tell you, but Faith is dead, honey. Marie is in the hospital. She's critical, but they say she'll be okay."

The world fell out from beneath her. She swayed. Murphy anchored her to the chair.

"No," she whispered. "It can't be true. Not ... not Faith."

Roy came around the table to stand beside her. Everyone seemed to be holding their breath. Kelsey knelt at Libby's other side. It was true.

"My sister—" Libby couldn't finish. The words stuck in her throat.

"I'm so sorry." Kelsey hugged her tight.

"I'm sorry, but there's more." Murphy rubbed a quick hand over his face. "There was a shootout at your parent's place, too. Your dad had a heart attack in the middle of all the gunfire. He's in the hospital."

"My dad?" Libby couldn't believe she had heard correctly. This was too much. *Faith dead? Shootout? Heart attack? Dad?*

"He's in critical condition, honey. Your mother is with him. She wants you to call first chance you get."

Libby pulled away from Kelsey. "I've got to go home. My Mom and Faith … I have to leave." She walked to the stairs, oddly energized. There was so much to do. Her mother needed her. Marie needed her. The house probably needed cleaning. Before she reached the steps, she turned back to Kelsey. "I can't finish the rocking horses. I'm sorry, but I have to—"

She stood there blinking in dazed confusion. Her world had just imploded. What was she thinking? Her discombobulated mind told her to stay and help Kelsey at the same time that it told her to run home. She took a step toward her friends even as her hand on the banister held firm. *I have to leave. I have to stay.*

In a second, Kelsey had hold of her. "Let's get you upstairs, Libby," she said quietly.

They walked up the steps into the kitchen together. Murphy and Roy followed on their cell phones, walking to different rooms in the house as they gathered information. Within minutes, Murphy joined Libby and Kelsey at the table, his face grim as he reached for Libby's hand, big tears in his eyes.

"You've got one helluva mother, you know that, don't you?"

Libby nodded. Her mother was the heart of her family.

He wiped his face, still clenching her knuckles. "These cartel guys used RPGs on the safe house. You know what an RPG is?"

Libby gulped. "That's what … killed Jonathan."

"That's right. I don't know how they got hold of all the firepower, but it sounds like they came prepared for a battle. Your parents decided to stay in their home and shoot it out. You need to know your mother was doing her fair share of shooting right along with your Dad. With their help, Alex and his team stopped the Russians. He's damn proud of your Mom and Dad. He says to tell you he's sure sorry about Faith."

Libby nodded. That sounded like her parents. One was as stubborn and determined as the other. But poor Faith. Tears flooded her eyes at the thought of her sweet sister. Faith wanted to be a dental hygienist. She was in college. But now ….

Gradually Murphy's words sunk in. *Shoot it out. His team. RPGs.* She squeezed his hand, afraid to ask. "Mark?" she asked in a whisper.

"He's fine. He and Alex took down a couple dozen Russians all by themselves."

Knowing Mark was safe was her undoing. Libby buried her face in Murphy's shoulder and wept.

Waiting sucked.

Mark stood clenching and unclenching his fists, the only thing he could do to alleviate the adrenaline in his system. And fume. The ambulance had long since screamed off with Jerry and Rosemary. Mark was ready to hunt the rest of the Russians down and finish the job. Mother had already relayed their exact location, headed south. If *The TEAM* was to intercept, they needed to move soon.

Unfortunately, the local authorities had a different agenda. As soon as the Wisconsin state police rolled onto the scene, The TEAM's plan to apprehend fell apart. With all the dead or wounded Russians laying all over Jerry's farm, the sheriff's department quickly jumped to the wrong conclusion.

Just as quickly, they took Alex, Mark, and Zack into custody, confiscated their weapons, and bagged everything in their pockets as evidence. Since all three wore cargo pants, all those pockets provided a lot of evidence. Ammo. Handguns. Clips. Extra magazines. And more. At first glance, Alex and his team were simply hired guns without any authority to do everything they had done. By the looks of the place, they'd done plenty.

The sheriff in charge was on his phone verifying Alex's side of the story, while Alex was on his phone with the FBI in D.C. For some reason, he was the only one allowed to keep his phone.

"I don't care about your sonofabitchin protocol. You cost one civilian her life." Alex stilled barely long enough for a reply from whoever was on the receiving end of the line. "That's the whole point. You shouldn't have lost anyone!"

In aggravation, he slapped his phone shut and barked at Zack simply because he stood the closest. "We're never working with the FBI again."

Zack shrugged and turned away. Mark stepped away, too. His boss radiated hostility, but Mark had enough of his own. Grinding his teeth, he clenched his fists again, then spread his fingers wide. This whole operation had turned into a nightmare, and Libby was in the middle of the firestorm. Something had to give.

Searchlights flashed through the upper level of Jerry's once pristine barn. The dairy herd inside was probably never going to give milk again after the ruckus of the night, but at least the Russians hadn't set the barn on fire. The state medical examiner was busy with his forensic team. An array of lights displayed the carnage that Mark caused when he'd shot the crate full of grenades. He didn't think twice about it then, and he didn't care now. Every single one of those men was responsible for murdering Faith. He'd do it all again.

But why Libby's parents? And why breach a safe house in a sleepy farming community that held two elderly people and two young women? It seemed the cartel had zeroed in on the Clifton family. Nothing made sense. Logically, Mark could understand if the hit had been against Jonathan's parent's home if only because the dope was buried in their son's casket. That would have made sense, but how did the cartel know where the safe house was? The simple problem of a drug lord out to retrieve his stolen dope was not so simple anymore. When did the cartel get so smart?

Too many questions, and Mark had no answers. More than all the armed soldiers behind the barn, it was the man with the laptop that bothered him the most. That guy was obviously their communications man, but exactly who was he communicating with? What else did he know, and how did he know so much? These guys had to be inside The TEAM's server. Maybe the FBI's too. Nobody was safe.

Mark shuddered. An instinctive need to protect Libby flooded his normally rationale mind. She was safe on the other side of the country, but he needed to hear her voice to make sure.

"Do we know what happened at the cemetery yet?" Alex snapped.

"FBI had agents staked out there," Zack offered. "Haven't heard what happened though. Been kinda busy."

Alex stabbed another number into his cell phone just as the sheriff in charge ambled over, interrupting the call. Mark sized him up. Sheriff Dawson looked like just another farmer, tanned and tired. He walked with a slight limp that didn't seem to slow him down, but his calm demeanor did not reflect in his sharp eyes. This was his crime scene, no ifs, ands, or buts about it.

"Your story checks out, Mr. Stewart." He nodded to another officer to return their property. "Honest mistake. Thought you might have been the guys who killed that family in West Virginia the other day."

"Understood." Alex snapped his thigh holster where it belonged, sinking his SIG into its place. "Are we free to leave?"

Sheriff Dawson didn't answer. "You and your men did a good job protecting Jerry and Rosemary. Sure wish you would have been at that first house though."

"We should've been there," Alex said brusquely. "What about the cemetery? The FBI get hit there, too?"

"I've been busy processing the safe house, but from what I hear, the FBI agents are still on site. They've had a quiet night. Looks like these Russian were only after the safe house and this place." He dusted his hat against his leg as he shot a scrutinizing look at Alex. "You wouldn't happen to know why, would you?"

"No." Alex glanced at the Clifton's damaged home. "FBI said the cartel was headed for the cemetery. Not here."

"Seems to me this little war of yours ain't about the drugs at all. If what the FBI told me is the truth, all the opium in Jon Wells' casket is still six feet under." The sheriff looked around at the tremendous crime scene. "Guess when you're dealing with folks like these Russians, you never know what's going to happen next do you?"

"Are we free to leave?" Alex asked again, annoyed.

For once, Mark agreed with him. They needed to move.

"No." The sheriff stared at Alex. "I need you and your men to stay put for the next twenty-four hours. FBI is supposed to call me back. I want you guys handy when they do."

Stay? Mark cringed, his blood pressure already pounding loud and clear. *No way. Wrong answer. Alex is gonna kick your—*

"Well, okay then." Alex glanced at his weary men. "Mark. You know the town. Get us a room."

Nineteen

"Bastard," Alex muttered.

It was late morning by the time the sheriff let Mark, Alex, and Zack leave the crime scene. By then, they had been grilled a dozen ways to Sunday as to precisely what transpired during the confrontation with the cartel, who did what to who, and where they did it. Alex and Sheriff Dawson were on a first name basis. Maybe not Christian names, but names nonetheless. Whether they wanted it or not, The TEAM was forced to retreat to the only hotel in Spencer to wait out the twenty-four hour hold.

Mark drove while Alex's speakerphone got a nonstop workout.

"I'm telling you there is absolutely no way anyone hacked my firewall, Boss," Mother insisted. Until now, Mark had no idea she was every bit as stubborn as Alex, or that she sassed him the way she did. The two of them sounded like they were married.

"Well, someone got hacked, and it better damn well not have been us."

"It wasn't." Mother sounded sure.

"Make damn sure," Alex growled. "The FBI will be all over—"

"And I'm telling you for the last time. It isn't possible. It wasn't us."

"Just do it." Alex snapped his phone shut, glaring at Mark. "For two cents, I'd ...."

Mark caught the implied threat that Alex didn't finish. A bossy woman like Mother wouldn't have lasted two seconds in the Corps. One mouthy reply, and she would have been transferred or discharged. Harley insisted she was pure genius, but Mark wasn't convinced.

He pulled their rental up to the motel, parked and unloaded their gear and backpacks. The motel wasn't much, but it would give him the privacy and time to make a very urgent call. He hated having to break more bad news to Libby, but if anyone had to do it, it should be him. Poor girl. His heart ached all over again for her and her family.

Zack bumped him as he picked up his gear. "I'm hitting the shower and then the bed. Do me a favor. Don't bug me."

"I'm calling Libby," Mark answered. "Anything you need me to tell Murphy, Boss?"

"Already talked with him." Alex slung his backpack over a shoulder. "Libby knows."

Mark's jaw dropped. "When did you do that?"

"You didn't think I'd let you make that kind of a call, did you?" Alex shot him a hard look. "I called while we were standing around waiting for the sheriff to wake up and let us leave."

"But I—"

"No. You should not have been the one to make that call." Alex cut him off. "That's not your place. It's my team. My error. My call."

"But I—"

Alex's glare silenced Mark. The subject was non-negotiable.

"Fine. I'm going to the hospital then. I need to see Libby's mother."

"Make it quick," Alex growled. "First chance we get, we're out of here."

Mark went to his room and stowed his equipment, but instead of leaving right away, he called Libby. Her cell phone rang, but no one answered.

"Come on," he muttered. He needed to hear her voice, to know how she was handling this awful news. "Please answer. Talk to me."

Her image came to him like a punch to his solar plexus. She was crying. He could feel it. Mark redialed, in case he had called a wrong number. Still, no one answered. *Where are you, Libby?*

Aggravated, he pocketed his cell phone and hurried out the door. He'd call again after he visited with Rosemary. Maybe then, he would have a little bit of good news. It was with a weary heart he drove to the hospital and tracked Libby's mother to the emergency room, nearly noon when he found her. She stood alone at the end of Marie's bed, staring at her unconscious daughter. He placed a gentle hand on Rosemary's shoulder so as not to startle her.

"Oh, Mark," she whispered when she saw him. "You didn't have to come."

"Yes, I did. How is she?" He put his arm around her shoulders.

"The doctor thinks it's only a concussion," she answered very matter-of-factly as she leaned into him. "They've run some tests and done an MRI. She doesn't have a broken back or neck like they first thought, so that's good."

"She hasn't regained consciousness yet though?"

"Not yet. I guess it's just a matter of time."

"Come on." He pulled her to a nearby chair. "Let's sit down so we can talk."

She agreed, and Mark located another chair so he could sit with her.

"How's Jerry?"

She scowled at that question. "He sure picked a heck of a time for a heart attack, didn't he?" Rosemary was still plenty feisty.

"Is he okay?"

She sighed deeply. "He'll be fine. They've taken him somewhere upstairs to do an angioplasty. I should be with him, but I was hoping Marie would wake up. I don't want her to be alone when she comes to."

"His attack wasn't serious?" It sounded plenty serious to Mark.

"Oh, yeah." Her eyes lit up. "It's serious all right. After the angioplasty, he'll need a valve replacement. That will set him back a couple weeks. Maybe months. Don't look so worried, son." Rosemary patted his arm. "Nothing can keep my Jerry down. You'll see."

They sat in silence. Faith's death was the tender subject he did not want to broach, but something needed to be said. Rosemary patted his arm again, a sad twinkle in her eye as if she had read his mind. "I might need your help with another funeral though."

"Yes, ma'am." Tears sprang to his eyes. Libby's mother had a no-nonsense way about her, but losing a daughter was still hard. He hurt for her. His mother's death still haunted him after all these years. Somehow, losing a child had to be so much worse. Mark remembered Faith's sweet flirtation.

Her box of unopened stationary was somewhere in his new apartment in Virginia; he didn't know where. Now he wished he had written at least one letter to her.

"You've raised a good family," he said.

"I have," she agreed. "My three girls have filled my house with nothing but love and laughter. I couldn't ask for more."

"You've always made me feel at home, too."

"You're always welcome at our place, I hope you know that. Course I might need some remodeling done." She thumped his knee with a gentle fist. "Libby's my youngest daughter. Did you know that?"

"She is?"

"Faith was my first. Along came Marie a year later, and then little Libby a year after that." Rosemary chuckled quietly. "We couldn't wait to have our big family. For awhile, I was pregnant every year."

Mark let her talk.

"Jerry named her Liberty. He always liked that name so that's what's on her birth certificate," she said. "'Course we call her Libby. You know that."

"I always thought she was your oldest."

"She does act old for her age, doesn't she? Jonathan did that to her. Made her old before her time with all those lies he told her."

"You knew?"

Rosemary nodded. "Sure I did. A mother knows a lot more than her children ever give her credit for. Libby had to figure that out for herself."

"You're a very wise mother."

"Not really. Jonathan caused his own problems. He could've been cutting alfalfa right this very minute instead of pushing up daisies. Folks don't realize all the lies they tell will catch up with them sooner or later. He was a foolish boy."

Mark listened.

"It's the law of the universe is all it is." She sighed. "That old scripture is right. We do reap what we sow. Sometimes it takes a few years; sometimes it takes a lifetime. I can't help thinking if that boy would've been honest with my Libby, he would still be alive today."

"You didn't sow this," Mark said quietly as he glanced at Marie. She hadn't moved, but her monitor registered positive feedback. At least that was a good sign.

"No. No, I didn't. That's the truth." Rosemary straightened in her chair. "But I've lived long enough to know the good Lord has a hand in everything."

Mark had heard these same words during his mother's funeral. If the good Lord had a plan, it was darn tough sometimes.

"You know what I'm talking about." She rapped him a little harder on the knee. "I imagine you've seen men fall while you were in the service over there in Afghanistan. You've seen your share of death."

"Yes, ma'am. I have."

"And what did you do? Did you sit down and waste your time crying?"

"Sometimes," he admitted softly.

She gave him an unexpected hug. "Well, that's okay, son. Sometimes we all need a good cry, don't we? But what did you do then?"

"Got up. Kept on keeping on, I guess."

She nodded. The sad twinkle was back in her eye. "That's all any of us can do. We keep on getting up, and we go back to work. That's what gets us back to living again."

Rosemary drew a deep breath before she stood and went to Marie's bedside again. He watched her with a new appreciation. She might have been dealt a tough blow, but she wasn't out of the fight. She surprised him when she turned with a small smile.

"Something good always comes out of the bad times, Mark. Like you."

"Libby?"

"Mark."

The conversation deteriorated at that point.

"I'm sorry," he whispered, but all he heard was the muffled sounds of the woman he loved a thousand miles away and grieving for her family. How does a man stand and listen to heartbreak? He couldn't. Mark sank to the edge of his bed and cried with her. "I just talked with your mom."

"Me, too," she squeaked out a quiet answer. "Marie is going to be okay."

"She is." Mark heard the words Libby did not say. *But Faith is gone.* "And your dad is having open-heart surgery tomorrow morning."

She gasped, and every muscle in Mark's body yearned to hold her. Libby didn't speak so he continued, hoping he could offer some encouragement. "Alex wants you to come home."

"He does?"

"Yes. Roy and Murphy convinced him that you need to be here with your mother." He listened to more sobbing before she could speak.

"Mark."

"Yes, babe? I'm here. What do you need?"

"Please, please be safe. I love you so much. I couldn't stand it if ... I'll die if ...."

"Shhhhh," he crooned. "Don't worry. You'll be in my arms in a couple hours. I love you Libby."

"You take your time," Murphy said. "I'll be right here."

Libby made her way into the crowded women's restroom at O'Hare Airport. A throng of noisy girls in blue and black checkered school uniforms were busy at the row of sinks, brushing their hair, applying make-up, and chattering. Their bags were scattered under the sinks and along the wall behind them as she passed by. None of the girls looked up. Just as well.

As quick as she could get into a stall and shut the door behind her, Libby threw up. Funny how so little going down could hurt so badly coming back up. She swiped her mouth with a handful of toilet paper and waited to make sure she was through. That's all she had done when she'd gotten the news about Jonathan's death too—throw up, cry her heart out, and throw up some more. Nothing stayed down. It took well over a week before she had been able to eat something as simple as saltine crackers.

Her stomach clenched, but the extra saliva at the back of her throat that precipitated vomiting did not occur. She spit the rancid taste out of her mouth, and leaned against the stall door. *Good. I'm done. For now.*

Just like last time, the tears wouldn't stop. Her head ached, her eyes burned from too much crying, and she looked awful. This time was so much worse. She missed her sisters, she was scared for her dad, and she wanted her mom.

The noisy girls laughed. One of them joked about a boy named Josh, and how he had humongous pecs and big arms. That's all it took for Libby to summon the feel of Mark's strong arms around her. She stood in Kelsey's bathroom once again, surrounded by his half-naked body. She'd never been more sheltered, protected, or loved. For one brief moment, life had seemed perfect.

The scent of Mark had enveloped her then, that musky fragrance of cedar, freshly mown lawn, and shaving cream. Part of that smell was left over from the wrestling match with Alex's dogs. Mark had been such a good sport. If nothing else, it had given her an excuse to put her hands on him. She wanted him then; she needed him now.

If only he had stayed with her. If only the cartel hadn't come to America. If only the drug smugglers hadn't stolen all that opium. She pushed the pain away. So many if onlys.

Holding onto the feel of Mark, she could breathe. The pack of noisy girls rolled their luggage out the door, still chattering like one big moving, talking machine. Libby listened to the noise leave with them before she stepped out of the stall and walked to the sink.

An old cleaning woman wiped the counter tops. At least she was quiet. She stood with her back to Libby and a black plastic garbage can in the way, several plastic bottles hung on the handle. Libby was too tired to notice anything else. Dipping her hands under the faucet, she splashed cool water on her face and spit into the sink. The nasty taste of vomit went down the drain with it.

A stranger looked back from her reflection in the mirror. The lack of concealer around her sunken eyes accentuated her gaunt expression. With her hair pulled back in an elastic band, Libby looked like she belonged in a horror movie. She pinched her cheeks, more to feel the pain than to add a healthy glow. Color didn't matter. Blush was for fairytales and happy lives. Not her. Not zombie girl. Lifeless. Soulless. Hopeless.

Libby had never contemplated suicide before, but she thought of it now. Standing there face to face with her sad self, she understood why people did it. They couldn't handle their pain. They gave up.

Her zombie self stared back. Enticed. Offered an easy way out. She traced a frame around it in the mirror with a damp index finger. *I'm not like you. Suicide would hurt my Mom. My Dad. Mark.* She clung to that one strand of a silver lining.

Dark hollow eyes persisted.

Go away. Libby stared her zombie self down. She didn't have time for this. She had work to do. Her mother needed her to be strong, and by golly, she could do it. She would go home, take care of her father and sister, and somehow, everything would turn out the way it was supposed to. Yes, things would be hard, but she was a Clifton. If the shootout proved anything at all, it proved the Cliftons didn't go down without a fight. *There. Take that.*

The stark zombie eyes faded into sad blue. Her pep talk actually helped. Feeling a tiny bit better, Libby tore a couple paper towels off the roller, wiped her face, and dried her hands. She might not eat for a few days, but that didn't matter. Food she could live without. She nodded encouragingly to her reflection.

Zombie girl was gone. Only Libby Clifton smiled back. It might be a pitiful smile for now, but she could do it. She was sure of it.

Until that strange old cleaning woman punched her in the chest.

Twenty

"It's about time."

Mark handed Zack his gear to stow in the back of their rented Yukon. True to his word, the sheriff released them exactly twenty-four hours later. Mark was raring to go. After he'd gotten through to Libby, he had showered and lay down on his bed. He slept hard and fast, a habit picked up from his time in the Corps when sleep had been a rare commodity sandwiched between incoming fire and outgoing missions.

When Alex called, Mark was dressed and out the door, waiting to get this part of the operation finished, hopefully by the time Libby's plane touched down. She was in the air and on her way. Once she, Roy, and Murphy landed in Chicago, they would catch an express flight to Eau Claire, and she would be in his arms again. Mark had already told Alex he'd be the one waiting at the airport for her. For once, Alex agreed.

Knowing that Libby was safe in the air took the pressure off Mark, not to mention that the sheriff had posted extra guards at the hospital. No one stood a chance of getting past them to Libby's father. Even the FBI had anteed up with a dozen more agents. Mark sighed. Yesterday sucked, but once he had Libby in his arms, everything would begin to get better.

Mother and Ember were still reviewing their system protocols and denying they'd had a hacked. Mark didn't buy it. How else would the cartel have known exactly where the Cliftons were? The only question now was—why them? Did the cartel have a grudge against Jon for some reason and take it out on his fiancée? Was he the missing link to this whole fiasco? That didn't make sense. No way.

Mark and Zack had just finished loading when Alex showed up, his cell phone glued to his ear as always.

"What?"

Mark felt the crack of fury in Alex's voice. It held all the power of a close lightning strike. He could've sworn he smelled ozone. In that instant, he was physically connected with his very angry boss. Every nerve zapped into high alert. His heart thumped inexplicably loud in his chest. Mark stopped breathing.

"How the hell did that happen?" Alex turned his back on Mark and Zack as he bellowed. "When? Sonofabitch!"

Mark's stress level ratcheted higher. He wasn't prepared for what happened next. Cursing vehemently, Alex fast-balled his cell phone into the side of the Yukon. The phone shattered upon impact.

Mark froze. He could take a kill shot without a second thought. He'd walked point on patrol through enemy streets and towns. Those things didn't scare him. He had undergone months of training, and, in the process, developed some kind of weird sixth sense that went with the job of being a sniper. But fear washed over him now. There wasn't a molecule of saliva left to swallow. His body went rigid. Evil approached. There wasn't a thing he could do to stop it.

Alex stared at him. "Castor's got Libby."

"He what?" Mark heard the question shriek out of his mouth.

Snapping a finger at Zack, Alex brushed beside Mark. Zack tossed his cell phone and Alex caught it. He stabbed in several numbers. "Mother."

The phone was already on speakerphone.

"Yes, Boss."

"Where are they?"

"As near as we can tell, O'Hare."

"You don't have visual?"

"No. They—"

"Why not?" he roared.

"Not every inch of the terminals is covered by security cameras." Mother's voice maintained a cool, calm tone despite the nasty man screaming at her. "We lost sight when they entered the parking garage. Ember is working to triangulate their cell phone calls. At least they're talking a lot."

"Find out what the FBI really knows." Alex raked his hand through his hair in frustration. "I'm sick of their bullshit."

"Already on it. Also tracking GPS—"

"Satellite coverage."

"Already on that, too. You need to know—"

"What?" Alex couldn't seem to let her finish a sentence.

Mother took a deep breath. "Boss. Murphy called us, too. We're doing everything we can to find Libby Clifton. You've got to give us time." Her calm tone was as much chastisement as explanation.

Alex stilled. He glanced at Mark, for a moment looking like he might actually apologize.

Mother's disembodied voice spoke from the cell phone again. "Boss? Are you still there?"

"Copy that." He blew out a huff.

"Like I said, Ember triangulated their cell phones. I'm sending coordinates to you now."

"Stop. Send them to Zack's number instead. Anything else?"

The phone was dead. Mother had hung up on Alex first.

"I never should've left."

Mark stood with Zack at the car, waiting for Alex, who was once again on line with someone back in D.C., and still mad as hell. But Mark was angry, too. He needed something to hit. "I should've stayed with her."

"Man, this is no one's fault," Zack said steadily. "No one saw this coming."

"The FBI knew there were two dozen of them."

Zack nodded. "I don't guess they expected them to show up all at once or in the same place."

"What the hell good's the FBI if they can't do simple recon?" Mark's frustration spiked higher. This explained why Alex disliked this particular federal entity. They sucked. Mother too. She was as much to blame. "There has to be a hacker. How else could the Russians have known when and where to grab Libby?"

Zack nodded again. "Alex thinks so."

"And what's wrong with Mother?" Mark fumed.

"She's a genius and she—"

"She's no genius if she just got hacked." Mark turned away sick and tired of excuses. Zack's calm demeanor didn't help.

He put a hand on Mark's shoulder. "How could anyone have—?"

"Because she would have been with me!" Mark punched the side of the Yukon. Something cracked inside his knuckles. He didn't care. The pain made him angrier. "One minute she's in my arms. The next minute—this!"

Zack didn't say another word.

"What the hell's keeping him?" Mark kicked the vehicle's tires. His hand hurt. And now his foot hurt, but neither as much as his heart. "Doesn't he know we've got to get going?"

"He's on the phone with Mother." Zack's voice was firm and low. "She's tracking Castor's vehicle. Maybe we can get Libby back today."

"Why did they grab her in the first place, huh? How'd they even know where she was?" Mark snapped. So many questions ate him alive. "And why attack Libby's parent's farm? There weren't any drugs there."

"You're right. They didn't go after the drugs in West Virginia either."

"What?" He turned on Zack at that revelation. "When the hell was Alex going to let us in on that little piece of news?"

"Because the FBI just got around to sharing *that little piece of news* with me." Alex strode briskly up behind them, his words clipped and cold.

"So they killed that mother and her kids for what? For nothing? For the fun of it?" Mark faced Alex, his fist clenched and dripping blood. "What else aren't you telling us?"

Alex turned to Zack, ignoring his junior agent. "Are we ready to go?"

Zack handed Alex his holstered SIG.

"I won't need it. Mark. You're riding shotgun." Alex climbed into the driver's seat and slammed the door. "Castor is northbound on the highway, headed our way. Get in. We're going hunting."

Mark hesitated, still waiting for answers.

"You waiting for a damned invitation, Houston?" Alex snarled.

Mark was barely seated alongside his boss when Alex had his foot in the accelerator. The vehicle bounced off the curb and swerved into traffic. They were southbound on the highway when Zack's cell phone rang.

"What?" Alex barked into the receiver.

"Your target is coming straight to you." Mother's voice spoke clearly and patiently over the speakerphone. "You're about thirty miles from the interchange. Traffic is light."

"What are they driving?"

"SUV. Possibly a Jeep or Honda. Dark color."

"Not much help, Mother."

"Working on it, Boss."

"Work faster."

The second Alex set the phone down it rang again. "Now what?" he snapped.

It was a deeper voice on the speaker this time. "Is this Mr. Alexander Stewart I might be speaking to?"

"Who's this?"

"Is me. Is Yuri. My boss, Boris, say you fight pretty good for old man."

Alex locked up the brakes and pulled the car to the shoulder. "Where are you?"

The Russian didn't answer. "I think I might have something you vant, Mr. Alexander Stewart. I think you will vant this thing I have stolen from you very, very much. Is a very leetle girl with curly blond hair."

"Where is she?"

Mark stilled when Yuri groaned. "Ahh. She smells like peaches I think. Like peaches and cream, maybe with a sweet taste of sugar and honey." He murmured a low guttural rumble. "Makes a man vant to take a big mouthful, she smells so good."

"Give me that phone," Mark ground out, reaching for the cell phone, ready to take over the conversation.

Alex stuck his elbow in Mark's face and turned away.

"Do I have your attention now?" Yuri's voice changed to silk. "Are you listening very carefully to me? You should know that I am big man vith very big appetite."

"What do you want?" Alex rasped.

"Ahh," Yuri gloated. "Boris said you always vere fast learner. That is good thing."

"What do you want?" Alex asked again, his voice suppressed and tight.

It was all Mark could do to not shove him out of the way, take the phone, and finish the conversation. His boss was no contest, wouldn't last one minute in a face to face. Only the threat to Libby stopped him.

"I vant you to know I hold all the aces in the holes. I think is how you say it in America vhen you play poker. No?"

Alex blew up. "You hurt one hair on her head and, so help me, there's no place deep enough I can't find you."

"Give me the damn phone," Mark snarled, ready to push Alex out of his way.

"Ahh," Yuri said calmly. "Is not up to me if she gets hurt. Is up to my boss, and he is very—"

"Then stop wasting my time and get your boss on the line. I don't talk to lackeys!"

Yuri chuckled another deep growl. "But you vill talk to me, I think. If you bring me all opium that stupid Mr. Castor thought he could steal, I vill give your leetle girl back. At least, I vill tell you vhere to find her. If not—"

"Where? When?"

"I think maybe you vill need two days to do it. No?"

"I can get you that amount of opium in less. Where should I bring it?"

"Good," Yuri purred. "I vill call and tell you location, but one more rule to this game ve are playing."

"What?"

Mark held his breath. *Please don't hurt her.*

"You must come alone."

"Fine." Alex stared at Mark, his eyes flashing sparks. "Tell me where and when. I'll be there."

"There must be not one single other person with you," Yuri instructed. "Not even those two soldiers you have in car with you now."

Mark jerked his head around. That Russian pig knew exactly where they were. *Where is he?*

"Are you going to tell me when?" Alex asked.

Mark read the truth in his boss's eyes. This was nothing more than a trap. Alex was going to walk right into it.

"I vill be in touch."

"Wait!"

The phone went dead. Alex no more than set it down when it rang again.

Mother didn't waste time on hello. "The car is approaching your twenty in two minutes. It's northbound and driving fast. There's an exit five miles south of your current position. If you—"

Alex dropped the phone and gunned the engine. Hand over hand on the steering wheel, and within seconds, they were back on pavement and screaming south.

"Black Honda Pilot." Mark pointed to the other side of the freeway. The black vehicle raced past in the passing lane, swerving to the shoulder to make its getaway.

"Got it." Alex turned the steering wheel sharply to the left and executed a screeching U-turn that by all rights should have sent their vehicle rolling. Instead, the Yukon's tires slid across the tall grass in the median between the freeway lanes. In a cloud of dust and smoke, they charged northbound, minutes behind the car that held Libby captive.

Yuri wasn't going down without a fight. Shots rang out across the highway when the Honda hit the one hundred mile per hour mark. Both Russians in the back seat of the fleeing vehicle fired out their windows. The concept of riding shotgun took a realistic turn as Mark returned fire. With slow and steady concentration, he centered the tires of the fleeing vehicle in his scope. It was a tough shot. No allowance for the smallest mistakes. Libby was in that car.

He summoned the calm of the universe to him now. *God, don't let me miss.*

The Russians got off a lucky shot. The Yukon's windshield shattered. Mark re-steadied his rifle, took a deep breath, and aimed for the rear tire again. With another curse, Alex swerved to the left and gunned the accelerator.

Mark's first shot missed. Undeterred and as patient as sin, he aimed again. *I can do this.*

His second shot hit the rear tire exactly as planned. The Honda swerved across all lanes of the highway. Cars scattered, all except the one Alex handled. He rammed the left edge of the Pilot's rear bumper, forcing the SUV off the freeway sideways in a cloud of dust. It fishtailed once, twice, before careening into the ditch to rest on all four tires.

Mark scrambled to his feet, steadying his weapon through his open door window frame. The two Russians in the rear seat of the Honda tumbled out with guns drawn. They didn't get a shot off. Mark took out the one on the left. Zack downed the other. Neither man in the front seat made a move. Mark, Alex and Zack approached with guns drawn, Alex on the driver's side.

Mike Castor had his hands up in the passenger seat. The driver had to be Yuri.

"Get out!" Alex shouted. "On the ground. Now! Face down!"

Both men complied. Castor glanced up. The stark look in his eyes jolted Mark.

Damn it.

Libby wasn't there.

Twenty-One

Why am I in Mom's basement pantry?

Libby tried to think. The musty smell of concrete wrapped around her with its clammy fingers. She shivered. It was always chilly in the basement. Her head hurt. Thinking was hard.

Did she want applesauce or onions? Libby giggled at her foolish forgetful memory. The chuckle that filled her ears sounded hollow.

Very slowly the fog in her brain faded. She woke to a splitting headache, every part of her body aching. She was underwater somehow, but that couldn't be. Her thinking was so muddled and disconnected. It was hard to focus, much less see. Besides, she had forgotten to turn the light on. *Do all basements smell this damp and stuffy?* Wriggling awake, her back hurt too. Plus there was something sharp gouging her right shoulder blade. She could barely move.

What on earth am I sleeping on? How did anything so sharp get into my bed?

She reached behind her shoulder. Her elbow collided with an immoveable wall above her.

"Mom!" Even her voice sounded odd this morning.

Frightened, she placed both hands to the wall in front of her face. Cold stone lay within inches of her nose. Similar concrete pressed against her sides, knees and feet. She had barely inches to move. The pitch-black darkness stifled. She gasped, suffocating, trapped in a concrete box with no room to move and no air to breathe.

"Somebody help me!" she screamed with all her might. "My God, somebody help me!"

Her screams filled the small narrow space. Nightmarish shrieks that she could not stop poured out of her mouth. Panic flooded her brain, numbing her to reason. The awful noise was too much. At last, she clamped her hand over her mouth. Screaming didn't help. It hurt.

Her knees banged against the stone. Terror slithered up her throat. The shakes were something else. She tried to hold still, but steeling her muscles only made it worse. She lay exhausted. There was nothing to be done. She was buried alive.

The creep of panic was only a second away. As quickly as she was quiet, she screamed again, out of control and scared to death. Her terror came in waves, each scream louder than the next until her head pounded. This had to stop. It didn't help. She covered her mouth again, biting her fingers to keep her teeth from chattering.

Panting to regain a shred of composure, she tried to think. What happened? Oh yeah, that old cleaning woman in the restroom. She had an odd look about her, but Libby had been too busy with her own problems to care. Too late. The odd, old woman was really a man.

He punched me in the chest. I fell. He stuck something in my face. And now I'm ... here.

Tears ran down the sides of her head and into her ears. She forced herself to focus.

"Dad," she said softly into the darkness. "Daddy. Can you hear me?" Hearing his name brought a tiny sliver of comfort even though she knew he wouldn't answer.

"Mom," she choked. The enormity of her situation overwhelmed her.

"Mark." Rising fear clamped at her throat again.

"Oh, God," she pleaded between chattering teeth, her lips bitten and bleeding. Terror stormed over her again. "Please. Please help me!"

Mark was not allowed near the prisoners.

He and Zack were glued to the one-way glass window in the observation room. Fortunately, Alex had been given FBI clearance to interrogate, at least for now. Usually The TEAM's authority did not include interrogating prisoners, but given the fiasco in Spencer, and a timely call from Jed McCormack, Alex's friend and senatorial advocate, the FBI had no choice. Jed simply had more influence than the Bureau's Director.

"You Americans think you are so clever." Yuri was a big man, more that twice the girth of Alex. His ham hock hands with sausage fingers decorated in gold rings were relaxed despite the cuffs chaining him to the table. Shackles at his ankles held him to the floor, but the big man did not seem perturbed with his tenuous situation. He nodded his chin toward Alex as if it was his turn to play at this very dangerous game.

"I'm only asking one more time, Yuri Grigoryev." Alex spit the Russian's name out of his mouth. "Where is she?"

"I tell you vhat." Yuri reached for the tablet on the table. Instead of a confession, he scribbled two addresses down, tore the sheet off the tablet, and tossed it at Alex.

Alex glanced at the writing, not falling for Yuri's taunt.

"Is all same to me." The Russian relaxed back in his chair, folding his huge hands on the table. "Read it. That is vhere opium is buried that Mikey stole from my boss. New York. Oregon. Idaho. Visconsin. You dig up. You bring to me. Maybe then we make vhat you call a deal."

"You're not listening. The only deal happening here today is her life for yours. You tell me where she is, and maybe I'll let you live the rest of your worthless life some place besides Guantanamo."

Yuri continued as if Alex hadn't said a word. "You must bring to me opium from your United States of Vest Virginia, too. Maybe still be time for more discussion then. You vant I give you that address, too?"

Mark stood with his fist against the window, fighting the urge to pound the glass to get Alex's attention. There was no way he'd get into the room with Yuri, but if he could, just for one minute—

He stowed his desperation in exchange for a whispered command to his boss. "Make him talk, Boss. Bust him up. Hurt him. Make him."

"If anyone can get through to these guys, it's Alex." Zack stood quietly at his side.

Mark didn't take his eyes off the confrontation in the other room.

"There will be no discussion." Alex stared at the insolent man in front of him for a full minute before he continued. When he did, his voice dripped venom. "Unless you tell me where the girl is, we're done."

Yuri shrugged. "Is not my problem. Is yours."

"It is your problem!" Alex jumped to his feet, his fists clenched. The man was holding back. By the looks of him, Alex wanted to slap the arrogant look off this Russian's face as much as Mark did. *You can take him, Boss. Hit him. Hurt him. Do whatever it takes. Find Libby.*

"No, no. I do not think is my problem. You vill bring opium, and you vill provide safe passage back to Kabul. Only then vill I tell you vhere leetle girl is." Yuri made a sweeping motion with his fingers as if urging Alex out the door. "I think maybe she has forty-eight hours to live, maybe less by now. Then air vill run out. You are vasting time."

Mark's heart stalled. *Forty-eight hours before air runs out? My God, where is she?* He whirled on Zack. "What have they done?"

"Sounds like they're holding her in some kind of a container or—"

"They've buried her alive." Mark gasped at the implication. "Just like the drugs. She's in a coffin!"

"We don't know that." Zack gripped Mark's shoulder.

The voice of their enraged boss caught their attention again.

"Forty-eight hours?" Alex roared. "What do you mean? Are you telling me—?"

"I telling you vill never see her alive again." Yuri leaned over the table, his fingers laced together very calmly in front of him. "Is too bad. She is pretty leetle thing. Is a very hard vay to die without—"

Alex launched across the table, his fists on Yuri's collar until he was nose to nose with the man. Mark panicked. Muscles stood taut in Alex's neck.

"Don't kill him," Mark said to the glass window, knowing that's exactly what he wanted to do. "Not yet."

"Listen to me. I've got the best task force in the country looking for that little girl," Alex hissed, his words more promise than threat. "So you sit here on your fat ass, and you hold your breath waiting for that opium. Because when we find her, and we will, I'm personally going to make sure you never see the light of day."

Hit him, Boss. Mark's own hand clenched in sync with his boss's. *That's all he understands. Make him bleed. Make him talk.*

Yuri grunted, a smile wrinkling his wide flat nose.

He's playing with you, Boss. Mark groaned, hoping Alex had more up his sleeve than useless threats.

"You think your friend Mikey's gonna turn my deal down? Do you?" Alex pushed back from the table so quickly that his chair crashed to the floor.

Yuri chuckled, but the big man's nostril flared. A barely perceptible squint fluttered over his eyelid.

Mark's heart picked up hope. *Keep going, Boss. Don't stop. You can do it.*

"You think a conniving weasel like Mikey can take this kind of pressure?" Alex leaned forward on both clenched fists, barely planted on the balls of his feet. "You think a two-bit punk who runs at the first sign of trouble has the balls for this kind of conversation?"

Again Yuri blinked.

Tell us where she is. Tell us.

Yuri sneered, his voice as cold as ice. "I think you got nothing. Mikey is same like me. Go see." He nodded his chin toward the door. "Ask him. See for yourself. He knows vhat vill happen if he talks."

Alex stalked out the door.

Mark went ballistic. "That's all? You call that an interrogation? He chats the man up like—"

Zack still gripped Mark's shoulder. "It's not over yet."

"We don't have time for games," Mark roared. "Forty-eight hours. That's all we've got!" He shrugged Zack's hand off his shoulder and headed for the door to confront his worthless boss.

Zack stepped into his way.

"Get out of my way, Lennox," Mark rasped, "or so help me—"

"Mark." Zack blocked the door; his voice clear and calm. For the moment, they were two heavyweights squared off and ready to rumble. Mark scanned his opponent. He could take him. No sweat. Right now. Right here.

"You saw him with Yuri. Now let's watch him with an ex-Marine."

Mark glared at Zack, his self-control on empty, and his emotions running the show. Zack's brown eyes pierced through the storm in his head. Zack made sense. For now.

"Alex is doing everything he can. Right now, he's the only one who can help Libby." He clapped Mark's shoulder hard, an unspoken threat in his eye. "Do you think any of us would even be watching this interview if the FBI was running the show?"

Mark stilled. The answer to Zack's question was easily an unequivocal *hell no*. They would have to read about it in the newspapers along with the rest of the world, after all was said and done, how the FBI failed. How a young woman lost her life because they couldn't find her in time. Mark licked his lips and sucked in a deep breath.

"Alex will find her." Zack nodded to the door behind him. "Get your ass into the other observation room."

Mark blew out a shuddering breath. Zack might be right.

They stepped across the hall to watch one ex-Marine tear into another.

It didn't take Alex long.

He circled the table in the room where Michael Castor sat handcuffed with his feet manacled and chained to the floor like Yuri's had been. An average-sized man with a shock of light brown hair falling into nervous eyes, Castor licked his lips continually. Alex prowled behind him. Castor's eyes rolled from side to side as if he could in any way anticipate where Alex would strike. He cringed, his shoulders tensed as if waiting to be hit.

Alex circled the table again, his eyes hard and dark. Once more, he paused directly behind Castor and waited.

Mark stood on the other side of the glass with the exact same expression as Alex, his arms folded across his chest and his jaw clenched.

Castor was the key to saving Libby. He had to be.

"You nervous, Marine?" Alex asked very quietly.

Castor jumped, his nerves strung tighter than tight. "Ah, no, sir, ah—"

"I asked ARE YOU NERVOUS, MARINE?" Alex bellowed at the back of Castor's head. "You mean to tell me you smuggle opium, you steal from a dangerous cartel boss, you hide your buddy's decapitated head in a casket, you kidnap an innocent woman—AND YOU'RE NOT NERVOUS?"

Castor clenched his forehead in his hands. "Yes, sir. I am. I guess, umm, I am nervous."

"I don't care!" Alex roared, still standing behind the man. "All the hell I want to know is where you dumped Libby Clifton. You tell me that, and then maybe we'll talk. MAYBE."

Castor cowered, leaning his face into his knotted fingers.

"Man up!" Alex stepped to his side, and slapped Castor's hands away from his face. "Look at me when I'm talking to you."

He obeyed, facing Alex and blinking through the sweat in his eyes. "Yes, sir. I'm—"

"And don't call me sir again," Alex hollered. "I'm not your commanding officer, and I'm not your drill sergeant. They might have cared about you. I don't. I'm just the man who's gonna watch you hang."

Castor nodded once.

"You'd better listen, you stinking excuse for a man." Alex continued badgering. "Your friend's on his way to GITMO, and so are you if you don't cooperate. Right now, you're the same as him. DO YOU HEAR ME, MARINE?"

Castor could barely sit still in his chair. "I hear—"

"You what?"

"I HEAR YOU!" This time Castor screamed back. Growling with frustration, he yanked the chains at his hands and feet, thrashing as if he could shake himself free. He couldn't. Angrily, he kicked his shackled feet. Chains rattled. His efforts made no more difference to the table bolted to the concrete floor than they did to Alex.

"WHERE IS SHE?"

"No!" Castor glared back at Alex. "You hafta do what Yuri said. Get the opium. Dig it up. Then he'll tell you what you want to know. Just do it."

Alex leaned into his prisoner's face, one hand on the table, the other at the back of his chair, and his nose nearly touching the side of Castor's head. "You need to understand one thing. You're a dead man if she dies."

Castor nodded vehemently. "Yes. I ... I understand."

"I don't think you do, *Mikey*. Guantanamo is no place for an ex-Marine. You know that? You think those guards down there are going to understand a jarhead working for a Russian mob boss? Hell, you won't even make it to your cell before they throw you a party."

Fear glittered in Castor's eyes. His tongue darted out of his mouth to dampen his lips again and again.

"And trust me, Marine. GITMO will be a freaking vacation if that little girl dies. I'm only making one deal. It goes to whoever talks first. Where is she?"

Michael Castor was falling apart. Even Mark could see that. Sweat poured off the man's face and neck. He blinked to keep Alex in his line of sight, his hands raised protectively between him and his tormentor, like that would prevent more abuse. Castor was the weak link, but Mark knew better. Even a weak link had to be strong enough to know when to break.

"Round one looks like it's going to Alex," Zack commented quietly. "Castor's falling apart."

Mark didn't answer. Alex might take round one, but Libby was still missing. He saw it clearly now. Zack was wrong. Castor was in a no-win situation. Either way, he was headed for a death sentence. GITMO or Seinkevitz, it made no difference who did the deed. He was the epitome of a dead man walking. He'd never talk. Neither would Yuri.

"You've got one minute." Alex slammed his fist onto the table.

Castor jumped. He blinked big, wide, scared-to-death eyes while tears trickled down his face. "I can't," he sniveled. "I just can't."

"Then you're no damn good to me." Alex turned on his heel and exited the interrogation room.

Mark's heart sank.

It's happening again.

Twenty-Two

Mark's mind was a million miles away.

It was the same scenario all over again, an instant replay of an earlier tragedy he couldn't prevent either. The dark eyes of his sweet mother gazed back at him from her deathbed. Once again, time ticked away exactly like it had all those years ago. The only difference was that he got to hold his mother's hand while she died. He had time to tell her how much he loved her. She must have tired from hearing it so many times, but right up to the end, she had held onto his hand. Each time he'd cried, she told him to be brave, that he was the best part of her life.

She still died.

"I love you, Markie," she had rasped, her breath sour and old in his face. "You know that, don't you?"

"I do, Mama." He had tried to be brave. He didn't want to scare her in case she didn't know she was dying. It was hard. She was everything.

Pulling her only child to her breast, she had kissed his eleven-year old forehead one last time. "You're a lucky little boy."

He was sure he'd heard wrong. How could a child with no mother be lucky? How could being left behind with his father, a cruel man who couldn't be bothered with his wife dying in his bed, ever equate to being a lucky little boy?

"Why?" He had stifled his tears. *Big boys don't cry.*

"Because ... now I'll be ... your guardian angel ... mama."

The memory chilled him all over again. Life had left her body so slowly, like a bicycle tire with a leak, so slight it might go unnoticed until the rider was left stranded in the middle of nowhere. And he'd been stranded ever since.

Until the Marines.

Until Jon Wells.

Until Libby.

With his jaw clenched, Mark watched the end of the useless interrogations of two cold-hearted men by another cold-hearted man. Only this time there was no hand to hold, no way to say good-bye, and no final breath to hear. No one had a clue where Libby was, and the men who knew would not tell.

Mark hated the world of men. They were cold like his father, heartless like Alex, liars like Jon, and murderers like the Russian. And he was one of them.

Alex slammed the door of the interview room behind him, oblivious that Mark stood watching. He flipped his cell phone open and stabbed a button, as usual, abrupt and rude.

"Mother. Get that bastard Seinkevitz on the line. Now."

He paced a tight circle, his face hard as steel. Alex Stewart was a complex man. Gentle with his wife and Libby, yet tough enough that he had killed all those men at Spencer. He looked the part of a predator, stalking, his fingers squeezed to his temple while he planned more death.

I'm as bad as he is. I would kill them all again.

"Seinkevitz?" Alex actually chuckled when he spoke the man's name, but Mark heard the tension in the levity. "I think we got off on the wrong foot, because THERE IS NO WAY IN HELL YOU'LL GET YOUR DOPE."

Alex stilled only as long as it took the man in Afghanistan to answer. "You don't get it, do you? I don't negotiate. Shut up and listen for a change."

Any other time, this would have been a moment of entertainment to watch his boss take on the psychotic monster across the world. Not today. It made Mark sick. Neither Yuri nor Castor had given any indication of Libby's whereabouts. Mother with all her high tech satellite images couldn't find her. Threatening the man behind this nightmare would not get her back.

"Yeah. I've got 'em. What's left of them. Yuri the best you got?" Alex's voice poured acid into the phone. He was taking no quarter.

The nasty tone set Mark on edge. *She's dying. Don't make it worse. Can't you see? You're letting her die.*

"Well, listen up. There is no ransom. You got that? Nothing. Not one ounce of your hundreds of kilos of opium, and I'll do you one better. I'll personally kill all you can send. Hell! Send 'em all!" Alex punched his fist into the air as he spit the last words into the phone.

Mark gulped. The tension in the hallway choked him. This was not negotiation. This was ego on steroids, plain, simple, and proud.

"You think you've got the balls, you just try me." With his final insult hurled, Alex snapped the phone shut, but then he froze. For a second he stood stock-still and stared at the phone in his hand. He combed a hand through his hair like he'd never seen that cell phone before. Then he stabbed it again. Without any preliminary greeting, he verbally attacked the person he had just dialed.

"Find out where that bastard came from."

It had to be Mother who Alex was barking at again. Poor Mother.

"No. I don't want a new phone. Do what I asked! I want to know where Seinkevitz lived before he turned up in Afghanistan." Alex paced a tight circle from one side of the hall to the next. "I've already got the intel from Mark and Harley. I need more. Now! I need—"

He scrubbed a hand over his head again in silence as he listened.

"Where? Are you sure?" He resumed pacing. "That sonofabitch!" he hissed.

More tight circles in the hall and Mark could not understand what had just happened.

"Okay, good," Alex muttered. "Yes, Mother. Send me all you've got. Tell Ember thanks."

His tone calmed, but all Mark saw was the man who'd just signed Libby's death warrant.

It wasn't until Alex hung up again that he noticed he was not alone in the hall. Instantly, his countenance changed. He glared at his junior agent. "We are going to find her."

Mark stared back, helpless, used, and just plain scared to death. There was no way to find Libby now. They had no leverage—they had nothing. Like a dumb ass, Alex had just thrown it all away.

"No ransom?" he bellowed. "How will we find her then? Where is she, Boss? If you're so damned smart, where is she? Who's the real asshole here?"

Alex crossed the few steps between them, and grabbed Mark's shoulders. "Now you listen. You need to trust me. I am NOT going to lose Libby. Neither are you. Understand?"

Mark couldn't answer. He didn't trust Alex. He had no reason to believe him either. Worst of all, there was nothing he could do to help Libby. The last time he had stood at this grave, he'd lost everything. His mind played a wicked trick as the smell of chrysanthemums floated around him. Funeral flowers.

Alex's blue eyes flashed.

"Don't you dare give up."

Mark turned away.

It's happening all over again.

I'm bleeding.

Libby tasted the salty metallic flavor on her tongue. It was a good thing. Bleeding and pain meant life. Besides, she was thirsty. Cold too. All signs that she could still feel, that she was alive, and life was good. *Wasn't it?*

Her stomach gurgled. *Oh yeah, I'm hungry to, but that's okay. I don't need food. I would probably just throw up.*

The silence of her tomb deafened her as much as her screaming had earlier. The hours crept by. She had already wrestled with the demons of suffocation and claustrophobia. With all her might, she'd tried to stay calm, and focus her mind on something good. Sometimes it actually worked. Still, it was hard to slow the freight train of panic that rolled over her time and time again. Her mind pinged from desperation to terror and back to desperation again with very few rest stops in between.

Hysteria will drive me insane. I don't want to be insane, do I?

She didn't know anymore. Her mind worked in curious ways under this extreme condition. It lied to her one minute, telling her there was hope, but the next, it convinced her that insanity wouldn't be so bad after all.

How will I know if I go insane?

Closing her eyes, she concentrated on the night in Kelsey's back yard. That was real. It had happened, didn't it? Taking slow breaths in, she forced herself to exhale just as slowly out. *Think of Mark. Think of Mark.* So she did. His Camaro key came to mind and his dog tags too. They still hung at her neck. She clutched them in both hands now. With that tender image of him locked firmly in her mind, her brain stopped running in panic mode.

Think of Mark. Think of Mark.

Libby took a long cleansing breath, determined she would not give into hysteria anymore. Repeating the mantra got her heart rate to slow. The panic subsided.

Good. This is better. I'm ... going to be rescued pretty soon and ... I'm going to be rescued pretty soon. Mark will save me like he did at Georgetown. I'm going to be rescued pretty soon. Think of Mark. Think of Mark. Inhale slowly. Exhale slowly. Okay. I can do this.

She went over the events of the day, talking out loud as calmly as possible. Even the slightest hint of fear could toss her self-control away. She focused and tried to remember every little detail.

"I flew with Murphy and Roy. We had first class seats. Murphy sat in the aisle seat, and made me sit by the window so I could see everything, only I think he wanted the aisle seat so he could go to the restroom." She recalled the smooth landing at O'Hare and the crush of people in the terminal. Murphy had steered her off the jetway to the nearest restroom. He promised he would wait for her.

Poor Murphy. What he must have gone through when he discovered she was gone. *He's probably going out of his mind. Like me.* Pushing that bleak impression back into the depths of her soul, she focused again. Another deep breath in followed by equally deep exhalation out, and she tried again.

"How did I get out of that bathroom? Oh yeah, that cleaning woman was a man, and she – he punched me." The sweet cloying odor of chloroform reminded her of exactly what had happened. And the garbage can. That must have been how he got her out of the bathroom. He had dumped her in with the trash. That mean man wheeled her right out of the women's restroom under Murphy's nose. Poor Murphy.

"But why? My parents aren't rich. They can't afford to pay ransom." It had to be related to the cartel Mark had warned her about.

Panic peeked around the edges of her very rational argument, like a thief come to steal her momentary hold peace. *Deep slow breaths. There now. I'm cold, but I'm okay.* She quelled the suffocating feeling that accompanied fear and focused on analyzing why this had happened.

If the drug cartel had done this, then Mark and his team were surely searching for her. They might even be close to finding her at this very minute. *Think of Mark. Think of Mark.*

"I can make it. I know I can," she encouraged herself. "Focus, Libby. Breathe. Relax. This is hard, but Mark is coming. I know it. I can hold on 'til then. Yes. I can."

But her mind worked against her as much as it worked for her. Will it be painful to suffocate?

"No," she answered her question out loud. "I don't think so. When oxygen is depleted, I'll keep breathing only I'll be breathing carbon dioxide. I'll get sleepy, and then ...."

I'll die.

"Okay. That's not helping," she scolded herself. "I've lived a good life. I've been blessed with a lot. Think positive, Libby."

Stifling a sob, she forced herself to concentrate again. But there was so much more she wanted to do, so much more life she wanted to live. Her pulse quickened. What were her mother and father going through? A huge hiccup wrenched out of her. Every good thought turned toward death.

Think of Mark. Think of Mark. Think of Mark. Oh, God, help me think of Mark.

Tears came even as she chanted her calming mantra. He had felt so strong and warm under her hands. When he set her on the bathroom counter, her heart all but stalled. He'd never even slipped a finger under the waistband to her pantyhose. She bit her lip. Tears slid freely down the sides of her head. If he would've hinted just a little bit that he wanted more, she would have complied. Libby knew it to her core. She would've made love with him, right then and there. Willingly. Happily. Anywhere.

That knowledge brought another wave of panic. All they had done was kiss and hug. She wanted to do a lot more with Mark. To Mark. She wanted—more.

"I'm not done yet," she whispered to the cold, dark silence.

Be thankful for what you already have before you go asking for more. Her mother's words came back to her now. Sweet Rosemary, as practical as she was loving.

That thought gave Libby the shred of hope she needed to control her hysteria. She took a deep breath. *Okay then. All I have to do is stay calm. Mark is coming. I can do it.* She squeezed her eyes tight. *I know what I'll do. I'll close my eyes and pretend I'm home again. I'm in my Mom's kitchen. We're making cookies.*

The warm memory of her mother's kitchen came to mind. So many happy moments were spent there. Libby took a deep breath and let her mind rest in happier days spent canning cinnamon applesauce, baking pumpkin pies, and Christmas sugar cookies, all done to the backdrop music of sisterly chatter with Faith and Marie.

Faith ….

"My sister's dead." The hole in her heart hurt so bad that she wanted to die, too. "Why me? Why my Mom and Dad? Why is this happening to us?"

The fragile bubble of hope she had fooled herself into believing popped.

"I don't want to be in here," she screamed, thrashing until every bone and muscle hurt all over again.

Control fled.

"I want to go home!"

This wave of panic stifled worse than the others before it. The bleakness of her predicament choked the life out of her.

"Mom! I want to come home!"

Twenty-Three

Alex must be running out of options.

Mark sat across from Mike Castor.

This was the second interview. Libby's last chance. One way or the other, Castor or Mark would break. He'd been warned not to touch the prisoner, so he gripped the edge of the table, only because it kept him from wrapping his fingers around Castor's neck.

Fear clutched every breath. Time was slipping away. His heartbeat throbbed its dismal cadence, *'Libby's dying. My Libby. My life.'*

Zack was right though. Castor was falling apart. Anyone could see that. He licked his lips and couldn't seem to hold still. The man's lips were chapped and sore. Apparently he'd been scared to death for quite a while.

I don't care. My Libby's dying.

But Mark knew better. The only reason Alex had allowed him into the same room with Castor was to pacify him. Alex was also using Mark as a Threat Level DELTA tactic. He made two of Castor. Alex was still playing. Mark wasn't.

When he'd entered the small interrogation room, he caught the look of terror in the man's eyes. A young man didn't toss hay bales all his life, wrestle cattle for branding, or walk miles to school each day and turn out to be a wimp. Mark was the proverbial gorilla in the room, and right now, he wanted to use every ounce of that muscle to pound the truth out of the coward in front of him. His hold on the ethical treatment of prisoners was very thin. Mark glanced at Alex. If push came to shove, not even his domineering boss could stop him.

She's dying, Boss. It's all your fault.

Alex didn't ask a single question. He waited. Mark followed his cue, trying hard to not jump the gun. Castor fidgeted and looked everywhere but at Alex and Mark.

The second Alex leaned forward Mark held his breath. Game time. Castor was going to lose. He had to.

"I want you to meet Libby's friend," Alex said calmly. "This is Mark Houston."

Castor glanced up, but immediately bowed his head onto his arms again.

"Look at him, Marine." One minute Alex was respectful, the next he turned belligerent. It worked.

Castor looked up at Mark, shaking but not breaking eye contact. "Why? You gonna beat me to death?"

As a matter of fact, yeah. Mark grunted, his knuckles tight on the edge of the table. Now was not the moment to bait him.

"He's not here to hurt—" Alex barely spoke when Castor exploded.

"Cuz that's what you're gonna have to do!"

That's all it took. One minute, Mark was sitting. The next he was on his feet, reaching across the table with both Alex's hands in the middle of his chest. He would've had him too, if Castor had known when to shut up.

"Kill me. Do it. I wish you would!" Castor bellowed. "You're a big guy. At least with you, all this bullshit would be over. Do it. God, just beat me to death right here and now. Choke me. Break my neck. Just freaking kill me!"

His plea took the wind out of Mark's sails. Common sense re-engaged. He still towered over Castor, his rage filling the small room, and by the looks of him, Castor felt it. But he wasn't taunting Mark. The man really wanted to die. Fear glistened in his eyes and all over his damp sweaty body.

"Tell me where she is," Mark ground out. Alex's hands were still nailed to his pectorals, pushing him back into his seat. He shrugged it off, half wanting to knock his boss on his butt, too. "Where'd you guys stick her? What'd you do with her?"

"Sit down," Alex commanded.

Mark stared at Alex, but the damn smug man did not even look up to meet his eye. He assumed Mark would simply obey because he was boss. *Well, guess again.* Breathing hard, Mark took another second to think. Alex was no match for him. He might get a sandwich, but Mark could make a meal of him if he wanted to. And he did.

Mark dusted his boss's hands off his chest. Alex finally decided to look up at him. Castor had just tossed a wrench into the works. You can't intimidate a man who wants you to kill him. Mark swallowed hard and sat, glaring at Castor.

"How about a deal, Mike?" Alex sat, pulling his chair closer to the table. He'd turned into the good cop, even using Castor's real first name.

"I got nothing to say," Castor whispered, his furtive gaze on Mark before it hit the table again.

"You might want to reconsider. There's no way out of this mess." Alex was extremely calm, compared to the scene

Mark had witnessed earlier. "Your next stop is prison. Hard time."

Castor grunted, his eyes full of tears. "I wish."

Alex leaned forward like a good used-car salesman. "Listen to me. I've got one deal to make. Only one. I'm talking to you first because frankly, I hate that sonofabitchin Russian friend of yours. I can't keep you out of prison, but I can make sure you live."

"How?"

"I have some influence. I can ensure that you'll serve your sentence in a secure facility."

For a second, Mark saw a flicker of hope in Castor's eyes, but the man was simply too scared to think. His chest rose with short, hurried breaths, and his tongue continually skimmed both lips when he wasn't biting them. He started rocking from side to side, his foot tapping hard against the table leg.

"Tell me what you need." Alex changed tactics. "What can I do to sweeten the deal?"

Castor rolled his shoulders, blinking away his tears. "You feds. You don't get it, do you?"

"What don't I get?"

"No! No! I'm not saying anything." By now his chair bounced off two legs each time he rocked. "I can't."

It dawned on Mark slowly. Hitting this man wasn't going to get him what he needed. Killing him? No way. His heart plummeted. Mike Castor would go to his grave before he'd confess where Libby was hidden. It was his life or hers.

"Then we're done here." Alex stood to leave. Castor had stopped rocking and buried his face in his arms again.

Mark couldn't get out of that room fast enough. Nothing Alex had said or done had helped. Both Yuri and Castor were dead ends. Time was running out. The clock was ticking. Wherever she was, Libby was suffocating to death right this very minute. She couldn't breathe. Neither could he.

"Mark."

He heard Alex say his name, but he shoved past him. *Libby's dying.*

"Mark!" Alex called to him again.

Mark walked away. He had nothing decent to say. Quick strides took him down the hall. He had to get out of this building. Her lack of oxygen stifled him. Her panic flooded his senses. Across the essence of time he could feel all she was going through—her panic, her fear, the dark smothering darkness of whatever they'd buried her in. Sympathetic claustrophobia brought the walls of the police station crashing in too close. *She's dying!*

With a shove, he burst through the nearest exit doors, pushing them wide open. Air gushed into his lungs, but he'd nearly hit the pretty woman coming up the stairs. Kelsey.

"I'm sorry," tumbled off his lips.

"Mark." Her brown eyes filled with tenderness the moment she looked up.

He choked at his thoughtless action. He'd almost hurt her. "Ma'am. I'm sorry. I—"

In less than a second, she had hold of him, her hands barely circling his muscular forearms. "I'm so sorry," she whispered, her eyes bright with tears. "We thought Libby needed to be with her mother."

"I know," was all he could manage to speak. "I understand ... that."

"Alex will find her." Tears covered her cheeks. She meant encouragement, but she hadn't seen what he had just witnessed.

"No," he croaked. *Not true. Castor and Yuri won't talk. Yuri wants his drugs. Castor wants to live. Alex won't negotiate. Libby's dying!*

Mark pushed Kelsey gently out of his arms and set her aside before he bolted down the stairs.

I. Have. To. Go!

Libby squeezed her eyes shut against the darkness. She had already prayed so many prayers, but with every bright, positive picture she had conjured, an uglier one stood in the shadows, like a bucket of ice water ready to drown any glimmer of hope. She had found moments of sanity by repeating favorite songs and poems she'd memorized in school. It helped divert her mind from her awful conditions.

No light. No heat. No water. No Mark.

She revisited them now with meticulous attention, trying not to shiver, trying to lick her dry lips with her moisture deprived tongue. There were so many poems she had loved over the years. Like long practiced prayers, she set her mind in a loop and repeated Robert Frost's words over and over. Her English teacher would be proud how she had dissected and analyzed those poems.

Eerily, her mind returned to the hopelessness of '*the darkest evening of the year.*' Again and again she focused on the lovely woods, the downy flake, or the poor little horse out in the cold wintry weather, but her mind circled relentlessly back to *'the darkest evening of the year.'*

I'm in the darkest evening. Stuck in blackest night and hopeless day, but Mark will find me. He's coming for me now. I feel it. I know it.

Fear pushed against the faint pulse of hope in her heart.

Fight it. Push it back before it takes over again.

Gulping a quick breath, she pushed back one more time and started to recite another poem, her teeth chattering through the lovely verses of Rudyard Kipling. She used to love the world of possibilities contained in the little word *'if.'*

Her teacher would be so proud.

Mark ran.

He'd become a human volcano primed to blow, and he didn't want to do that around Kelsey. He hit the sidewalk with one intention only. Get as far away from Alex as possible. The only thing he could do right now was pray, and his mind was already hell bent on heaven. It just wasn't enough.

Mark headed east and away from the police station. Kelsey would tell Alex which direction he'd gone. He didn't care. Right now, he needed room to breathe. He couldn't take the not knowing anymore. He had to find some place to think before he tore the police station apart and Alex with it.

The blocks flew swiftly by as his legs became fiery pistons pounding the sidewalk, eating up the anger stored too long inside.

I can't lose her. Not Libby. Not again. Please. Not again.

He poured all of his angst into running. Sweat poured down his face, neck, and chest, but still he ran. People stepped out of his way. Traffic held at intersections when he disregarded crosswalks and stoplights. Stores, service stations, restaurants and cafes—everything blurred as the sidewalk became a treadmill through town.

God. Help me. Help me find a way.

His marathon ended at the manicured baseball diamond of the local sports park. Grinding to a halt at home plate, Mark bowed his hands to his knees, panting and gasping for air that didn't bring any relief. The burn in his lungs matched the pain in his side, but they were nothing compared to the gaping hole in his heart. He was drenched to the bone with sweat, tears, and the dirty feeling of despair.

Light glimmered from the few lampposts in the park. He dropped to his knees and sobbed like a baby with his face in the dirt. The place was quiet. No one witnessed him heave and vomit—he hoped. The irony did not escape him. This was home plate, the place where winners were made – and losers. And he, the biggest loser of them all.

God, anything. Please let her live. This time—please let her live. Don't take Libby, too. Bitter tears fell into the dust. Hopelessness settled in. *Take me instead. I deserve to die. Not Libby. Take me.*

Instead of the wise voice of God, he heard his father again. John Houston, the angriest man in the world. Mark had never known what made his father so mean, but he was. The tragedy was that he owned the best farm in the county. He had a good life, a wife that adored him, and a son that forever tried to please. If he'd ever once looked up from his angry path, he might have seen all that, but he didn't. Not once. He was locked into looking down.

Get used to it, you damn baby. You're a worthless excuse for a son. Grow up.

That was the bitter man's version of consolation the day of JayJay's funeral.

God, how Mark missed his mom.

Endless stretches of stony silence followed, punctuated with outbursts of contempt and derision. The old man kept himself absent and occupied, turning his dairy farm into a twenty-four seven workload and avoiding his only child in the process.

Never knew what she saw in you. You ain't nothing but trouble and another mouth to feed.

Mark blocked the relentless words. Still, they came.

What'd she think dying like that? I was gonna raise a snot-nosed kid by myself? Why do you even bother coming home?

Young Mark had withered before his father's suffocating reproach. He became an invisible child, a burden and a millstone around a hateful man's neck. In the hopelessness of utter rejection, the boy spent his time proving himself, making up for failures that weren't his to make up for. It was never enough. Nothing mattered, not excellent grades at school or how many bales of hay he could toss in a day. His father looked through his only son like smoke. The boy was never seen again.

Those ugly memories crushed the hope out of Mark again. His father was right. Mark was nothing. He deserved nothing. Unloved meant unlovable. He could not change his fate anymore than he could find Libby. He wasn't worthy.

That's why he had lost his mother then, and why he would lose Libby now.

Stupid boy.

So lost in the hate-filled rant in his head, Mark didn't hear the quiet footfall behind him until a hand rested on his shoulder. It was a man's hand. A strong hand. *Damn.*

Alex.

"What do you want?" Mark twisted away from the touch. The last person he needed was his boss. Harley or Zack maybe, but Alex? Never. Hell. He was the problem.

"Come on, Mark. We've got work to do."

And he was so freaking calm.

"Let me be." Mark jerked his shoulder out from under Alex's hand.

Alex ignored him, brushed the dirt off Mark's shirt, and hooked his hand through Mark's arm to pull him to his feet. That was the last straw. He pushed Alex away again with an elbow flying. He wiped his face as he finished getting to his feet by himself, and he came up swinging. Half of him wanted to knock Alex down, maybe even knock him out. He could take Alex. Maybe then he'd feel a little better.

But the other half wanted so much to believe. Harley and Zack trusted Alex. Murphy and Roy, too. Not Mark. He didn't respect Alex, and he didn't like him, especially now that he had given away their only leverage. No ransom? How would they ever get Libby back now?

But Mark trusted Harley and Zack. That's all that restrained him now. Like it or not, it was Alex who stood on home base with him. *Damn.*

"Why'd you tell him no ransom?" Mark demanded.

"They're not going to give her back." Alex was as calm as Mark was angry. "You already know that."

"No, I don't. I don't know anything for sure. Neither do you. I could get that dope out of Jon's casket. It's only a couple hours away. You could work with the FBI to open the rest of those graves. We could get it done today. I know we could. They'd get what they wanted. They could tell us where she is and then—"

"They have no intention of giving her back, Mark." The calm turned to steel in Alex's voice. "We have to find Libby ourselves."

"But you don't know that." He shoved Alex away. "God! You're so damn sure of everything, aren't you? Well, I'm not. I have to try. I have to do something. We don't even have to dig that crap up. You could get your hands on that much opium from the FBI. Couldn't you? They keep some on hand for things like this. They'd give it to you. I know they would."

"Think about it, Mark." Alex met him head on. "The Russians killed the family in West Virginia for no reason. They hit the safe house in Spencer for no reason. They never went near the cemeteries where the dope's buried. Nothing about this has to do with recovering the opium. It might have started out that way, but that's not what is going on now."

Mark stared at his boss. Logic penetrated his out of control emotions.

"We are going to find her." Alex still sounded so sure of himself.

Mark's last shred of resolve evaporated into outright panic. "I can't do this anymore," he ground out. "God, Boss!

I can't sit here and wait for her to die. That's all I'm doing. I can't do it! Not again!"

Alex stared, and Mark stared back. In his frustration, he had just revealed too much of his soul to the man he wanted to hate. Neither blinked.

"You might not believe this," Alex began softly, "but I can be an ignorant ass."

Mark looked twice at that incredible understatement. *Yeah. That's one of the words I've used for you.*

"I've only given up twice in my life, once when I lost my wife and daughter, and once with Kelsey. I'm not letting you make the same mistake."

"I don't care what you think," Mark said. Nothing made sense right now, especially the words coming out of his boss's mouth.

"Then maybe I don't know you like I thought I did," Alex said quietly.

With a frustrated swipe over his face, Mark tried to concentrate. Alex finally said something right—he didn't know a damn thing.

"Let me tell you what I see. First of all, son, you are no quitter. You're a damned fine sniper. That doesn't say quitter in my book, not by a long shot. Speaking of which, I happen to know you held the record for the long shot in your unit. Second of all, that little girl loves you, Mark. Anyone can see that. And she's out there somewhere. What do you think she's doing right now?"

"She's dying." Mark's voice cracked as his fear poured out. He squeezed his head between both hands like that could ease the failure that consumed him from the inside out. "God! She's dying because I can't find her. What do you think she's doing?" He hurled his words like a fistful of daggers, wishing they'd mow Alex down like the house of cards he was.

Alex steadied him with a hard grip on his shoulder, his voice as stern and tough. "No. No. No. That's not what she's doing. Get that out of your hard head once and for all. Think better, Mark. Think. Picture Libby. Do you honestly believe that little girl of yours has given up?"

Mark looked straight into those icy blues. They seemed to pierce straight into his soul, as if Alex could see what he was thinking, what he was truly made of instead of the emotional mess he'd turned himself into. His eyes and ears opened. There was something else mixed with that raw power that Alex wielded so effectively, something Mark hadn't seen until now. Something he needed more than anything else.

Alex said that little girl loves me.

The memory of Libby swimming at Lake Wissota flashed into his mind. She was a competitive swimmer, even against two men who could easily out distance her. Man, did she give them a run for their money. She was so gorgeous in her red swimsuit, her gold hair piled high on the top of her head, always working at getting her way with that teasing smile. She'd charmed him and Jon both. They were both head over heels in love with her.

What would Libby be doing right now? What would she be thinking? Would she give up? Would she just quit breathing? Would she wish to die? He couldn't imagine her doing that, not for the life of him. Nothing about her said quit. Like mother – like daughter.

The image of Rosemary patiently waiting at the hospital for Marie to wake up crystallized in his mind. Wherever

Libby was, she was waiting, too. For him. She had faith. She believed.

Alex said I'm a damn fine sniper.

Alex had been so full of rage on the drive to Spencer, but he had selected Mark to go with him into the cornfield. Not Zack.

Alex called me son.

Mark stilled. It was Alex standing with him now, no one else. Right on cue, Alex gripped his shoulder. They stood eye to eye.

"Come on, Mark. I can't do this alone. Get your head back in the game. Focus. Let me work on Castor one more hour. He knows where Libby is. I'm sure of it."

Mark dusted the dirt off his pants, wiped his face with the tail of his shirt, and looked his boss over one more time. For the first time, he saw the wicked scar along the length of his boss's left jaw line. Alex had obviously broken his nose once or twice, too. It was crooked as hell.

"Okay." Mark blew out a deep breath and planted his feet. "Let's get outta here, Boss."

They turned toward the Yukon where sweet Kelsey waited for the men in her life.

"Remember that equalizer you were telling me about at the picnic?" Alex asked before he opened the driver's side door.

"Yes," Mark said quietly, still sniffing and wiping his face. Kelsey didn't need to see him like this.

"Good." Alex leaned across the roof of the vehicle. "That just might be the best decision you ever made."

Twenty-Four

A light!

Libby jolted awake. Am I saved? Is Mark here? She hadn't really seen a light, had she? It happened again. She chuckled. Maybe it's Tinkerbelle? Hmm. So this is how insanity feels. It's not too bad.

When the air inside her dungeon turned colder, her skin grew warmer. Inhaling hurt as much exhaling. Sick. Delirious. Buried alive. It couldn't get much worse. At least she wasn't hypothermic. Shivering was supposed to be a good thing and she was doing plenty of that.

Dreams and images invaded every prayer or poem. She was never sure if she actually slept anymore, the line between day and night non-existent.

So this is how I'll die – sick, alone, and insane.

Like an out of control carnival ride, her fevered mind took her up through childhood memories and down into high school dances. The prom. One minute she was twirling like a top on the dance floor with Mark, and the next she was riding the tilt-a-whirl with Faith and Marie, screaming their heads off like they did every year when the fair came to town.

Libby drifted. She was tired. And sick. She dozed, content to let the illness have its way.

"Come on Peewee. We don't have all day."

Faith?

Libby awakened in the middle of the huge Clifton vegetable garden alongside – Faith? Nah. It couldn't be?

"You're supposed to help me weed today, remember."

But Faith is dead. Isn't she?

Libby reached for her sister's white gold hair to confirm this was only apparition. Instead of cold stone, she touched carefully plaited braids beneath her fingertips.

"Hey! Get your mitts off my hair. I just washed it." Faith tilted her head up to show off her hair. "Marie helped me with the braids. It kinda gives me a Jamaican look, don't you think?"

Libby couldn't speak. The orange beads mingled in Faith's braid did look exotic, but – Faith? Is this real? Am I already dead?

Faith looked up from where she knelt weeding. She winked like they shared some wonderful sisterly secret. In a heartbeat, Libby believed. This was real. The darkness in her soul lifted as the wonderful Wisconsin sunshine poured down upon her.

I don't know how this happened, but I'm okay. She called me Peewee. I can do this. Weeding is fun with Faith.

The normalcy of her surroundings confirmed her conclusion. As usual, they sang while they worked, simple silly songs that made the chore go faster. I've Been Working on the Railroad, and then Old McDonald Had a Farm, E-I-E-I-O. Libby sang her heart out. This was real, the most real thing she'd ever felt. Faith could call her whatever she wanted.

The music lifted Libby's heart. Her voice blended perfectly with her older sister's. They were two crystal sopranos singing in the garden, her father's own songbirds.

Faith worked down her row of string beans so much faster than Libby. Further and further she went until Libby lost sight. All she could hear was, E-I-E-I-O just around the corner of the tall bean poles.

"Don't go so fast," she complained.

Like a little sister lost in the supermarket, she ran to catch up. Faith was already around the next corner of the tomato cages, singing like she hadn't gone anywhere. E-I-E-I-O. The garden turned into a maze. Faith kept weeding and singing. Libby kept running to catch up.

"Not fair!" She plopped down, digging her bare toes into the warm garden soil. "You're not playing fair, Faith."

In the midst of her pity party, a yellow dandelion, dirt clod and all, sailed over the high tomato cages and bonked her on the head. She jumped to her feet. "Faith. Come back."

Peeking through the tomato vines were the glorious blue eyes of the older, wiser sister. Like a beacon from home, they met the searching blue eyes of the younger sister who had been left behind.

"Don't leave." Libby stretched to touch Faith—one more time.

In the clearest voice, her sister answered in her usual I'm-so-much-smarter-than-you voice, "I'm gonna tell Mom if you don't stop following me."

Libby woke to the cold dungeon of her reality. It was only a dream, but the heavy fragrance of sun-warmed tomato vines and good loamy earth still filled her nose. She drew a deep breath, pulling it into the deepest part of her lungs.

Faith is going to tell Mom.

How many times had Libby heard that in her short life? Those were her older sister's real words, exactly what Faith would have said if she'd actually been there. Any other time they would have stung, but now they wrapped around Libby like a comforter sent from home.

She shook the chill off her arms. She understood now. Faith had gone on ahead. It wasn't Libby's turn to follow.

Not yet.

Alex surprised Mark.

It was Kelsey in that interrogation room.

"I don't know about this." Mark brushed a hand over his head.

Alex hadn't taken his eyes off his wife. "Kelsey's good with people. Give her a chance."

And then what? She was in there all by herself with a cold-blooded murderer. The poor woman's feet tapped a relentless beat on the linoleum the second she sat down. She had taken two things in with her, a folder and a hair clip. The clip kept snapping opened and closed.

Mark held his breath, calculating how fast he could get in there if Castor made one wrong move. The man had gone from a slouching deadbeat to an all out pervert, looking her up and down like she was in anyway a possibility in his pathetic life.

She's way out of your league, dirt bag. Touch her, you die.

From the moment she entered the room, Castor did sit up a little straighter and paid attention a little differently. He smoothed his hair off his face, at least the portion he could reach with his hands still in cuffs and chained to the table. He didn't exactly volunteer information, but he did look her in the eye, which was more than he had done with Alex.

Kelsey offered a tentative first move. "Do you, umm, mind if I talk with you for awhile?"

"Knock yourself out," Castor snorted. "I ain't going nowhere."

"Would you like some coffee? I could get a cup for you if you'd like."

"Yeah, right," he muttered. "You Feds are pretty dumb if you think I'm falling for the good cop, bad cop routine again."

"I'm not a Fed or FBI." Kelsey glanced at the two-way window, trepidation written all over her face. "I'm just Kelsey. I teach kindergarten."

Mark growled. "I don't like this, Boss. What if—"

"Knock it off." Alex stared at his wife. "She's just getting started. Let her be."

She shifted her feet, crossing them at the ankles and uncrossing them again. The clip in her hand snapped open and closed a few more times. "Okay, so, umm, the reason I'm here is because I think you're a nice person. Deep down inside, you're a good guy."

"You don't even know me, lady." Castor looked away.

Mark's heart went out to her. Round one had definitely gone to Castor. What was Alex thinking?

Instead of saying anything more, she swept her hair up and clipped it high on her head so only a few tendrils hung down. Castor glanced at her, and did a quick double take. Pulling her hair up like that made her look elegant, but it also revealed the scars on her forehead and her left cheekbone.

Want to or not, he watched her a little closer. She had Mark's attention, too.

"Anyway." She blew out a big breath like that simple act of putting her hair up took a lot of courage. "I can tell you're a good man by the way you talk. It's in your voice."

"You been listening to me talk a lot, have you?" he snarled.

Round two, Castor. Kelsey, zip. Mark grimaced. She had better come up with something more than her opinion if she intended swaying this dirtbag.

She shook her head. "No, but like right now, just the way you looked at me when you said that, I can see it in your eyes. You don't have a mean bone in your body. Not really."

"What do you know about mean? Ask that guy who was just in here." Castor nodded toward the door. "He'll tell you. All Marines are mean bastards."

"Well, umm." She gulped. "I know the difference because I used to be married to a mean man." She traced a line over her eyebrow and down her cheek, exposing the side of her lovely face to this predator. Her hand shook, and Mark groaned. This was such a bad idea.

"What happened?" Castor's tone softened when he actually looked at her.

"W-w-well," she stuttered under his close scrutiny. "I guess you could say he didn't see me like I was a real person. I was just something he used to make himself feel powerful."

Castor shifted in his seat. "He hurt you? Bad?"

"He was a coward, Mike." Kelsey spoke more confidently now. "He wasn't like you at all."

Mark's ears perked up. She had just called Libby's kidnapper by his first name.

"But you don't know me," Castor whispered.

Mark saw it now. Kelsey was playing to his good side, like he actually had one. In her gentle way, she was helping him remember the man he might have been.

"No. You're right. I don't know you. I mean I've never met you before today, but I can see it in your eyes. I really can."

"What?" Castor asked sincerely. "What do you think you see?"

Kelsey leaned across the table and locked eyes with Michael Louis Castor. Mark froze. She had just put herself in the danger zone.

"I see a very strong man who doesn't know who to trust," she said softly. "I see a good man who wants to do the right thing. He just doesn't know how."

Mark held his breath. She sure saw something he didn't.

"But I need to know something, and maybe you can tell me," she continued. "How can a man as handsome and strong as you hurt someone like me?"

Castor gasped. The hard look flashed back over his face. Mark cringed. Why on earth did she have to go and ask something like that? She had just blown it with that question. Big time. Game over.

Kelsey leaned across the table, still searching Castor's ugly face for what Mark didn't know. She hadn't asked that question with any anger in her voice. Instead, it came across like a sad curiosity. It hung there unanswered between the abuser and the abused, between the strong and the weak. Now it was Mike's turn to shift nervously in his chair as Kelsey put a face to his crime. Mark held his breath while the drama unfolded between a sweet angel and a man headed to hell.

"I don't know," Castor finally whispered.

"I don't know either," she said quietly.

"Why are you asking me crap like that, lady?"

Kelsey blew out a small sigh. "I guess because he killed my little boys, Mike, and sometimes it's all I think about."

"Damn it, Kelsey. Not that." Alex stood with his arms crossed, one fist raised to his chin, and his eyes locked on his wife. Mark never thought he'd live to see the day. Alex was biting his thumbnail.

She kept going, her voice filled with quiet anguish. "I guess there doesn't have to be a good reason to hurt another person. It's kind of like a snowball. Once it gets pushed down the hill, it just keeps rolling, doesn't it?"

Castor readjusted his sitting position, straightening one leg, and then the other until they were both pushed to the end of their shackles.

"Why'd he do that to you?" he asked quietly. "How could anyone hurt you?"

"I don't think he meant to at first." She wiped her eyes. "He always said he was sorry afterwards, but it's like he was broken inside, like he never knew what a happy family was about."

"Like hell he didn't," Alex muttered. "He had her and the boys until he—" He froze, straining to hear the conversation from the other room.

"I'm sorry." Castor's voice had softened. "I mean it. I'm sorry."

Mark stepped back from the window. He couldn't watch Kelsey anymore, so he watched Alex instead. The man was wound tight as a drum. The depth of his love for his wife radiated from him like an ocean wave, but there was something more. Mark blinked as the truth hit him. At some deeper level, Alex believed he was a lot like Mike.

"Me, too," Kelsey whispered. "Losing a child is the worst pain in the world. I used to ask God to let me die, it hurt so much."

"She's got five more minutes, and this is over," Alex muttered.

"I don't see how anyone could hurt you." Castor shifted nervously again.

"Are you married, Mike?"

"No. I've been kinda busy." He calmed as the conversation turned to a more normal topic. "You know, I was a Marine, and work and all."

"That's too bad." She studied the grain in the tabletop with her index fingernail. "I bet you would be a good husband. A good father, too."

He shrugged, offering a sad smile. "I had a girl once."

"You did?" Kelsey brightened. "What was her name?"

"Juliette. She left me."

"Oh, no."

Her sincerity surprised Mark. She wasn't playing this guy. It sounded like she really felt bad for the jerk.

"How about you?" Castor asked. "You got a good man now, someone who treats you right?"

"I do." She nodded to confirm her words. "I don't know what I would do without him. He's taught me what real happiness is about."

"You love him?"

Castor's question surprised Mark. It sounded like he cared.

"I do. With all my heart, Mike. He's my reason for living."

Alex glanced at Mark again, his eyes bright with emotion. "This is not what I expected when she asked to talk to him."

"But he's talking," Mark said. "She's doing better in there than we did."

Alex shook his head. "Yeah, but two more minutes, and—"

Right on cue, Kelsey opened the folder in her hand. She slid an eight-by-ten photo of Libby across the table, one that Murphy had taken during the picnic. It showed Libby snuggled under Mark's arm, smiling with a look of total adoration in her eyes.

Castor glanced at the photo, and then at Kelsey, his eyes narrowed in suspicion. "Yeah. I seen her. That's the gal I grabbed at the airport."

"Her name is Libby Clifton, Mike. I talked with her mom." Kelsey brushed a tear off her cheek. "Rosemary's scared that she might never see her little girl again."

Castor bowed his head.

"Libby likes hummingbirds and cardinals. She's a competitive swimmer, and she's in love with—"

"That guy, that Mark Houston guy." Castor remembered. "Right?"

Mark stood at the window again, his heart in his throat.

"What did she do to you?" Kelsey asked.

"Nothing. Yuri pointed her out and ...." He shoved the photo back across the table. "Look lady, this wasn't personal."

She rubbed the scar over her brow. "It was personal to me."

Mark blew out a deep breath right along with Castor. "Please tell Kelsey where Libby is," he whispered. "Be the man she thinks you are. Please."

Castor scratched his ear, tugging on his earlobe and then his chin like he needed to deliberate. "I want to help you. I really do, but I can't."

She leaned toward him. "But you're the only one who knows where Libby is, and she's just a little girl. She won't last much longer in this cold. I don't think she even has a coat."

"She had a light blue sweater," he said quietly. "Least, she did the last time I saw her."

When Kelsey didn't respond, he looked around the room, his eyes darting back to her as he bit his lower lip. He leaned toward her. "Really, I want to help you. I do, but it's not that easy. They'll kill me the minute I walk out of here."

"They won't kill you, Mike. I'm sure—"

"No, not your folks. I'm not worried about them."

"Is it your friend then, the one they call Yuri?"

"He's not my friend," Castor snapped, his eyes suddenly hard. "He's a cold-blooded killer. Did you see what he did to those folks in West Virginia? And that little boy? Every time I close my eyes, I see that poor little boy with his throat cut, and—"

Kelsey gasped. She blanched white, and Mark glanced sideway at his boss. Apparently, Alex hadn't told his wife about the gruesome details of what happened in West Virginia.

Alex was already out the door. Mark followed. When they burst into the interrogation room, Castor had hold of Kelsey's hand. They both looked up in surprise.

"We're still talking," she said simply, not moving her hand.

Alex shook his head. "No. You're done."

"But Alex—"

"He's your husband?" Castor gasped. "He's the guy you live for?"

Kelsey nodded, her eyes bright with tears. "He is."

"Enough," Alex ordered. "Let her go. Now."

Castor looked to Kelsey, several emotions playing across his face as he held onto her fingers. Mark noticed she squeezed his fingers, too, but he also saw the different look in Castor's eyes. He wasn't scared anymore. He'd changed into a drowning man holding onto a lifeline that he couldn't bring himself to let go of. Not yet.

"Let her go, Mike." Alex sat at the opposite end of the table, his voice restrained. "What if I made Seinkevitz go away?"

"You would've saved that little boy, wouldn't you?" Kelsey asked at the same time, leaning toward Castor again.

He chose to answer her instead of Alex. "Yes, ma'am. I would never hurt anyone, not like that. Jose and me were stupid, but we weren't killers. We only wanted to get rich. That's all."

He glanced at Alex and, just like that, he let Kelsey go and pushed away from the table as far as the chains allowed. The nervousness was gone.

"Honest. I never thought they'd hurt that family like they did. Yuri's a cold-blooded psychopath. He even laughed when he did it."

"And that's why I'm talking with you," Alex said grimly.

"Yes, sir." Castor bowed his head and sucked in a deep breath. "But I can't help you. I'm sorry. I just can't."

Mark reached for Kelsey's chair as she stood. Grasping her elbow, he meant to escort her out, but just as they reached the door, she turned to the prisoner one last time.

"Mike?"

He looked up in surprise.

"Would it be okay if I wrote to you while you're in prison?"

His eyes glistened. "Yes, ma'am. That would mean a lot."

For the first time, Mark felt sorry for him. Yeah, Kelsey might actually write to him, but other than that, the man had nothing to look forward to.

Twenty-Five

I have to be dreaming.

A summer raft floated just beyond her reach.

Jonathan and Mark stood waving to her like silly boys, both so handsome it was hard to know which to swim to. The water splashed over her eyes, blurring their faces. Straight and true, she pushed against the waves. Each stroke became a decision. Mark or Jonathan? Jonathan or Mark? The element of nature that she loved so much spoke to her now, each lapping wave a whisper to, *'Think of Mark. Think of Mark.'*

She reached the raft. A strong hand reached for her. It was Mark who pulled her up and out of the lake with a single move. Jonathan was gone. Warmth flooded her soul.

'My home. My car. And my heart.'

She woke. There was no Mark. No raft. Only stone cold dark. Her resolve crumbled.

"Help me, somebody help me!" She scratched the concrete barrier and screamed, "I'm in here! Mark! Get me out! Somebody help me!"

Claustrophobia suffocated her. The walls closed in. Panic ruled.

"Help me. I don't wanna die in here. I'm scared, and I don't wanna die." Tears ran into her hair and down her neck. "Mama!"

As quick as the panic attack stormed over her, it was gone. Like a deflated balloon, Libby lay limp and exhausted by the useless waste of energy, all hope sucked out of her.

As her awful reality settled itself alongside her in the coffin, she felt sad and sorry for her father, her mother, and both of her sisters. Most of all she felt sorry for herself, shut up in the deep dark wherever she was. She'd never be a nurse, a wife, or a mother. Neither would there be a marriage, a wedding night, or a honeymoon. For sure, there'd never be a birth. No babies would call her Mama. No husband would make love to her and call her darling, sweetheart, or dear.

She tried to lick her parched lips. Even saliva had deserted her.

All there was—was nothing. All there would ever be— was death. Her death. She would die in this box. Her future held only a hollowed shell of skin and bones, no life within, and no life without. All she'd ever be was a shriveled, mummified corpse. Like the sick, scared girl she was, she cried.

It was the saddest sound she had ever heard.

For the first time, Mark dared to hope.

"What if I could take that Russian bastard out of the picture?" Alex got right to the point.

"What do you mean?" Castor asked wearily. "He's in Afghanistan. You're here."

"I mean eliminate him. That deal's still on the table. You help me. I'll help you."

Mark shot Alex a glance. He intended to use that equalizer Mark and Harley had left inside the Russian's compound. Hell, yeah.

"You don't know what you're asking me to do."

"I'm asking you to be half the man my wife thinks you are."

"Then what?"

"Then you'll go to trial, most likely to jail for the rest of your life, but I've got some influence. I can promise protection for whatever time you'll serve." Alex signaled Mark.

He hurried to retrieve a portable television. This guy was cracking. He could feel it.

"Can you see that okay?" Mark asked when he positioned the TV at the end of the table.

Castor looked up at him, suspicion still in his eyes. "Yeah, sure. What's going on?"

Mark dialed his friend in Afghanistan. Late night in Wisconsin meant early morning there. *Come on, Harley. Answer the phone.*

"Morning." Harley's cheerful voice instantly calmed Mark. He breathed a sigh of relief. His buddy was about to make a big impression.

"Good to hear you, Harley. Can you send me the feed to camera five?"

"You bet."

Mark listened to shuffling as his request was attended to. The screen flickered to life with input from camera five, showing an ornate building on the outskirts of Arzad's little village. The upper balcony door opened. Boris stepped out, a phone to his ear and that arrogant sneer on his ugly face.

Mark steeled his nerves as the camera Harley had placed high in the tree shifted to a close-up view.

He saw it then. Mukhtar flashed to his mind.

"You receiving?" Harley asked.

"Clear as a bell. Tell me something though. Have you ever seen any of his men with a scabbard?"

"Nope," Harley answered quickly. "Your buddy is the only one. There's a Japanese Samurai Katana sword inside of it, a forty-one inch full tang blade. He keeps it battle ready. I've been watching him. The joker practices every night on his balcony like he's some kind of a martial arts expert."

"I'll bet that blade makes quite the surgical cut, don't you think?"

"You bet," Harley agreed. "You might say a man could lose his head over it."

"Or his fingers," Mark muttered, his throat dry at what Jose and Mukhtar had suffered. "Hold on."

"Copy that."

"That's him," Castor whispered in disbelief.

"Seinkevitz?" Alex switched his speakerphone on. "Or should I call you Rod Kensington?"

Mark's jaw dropped. *Alex knows this guy?*

The bearded man on the balcony looked around as if he might see someone lurking in the shadows. He dropped the heavy Russian accent. "Where you at Stewart? Show yourself."

"This explains a helluva lot," Alex answered calmly. "None of this has been about the opium at all, has it?"

"You always were quick on the uptake." Kensington leaned against the wrought iron railing, his voice casual like he was talking about Monday night football. "I gotta be honest. It was about the drugs until I heard you and that piece of crap business of yours were involved. Then it was just for the fun of watching you jump through your ass."

"You killed a mother and her children for fun."

Kensington shrugged. "Mostly. Yeah. You gotta admit. I've kept you busy."

"Then you abducted an innocent young woman and buried her alive," Alex hissed. "You're a twisted bastard."

"You don't know a thing about me. Never did." Kensington glanced around his compound like he still expected Alex to stroll out from behind his garage.

"I know you recruited your army in Leningrad."

"All that means is you still got Mother working for you. She's the only one who could've found me. Is Mortimer still working for you, too? He still snorting that crap up his nose?"

"Mother's good, but Harley's better."

Mark smiled. So that was what Mother was telling Alex during that conversation in the hallway. That must've been when Alex found out who Boris really was – this Kensington guy. Well good, because in a few minutes, Harley was going to be damn great. If Kensington only knew.

"You've gone too far, Rod."

The wanna-be Russian grunted. "What? That little girl I got stashed mean something to you?"

Mark stiffened, but Alex ignored the question. "How many more men are you sending to finish your dirty work?"

"Yeah, right. Like I'd blow my game plan." Kensington squeezed the bridge of his nose with two fingers. "Thought you were smarter than that."

"You're still using, aren't you?"

"You see, now that's the best part about not working for you." He looked around again. "I don't hafta worry about your dumb-assed rules. Hell. I made my own. You wanna know what my first rule is? Huh? Do you? Well, I'll tell you. I do as I damn well please." Kensington stiffened at his railing as he ranted. "You got eyes on me. Do I look like I need anything? I don't think so. I'm living the dream, but you? You're still trying to get that stinking covert op piece of crap business off the ground, ain't you?"

"You haven't changed at all."

"Why should I? There's better things than living in the good old U. S. of A. You ought to get out of the country once in awhile. Live a little."

Mark watched Alex's demeanor change. The calm was gone.

"You killed innocent people. If I could've found you then, I'd have shot you myself."

Kensington kicked his railing. "They were nothing but a bunch of rag heads. There's plenty more where they came from. You oughta know that. How's that cute little Najela chic? You think I don't know about her? I got news for you. She oughta be close to marrying age, ain't she? At least she's old enough to—"

"Rod." Alex's voice turned lethal. "Leave her out of this."

"What you gonna do, fire me again?" Kensington stabbed his finger toward the west as if Alex stood there. "You oughta know better than to make threats you can't keep, old man. You just wait. My guys are coming for you. You're next. You hear me?"

Alex nodded somberly to Mark and hung up his phone. "Finish it."

The video turned into a silent movie. Kensington ranted into dead air.

Once more, Mark put the phone to his ear. "Are we clear to strike?"

"Waiting on you," Harley answered. "Just so you know, the staff cleared out the day they saw those footprints you planted. Good call, Houston. I didn't know these folks believed in giants."

Mark closed his eyes and sent a silent prayer. *I'm coming Libby. Hold on, honey. Please hold on.*

"Make it rain," he whispered. "Send that bastard back to hell."

"Copy that," Harley confirmed. "One bastard and his minions going down."

Mark tilted the TV stand so Castor had optimum viewing. The Russian had tossed his phone into the open door behind him, still looking for the hidden cameras. Suddenly, the screen filled with static until, little by little, an image emerged through billowing dust and smoke. This one was not from camera five though. It had to be camera twenty-one, the lucky camera a half-mile away from what used to be an evil man's lair. Mark held his breath while Harley provided a close up view. Nothing remained. No barracks. No turret. No Seinkevitz.

"What the-?" Castor sat glued to the screen, speechless.

Mark held his breath. The world had stopped turning on its axis. Everyone waited for Michael Castor.

He blew out a long sigh before he glanced at Alex and then the double-sided window. "Sir, may I, umm, talk with your wife?"

Alex shook his head. "No. She's had enough for one day."

"But." His whispered voice caught. "She believed in me. Please."

Alex hesitated, then motioned Mark.

He found her watching in the observation room, her eyes full of tears. If she had ever doubted what The TEAM stood for, she didn't anymore. She had just witnessed her husband order the death of a man.

"Mark." She reached for his hand.

"Yes, ma'am." He swallowed past the guilt stuck in his throat. Neither he nor his boss deserved these precious women who loved them.

"I'm going with you to get Libby."

Mark couldn't get to his car fast enough. Alex bee-lined to their other vehicle with Kelsey on his arm and his cell phone to his ear. They knew exactly where they were going. And why.

Mike Castor and Jose Gutierrez didn't just smuggle opium for Seinkevitz; they had cheated him. Castor skimmed a little off each shipment before he made the drop to a derelict building in downtown Dover, Delaware. He never saw who picked it up, so he was not able to close that end of the smuggling ring.

When he and Jose figured they'd gotten enough opium set aside, they'd planned to disappear. Castor thought he could live undetected in Baja for the rest of his life. Gutierrez had his eye on a vineyard in the south of France. Like crooks the world over, they planned to live the high life. Also like men foolish enough to believe they could get off scot-free, neither of them realized how psychotic Kensington was. In the end, he gave them just enough rope to hang themselves. Then he did it for them.

Once Kensington found out Alex and his team were involved, the game changed. Murdering the family in West Virginia was only a sadistic ploy to draw Alex in. Once The TEAM was involved, Kensington knew Alex would never quit. It all came down to revenge for something that had happened years ago.

Mark didn't have all the answers. Apparently, there was bad blood between Alex and this Rod Kensington guy. Mark only knew that once Castor had Libby, Yuri forced him to pull over into a wayside, the Wisconsin version of a rest stop. The wayside was barricaded and closed for repair. Stacks of rectangular concrete planters had been stockpiled for a beautification project. Since no work crew was on-site, Yuri had simply dropped his unconscious victim into one of the planters, and covered her with another, using the front-end loader on site. It was convenient, quick, and a tremendous bit of luck—for the Russians.

Mark grimaced when Castor told them the exact location, only twenty miles south of the mile marker where they had intercepted the Russians.

He'd been so close to Libby and hadn't known it.

Cold ....

Can't feel ... feet. Everything ... aches. Aspirin ... sure be nice.

Wish I could ... sleep.

Mom. You seen my red sweater? Wait. Oh, yeah. You're not here ... either.

So very ... tired. Can't wait ... anymore.

Leave me alone. It's time.

I quit.

Twenty-Six

Mark screeched into the construction site amidst a cloud of flying gravel and dust with Zack at his side and Alex and Kelsey on his bumper. The police weren't far behind. The life flight helicopter already searched for a nearby place to land.

Mark ran to the rows of planters.

Zack ran for the frontend loader. "There's no damn keys!" he roared.

Just like Castor said, the planters were stacked three high in ten neat rows—thirty planters that created twenty ready-made tombs. But which one? Libby was right here, but still out of reach. They needed the frontend loader.

"Libby!" Mark bellowed. "Libby!"

If she would just make a sound or scream for help. Anything. He grabbed the first planter on the end of the stack. It didn't move. The damn things were nested into each other, the base of each fitted into the lip of the one below. Applying his shoulder, he went at it again. They had to be moved carefully, or risk crushing her, but damn. It wouldn't budge.

"Why couldn't he tell us which one she's in?" Zack added his muscle to Mark's.

"Yuri didn't trust Castor. He blindfolded him once they got here." Alex joined in. "I called Mother. She contacted the governor. Someone's on their way with the key."

The knowledge that Yuri had blindfolded Castor sent a cold chill washing down Mark's back. Yuri could've killed Libby, could have shot her and left Castor thinking she was alive. The planters might be another lie. She might not be here. Panic seized his gut, adding strength even as his eyes combed the landscape for any sign of a body.

It took all three men to work the top planter off the stack, inch-by-inch and grunt-by-grunt. At last it fell.

No Libby.

Mark groaned. Suffocation swelled up inside of him. Hypothermia shivered into his soul. *She's here. I know she is.* He brushed the sweat out of his eyes and attacked the next planter in the same stack. *Hold on. I'm coming, babe.*

Zack took the other end. Alex braced himself against the toppled planter and took the middle. No words. The three men pushed and pulled. This one was lower to the ground; it offered more resistance. Mark's legs trembled. Sheer brute force might not be enough. *I'm not letting her die.* A roar blasted out of him. The planter toppled over. Alex dodged it just in time.

No Libby.

"Where is she?" Mark growled as he ran to the other end of the stack. The end planters seemed the most logical. They were easy to reach with a frontend loader. But if Castor only knew the lies that Yuri had told him ….

Mark pushed the evil thought away. *No. She's here. I know it.*

Alex and Zack were quick to his side. Each planter became heavier and harder to wrangle. They were fighting time as well as their own strength. Mark's hand slipped. The concrete sanded a patch of skin off his palm. He glanced at

Zack and Alex. Sweat glistened on their faces. Both men shook from their efforts, panting like draft horses, their faces contorted in sheer determination and resolve. He'd seen these exact same looks on other brothers before—in Afghanistan, and here they were again, in it to the end with him. For her.

If they believed, then so did he.

"Almost got it." Zack's huge biceps bulged beneath his shirt. The cords in his neck tightened. Alex gripped the opposing side and leveraged his weight against it, groaning as it tipped toward him. He danced out of its way when it finally fell to earth.

"Damn it to hell," he muttered, blowing out a huge breath.

Libby was not there.

"If that sonofabitch lied, I'll kill him." Mark fumed out of control. Three down. Seventeen planters to go. Doubt niggled.

"Come on, guys. We can do this." Alex stood panting with his hands on his knees at the end of the next planter, sucking in great draughts of air and shaking. They were all beat, working past their exhaustion. "One more time. This is the one."

"We're running out of steam." Zack wiped the sweat off his face, still blowing out huge breaths to restore his oxygen level. He scanned the work site. "There's got to be something we can use for a lever around here."

Even Mark felt it, that human frailty called weakness creeping into his body. The muscles in his thighs and buttocks twitched. Everything else burned. Who was he kidding? They were just three men thinking they could do the impossible, and she might not even be here. They were fools to have believed Castor.

He shrugged his doubts away yet one more time. If nothing else, he would die trying. Bracing himself against the next planter down, he launched another attack, his shoulder to the hard cold concrete and his fingers grasping for purchase on its smooth outer wall. *Where there's a will, there's a freaking way!*

Arghhh! He squeezed his eyes and summoned every last sinew to give its all. Nothing happened. The heavy planter didn't budge. He clenched all the way to his soul. His all wasn't good enough. It was gone.

No! Libby's not dying like this. No way.

Suddenly, another pair of hands clamped over his. The planter shifted. He blinked. Three had become six. The paramedics stood with them now, adding their will to the fight. More grunts and groans. At last, it toppled to the side.

Libby!

"Got her," Zack sighed.

"I'm here, baby. I'm right here. Please be okay." Mark dropped to his knees.

She looked up at him, her blue eyes dazed and clouded. Unseeing. He lifted her out of the concrete box, cradling her against him. Her hand reached up, making contact with his cheek, but not reaching for him; just reaching, the way a blind woman might accidentally bump whatever stood in her way. Or whoever. Bloody fingers smeared his cheek.

"Mark." She blinked twice, dropped her hand, and closed her eyes.

"Libby, I've got you," he murmured, his hands smoothing over her cold arms to get a reaction from her. Anything. He pinched, pressed, and squeezed. Nothing.

The paramedics moved in to do their work. Very gently, they eased her out of his arms and moved her onto their portable gurney. He clung to her ragged hand.

"Come on, babe. We're swimming, remember? We're going together. You and me. You say when. You say—" He choked. This was that awful moment. She was leaving him. Dying. This was—when.

While one medic wrapped her in heated blankets, another inserted an IV line into her arm. The third medic took her vitals and relayed those statistics into the two-way radio at his collar. Everything they said sounded so grim. Mark stood in the way. His heart in his throat.

"You have to let us do our job," one of the medics said gently, but then he met Mark's eye. He handed him a large squeeze tube. "Put this on her fingers. Use it all. It'll stop the pain."

Tears dripped down Mark's face as he lifted her hand again. This tiny little hand was all that had saved him that summer night on the raft. But now ….

A solid hand landed on his shoulder. He glanced into the sad eyes of Alex. Kelsey stood at his side. Mark had no words. They'd done all they could.

"She's alive, Mark." Kelsey snaked her arm around his waist. He heard the gentle admonition in her voice to keep believing. "She knew you would come."

"Sometimes cold is a good thing," the medic offered.

Mark glanced up at that hopeful comment. "I'm going with her."

"Wouldn't have it any other way, sir."

He stood as the medics transferred her into the helicopter. Alex, Kelsey, and Zack were with him, but he couldn't take his eyes off Libby. Alex clapped one last hand to his shoulder. Mark tossed Zack his car keys and scrambled onboard.

The chopper headed north.

"Oh my," Rosemary's voice was tight on the other end of the telephone line. "I can't get away, Mark. I'm already running back and forth to the rehabilitation center and the hospital. Marie hasn't come home yet, you know."

"How is she?" Mark could feel the weight of the world on Rosemary's shoulders.

"She gets a little better everyday. I'm told she'll be released maybe tomorrow."

"Where will you take her?"

Rosemary's voice cracked. "I haven't had time to think about the house yet."

"I can cover your motel room if that's where you decide to move Jerry and Marie," he offered. "At least let me do that."

"Oh, no. You're doing plenty right there with my daughter. You'll stay with Libby, won't you?"

"Yes." His voice caught. *Sure glad this isn't a video call.* "I'm not going anywhere."

"And you'll call every day so I know what's going on?"

"There's no way I'm leaving her, Mrs. Clifton."

Her next question caught him by surprise. "You love my little Libby, don't you?"

He choked. *Wow. What an understatement.* "Yes, ma'am. I do." he admitted.

Rosemary was quiet for a minute. She was crying, too. "I'm ashamed to say this because she needs me. I should be there with her, but I'm only one person. I'm planning Faith's funeral, too."

Mark hurt for Libby's mother. "It's okay, ma'am. I won't leave Libby."

"Jerry and I always wanted a son," she said softly.

He couldn't respond. Libby's mother and father had treated him like family the moment he had stepped through their front door.

"You give my little girl a hug for me, okay? You tell her I love her."

Mark nodded.

"And Mark."

His voice cracked with his one syllable reply. "Yes?"

"I love you, too, young man." Mrs. Clifton cried openly now. "Thank you for loving my Libby. One way or the other, I'll be seeing you kids soon."

"Yes, ma'am." He hung up the phone and wiped his face before he turned to Libby. She lay pale and lifeless on the stark white of the hospital bed. He lifted her bandaged hand.

"You probably heard me tell your mother," he whispered against her cheek, "but I love you with all my heart. I'm not going anywhere. Please come back to me."

"How is she?" Kelsey asked quietly.

She and Alex were the first visitors of the day and a welcome sight. One of the orderlies had pushed a recliner into Libby's room so Mark could actually get some rest during the night. It didn't help. She was a critical case, so doctors and nurses came and went all night, checking, monitoring, and just generally caring for her. Recliner or not, he couldn't sleep. He had to know what they were doing, thinking, and what meds they were giving her.

"She's better." He stretched his aching back as he stood. Movement didn't help either. His only relief came from the steady readout of Libby's bedside monitor. "Her body temp's normal, but the pneumonia's kicking her butt. Her oxygen saturation could be a lot better."

"They've got wonder drugs for pneumonia these days," Kelsey offered.

"That's what they tell me." He took Libby's bandaged hand in his and rubbed a gentle thumb over the layers of gauze where her knuckles might be. "For now she's in a hold pattern. The meds are supposed to reduce her congestion. If not, the doctor plans to aspirate."

"Has she come around yet?" Alex asked.

"No." Mark bit his lip. The pale lady at his fingertips didn't even know he was there. "I thought once we got her warmed up, she would snap out of it. I guess she needs more time."

"It's hard waiting, isn't it?" Kelsey looped her hand over his arm, patting his bicep with her other hand. "She's very lucky you're here to watch out for her."

"Yes, ma'am." He caught himself. "I mean, Kelsey. I mean ...." He scrubbed a hand over his head. It had been a helluva week. He didn't know what he meant anymore.

"She'll come out of it," Kelsey reassured him. "You'll see. Have you had time to call her mother yet?"

"I did. Jerry and Marie are both going to be released next week."

"How's that going to work?" Alex asked. "Their home's demolished. What's she thinking?"

"I honestly don't know, Boss. She's going to need help, that's for sure."

"Let me take care of that." Alex clapped his back. "You worry about Libby. Come on. Let's get some breakfast and maybe get you a shower."

"Nah. I'm fine." Mark shook his head. *Besides, she might wake up. I need to be here.*

"I'll stay with her. You guys go on." Kelsey patted his arm encouragingly. "It won't help if you get sick, too."

"But I can't leave." He hadn't come this far to desert Libby now. "Really. I'm good. They said I could use the shower in her bathroom and—"

Kelsey's smiling brown eyes melted the argument right out from under him. Yeah. Libby couldn't be in better hands. A tired tear came to his eye. He brushed it away before anyone else saw it. Damn. He wasn't carrying the weight of the world all by himself anymore. Other people actually cared.

"Well, okay." He nodded, brushing a hand over his face again.

"I'll take good care of her. You know I will." Kelsey wasn't playing fair. Everything she said was so kind and so sweet and ....

He wiped another tear, hoping for control before he had to face his boss.

"Come on, son. You look like hell." Leave it to Alex to offset Kelsey's sweetness with his sour. "Let's go. I'm hungry."

Mark nodded. "Okay. Guess you're right."

"Of course I'm right." Alex steered him toward the door with a glance over his shoulder to the women. "We won't be long."

"I'll be right back," Mark informed Kelsey like she didn't already know that.

"Take your time." Kelsey waved them off. "Us girls will be fine."

Mark choked. He had just left his angel with another angel. Yeah. Libby would be fine.

Twenty-Seven

The shower felt fine, but man, real food felt so much better.

Mark stabbed another pork chop and two more slices of buttered toast. Alex obviously knew all about that 'breakfast being the most important meal of the day' propaganda. He hadn't just bought a meal. He'd bought a feast.

"Slow down." He smirked. "She'll be there when you get done."

Zack showed up in time to help himself. Alex poured another round of coffee from the carafe the waitress had left at their table. That was another thing. Hospital coffee really sucked.

"I see you like a little coffee with your cream." Alex spiked a brow at Zack's very light brown coffee.

"I likes what I likes." Zack snagged another one of those single servings of vanilla flavored creamers. This was his third. "You ever try one?"

Alex shook his head, sipping his coffee black, strong, and hot. "Hell no. I like the real stuff."

Zack grunted, then turned to Mark. "I stopped by the hospital. Kelsey said you guys would probably be here. Libby's looking better."

"Is she awake?" Mark straightened in his chair.

"No, but she's not so gray today. Kelsey was reading to her."

Mark blew out a big sigh. He needed to get back to Libby's bedside, but something else nagged at him. "Who was this Kensington fellow, Boss? It sure sounded like you knew him."

"A mistake." Alex grunted.

"Why's that?"

Zack shot Mark a look. "Rod was a screw-up from the get go. You've seen plenty of them in the Corps. Macho boneheads with a gun. That's all he was."

Mark nodded. He knew the type. Armed and stupid in uniform were never a good combination. That he had used a sword to personally commit his atrocities only made him that much more evil.

"The problem started when I sent him on a simple op to Afghanistan." Alex sipped his coffee. "All he had to do was watch a couple caves northeast of Bagram. He stopped checking in three days after he got there. Then he sent bad intel to the Air Force."

"He liked the dope, huh?" Mark asked. He'd seen the signs. Rod was a user.

Zack nodded even as he stuffed a forkful of pancakes into his mouth.

"That wasn't the worst of it," Alex said. "I missed something when I hired him. Not going to make that mistake again. Now I look my men in the eye like I did with you."

That explained a lot. Murphy had been the one who originally approached Mark while he was still in the Corps, said he was looking for a few good men or some other line of BS like that. The job seemed promising and offered over the top benefits, which made it hard for a man coming home from the war to pass up. All Mark had to do was show up and, if he passed muster, the job was his. When he did show up, Alex hadn't even bothered to shake Mark's hand. No nice to meet you, thanks for stopping by, nothing. He stood in The TEAM's open bay like he had other places to be and barked, "What's the right time to take a kill shot?"

Mark hadn't thought twice. It was the dumbest question he had ever heard. He'd hoped he had kept the insolence out of his voice when he gave his one word answer to the jerk asking. "Never."

At that point, Alex had walked out, leaving Mark wondering what the hell had just happened. The only thing that told him he'd passed muster was the twinkle in old man Murphy's eye.

"Kensington enjoyed the killing," Alex continued. "He was mean. I don't want that kind of man around me, much less on my payroll. I'm looking for the kind of guy who'll look for every last reason *not* to take the shot. You two know what I mean."

"And here I thought you hired me for my long-shot record." Mark smiled. He caught Zack's wink and silent toast with his coffee cup. There it was again, that brotherhood thing. That family thing.

"Don't get me wrong. Records are good to know, but I'm only hiring the best men. There's damn few of them around."

Mark heard the gentle praise in Alex's words. His boss might be a hard man to work for, but he was a good man, too. A real good man.

"So why did he go after the Cliftons? Jon wasn't involved in drugs," Zack asked.

Alex sighed deeply, his stare piercing Mark. "I'm not one hundred percent sure. Mother is still fighting me on this, but I think Kensington got inside our server. Once he figured out that I had two men in Afghanistan, he decided to play god. It only got better when he discovered some of his dope was buried in your buddy's coffin, Mark. That put you on his radar, big time."

Mark's throat dried up. "He came after Libby because of me?"

"I doubt that." Alex shook his head. "No way he could have known how you felt about Libby, but I do think that striking Jon's fiancée and her family was Rod's way of getting to me. Think about it. He could've destroyed this team from the inside out if he'd gotten to you."

"He almost did. He could've—"

"No." Alex stopped Mark cold. "This kind of a man is predictable. You knew that going in country, or you never would've taken those fancy fireworks with you."

Mark stared at Alex. So many chess moves. So much risk. Yet this man moved through it like he always knew the outcome.

"Besides." Alex smirked. "I never doubted you. Not for one damn minute."

What could he say? There were no words, so Mark simply nodded. Humility swarmed up from his boots. This was why men were willing to follow Alex Stewart into death, maybe even beyond. He was a sonofabitch all right—the very best kind.

"Harley called," Zack interrupted. "Guess your little surgical strike did not go unnoticed by the folks at Bagram."

Alex grunted. "I'll call the commander over there. He'll understand."

"The FBI's happy though."

Again, Alex grunted, this time Mark, too. Who cared what the FBI thought? He didn't.

"So when are you going home?" Mark asked.

"When Libby wakes up. Why?" Alex replied.

"Guess I thought someone should be back at the office, that's all."

"Not your problem. Mother and Ember will call if they need anything. Right now, they're just glad we got to Libby in time."

"Yeah, about that." Mark cleared his throat. "Thanks."

"No thanks needed."

Zack dragged his napkin over his mouth and settled back into his chair. "What did you think? We'd let you run off and save the girl all by yourself?"

Mark shook his head, but yeah. That fear had crossed his mind. He'd been alone too long, always fighting uphill battles by himself. The Corps had been the closest thing to a family since his mother died. The TEAM? Not so much until now.

"What's really going on?" Piercing blues stabbed Mark with their x-ray vision.

Mark hesitated. Something else needed to be said, only not to these guys. This was tough. Every instinct told him to get his butt back to Libby's side, and yet, Jon's voice nagged at him from beyond the grave.

"I have to visit a friend. I need a couple hours."

Alex never blinked. "Do what you need to do. Kelsey loves sitting with Libby. You know that. Zack and I will go keep them company. Heck, we might even see Murphy and Roy today."

"We'll miss you." Zack shot him an exaggerated smile. "But we'll manage."

Mark tossed a couple bills on the table.

Alex tossed them back.

"Get the hell out of here, son."

**JONATHAN W. WELLS
BELOVED SON
USMC
Semper Fi**

Mark stood in the bright October sun remembering. It had only been four months. It seemed like a year. Jon's grave lay peaceful and serene, undisturbed by the cartel. Kilos of opium still rested six feet under. No doubt the FBI would remedy that before long, but the drugs were the farthest things from Mark's mind.

This moment was all about his friend, the happy-go-lucky man who used to put a positive spin on a crappy day and make everyone laugh in the process. Jon was a born gambler, a smart-alec when he bluffed during poker, and what they called an indirect leader. Even without the rank, he seemed to know how to reach his Marine brothers; how to inspire and cajole so a guy didn't even realize his attitude was being changed.

No wonder Libby had fallen in love with him. Heck, everyone did.

At least that's the man Mark thought he knew. He sat cross-legged in front of the headstone, resting his hand at the top of it like he would if it had been his buddy's shoulder. All the evidence was stacked, weighed, and sorted. Jon had loved the Corps. Many men did. It was an honorable career choice. No doubt about it.

"Hey, Jon," he said softly, not knowing how else to begin a conversation with a dead man. Still, things needed to be said, and Jon needed to hear them wherever he was. "I thought I knew you."

A dog barked far away, reminding Mark he was in a quiet country town. Just down the road from the Clifton's farm. The Wells household. The real world. Not Afghanistan.

"You were always smarter than me. You had everything I wanted. Hell, you had parents who loved you, and a girl who thought you walked on water. I saw the way she used to look at you. Heck. Libby probably still loves you."

A train whistled along the line that ran through central Wisconsin. It sounded as far away as the barking dog. Mark scrubbed a hand over his face, wondering why he was here. His friend couldn't hear him, could he?

"I guess I'm here today because you had us both believing you were going to marry her, but you weren't. Once you hit Lejeune, you had no intentions of coming back to this dusty little town, did you?"

A simple, white cabbage butterfly floated by. Mark watched it go. The poor thing would be dead within the month, frozen in the first blast of a northern breeze out of Canada. It didn't know that now. All it knew was that today, it lived. The sun shone. Life was good.

"She would have waited forever, and you would've let her. Heck, you'd already rescheduled your own wedding, what? Three times? How does a guy do that to the woman he loves?"

Mark fingered the final words on the headstone in front of him. This was the dumbest thing he had ever done. He could see his friend clearly, handsome, cocky, and charming to a fault, but Jon Wells was dead. There would be no voice from the grave, no specter to sit and chat with him like they did in the movies. Still....

"If you wanted the Marine Corps life instead of her, you should've told her. If you didn't want to get married, if you didn't love her anymore, you should've told her. Hell, Jon. It might have hurt her feelings, but you should've been square with her. Instead, you lied. You lied to me, too. You put this family through hell."

The longer he sat there, the angrier he got. Mark clenched his fist, wanting to strike that marble headstone hard enough Jon could feel it wherever he was. Instead, Mark blew his anger away with a deliberate breath. After all was said and done, Jon wasn't the lucky one.

Yeah, death pretty much summed up the worst of it, but he'd also tossed Libby's love aside like it was nothing. He'd chosen the chaff of adventure for the gold of a sweet woman's heart. Mark knew all about being tossed aside. Jon was a stupid, stupid man.

"Anyway, guess I just wanted you to know that I'm going to ask Libby to marry me. She's hurting right now, but you know how she is. Libby's tough. She'll pull through. She'll dance on that beach again. You'll see."

Mark stared across the cemetery grounds. So many ghosts lingered here. He could almost feel them. The smiling face of his buddy came to mind. He and Jon were brothers through and through—peacetime, wartime, and a heck of a lot of in-between times, too. He didn't want to part enemies now.

With one final friendly smack to the headstone like he would have given to the side of his buddy's head, Mark pushed off the ground.

"Libby loves you, too. We both do. You need to know that."

He faced the grave, stiffened his back, and cocked his arm in a final salute to his friend.

"Talk to you later, Jon. Semper Fi."

Twenty-Eight

Where am I?

Libby opened her eyes in the dark, her mind feeling for the edge of her unyielding stone universe. It was not there. Only a void of dark nothingness surrounded her.

Did I die? Am I dead?

She expected cold stone. Not this. Warmth caressed her face while softness lay lightly against her chin. She took a deep breath into congested lungs that coughed and wheezed for air, but she wasn't cold. The knife of pneumonia in her chest wasn't gone, but it had lessened. A bouquet of bright yellow flowers hovered beside her.

Am I dreaming? Are those flowers real?

The gray receded. The black walls of her tomb were gone, replaced with soft lights from the wall behind her. The flowers stood on an actual table. They weren't floating. She was alive, but a shadow loomed overhead. The stone coffin lid tilted closed, and—

"Hey, there," a gentle voice whispered. "You're awake."

"Mark?" she croaked, afraid to believe her eyes.

He pressed his forehead against hers. "You're safe. I've got you now."

She clutched his shirt. If she could have climbed inside of it with him, she would have. "I knew you would come," she rasped hoarsely. "I knew it."

He kissed her forehead and then her nose, but he was too close. She turned away from him, gasping for air. He backed off, but the minute he did, she grabbed his hand, realizing for the first time that hers were wrapped in thick white mittens. Bandages. She clung to him anyway, afraid this was another dream; that he might turn into concrete if she let him go. Dreams had lied to her before.

"Don't leave me," she croaked.

He lay in the bed alongside of her. "I'm not going anywhere. I've been waiting for you to wake up, honey." Very deliberately, he kissed her cheek and rested with his face in her hair, his breath warm and steady on her cheek.

She rolled to her side to see him better. The suffocating feeling returned. She arched away. Hurt glittered in his eyes, but—

I can't breathe. She clenched his hand and squeezed her eyes shut.

"It's okay," he crooned soft and low. "Open your eyes, babe. You aren't buried anymore. You're here with me."

She sucked in a deep breath, squinting through barely opened eyelids.

"Slow and easy," he said softly. "There is plenty of air. You're safe now."

"But I was scared," she cried. "It was so dark, and I couldn't move."

"I know. I was scared, too. I thought I'd lost you." He caressed her cheek. "Settle down. Breathe slow and easy."

"I couldn't get out, Mark. I tried so hard."

"I know," he said calmly, "but you're out now. You're just having a panic attack. It's okay. You're here with me."

"And ... and ... I was all alone." She burst into tears all over again, burrowing into his arms and chest, afraid he was just another illusion like Tinkerbelle.

Her mind offered instant comparisons. If he was an illusion, he was a nice warm illusion for a change. Her panicky breathing slowed as she inhaled the fragrance of soap and manly deodorant instead of concrete, blood, and fear. She was clean, too, the filth of her tomb washed away. His arms around her were strong and comforting. She burrowed in closer, needing to hear his heartbeat.

Thump, thump. Thump, thump. She stilled to hear it better. *Thump, thump. Thump, thump.* Her panic faded. The rhythm of his heart turned into her mantra. *Think of Mark. Think of Mark.* He placed kisses to the top of her head. Steady as a workhorse, he kept on rocking and holding her.

"You saved me," she murmured.

"You bet," he whispered. "Me, Alex, Kelsey and Zack. We all saved you."

"How long ... was I gone?"

"You were kidnapped four days ago. The Russians grabbed you at O'Hare. They stuck you in a concrete planter. It probably felt like a coffin, huh?"

"It was really cold. I prayed and prayed and ... I was scared." She burst into tears again.

Mark kept on rocking and talking. "You cry all you want, babe. I've got you now."

She settled down again. Rocking felt comforting. Safe.

"You're very sick, and you need a lot more rest."

With those words, she tightened her grip. "But you aren't leaving me, are you?"

Mark enveloped her with both arms, one hand pressing her head to his chest. "I am never leaving you again, Libby Clifton."

"Did she wake up?" The red-haired nurse asked.

Mark nodded from his prone position beside Libby, not wanting to disturb her sleep. She was hot and sweating, but still gripped his hand tightly against her chest.

The nurse pushed the side table away to check her IV and monitor. "Can I get you anything?" she whispered, peering over Mark's shoulder at her patient. "Or do you already have everything you need?"

He glanced back to the smile in her emerald green eyes. "It's stuffy in here. Could you lower the thermostat? Would that be okay?"

"How about if I open the window instead?" She drew the blinds open just enough to crack the window. Cool air wafted across the room. "I'm Judy O'Brien by the way. Buzz if you need anything." She moved the call button within reach and patted his arm one last time before she left.

Nurse Judy had just hit the nail on the head. He did have everything he needed. The reality of all he could have lost shuddered through him. Mark tightened his grip, but relaxed it just as quickly. No more restraints for Libby. Never again. Only blue skies, sunny days, and whatever else he could do to make her smile.

He kept his nose in her hair. Kelsey had brushed and braided a swatch of it to control the unruly curls. The lovely scent of shampoo filled his cup to overflowing. This sweet, gentle, tender woman was his whole world. He couldn't breathe without her. Hell, he couldn't think. Every last ounce of his body, mind, and soul belonged to her whether she knew it or not.

Despite her fragile condition, Libby's slender body tucked into his like they were made for each other, and that was the problem. All his hopes and wishes were now face to face with a lifetime of doubt. How could this delightful creature love him? How could anyone? She had said it before, and he'd seen it shining in her eyes, but really? Him?

Mark squeezed his eyes tight against the ghost of his father. His mother's sweet smile glimmered through the gloom. She had loved birds. He recalled how she would run through the house at the first clarion call of the morning meadowlark in summer, flinging windows and doors wide open so she wouldn't miss the next song. He had helped, thrilled for the game of playing with his Mom and letting the outdoors in. She danced with him, a silly happy jig like they were both little kids, like he couldn't do anything to make her not love him.

"I love you," he whispered quietly to his mother's memory, still holding Libby against his heart. "I always will."

"Hmmm." Libby grunted softly. Her arm reached up to circle his head. She pushed her backside into his hips. "Don't ever leave me, okay? I love you so much."

One sweet clear strain of a meadowlark's prayer called to him from the sunshine of the world outside. Mark blinked hard against the tears. Could it be possible?

Maybe.

"No-o-o!"

With the first shriek, Mark was off the chair and on his feet. Libby lay in bed thrashing, both hands in front of her face. He tried to calm her. She had already wrenched the IV line out of her arm.

"I'm here, Libby. I'm right here." Cursing himself for thinking she might rest easier in bed, he tried to capture her flailing arms. She struck him full in the face with the heel of her hand.

Crunch. Ouch! Blood gushed down his neck.

"No-o-o!"

The night nurse stood at the door. She left only to return with a restraining belt.

"No way," Mark yelled. "Get that thing out of here."

"But this will keep both of you safe," she insisted.

The nurse was probably the smarter of the two, but there was no way he was doing that to Libby. Still trying to hold her with one hand, he staunched a wad of tissues to his nose with the other.

Luckily, Judy showed up. "I can give her something to calm her down."

"No drugs." Mark leaned into Libby to keep her still. "She's having a nightmare. That's all."

"She's burning up, too. I'm calling her doctor." Judy turned away to place the call.

"It's okay baby," Mark crooned against Libby's cheek. She was definitely feverish. *Damn. Not again.*

"If you can hold her still," Judy said when she finished the call, "I'm going to draw some blood. We need to know what's causing the fever."

Mark worked to calm Libby, but all he could do was exactly what he didn't want to do, hold her tight while Judy drew the sample.

Libby hissed through clenched teeth. She pushed and grunted, fighting him tooth and nail. Blood splashed from his nose to the white bed covers making the struggle seem more horrific.

"I'll be right back." Judy left with the vials of blood.

"Come on, sweetheart. Talk to me. I promise. You're okay."

"No! No! No-o-o-o! I want out. I want out," she screamed.

Out of where? His heart melted. She must be dreaming she was buried alive again.

"Libby," Mark shouted as she took another raspy breath to scream. "I found you, remember? You're not buried alive anymore."

She blinked. Before she could get that scream out of her mouth, he called to her again. "I've got you. You're safe. You're in the hospital. Please wake up."

Her eyes began to focus, but she was burning up. Where was Judy? One more time, he spoke loudly. "You're safe, remember? You're with me."

"I'm ... I'm ... here." She peered up at him, her eyes full of fever. "Someone ... was screaming."

"That was you," he soothed. "You were having a bad dream. That's all."

She touched his bloody face with hot fingers and palms wet with perspiration. "What happened ... to you?"

"Nothing. Just got my nose in the way, that's all. I'm fine. How are you?"

"Bad," she rasped.

Judy marched into the room with a new IV and an ice compress for Mark's nose.

"I see you're awake," she whispered as she put the new line in Libby's arm and pressed her stethoscope to her chest.

"It hurts ... to breathe." Tears trickled down the side of Libby's head.

"I'm hearing a lot of congestion," Judy said. "Your doctor's on his way. We'll know what's going on when the lab calls."

Mark held the compress tenderly against his nose, his other hand clenching Libby's. He kissed her forehead, careful not to bleed on her.

Judy left the room momentarily, but came back in a quick minute and pushed a hypo into the IV line. And another. Before the second hypo, Libby's eyes closed.

"She's fighting two strains of pneumonia. I've given her a stronger antibiotic along with something to help her rest." Judy slid an oxygen mask over Libby's face and placed a cold compress on her forehead, another at the back of her neck. "We may need to move her to intensive care if we can't get a handle on it here. I'm sorry about the restraints, but my nurse was following normal protocol. You scared poor Cassandra to death."

He shook his head. "Libby's had enough. I couldn't do that to her again."

Judy didn't pursue the argument. "Do you want a doctor to look at your nose?"

"Nah. It's just a nose." He leaned his head back to stop the bleeding. It hurt, but he wasn't about to admit it, not with Libby as sick as she was. A bloody nose was nothing.

"Don't do that. You don't want the blood in your stomach. Come here." Judy steered him into the bathroom and had him lean over the sink, demonstrating where he needed to squeeze his nose. He winced the minute she touched it. The damn thing hurt like a son-of-a-gun.

"It's broken, isn't it?" she asked?

"Ah, yeah." No kidding. He squinted through teary eyes. Definitely broken. Harley and Zack would never let him live this down, a big guy like him trounced by a dainty little girl.

"You'll have two black eyes by the morning."

"Cool, huh?" He grinned through the bloody tissues.

Judy frowned, both hands on her hips. "Cool?"

"Yeah. My Libby's just like her Mom" Sick as she was, he was proud that his girl had a mean left hook. "She doesn't know how to quit. You'll see."

Twenty-Nine

Libby squeaked one eye open, waking slowly. The cellophane crackle of congestion in her lungs was gone, along with her strength. Still, she felt better. Breathing was one of those things people took for granted. Not her. Not today. Pulling in a full breath, she eased into a sitting position.

Poor Mark. The room was dark, but there he was, sprawled in the recliner, a curled fist to his forehead and sound asleep. *Aw. How sweet.*

Libby pushed her tangled hair out of her eyes, really wanting to brush her teeth. That had to be a sign that she was better, wasn't it? Several bright bouquets decorated the desk and countertops. An especially elegant crystal vase filled with the prettiest roses she had ever seen occupied her nightstand. Those had to be from Mark. Red roses for love – but no toothpaste anywhere in sight.

Libby reached for her water bottle, shaking with the extremely small effort it took to reach it. Even the room temperature water in her bottle tasted good. She took another breath and planned accordingly. If she took it slow and easy, she could make it to the bathroom and have her teeth brushed in no time, maybe run a comb through her messy hair, too. After all, there was a man in her room. It wouldn't do for him to see her like this.

At least the bed rail was already lowered, one less obstacle. She eased the covers off and pulled her hospital gown over her knees. Her plans came to a screeching halt. She pulled the blankets and sheet back over her legs, feeling foolish. A student nurse should've known better. Sick people have catheters. *Darn. I'm not going anywhere.*

"Going somewhere?" Dark eyes smiled from across the room. Mark hadn't moved an inch, but he was awake and watching, a definite smirk on his handsome face. Had he seen?

"I need a toothbrush and," she answered hoarsely, "I want to use the bathroom." *And a shower wouldn't hurt. I reek.*

He arched his back and stretched, both hands over his head. Ah, that body. Yeah. She must be feeling better. The sight of him working the sleep out of his muscles and joints was just plain delicious. Sheesh. Flat abs, tight shirt across his muscular chest, dark mussed hair and sleepy eyes – the man was handsome down to his stocking feet.

Her stomach gurgled. *Oh, and I'm hungry too.*

"Step on it, Mark." she teased with her raspy voice. "I want to get out of here. Today would be nice."

"You are feeling better." He placed both hands on his knees as he pushed out of the chair.

Now that she could see him better, she blinked, not sure what she was looking at. "What happened to you?"

He crossed the room in a few quick steps and sat on the edge of her bed, winking through two black eyes and a strip of flesh-colored tape over the bridge of his nose. "I learned a very important lesson last night."

"Oh, my gosh. Who hit you?" She cupped his cheek in her palm.

"You did." He took her bandaged hand in his and raised it to his lips for a quick kiss. The smile on his face took her breath.

"I hit you?"

"You didn't mean to, but yeah. You've got a mean left hook."

"Why? How?" She didn't know where to start.

"Forget it." He grinned. "But now I know. When you want fudge, I'd better jump. You said to get a couple dozen roses while I was at it. Guess I was a little slow and—"

"I didn't do that." She knew better. He was teasing. If there was one lesson the Clifton girls learned early, it was to keep their hands to themselves. She had never hit anyone in her life. Well, okay, maybe that mean rooster in the hen house, but he had it coming.

"Oh, yes you did." The smile on this handsome guy's face drew her in. He leaned in for a kiss and her morning-breath alarm went off. She ducked her head into her shoulders and covered her lips with the edge of the sheet. No way was he getting any closer with her teeth still furry and her mouth full of halitosis. *No way.*

Her heart stalled. He was irresistible, and she had punched him, and he did have two black eyes that made him look rakishly good, and—

Oh, my gosh. Okay. Just this once.

She met him halfway. His lips grazed hers, soft and incredibly tender. All her good intentions melted. She wrapped both arms around his neck and a nice, warm tingle invaded her chest, telegraphing sparks all the way to her toes.

He smiled against her lips. "Yep. You're definitely feeling better."

"I told you we should've knocked."

Libby pulled back, her arms still latched around Mark's neck. Kelsey and Alex stood at her open door. They looked as surprised as she was.

"Hi," she offered weakly, but she didn't let go of her man, and he didn't let go of her.

"We're kind of busy here, Boss," Mark said. "Could you two come back a little—"

"No." Libby bit her lip. *Oh, my gosh.* Her face had to be ten shades of red. It felt hot enough. "Come in. We were just—"

"I've got eyes. I see what you were doing." Alex smirked that cheeky smile of his and waved her explanation off.

Mark still hadn't moved. Instead, he bumped her with his hip, so she made room for him to sit. Wow. He was sitting on her bed; his leg stretched along the length of hers like it was no big deal. Sure, there were plenty of blankets between them, but, wow. He was sitting on her bed, and she was in it—with him. A vague memory flitted through her mind so fast she couldn't catch hold of it. Had he done this before? Come to think of it, what day was it? How long had she been in the hospital?

"Can you spare a few minutes to talk shop?" Alex asked Mark, one brow arched as he nodded toward the door. "Unless you kids are too busy."

"Sure." Mark planted a quick kiss into her hair before he bounced off the bed and followed his boss into the hall.

Kelsey came to her side. "My goodness. That new antibiotic did wonders. You look a hundred percent better."

"I feel good." Libby ran a hand through her tangled locks. "How long have I been in here?"

"A couple days." Kelsey sat beside her. "You had a relapse. Scared the daylights out of us, especially Mark."

"And I hit him?" Libby still couldn't believe she had really done that.

"I think you bumped his nose by accident. He was trying to calm you in the middle of a nightmare. That's all."

Libby blew out a big breath. Her memory had turned into Swiss cheese with lots of holes.

"Would you mind if I brushed your hair?"

"Oh, please. Yes." Libby glanced at the bathroom door. "Do you think there's a toothbrush and toothpaste around here?"

"I'll check. I brought some clothes for you when you're ready to leave, too."

"I'm ready now." Libby breathed out a big sigh. *I'm so ready. My Mom needs me. I want to go home.*

By the time the men returned, her breath was minty fresh, and her hair was tamed within the braid piled high on her head. She was on her way to a full recovery. The minute a nurse showed up, that catheter thingee was a goner, and Libby would be halfway out the door and on her way home.

Mark stood at the end of her bed with his boss, their eyes twinkling like they shared a secret. Kelsey sat in the chair next to her, and Libby had to admit, she was getting tired. The simple things she'd just done had worn her out. Her hopes were fading. Even without the catheter, her doctor would probably not let her leave yet. Her emotions were getting the best of her. *I want my Mom.*

"I don't know." Alex studied her intently. "It may be too soon."

"No." Mark beamed. "She can do it. Trust me."

Libby sighed. These guys were teasing, and she wasn't up to it. All her previous energy had fled. She bit her lip. "What's going on?"

"Alex wants to take you home today," Kelsey said quietly.

"He does?" Okay, that worked wonders. Libby straightened. "Great. I'm ready."

"No, you're not." Mark came to her side. "You're still sick, so there are conditions."

Libby looked to Alex.

"You will have a full-time nurse," he said evenly.

She nodded. "Okay. What else?"

"You'll have to do what she tells you to do." A smile tugged at his lips.

"I can do that," she agreed quickly, anything to get out of this place.

There was that smirk again. The man could be so annoying. Something else was still unsaid, and she was too tired to play along. At last Alex spoke again. "Mark will stay with you."

Best plan ever!

"Mom. I'm home."

Mark angled Libby through the completely restored front door of her parent's home. Like the stubborn woman he was learning she could be, she had wanted to walk instead of him carrying her. He might not be the brightest bulb in the box, like Harley would say, but he was no dummy. A man didn't pass up the chance to carry a pretty woman.

Rosemary had her daughter in her arms in short order. He turned to view the restoration work, so they wouldn't see his face and know that he was as emotional as they were.

True to his word, Alex had stepped in and completely restored the Clifton home before Rosemary had a second to think twice. The porch was rebuilt with new wicker furniture exactly like Mark remembered. Another hundred-year old oak door barricaded the entrance, and somehow, Alex had managed to replace the brass doorknob with the exact same fixture that had been lost in the fire. Several rooms still needed painting, but for now, Jerry and Marie rested comfortably in their own beds. Two private nurses ensured Rosemary had plenty of help, and another followed to provide care to Libby.

Libby's father shuffled out of the kitchen, and before he knew it, Mark was shaking his hand. Jerry's hand seemed thinner, his grasp firm, but not as strong as before. If Mark thought Rosemary and Libby were emotional, now he faced the man who'd thought he had lost two daughters.

Jerry gripped Mark's shoulder with his other hand and shook his head, breathing hard from his short walk.

"Morning, Mr. Clifton." Mark hoped that would be enough, but Jerry kept shaking his head. A single tear trickled down his cheek. Mark gritted his teeth. He'd done enough crying.

"Son," Jerry ground the word out.

The battle was lost. Mark couldn't hold back his feelings. Tears filled his eyes, too.

Libby Clifton was home, safe and sound.

Mark sprawled across the huge four-poster bed alongside Libby, the same as he'd done every day since she had come home from the hospital. Rosemary had set him up in his own room down the hall, but he was never far away. If Libby needed her curtains opened to let in the sun, he was the man for the job. He helped her walk down the hall to the bathroom, and made sure she was steady on her feet before he closed the door to give her privacy. Happy to help and willing to do anything she needed, he catered to her like she was queen and fairytale princess all rolled into one.

Because—she was.

They had just returned from a short walk around the yard. She'd wanted to see how everything looked since the painters had finished. By now, her parent's home looked more like it belonged in the *Better Homes and Gardens* magazine instead of the rural town of Spencer, Wisconsin. Alex insisted it was the least they could do, and Mark was proud of his boss.

As Mark lounged next to her with the latest copy of *Field and Stream* under his nose, Libby pushed her hip against him. She was getting stronger every day. Instead of needing a nap, the walk they had taken energized her. Her color was good, her breathing back to normal, and keeping his hands to himself was getting more and more difficult. Judging by the second hip-bump he just received, she had the same problem.

"Are you trying to tell me something?" He looked up from his reading, trying and failing to look stern.

She shot him that dazzling smile and promptly pushed him flat to his back. Hopeful anticipation lit her eyes. Before he knew what hit him, her lips covered his. This wasn't their usual little kiss that he had settled for while she was recuperating though. No. She kissed him slowly and thoroughly, letting her tongue explore his lips before she pressed him for more. And then a little more. With each tender thrust of her body, she made her intentions perfectly clear.

"Come here, you," he whispered huskily.

With her breath hot on his neck, he let his hands roam over her shoulders and down her back before they came to rest at her hips. Warmth surged through him when she arched into his touch. Even in denim jeans, his body was making his intentions clear, maybe a little too clear. His fingers strayed beneath the waistband to her jeans, and he groaned. So much fire sparked from her to his fingertips. He wanted her. Now.

"We need to talk," he ground out the words he didn't really feel like saying.

She didn't seem to hear him. Instead, she pressed hot, moist kisses into his neck, her hands holding each side of his head as she pushed her breasts against him, and in the process, lifted her backside away. Mark cocked his head as her tender lips worked a sweet line of warmth along his collarbone.

His mind automatically planned his next move, which had everything to do with what color bra and panties she wore underneath her Mickey Mouse sweatshirt and the zipper on her jeans. Well, at least the ones she wore at the moment, because very soon—

He groaned again, torturing himself with the pleasant softness of her body. Libby was too tempting for his current level of control, which was pretty much zero spelled with a capital Z-E-R-O.

"Do you hear me, babe?" he asked hoarsely. He needed to get a very important topic out in the open before he let himself fall over the edge. Once he fell, all bets were off.

"I hear you," she said the right words, but she still wasn't listening.

With a herculean effort, he untangled her prowling hands from his neck and pushed her gently up and away. Looking into those deep blues didn't help. He was still falling.

"No more kissing." He kissed the end of her nose despite his words. "We need to talk."

"You want to *talk*? That's all? Really? Now?"

"Yes. I need to talk with you about something." He smiled as he sat up with her, pulled her off his legs, and positioned her alongside of him. Everything about her worked against what he had to say, the smell of her perfume and the way her breasts totally enhanced that ratty sweatshirt. Never had Mickey Mouse looked so good, or so three-dimensional.

"I'm listening already," she said impatiently with a flounce of her blond head. "What?"

"Do you know what I want most in the whole world?" he asked quietly.

"To talk?" Now she was being petulant. Cute, but petulant.

He grinned at this precocious woman. He'd loved her at a distance for so long. Now that she was healthy and in his arms, what on earth was he thinking?

"I want you to know that I love you." Mark chuckled at the wrinkly frown on her face. There was a solid ounce of brat mixed in with this womanly creature.

She smiled and leaned into him, her fingers instantly searching across his chest to the buttonholes on his shirt. "I love you, too, Mark. You know I do."

"Remember when I told you that my mother died?" He snared her hands before she got the best of him.

"Ah, huh." She licked her bottom lip. The soft, sweet gaze of a honey-blond seductress glowed back at him, and Mark forgot what he wanted to say. He leaned in to explore the rest of this goddess at his side—breasts, nipples, thighs, backside, and—

Arghhh! He caught himself just in time.

"Libby. Stop it. Sit right here." Mark pulled his knee onto the mattress and turned to face her. She reached her slender fingers to his knee, burning five little points of smoldering passion through his jeans and all the way to his groin.

With a deep breath, he began again, rambling through the script before he forgot it. The whole thing made logical sense when he had rehearsed it before, but now it came out like crap. "Okay, so when my mother died, my dad had no use for me and it was like I turned into nothing. Do you understand what I'm trying to say?"

"What does that have to do with us right now?" She whined like a little girl trying to get her way.

Ah, he was smitten through and through. Every single thing about this woman was plain adorable. This was going to be a lot tougher than he thought.

"What I'm trying to say is that this is the first time since I lost my Mom that I've been part of something wonderful, pure, and perfect. That something is you."

She cocked her head. Poor girl didn't have a clue where this conversation was headed.

"I don't want to ruin what we have, Libby. I don't want to rush this."

"What are you telling me?" she asked impatiently.

"I'm trying to tell you that … I don't think we should have sex until we're husband and wife." He blurted it out. That did it. He had her full attention now.

"Excuse me?" Those cobalt blues were wide, surprised, and maybe even a little hurt.

"Libby, I want all of you. You've got to know that by now." He hurried to explain. "But I don't just want to just make love with you; I want to make a *life* with you. I want to make our life, and maybe someday, our baby's life, too. Sex is a big deal. I guess what I'm saying is that I want to do this right, Libby. Once."

Her eyes were wide with shock, but then he made it worse. "In one year, Libby Clifton, will you please marry me—and make love with me—for the rest of our life together?"

Anger flashed across her face. She hadn't heard the marriage proposal at all.

"A year? A whole year? Like next October?"

He wanted to laugh. The poor girl wanted sex, and here he was, offering a year's worth of celibacy instead, and making it sound like it was a good deal, too. Three hundred and sixty-five days sounded awfully long to him now that he heard it out loud, but he was just as sure it was the right thing to do.

Mark wasn't kidding himself. She'd loved Jon. She needed time to grieve for him as well as Faith. As much as he loved her, Mark wasn't going to take advantage of her or her family. In a year she'd be in a better frame of mind. Besides, it would give them time to get to know each other better, to plan their life and their family. Maybe life would be more normal in the Clifton household in a year. That's all he wanted. Normal. It had always seemed like an impossible dream, and now that it seemed within reach, he didn't want to ruin it.

He held his breath as the real specter raised its ugly head again. How could this delightful, feminine creature really be in love with him? How could anyone? He had given her an out.

Would she take it?

Thirty

Libby looked deeply into Mark's brown eyes. This crazy man was thinking way too much, but something else glimmered there too. Hesitation? Fear?

"This doesn't make me happy, you know." She edged closer to him, one hand on his muscular thigh. Silly Mark. Did he think positioning that knee between them would stop her? She took her index and middle fingers and walked short little finger-steps up his inseam. "A year is a very long time."

He swallowed hard, his eyes glued to her walking fingers.

Libby took control of the situation. *You're in for it now.* With a flounce of her head, she pushed him onto his back again. He didn't offer any resistance, so she climbed on top, one knee at each side of his jean pockets.

Her blood pounded with what she was about to do. She and Jonathan hadn't sealed their love, but this was Mark. She had no doubt he loved her, wanted her. Love with him was rich and deep and true. He was her man; it was time he understood that.

She let him suffer as her fingers smoothed over his pecs and down his ribs, lingering over the place where his nipples might be. It was kind of hard to tell beneath his light cotton shirt and the T-shirt beneath. A moan escaped his lips. Oh, yeah. She'd just hit pay dirt.

Her blood ran hot and ready. His, too. Even now, his eyes flicked over her breasts, before they jerked back to her face. He was trying hard to maintain control, but she intended to demolish that line of resistance between them once and for all. As his eyes turned to molten obsidian, his breathing became more labored. Libby smiled. She might be a dainty woman, and he a heavy weight, but she wasn't going to give up this battle without a Clifton-sized fight.

"No, Libby. Come on." He tried to push her up and off, but all she had to do was wiggle against his zipper, and he stilled.

"Shush, Mr. Houston." She placed a finger to his lips. "You've had your say. Now it's my turn." *Oh, Mark. You are already mine.*

With her breath mere inches from his lips, his chin tilted automatically in anticipation. Libby paused right there, right at that one second to kiss position. She brushed her fingers through his sideburns, slowly massaging his scalp. He closed his eye, his hands on her hips again. She arched against him just once. It was enough. He'd risen to the challenge. *Oh, my.*

"So what I think you're telling me, and feel free to correct me if I'm wrong, but you want to refrain from making hot, passionate love to me for the next three hundred and sixty-five days. Is that right?" She stuck out her lip, willing all of her feminine wiles into play.

"Yes, ma'am." He removed his hands from her hips and clasped them behind his head. "You're right. A year is exactly three hundred and sixty-five days."

Hooded eyes met hers. So much electricity crackled between them that Libby wished now that she had locked her bedroom door. It wouldn't do to have her mother walk in on them, not like this. She shook her head, and let her hair fall over and around his face, knowing how much he loved that. He was right where she wanted him, trapped inside their secret compartment, their heavy breathing, and all that body heat.

"That's a very long time." Libby was the youngest of three children, the spoiled baby in the family. She knew how to get her way. If older sisters and parents could be coaxed, coerced, and finagled, this handsome ex-Marine could be, too.

"Are you sure that's what you want to do?" she asked breathlessly, her heart pounding for air and blood.

Mark closed his eyes. He was weakening. She could tell.

"Okay. Okay." His groan was incredibly deep and sexy in her ears, but now he'd covered his eyes with his arm.

Look at me Mark. You know you want this as much as I do.

"How about ... three hundred?" he rasped, his breathing heavy.

"Sixty." She countered the second the words left his mouth.

"No." He moved his arm as his eyes popped open. Now he smiled. "Too low. Two-forty."

"Never." She tossed her hair, her resolve shaken. Every little move he made only excited her more. If he didn't give in soon, she would combust. "Too high. Ninety."

She cringed. What had she just said? How on earth could she wait three months?

"Think about it," she said softly in his ear. "Two hundred and forty days is an awfully," she said as she licked the edge of his ear with just the tip of her tongue, ending at his ear lobe, "awfully long time."

He shivered. The groan that met her ears was the one she had been waiting for. He was cracking. Any minute now and—

"Okay. I give. You win." He bolted upright, sweeping her into his arms as he lifted her off her very comfortable position. It happened so fast. Her hair flew into her eyes when she found herself sitting on the edge of the bed again, her body aching for his.

He stepped back, took a deep breath, and knelt at her knee. She trembled. This was it, but she couldn't think clearly. Not yet. All she saw was the matching heat in his eyes. His panting matched hers, breath for breath. Energy arced between them. Mark wanted her. Even now, she could see him stifling the predator side of himself. She reached to caress that worried wrinkle from his brow.

Oh, Mark. How can you NOT make love to me?

He grasped both her prowling hands in his, his gaze scorching her from head to toe.

Kiss me. Just kiss me.

"Libby." He blew out a huge breath and started again. "Will you please ... please marry me in one hundred and eighty days?" Trembling, he pulled a gold diamond ring from his jeans pocket, and held it between them.

Libby could barely see, her eyes too steamed with wanton need that hadn't yet subsided. Hot blood throbbed through every vein. She had just tried to seduce the man she loved— and failed. She was as aroused as she could possibly get without having done any of the things she wanted with Mark.

And to Mark. And he had politely and kindly rejected her. She gathered her wits and fell into those dark, dark eyes.

You look so – hot.

But one hundred and eighty days was better than three hundred sixty-five. Wasn't it? Right now logic failed her. She couldn't count. One number sounded as good as the next. Breathlessly, she brushed her hair out of her eyes and saw the tender look of love in his. At last his ardent proposal registered. And then she saw the ring.

"Babe," he whispered hoarsely, the question shining in his eyes. There was that scared little boy look again, that ghost that seemed ready to slap him down the moment he got too close to her.

"Oh, Mark," she cried. "I don't know about one hundred and eighty days, but yes. I'll marry you. You know I will. I love you so much." She groaned. *Of all the times to become celibate!*

"Whew. That was tough." He rose off the floor, and sat at her side, kissing her chastely in the middle of her forehead. "That's only six months. We can make it to April. I know we can."

"You think so?" she asked with a petulant sigh when he pushed the ring over her knuckle.

Mark cupped her chin in one hand and gazed into her face, his eyes full of love. "Have you ever found your presents before Christmas morning?" he asked quietly.

"Yes." What did Christmas have to do with getting married?

"Didn't it spoil the magic of the day?"

Yes. Okay. She had to agree. That simple act of childish curiosity had ruined everything. There were no surprises, no anticipation, and .... *Oh. Yeah. Now I get it.*

"Making love with you is more important than Christmas." The sincerity in his voice took her breath away. "Maybe I'm old fashioned, but I think we both have a tremendous gift to give to each other, just once—on our wedding night."

She stilled. Where on earth had this darling man come from?

"I don't plan to simply love you, sweetheart." He kissed her forehead again. Somehow that simple act reached into the depths of her free-spirited soul. "I plan to cherish you every day for the rest of your life—and then some."

Mark was so tender as he poured his feelings out, but it was his vulnerability that touched her now. This man was unlike any other she had known. Something else dawned on her.

"I've never seen this side of you," she whispered. "Are you, umm, are you a—"

"Virgin?" he said the hard word for her.

"Yes." She was embarrassed and curious at the same time. How was it even possible? "I mean, umm, I am. Are you?"

"Yes, ma'am. I am." He never hesitated, his eyes still burning into hers.

All those arguments with Jonathan flashed back to her. She'd thought he had chosen the Corps over her because she wanted to wait. Now she was glad she had.

"You look surprised," he said, a bemused glitter in his eye.

"I guess ... I just assumed ... I mean ...." She didn't know what she meant. This made everything he had told her so much more—rare. "But you were a soldier."

"So?"

She studied the man beside her. Dark, handsome, and strong as an ox, Mark was the kind of guy most girls dreamed of, lusted after, and persuaded into marrying them. "I guess I thought you would be like all the other guys," she said softly.

"What? Horney?" He chuckled. "Believe me. I am like all the other guys. I'm no saint."

"Then why haven't you, umm, you know ... done it?" She bit her lip at her adolescent question.

"Because I've been waiting my whole life for you," he whispered reverently. "Just you."

Humility washed through her heart.

Six months was going to be a long time.

"What's up?" Mark turned his bedside lamp on as he answered his phone.

"We fly out today," Alex said. "Mother's got us booked out of Chicago to D.C., and from there we head back to Bagram."

"When?"

"Noon today. We'll be flying all night. Tell Zack. I'll pick you up at nine."

"Can I ask why?" Mark rubbed the sleep out of his eyes. He had planned on taking everyone out to dinner to announce his engagement to Libby.

Alex sighed. "We've had a security breach."

"A hacker?"

"Yes." He sounded less than pleased.

"Just like you suspected, huh?" Mark stifled the urge to call Mother and tell her, 'I told you so.'

"This guy is good. He hit the FBI server, too. That's how the Russians knew where the Clifton girls were. Name is Stanislav Egorov. He's one of Kensington's lieutenants. Right now he's out to avenge his boss. According to Harley's latest threat assessment, he's putting another army together. It's time we finished this."

"And he got Libby's flight information from our server?"

"Most likely." Alex explained his plan. "We'll bait him and eliminate him. Sound good?"

"Who'll stay here with the Cliftons?" Mark needed to know.

"Kelsey."

"Don't you think that's a little much?" he asked jokingly. With Seinkevitz and his henchmen out of the picture stateside, Mark's fears had been pretty much laid to rest.

"I figure between her and Rosemary, another Russian doesn't stand a chance at the Clifton farm. Besides, Kelsey's been known to hit a good tight pattern when she needs to. I've also asked Murphy and Roy to lend a hand, just in case."

"Okay then. See you at nine."

It was bound to happen one of these days. The easy mission in Wisconsin was at an end. Back to work. Mark rang Zack.

Then he rang Libby.

"But Mom."

Libby stood on the other side of Marie's empty bed helping strip the sheets to be laundered. Some things never changed at the Clifton household. Laundry always got washed, dried, and folded on Monday. Tuesday meant ironing and folding whatever lingered after Monday. Wednesday was all about gardening, canning, or freezing, depending on the season. The bread for the week turned from hard red wheat into golden loaves on Thursday.

Friday was an optional day that might entail grocery shopping, butter churning, or a dozen other little chores that needed doing. Saturday was the heavy-lifting day when floors were scrubbed, carpets shampooed, and everything else in the house dusted or polished. Last of all, Sunday was a day of well-deserved rest, but even that meant a morning spent at church, choir practice, and Sunday school lessons.

"It's important to your father." Rosemary used that scolding tone Libby remembered so well from her childhood. "It's good, rich farmland. He wants Mark to have it, so there's no sense arguing. Besides, he's awful proud of that young man of yours."

Libby's face warmed. She was pretty proud of Mark, too. "But he lives in Virginia. What will he do with twenty acres in Wisconsin?"

"It doesn't matter." Rosemary rolled the armful of dirty sheets into a pile and tossed it into the laundry basket at the foot of the bed. "It's a gift. He can do whatever he wants with it."

"Is Dad doing this to get him to stay here?"

"Now Libby Clifton." Rosemary's voice escalated a notch in dismay. "How could you say such a thing? Your father wants to make sure Mark knows he's part of the family. That's all."

Libby eyed her mother suspiciously. Something else was going on; she just couldn't put her finger on it. She floated the sun-bleached fitted sheet over the mattress pad for her mother to reach. Together, they tucked the corners, and then the sides. The top sheet went next.

The contentment of this simple chore soothed Libby. She had loved helping her mother ever since she could remember. Her near-death experience had given her a new outlook on all the things she had once found boring. She didn't mind gathering the eggs from the cranky chickens either. Even old Rufus, the mean Leghorn rooster, got a kind pat on his combed head this morning. Of course, then he had tried to scratch her legs with his three-inch spurs, and she had to thump him with the piece of one-by-one she always carried with her into the chicken pen. But for a minute there, she almost liked him, too.

"Mark asked me to wait for him." She smiled shyly at her mother.

Rosemary stopped fussing with the pillowcases. "Wait?"

"Yes, wait, as in wait for our wedding night. You know."

"Oh." Rosemary's eyes misted. "That kind of wait."

Embarrassed, Libby focused on stuffing Marie's pillow into its too tight pillowcase.

"That young man of yours is the best thing that ever happened to you," her mother whispered, "and to this family, too."

"He's ten times the man Jonathan was."

Libby looked at the doorway at that emphatic declaration.

Her opinionated father stood there with his hand on the door jam, balancing on shaky legs. "You hear me, young lady?"

"I'll always love Jonathan," she admitted openly. Jonathan was her first true love. How could she not love him? "But Mark holds my heart," she whispered shyly. "Everything's different with him."

Jerry nodded approvingly.

"But Dad." She had to know. "Why are you giving him twenty acres of your best south forty? It's not like he's going to move here and start farming, you know."

Her father's eyes twinkled. "Land is what a man gives a man. You oughta know that by now."

"But Dad—"

He cut her off. "'Sides, if I thought there was any chance that young man would move back here and take up farming with me, I'd give him a hundred."

Thirty-One

The flight back to Afghanistan was a long day's flight aboard an Air Force C-5 transport. It could've been worse. Could've been aboard a C-130. That would have taken days.

As the ramp lowered, Mark, Alex, and Zack were met with a pleasant breeze immediately spoiled by the forever present aroma of septic and dust. Harley waited by Arzad's rusty van, but Alex got right down to business.

"Status report."

"Egorov returned from Russia last week," Harley said as he stowed their gear in the back of the van. "He's got close to a dozen men as of yesterday. A couple more show up every day. Must have one heck of a recruiting program."

"Is the hotel ready?"

"Yes, Boss. One room. One night only. It'll be interesting to see what Imir actually gives you though. Arzad thinks he's working with the Russians."

Arzad nodded at Harley's comment. "Imir is not to be trusted, Mr. Alex."

"I'm not trusting him. Believe me. You know where we're going?"

"Yes. I drop Mr. Harley and Mr. Zack at market. I take you and Mr. Mark to hotel." Arzad grasped his friend's arm. "You sure about this?"

Alex looked him in the eye. "No worries, old friend."

"But this man is more worse."

"Why do you say that?" Alex asked.

"He's right," Harley intervened. "Egorov started a campaign of terror. We found Nasim yesterday. Egorov's men tied him to a stake in his field. This was tacked to his shirt." Harley handed a note to Alex.

"Translation?"

"It says *one man every day until someone talks.* Egorov wants to know what happened to his boss. He thinks these farmers had something to do with it."

"Is Nasim still alive?" Mark asked, his anger instantly red hot.

Harley nodded. "Yeah, but they roughed him up and broke a few of his fingers, like that was hard for a bunch of thugs to do to an old man."

Mark turned to Arzad. "As soon as this work is done, I need to see him. You will take me there, okay?"

Arzad nodded sadly. "I would like to take you now."

"Later, old friend." Alex stared at Arzad, a hard glint in his eye. "Let's get this over with once and for all."

Hurriedly, the men finished loading their gear. Within minutes, Arzad had dropped Harley and Zack at the market, then drove to the front door of the hotel. As he helped Alex with his gear, he asked again, "You so sure about this?"

His broken English made Mark smile. It was obvious that Arzad respected Alex as an equal, but he treated Mark, Zack, and Harley more like sons.

Alex clapped a hand to his friend's shoulder. "When this is done, you and your family must move to America. Will you make an old friend happy and consider that?"

Arzad shook his head, obviously distressed.

Just then Imir, a nervous man with an expensive three-piece suit and an oily smile, strolled out of the hotel doors and interrupted their friendly discussion. "Ah, so these are my new American guests." He clasped Alex's hand in both of his, the jowls on his chubby face quivering as he gushed. "It is not often that I have the honor of hosting the great Mr. Stewart and his fine associate."

Mark caught the conniving tone in the man's voice.

Alex pulled his hands out of Imir's clutches, retrieved his weapons case and turned to Arzad. "I'll be in touch."

"I will be here." Arzad nodded slightly and returned to his van.

"Do I understand you are only staying one night?" Imir played the gracious host to the hilt. "That is not enough time to see our wonderful city."

He ushered his guests past the registration counter and up the winding staircase, huffing and puffing all the way. At the first floor landing, he turned with a big smile and gestured toward an open door. "Here is the grandest room in the whole town, the presidential suite. Is it to your liking?"

He stood waiting for an answer that never came.

Alex entered first, and Mark behind him, his mind instantly strategizing points of egress and risk. Interestingly, the room faced the street where Arzad had just dropped them off. Its shuttered windows were wide open, as were the balcony doors in both street-facing bedrooms.

The lavish suite greatly exceeded what Harley had requested. An elegant Victorian design sofa and matching end tables dominated the wall next to the door. Espresso-colored easy chairs stood in opposite corners with an ornately carved wooden desk beneath the windows. In the final corner stood a wrought iron étagère. A leopard skin draped across a travel trunk that served as the coffee table in front of the couch. The room was designed for royalty, not two contractors on an over-night trip. Certainly, not for a war.

Alex glanced out the window while Mark dropped their gear beside the coffee table.

Imir still stood at the door waiting. "This room will give you an excellent view of the city. Yes?"

"It'll do," Alex replied curtly. He let his bag drop to the floor with a thud.

"Ah, yes. I believe it will do quite nicely. Because you are so well known in our fair city, dinner will be brought to your room this very evening. You will have a selection of the finest meats and—"

"Fine." Alex shot him a dark look.

Imir backed out of the room, still smiling. "If you need anything, please ring the desk and ask for me. I will be more than happy to—"

Alex pushed the door shut with his foot, already on his phone with Mother. When he hung up, he was all business. "Mother and Ember have back-tracked the hacker to Bagram, just like we suspected. They're triangulating an exact position. Should get back to us within the hour. If we get hit as hard as we did in Spencer, I want to make sure tonight turns out my way."

He went over the plan again. Harley and Zack would provide cover from their positions in the abandoned warehouse across the street. Alex was the bait. Mark was designated to cover Alex from inside. He would also maintain radio contact with Mother, Harley, and Zack while the operation went down.

"Eagle one." Mark's earpiece crackled to life with the first status report. "The turkeys have landed."

Leave it to Harley to make light at a time like this.

"See anything?" Alex ignored the comic relief.

"Just you, Mark, and a nice quiet view. You heard from Mother yet?"

"Soon. I'll let you know when she calls."

"Copy that." Harley signed off.

"I still think this is too risky." Mark was nervous enough for the four of them.

"We've already had this conversation." Alex opened the balcony door wider, making himself a ready target.

"Yeah, but—"

"It's done. Drop it." Alex caught the look on his face when he stifled his next comment. "You got something else to say?"

"Yes. I don't want to have to take your dead body back to Kelsey."

Alex smirked, like that was encouraging. "Do you think I would set myself in the bull's eye if I didn't have perfect faith in your talent to make sure I make it home to my sweet wife?"

Mark gulped. If that wasn't stress, nothing was.

"Remember son, I've got my best men with me. There's no way this can fail." His eyebrow spiked. "So don't let me down."

"Not going to happen." Mark gulped, sorry now that he had said anything.

A knock sounded at the door. He drew his pistol, stepped into the adjoining bedroom, and closed the door enough to still see through the crack. Alex answered. There stood an

Afghani waiter with a cart full of covered dinner trays, fruit and dessert bowls, as well as an ice bucket and two bottles of champagne. After he wheeled the cart into the room, Alex thanked him and handed him a generous tip.

When the waiter reached the doorway, he pulled a folded piece of paper from inside his sleeve, set it on the table, and turned to Alex. With his index finger to his lips, he nodded to Alex and quietly closed the door.

"What was that all about?" Mark scanned the scrap of paper from the table. "Does Stars of Allah mean anything to you?"

"Well, I'll be damned." Alex smiled as his phone rang.

"Twelve, maybe fifteen warm bodies headed your way," Mother announced quietly over the speakerphone.

"How far?"

"Inside of a mile. Closing fast."

"You're sure?"

"I am if I can trust the satellite feed and all the cell phone chatter."

"Thank you, Mother."

"You're welcome, Boss."

"What is this about?" Mark asked, still holding the paper. If something else was going on, he needed to know.

"Set up alongside me. I think you'll be surprised." Alex relayed the latest intel from Mother to Harley and Zack.

Mark did as he was told, fixing the sights of his scope on the streets below. The quiet evening had transformed. Everywhere he looked armed men waited in shadows and corners. The usual afternoon crowd had vanished. Switching back to Harley and Zack's positions, he detected Afghani friendlies standing alongside the two Americans, each carrying what appeared to be an AK-47.

"Stars of Allah was a group of freedom fighters during the Russian occupation," Alex explained quietly.

"It looks like they're still around today."

"Check out the man with Harley."

Mark focused across the road. There with rifle in hand and dressed in a long brown robe of the desert stood Arzad. He looked grim. Now Mark understood why the streets were empty. These men must have gotten the word out to friends and family.

He whistled softly under his breath. "Looks like Arzad's carrying a sniper rifle. Looks a lot like yours."

"It does, doesn't it?"

Judging by the tone in Alex's voice, Mark suspected that came as no surprise. He looked into his scope again. Eleven men in gray camouflaged uniforms crept toward the hotel, their rifles and pistols in hand. They seemed aware of the absence of the usual crowd, but still proceeded. Imir ran out to meet the leading Russian who sported a red beret. Mark watched an envelope exchange hands.

"That's your man." Harley's disembodied voice came through Mark's earpieces. "The man in the red cap. Stanislav Egorov, in the flesh."

"Got him." Alex took aim.

Mark selected the man to Egorov's left and lined him up in the crosshairs. The time to hit the Russians was now, before they set foot inside. Imir grinned as he pivoted to go back inside the hotel. Egorov sneered behind his back.

Mark waited for Alex to take the first shot. He squeezed his finger to the trigger and—

A single shot rang out, but it did not come from Alex. Imir dropped dead.

"What the—?" Mark turned to Alex.

Alex nodded toward Harley's corner of the warehouse. There knelt Arzad, his rifle firing round after round while Harley stood beside him, his weapon butt to the floor between his boots. The elderly Afghani looked as calm as if he were kneeling on his prayer rug at home.

Other AK-47s joined the barrage. Within minutes the noise ceased. Gray smoke laced the air. Every Russian was down, injured or dead, including Stanislav Egorov. In the flesh.

"I'll be damned," Mark said softly, and maybe a little proudly, too.

No one from The Team had fired a single shot.

"Man. Did you see those guys?"

Zack had just run down several flights of stairs to meet up with Mark, Alex, and Harley in the street. Everyone was high on the adrenaline of the moment.

Arzad stepped out from the shadows of the abandoned warehouse. Their wise, old friend had the same easy-going smile on his wrinkled face as always.

"I am most humbly in your debt." Mark bowed his head in respect, looking a little closer at his friend. "Are all these men yours?"

"These men neighbors and friends. We fight Russians many years." Arzad spat on the ground as if he had spoken a distasteful word.

"I think since nineteen seventy-nine," Alex added.

"We never stopped fighting them. Our country is not for them. They must go." Arzad nodded proudly. His weary eyes glistened with strength Mark hadn't noticed before.

"You are full of many surprises." Harley clapped Arzad's back and began shaking the hands of all the other men in the crowd. As if on cue, they lifted their weapons over their heads and gave a loud victory yell.

"You are my honored guests tonight." Arzad motioned to the man at his side who promptly ran down the street, and shortly returned with the van.

Within the hour, they were securely removed to Arzad's humble home.

It was a good night on the rooftop. The impromptu operation was an impressive success. It seemed the Russians couldn't hack the age-old word of mouth method of communication. They never knew what hit them.

Alex and Arzad sat together like two old soldiers, telling stories and sipping chai while Gulnar and Najela made trip after trip with more fruit bowls, sweet bread, and meat trays. The little home was filled to overflowing with friends and fellow freedom fighters. Harley and Zack still mixed it up with the men celebrating outside where an occasional round of gunfire punctuated the calm evening. Mark sipped another cup of chai, content to sit back and watch.

When Arzad saw him by himself, he came to sit beside him. "Why you alone?"

"You have given me much to think about," Mark said, "That's why."

"That is a good thing." Arzad smiled mischievously.

"Have you ever really needed our help?"

He turned somber. "Many of these men would not be here tonight if not for you."

"Me?" Mark cocked his head, not understanding.

"Come. There is someone who wishes to see you."

Mark pulled himself out of the rickety chair and followed his host downstairs and out the door. There inside Arzad's van sat Nasim, his face black and blue from the beating he had received and his poor hands bandaged. He sat with a plate of sweet meats and cheeses on his lap and a big cup of chai in his bandaged hands.

"Nasim." Mark reached through the open van window and rested his hand gently on the elderly man's shoulder. "It is good to see you again."

"My son." The old man smiled to see Mark, his swollen eyes full of happiness.

"I see you are still fighting like a young man," Mark teased. "When will you learn? You need to carry a bigger stick."

"You are right." Nasim grinned. "I must do that."

"It is because of your kindness to Nasim that these men came to fight tonight," Arzad said. "They saw what you did for him in the market that day. Look." He pointed across the way. There stood Mukhtar with an old Kalashnikov across one arm. He nodded to Mark, offering a half-salute with his bandaged hand.

"Was he part of what happened in the village?" Mark asked.

Arzad's eyes gleamed. "You have many friends here. Many are getting out of the poppy business. Apricot and almond trees are all Nasim wants to grow. That is why Egorov went after him. He did not set a good example."

"Good for you." Mark clapped the elder Afghani gently on his boney back. "I hear the United Nations will send aid for every farmer who quits the poppy fields."

"That is what they told us," Nasim said mischievously, "last time."

"Let us hope they do it this time." Mark studied his friend's tired old face. Nasim was symbolic of so many men in the country, working all their lives to provide for their families and dying too young in the process.

"Tashakur."

"No." Mark stopped Nasim's kind words. "It is I who should be thanking you."

"Mr. Mark. Mr. Mark." Najela burst out of the house with Harley strolling right behind her. She skidded to a halt, nearly colliding into Mark.

"Little girl." Arzad chuckled. "Why so much noise?"

She blushed and stuck her arm out to Mark. "I make."

Harley stood beaming and watching while Mark took the proffered gift, a bracelet woven of blue, purple, and bright pink cords with green glass beads intertwined.

"My Mr. Harley help me make present for your ...." She turned back to Harley. "How I say it?"

"Girlfriend." Harley supplied the missing word.

Najela turned back with a big smile. "Girlfriend. That is right, yes?"

"Thank you, Najela." Mark accepted the gift. "This is beautiful. Libby will love it."

"I have one more." She glanced back to Harley again. "Is okay?"

He shrugged. "It's up to you."

It surprised Mark when she tumbled against him, wrapping her slender arms around his waist in an unexpected hug. "You my favorite American, too," she said. "My Mr. Harley and you."

Mark had to smile. Sweeter words were never spoken. He looked up into Arzad's sharp eyes.

"I think you not look same. You not same man," Arzad muttered. "You okay, Mr. Mark? You good?"

His question caught Mark by surprise and made him smile at the same time. How could this wise old man read him like that? Or could he? Was Arzad fishing or did he already know that Mark was on his way to the altar?

"I am okay. Thank you," Mark said noncommittally.

"But your Miss Libby. She is good, too?" he persisted, his brows furrowed as he peered closely into Mark's face.

The old man was getting nosey. What was he getting at? No one knew about Mark's upcoming wedding except Libby and himself.

"Yes. She is good. Harley told me that you prayed for us. Thank you." Mark turned back to Nasim, hoping to break the spell Arzad seemed to be under. Somehow this wise man had picked up on some tiny nuance from Mark. If he didn't already know about the upcoming nuptials, he would soon if he kept connecting the dots like he was.

"You will get married and have many children? Yes?"

Mark turned back at that question. Probing eyes glittered from Arzad's wrinkled face. The scoundrel. Somehow, he already knew the answer.

Mark hesitated. He was not prepared to spill the beans without Libby. She should be there by his side, but Arzad stood waiting. Harley still hung back by the door of the house, but he was watching now, too. Najela had gone inside with her grandmother, but Alex had joined the group. The only one missing was Zack. Everyone seemed to be holding their breath.

"Well, ah." Mark hesitated. He looked to Alex. The man stood with his arms crossed, a bemused smile on his face. Tonight, Alex would be flying back home to his sweet wife. He deserved to know. Mark bit his lip. Libby would understand. "Yes. I am getting married."

Arzad's eyes lit with joy, so Mark spilled the whole can of beans. "Libby and I will have that family you're always pestering me about. Would you consider a stateside visit to help us celebrate? How does next April sound?"

"Congratulations!" Alex said as he slapped half of Mark's back while Arzad slapped the other half. "Kelsey will be so happy to hear this."

Harley grabbed Mark in an emotional man hug. "Congrats, brother. When can I meet her?"

"She's in Wisconsin with her folks right now. I only asked her a couple weeks ago." Mark beamed. He had never been swamped by so much male appreciation before. "We were going to wait until you could be there, too. I want you to be my best man."

"Me?" Harley seemed so genuinely surprised. His eyes filled, and he blinked hard. "Yeah. Okay. Wow. I've never been anyone's best man before. I'd really like that."

Mark turned to Alex. Suddenly, he was standing back on home plate again.

"Boss." Instantly his eyes filled. Mark bit his lip. He had already called his father, but John Houston had flatly refused to attend the single most glorious day in his son's life. Mark had expected as much, but like a dutiful son, he'd asked. It was no big deal. Not really. His father hadn't attended his graduation from the Corps either. Mark shouldn't have cared. But he did.

Listening to the bitter man's paltry excuse why he couldn't attend the wedding, Mark finally heard the real reason. It was then that he was able let go of the thing that would never be, the unrealized expectation that had nagged him every day of his life – a son's craving for his father's love. Mark knew then. He didn't need a father anymore, but he did need a friend.

Alex stood waiting.

He's as bad as Arzad. He looks like he already knows what I'm going to ask.

Mark cleared his throat. "Sir. Would you consider being my best man, too?" He winced. The offending word had just tumbled out of his nervous mouth. *Sir.*

Alex nodded one curt, quick nod. "Hell, yeah. I'd be damned proud to stand with you and Libby."

"Thanks." Mark blinked hard, fighting emotions at that simple affirmative. He wiped a hand over his face.

Zack interrupted the emotional scene. Judging by the way he staggered over to lean against Harley, he was ready to call it a night. "These guys got hold of some v-v-very f-f-fine Ru-s-s-sian vodka. It's got a real shw-e-e-t kick. You wanna try some?"

"Old man Mark here is getting married," Alex announced.

Zack offered a wobbly thumbs-up. "Good on ya, Hous-s-ston."

"And now is time for you." Arzad arrowed a gnarled, bony finger at Harley. "Mr. Mark has done what is good."

Mark smirked, thankful for the change of subject. "Yeah, Harley. Settle down, why don't ya?"

"You his brother." Nasim piped up from inside the van, pointing to Mark. "You must to do same."

A kid with his hand stuck in the cookie jar could not have looked more on the spot than Harley did at that moment. "I'm working on it. Sheesh." He rolled his eyes. "You know Najela's the only girl for me, Arzad. I'm just waiting for her to get a little older."

"Oh, no! You may not marry my Najela." Arzad chuckled with glee, tsking as that bony finger waggled under Harley's nose. "You must find nice American girl with good personality."

Alex outright laughed. Zack sputtered. Mark slapped his friend's back extra hard. "Yeah, Mortimer, find a girl with a nice personality, why don't you?"

"Already met 'em," Harley muttered. "That's why I like my dogs."

Thirty-Two

Oh, my.

Libby gasped. All she could do was stare at her reflection in the full-length mirror. A stately fairy princess stared back at her instead of the common farm girl.

I look beautiful.

The gown encasing her body was a glamorous trumpet style with an empire waist. It accentuated her small figure in all the right places with exquisite ivory lace over champagne satin and swirls of beads sparkling against her lightly tanned skin. Even her curly blonde hair created a breath taking contrast against the creamy material, especially where it lay against the cap sleeves on her shoulders.

"Do you like it?" Kelsey asked, her eyes glowing.

Libby didn't know what to say. She and her mother had made the trip to the east coast at Kelsey's request. Their long week of shopping for wedding dresses had culminated at Hannah's Bridal Boutique, a charming out of the way treasure trove in old Alexandria.

"It's perfect," she murmured at last, smoothing her hands over the elegant fabric. Never in a million years could she believe she could look so pretty.

Rosemary beamed. "Oh, my," was all she could say, too.

The exuberant clerk knelt at her feet with an armful of shoeboxes. "These satin open-toed heels match your dress perfectly." She smiled up at Libby with her spectacles perched on her nose. "You do look lovely, my dear."

Kelsey came to Libby's side, her hands at her elbows as she peered into the mirror. "We can keep looking if you would like."

"No." Libby shook her head. "This is it, and yes, ma'am." She nodded to the poor woman on the floor. "I'll take those shoes, too."

"My little girl." Rosemary sighed, a tear in her eye.

"Mom. You can't cry over every dress," Libby teased, but she wanted to cry herself. She couldn't wait for Mark to see her in this gown, and then help her out of it. Heat scorched her cheeks. That man. Kelsey's husband sure kept him busy. She didn't know what country he was off to this week. It didn't matter. He held her heart no matter where he was.

"Mom's are supposed to do that." Kelsey planted a quick kiss on her cheek. "I'm so happy for you and Mark."

"Me too." Libby sighed. "Me too."

"Would you look at that?" The happy clerk pointed to the wide glass window of the second story loft where Libby had been trying on dresses. Outside a flurry of March snowflakes drifted lazily out of the spring sky.

Libby shivered.

Christmas was just around the corner.

Mark stood at the front of the chapel, alone, even though Alex and Harley were at his side. He couldn't breathe. Even his heart muscles seemed to hold off beating like they should.

Life had paused. Time stood still. He worried. *Was I right to make her wait so long? Was I gone too much from her side? Was six months unbearable? Is she still in love with me?*

He found himself leaning forward. He needed to be the first to see her.

What if she doesn't come? What if she changed her mind?

The organ's first notes pealed like bells throughout the vaulted chapel ceiling.

There she is. My Libby. My bride. My Life.

The second hand ticked. His heart beat again. All his questions were answered.

God, I love her so much.

Jerry Clifton escorted his youngest down the aisle, her hand resting lightly on his arm as joyful strains filled the air. He looked as spritely as ever having recovered from his heart surgery. The man swore he felt ten years younger, but Mark didn't see the tears in his eyes as this father gave his daughter away. Neither did he notice the elegant lace over satin, nor the sparkles of beads stitched across the bride's bodice and at her waist.

Cobalt blue held fast to darkest brown. She never looked away. Even the shoulder-length veil couldn't hide the love on her beautiful, smiling face. He felt the strength of that love transmitted from her soul to his. Air whooshed into his lungs. He could breathe again.

As Libby took his outstretched hand, he recalled the raft out on the lake, the moment she had first reached for him. Like that night so long ago she held his hand again, her slender fingers lost in his gentle grip. This was where she had always belonged. With a groan meant for her ears only, he pulled her hand up to his heart and held it against the thumping in his chest.

"I love you," he whispered, pressing her fingers to his lips. Let the world watch. Let the world know. He was someone because of her. No longer the invisible, the soldier, the lost—he was Mark Houston, the soul mate, the white knight and the protector of the most gracious creature to set foot on God's green earth.

He lifted her veil. If there was anyone else in the chapel, he did not see them. She took his breath away, tears glistening on her lashes and devotion aglow on her face.

His bishop commenced the wedding vows. They exchanged rings and promised eternity. Alex released two white doves from a gilded cage. Immediately, they flew home to roost in Jerry's barn.

Libby Clifton became Mrs. Mark Houston—forever.

Harley

Harley tilted his chair against the wall as he watched the couples on the dance floor. It gave his long legs a couple more inches to stretch. For some reason, he waxed philosophical at weddings. Arzad wasn't able to make it from Afghanistan, but he had sent an extraordinary gift for the happy couple, a leather-bound copy of the Quran. It was a huge gift for an impoverished Afghani to give, and it touched Mark and Libby. Harley, too.

He fingered the blue-beaded bracelets at his wrist, simple gifts from a shy brown-eyed little girl, sweet little Najela.

Harley wondered what her future held as her conflict-besieged country evolved. Arzad and his family were dear to Harley's heart. He would have stowed them away in his suitcase if he could've brought them back to America with him. He wished the wise little man were here today to witness the joyful celebration before him now. Without a doubt, Arzad would have danced with Libby, and possibly Mark as well. Heck, Arzad may even have danced with Alex. Harley smiled. That would have been a sight to see.

He tapped his long fingers on his knees. Someday, it might be his turn to take the plunge, but fate had not been particularly kind. That day would not be soon. He was no catch of a lifetime and neither was he much to look at by his standards. His legs were too long, and his brain still too scrambled. War had wreaked enough havoc with his head and the drugs he'd self-medicated with weren't much help either. For now, his life was a carefully followed regiment of the right diet, plenty of physical exercise, the perfect job, and a damned good counselor who understood post-traumatic stress.

Besides, he had his dogs, well, Alex's dogs really. Whisper and Smoke were his buddies and visiting with them meant he could visit Kelsey, too. The Stewart's place felt like home. Harley didn't kid himself. Women wanted the perfect man. Not him.

"Are you Harley Mortimer?"

He blinked, startled that he'd been approached by a particularly pretty woman with a truly radiant smile. Instantly on his feet, he tucked his white shirt back into the waist of his tuxedo slacks and smoothed his forever unruly hair.

"Why yes, ma'am," he replied in his best fake Texas drawl while accepting her very dainty outstretched hand in his. "Reckon I am. Harley Mortimer at your service. Who are you looking for?"

"I'm looking for you." She smiled so darn pretty that his heart skipped a beat. Maybe two. Her green eyes shone like soft emeralds against her creamy skin and light copper-colored hair. "You are Mark's best man, aren't you?"

His breath caught. This woman was gorgeous.

"I am," he answered. "And you are?"

"Judy O'Brien." She shook his hand with a surprisingly strong grip. "I had the chance to help Libby when she was recovering from her pneumonia."

"Oh. Yeah." He remembered that now. Mark had mentioned a nurse who'd taken charge of Libby's care, and that she was good looking. He must have forgotten to mention that she was some kind of an angel, too.

"I hate to be forward, but ...." She glanced at the dance floor that Harley avoided like the plague. "Would you care to dance with me?"

"I, ah ...." He looked at Alex with Kelsey out there holding onto each other, Mark and Libby too. They looked comfortable. He didn't want to upset the ambience of this special evening. A long-legged goof ball like him could seriously mess up the whole thing. "I don't usually dance unless I've had a few drinks, and, umm, I don't drink anymore, and .... "

He scratched the back of his head, puzzled with what might come out of his mouth next. And there it was. The idiot in him won. "Well, sure, little lady. Why not?"

"I promise I won't step on your feet." Judy placed her palm inside his, and away they went.

He actually danced. No, he glided. No, it felt more like he floated with his hand at her waist. The darnedest feeling overwhelmed him like he might be able to fly after all—with her.

"You've done this before." She had a way of making him feel like he actually knew what he was doing. Fred Astaire never looked so good.

"Yeah, but last time it didn't feel quite like this." Harley towered over this beautiful, bright woman at his fingertips. The fragrance of jasmine filled his nose. He blinked like a deer in the headlights as she smiled up at him and ....

He forgot all about Arzad.

Mark sighed. By tomorrow night, he and Libby would be watching the sunset over the Bahamas, and from there a new life awaited in Alexandria. Her happily-ever-after plan hadn't completely changed. Only one of the main characters was different. Him.

He smiled to think how tired she was, how her feet hurt from those heels she had kicked off earlier, and how they still had a long flight ahead of them tonight. She had given him the six months he'd asked of her, but they would be in the Bahamas long before they ever got to make that mad passionate love she had wanted so desperately months ago. It seemed strange that the consummation of their love remained, as yet, undone. He could not imagine loving her more.

Somehow in the past months, he had found a job and two families, the Cliftons and The TEAM. Oh yes, and he was starting his own, the Mark Houston family. It had a very nice ring to it. Who would have thought that a worthless little farm kid from out-in-the-middle-of-nowhere-Ohio could ever be so blessed? The miracle of the woman in his arms was more than he would ever understand, but he knew one thing for sure. She loved him.

Across the floor, he noticed Kelsey gazing up into her husband's eyes. She always looked at him that way, as if there was no one else on earth but the man in her arms. They acted like this was their wedding dance, Alex all debonair and flirting with his wife, and Kelsey blushing. Glowing.

Mark breathed contentedly into his wife's fragrant hair. Even as tired as she was, Libby was the epitome of radiant. He finally had what Alex and Kelsey had.

He had everything.

THE END

Thank you for reading Mark!

Be sure to check out the rest of the guys and gals of Irish Winters' series: *In the Company of Snipers*

Other Irish Winters' books:

King of Hearts, Deuces Wild Series, *#1*
Joker Joker, Deuces Wild Series, *#2*
Smoke, Hearts and Ashes Series, *#1*
Ash, Hearts and Ashes Series, *#2*

Coming soon!

Seth, In the Company of Snipers, #17
One-Eyed Jack, Deuces Wild Series, #3

YOU are the key to this book's success!

Please tell other readers why you liked Mark and Libby's story by leaving an honest review at the retail site where you purchased it.
Recommend it to your friends. Lend it.
Most of all, enjoy it!

The best way to keep up with my new releases, giveaways, and actionable intel is to sign up for my spam-free newsletter at IrishWinters.com.

About the Author

Irish Winters is an award winning, Amazon best-selling author who, when she isn't writing, dabbles in poetry, grandchildren, and rarely (as in extremely rarely) the kitchen. More prone to be outdoors than in, she grew up the quintessential tomboy on a dairy farm in rural Wisconsin, spent her teenage years in the Pacific Northwest, but calls the Wasatch Mountains of Northern Utah home. For now.

She believes in making every day count for something, and follows the wise admonition of her mother to, "Look out the window and see something!"

Connect with Irish!
On Facebook: https://www.facebook.com/author.irishwinters
On Twitter: https://twitter.com/irishwinters1
Or at www. IrishWinters.com